Dance OF THE Starlit Sea

To the girls who rescued me from Hell
while I was drowning, this is for you 🖤

Published by Peachtree Teen
An imprint of PEACHTREE PUBLISHING COMPANY INC.
1700 Chattahoochee Avenue
Atlanta, Georgia 30318-2112
PeachtreeBooks.com

Text © 2024 by Kiana Krystle
Jacket and interior illustrations © 2024 by Roy Trinh

Edited by Ashley Hearn
Design and composition by Lily Steele

Printed and bound in June 2024 at Sheridan, Chelsea, MI, USA.
10 9 8 7 6 5 4 3 2 1
First Edition
ISBN: 978-1-68263-465-3

Cataloging-in-Publication Data is available from the Library of Congress.

Dance OF THE Starlit Sea

KIANA KRYSTLE

PEACHTREE
Teen

Chapter
ONE

✦

The Atlantic pulls at my heartstrings, as fondly as a bouquet of jasmine blossoms tied up in a bow. I fall before the rising waves, collecting the pearlescent sea-foam. It's sacred, just for me, like a gift from a lover or my dearest friend.

When I was little, I used to run into the Pacific for a moment of peace. It scared my mother silly watching her only daughter dive into the water's wrath. But I adored the sharp cold, the strength of the undertow, the reckless rush of the currents. The ocean could never hurt me. We were one. We still are, no matter how far from home I've come. My mother always said that, like the sea, I was chaos incarnate.

Which is exactly how I ended up here, on Luna Island.

The waves dissolve into foaming petals, reminding me that something so powerful can also be quite fragile at the core. My eyes fall shut as I plot my return to the depths. If I weren't on my best behavior to impress my aunt, I'd run in deeper and let the waters reclaim me.

"Lee-la," Auntie Laina calls from the cottage window. "Come back inside, sweetie. There's something I want to talk to you about."

Her voice snaps me out of my daydream. "Coming!"

Reluctantly, I rise from the sand.

A burst of florals hypnotizes me towards the cottage. Sweet peas and moonflowers press through the porch's warped wood panels. I make my way up the whitewashed steps, and a velvet orchid wrapped around the banister tickles my hand. Twinkling sea glass wind chimes wreathed with roses send a shiver down my spine as I grip the tarnished doorknob, hopeful that this place will become familiar soon. After all, it is my home now.

With a deep breath, I make my way inside.

"What's up?" I say, taking a seat at the dining table.

An assortment of tea and sweets is laid out. Only the owner of Petals Tea Shop could arrange such a charming display. A smattering of preserves and jams in heart-shaped dishes are nestled between the crooks of crumpets, scones, and other pastries garnished with lavender. Laina grabs a Danish with buttercream frosting dripping from a flaky crescent roll. Crumbles of brown sugar tumble off as she takes a bite.

I pour a dash of cream into a teacup. The milk feathers out like a lotus blossom. In China, where my father is from, the lotus symbolizes honesty, goodness, and beauty.

I may be beautiful, but I'm not honest, and I've never been good.

"How are you feeling?" Laina asks. Her voice is lush and airy.

I trace the hand-painted buttercups beneath my thumb. "Better," I lie.

She smiles sweetly. "Do you want to tell me what happened yet?"

My father hasn't told her? Of course she'd want an explanation, especially since I was sent to live with her out of the blue. Laina and I are practically strangers.

"You don't—you don't know?"

She laughs. "My brother hasn't called in nearly eighteen years. Actually, none of your uptight aunties have since they moved to the mainland. And although your father hasn't had the decency of a 'hi, Laina,' or 'how ya doin', Laina?' I'm overjoyed to see my gem of a niece here after all this time. Frankly, whatever happened between you and your daddy, you deserve nothing but grace. He can be so cold sometimes. Believe me, Lila, I know."

I take a long sip of tea, letting the warm vanilla blend soothe my throat. My father has every right to hate me after what I've done. But there's comfort in Laina not knowing that. Not knowing me.

"Thank you," I manage to say.

"Of course, Peaches."

Laina releases a sigh and stretches back in her chair, extending her arms through the open window as if to collect the sunlight. Her long black hair tangles with the breeze, and the ribbon corralling her locks nearly slips out with the wind. I wonder what it's like to be that free—so placid in her happiness, aloof in her lemon-colored cottage. My aunties back home could never be so relaxed. Why did they move away from here? From Laina?

She's beautiful. She has the same eyes as my dad—upturned and almond shaped, brown, with a glint of amber in the sun. However, unlike my dad, she's full of softness and roseate warmth. Her eyes crinkle adoringly when she smiles, and the tips of her fringe kiss her lashes. She laughs again as her chair slams back onto the ground with a thud. I jump, rattling my teacup against its saucer.

Laina doesn't notice. Instead, she grabs my hand. "Look, I know being here is going to take some getting used to. So if there's anything I can do to make this change more comfortable, please let me know."

I hesitate, pulling my knees towards myself like a crustacean curling into its shell. I was supposed to graduate high school early this summer. Finish with a GED and join a preprofessional program for ballet. That was the dream. I don't think anything can make it right now. Not when I'm on Luna Island instead of where I should be. Besides, there's not even an audition for me to work towards after I ruined my reputation onstage.

"I'm alright," I say. "I'm just going to get settled in my room."

"Lila." She stops me from rising. "I can't let you waste away in there on your birthday."

I sit up taller in my seat. "You—you remembered?"

"Of course. It's today, right?"

"Yeah, it is." My voice drops. I don't want to think about how my parents sent me away right before I turned eighteen or how I don't know Laina other than the birthday card she sends each year. A rising heat spreads across my palms. My stiletto manicure sinks into the threads of my dress, crumpling the thin cotton to calm my racing pulse. I hate myself for fraying such a delicate piece of my wardrobe. I sigh, smoothing out the floral print. "Thank you for remembering."

Laina tilts her head to the side, offering a faint smile. "It's the least I could do after . . . you know. Honey, I'm really sorry about everything. I won't pry, but let me show you a good evening. Luna Island really is quite lovely if you give it a chance."

I tug at the locket around my neck, the only thing from my mother that I brought with me to Luna Island. "That's sweet of you, but I just want to settle in."

"Then settle in with me tonight at the Midsummer Ball!"

"The what?" The last thing I want right now is to be around anyone else, let alone attend a ball.

She leaps to her feet. "That's actually what I wanted to talk to you about. I don't mean to overwhelm you, but it really is a treat. The Midsummer Ball typically only happens every seven years, and you just happened to arrive during an anomaly. Besides, it'll be a good chance for you to get acquainted with the community. Luna Island rarely ever has visitors."

"So I've heard." I reach into my pocket, running my fingers over the frayed ferry ticket crumpled in the hollow of my cardigan. . . .

The ferryman on Virginia Beach had looked me up and down before boarding, examining my ditsy-print suitcase.

"You planning to stay awhile?" he'd snapped.

The bite in his voice made me jump. I looked down at my heels as if they were ruby slippers that could make me disappear with a click. "Um, I guess I don't really have a choice."

He scoffed, taking my ticket. "Good luck, kid."

"Excuse me?"

His eyes narrowed. "You really haven't heard the stories?"

Was I supposed to? My parents hadn't told me anything. "No," I said to the ground.

"Only a handful of visitors book a ticket every month. Usually lose it before they can even board. Or sometimes they just forget. Miss the ferry, something comes up. Whatever it is, hardly anyone ever makes it to Luna Island."

I glared at the crescent-shaped island in the distance. Was this why my parents had sent me here? To be swept away by the sea before even reaching my destination? I wouldn't blame them. Not after what I'd done. I tugged my cardigan around me tighter, limbs shaking. Pale green waters lapped beneath the dock, taunting me forward like spindly fingertips.

Lila, it called. *Come to me.*

My eyes shut, breath hitching as I dropped my suitcase. It was an overtone of a voice—twin echoes, not quite human. I had heard it only in my dreams, that liminal space between reality and the otherworld. Sometimes, the veil would part when I reached a void—cliffsides, the open ocean—coaxing me to follow.

It's true, I've always loved the sea. But I'd be lying if I said my intrusive nature didn't terrify me. Sometimes, I mistake the ocean as my friend. But she is not a friend, and she is not kind.

"N-no," I stammered, banishing the sea's echo and its hold over me. It can only hurt me if I let it.

The ferryman chuckled. "Just as I thought. Another flake."

"I—I meant, *no*, I'm not leaving."

His lips twisted into a smirk, pausing, as if I'd back out. "Hop on before fate changes its mind."

Clinking porcelain startles me back to reality. Laina laughs as she recovers the sugar dish she toppled over on the table. The memory disappears with the crystal grains she sweeps onto the floor.

"I hate to cut our tea short, but I have to get going soon." She tosses back the beach waves fanning her neck. "The town is in a tizzy. I've been scrambling all week to get these pastries ready for the ball. We usually have months to prepare, but one town meeting and *bam!* I'm slammed. It's amazing what we've managed to scrape together with only a few days' notice."

"I don't understand," I confess. "If the Midsummer Ball only happens every seven years, then why now?"

Laina rises, checking her watch and cursing beneath her breath. "Why don't you come with me! It'll be good for you. Girls your age always hang out on Main Street. Maybe you'll even make some friends."

I nearly laugh. If only she knew the girls back home would rather slip glass into my pointe shoes than be my friend. "Thanks, but I highly doubt that."

Her smile wavers as she sinks into the chair beside me. "Come on, Lila. Give it a chance. Pageant season is fun. It was my favorite tradition when I was your age."

"Pageant season?" I wince. I know it's not the same as ballet, but I can't stomach the thought of another competition right now.

"I'm sorry. I wasn't suggesting you participate after . . ." She shakes her head. My muscles tighten. So she knows about *that*.

Great. "All I meant is that it would be a good opportunity to get acquainted with the island, maybe meet a few people. Please, I won't allow you to waste away here all alone on your birthday."

My breath slows as I glance at the scabs that mark my palms like tiny crescent moons, branding me with the mistake that got me sent away.

I didn't mean it.

I was being impulsive.

I'm sorry.

I tremble, shoving my hands beneath my seat.

"That's sweet of you, Laina." She's trying, and I don't want to make her job any harder than it already is. "I guess I could come along."

"That's the spirit!" She wraps me in a hug and pulls me to my feet. "Here," she says, handing me a hundred-dollar bill. "We'll go into town, and you can pick out something nice while I finish up at the shop. The boat sets sail at eight o'clock, and you need to dress to impress!"

"But, I— What do you mean 'boat'?"

"The boat for the ball! The dock is right at the edge of Main Street. You can't miss it once you're in town."

My heartbeat quickens. It's one thing to be trapped here. It's another to wander the unfamiliar streets alone. I shake my head. "This is too much. And I can't take your money."

"Yes, yes, yes, you can!" she says, grabbing a knit shawl off a hook near the front door. After slipping a wicker basket stuffed with fresh-baked goods over her arm, she gently tugs me down the hall.

"Laina—"

She tears open the door. "Let's go." She presses a hand to my back, and I stumble onto the embroidered welcome mat. "You need the retail therapy. Trust me. Take a walk down Main Street. There's a dress shop over there. Pick out something pretty, and I'll meet you at the dock at eight. M'kay?"

"Wait—" I try to say, but the wind tosses my hair in my face. I pluck it from my glossy lips and sigh. Laina is already halfway down the cobbled walkway, her basket jostling at her hip. The crisp green bill she gave me flutters in my hand. I'd better make use of Laina's kindness before it slips away too.

✦

Main Street reminds me of several towns I once visited in Europe—a blend of Positano, Amsterdam, and Paris. Townsfolk parade down cobblestone steps, wearing long pastel dresses and carrying bouquets of bright flowers tied with a bow. Laughter fills the air as ladies chat with shop owners and sip their teas below lace-embellished verandas. A man carrying a loaf of bread stops to tie his dog to a Victorian streetlamp. The little terrier yaps as I walk by, wagging his tail.

I pause, embracing the warm scent of butter and cocoa as a little boy brings a chocolate croissant to his sticky lips. Then, the salty mist of the sea comes rolling in with the breeze, reminding me I'm still on Luna Island and not in a Parisian romance novel. I inhale the familiar brine, and a flock of butterflies emerges from the rose bushes. They circle me, tangoing with the ribbons of my dress. For a moment, I pretend like I'm deserving of this bliss.

And then I see it.

My breath shudders as I surrender to the island's charm.

Before me is the most beautiful boutique I've ever encoun-tered. It looks straight out of a fairytale. A garland of mauve roses adorns the top of the cottage-like shop, vines curling downwards and falling languidly over the windows. Hanging above the door is an oval sign with chipped paint that reads LUNA's LOVE SHACK in swirly cursive. As I draw closer, soft colors seep out of the window, revealing a dress display.

The romantic gowns with puff pastry sleeves remind me of the costumes I used to wear for ballet. My muscles tense, and I bite my tongue. Before coming here, it was my dream to become a prima ballerina. A deep resentment fills my stomach, for those dreams will never happen now. I steady myself against the window, channeling images of the sea, praying for some sort of release. Only, the ugly truth is too intense to vanquish with daydreams of escaping like a selkie in water.

I'll never be the perfect ballerina.

I'll never be worthy of my parents' love.

I exhale a defeated breath, imagining myself in the pink dress with glittering teardrop crystals, twirling around onstage as the Sugar Plum Fairy. Perhaps if I just try one on, I can pretend to be the principal dancer I almost was. Maybe then the pain of longing might settle. Even for just a moment.

A bell chimes as I open the door. It's even more magical inside than out. Spools of ribbon hang from the walls like the atelier of a fairy queen. Tiny jasmine buds lace through the curls of a crystal chandelier. Dresses fill the curves of antique wardrobes, as if this were a princess's closet and not a store.

A group of girls squeal as they browse the gowns. They're dressed almost otherworldly, so unlike the yoga pants and sweatshirts I'm used to in San Francisco. Instead, they're ornamented in seafoam trousers made of silk, lace corsets with ruffles across the bustier, satin slips with rose embroidery. They wear seashells in their hair and around their necks—an iridescent mollusk held together by a string of pearls, an abalone claw clip that flashes different colors beneath the light, pukas threaded between pastel sea glass.

"Do you think this will be enough to impress the angels?" one of them says, holding up a white-gold gown with flashes of magenta cascading between the layers of silk. "I really want to make a statement tonight. First impressions are everything."

Her friend shakes her head. "You're going to need more than that if you want to one-up Roisin. You know how she is with a sewing machine."

"Pick the one with the crystals," another girl cuts in. "The angels *love* anything that glitters."

Someone scoffs beside me and I turn, meeting a girl hanging new gowns on satin hangers. She seems about my age, with vibrant persimmon hair tumbling down to her waist. Her pinkish skin is dashed with freckles, and her frame is small and delicate.

"She's right," the girl mutters to herself, half hidden behind the racks. "They're going to need more than that to outdo me."

I look her up and down. She's lovely, like a rose-gold angel. "You mean for the pageant?"

She blinks, stumbling as our eyes lock. "Oh! I'm sorry. I didn't realize anyone was listening. Good tidings! How can I help you today?"

I hesitate, taking another look around the room. Foiled stars shimmer across the ceiling, hand painted with a glimmering sheen. It's almost like this place has been enchanted, and for a second, I even believe it is.

"I—I guess I'm looking for a dress for the Midsummer Ball."

She scrunches her button nose. "Wait, how do you know about the Midsummer Ball?"

"Oh. Well, I'm staying with my aunt for a while. Laina. She owns Petals Tea Shop."

"Interesting . . ." Her eyes trail over me. My throat tightens as her lashes flick up and down. "Your locket. It's from Luna Island, isn't it?"

I glance at my chest, grabbing the heart held around my neck by a golden chain. It's an antique made from a rare source of mother-of-pearl found near Luna Island's shore. It flashes lilac, green, and pink in the light.

"Yeah, it is. I was born here." I've had it with me since I was a baby. There's a picture of my parents inside. My mother said to wear it so I'd always know they're nearby. Though, it feels more like a noose now.

"Besides that, you're dressed like a total tourist." The girl laughs.

Heat rises to my cheeks. Sure, my sundress is simple, but I'd thought the tiny flowers on it were sweet. Now they just seem childish. "Is it really that obvious?"

"This is Luna Island, not Palm Beach. Good effort, but I'm sure I could help you find something better."

Her confidence makes me falter. "Yeah," I mutter, gathering my hair to the side. "Everyone here looks like—"

"An angel of the sea?"

"Angel . . ." That's what that other girl was saying earlier. *Something to impress the angels.*

"My." Roisin's fingers flutter to her lips. "I know you're new here, but your auntie really never mentioned the angels before?"

"No." I twist the locket once more. "What, are they like your mascot or something?"

"This isn't high school, silly. The angels are all around. You never know who might be one. If you're lucky, they visit you. Grant you wishes. Extend protection, charms, or gifts."

A scoff escapes my throat. "You're kidding, right?"

She stares me down with her hazel eyes, their color changing in the light.

"You should be thankful, Roisin," one of the local girls interrupts. Spiraling golden ringlets strung with tiny seashell beads frame her heart-shaped face. The slight sunburn on her nose gives her a sun-kissed glow. "One less pretty girl to compete with you for Angel of the Sea."

"Angel of the Sea," I say. "Is that the name of your pageant?"

The girls exchange knowing glances. I assume that's a yes.

"I'll see you tonight, Serena," Roisin says with a lilt. "Oh, and Ophelia was right. Go with the sparkles. Though you'll still need a bit more to outshine me. Perhaps an accessory? We have an array of jewelry in the back."

Serena sheds a sheepish smile, offering a friendly nod before turning to leave. And although she walks away politely, I've competed with girls long enough to know Roisin's confidence was enough to make Serena second-guess the dress entirely.

"You know, you're pretty good at this whole thing."

"What, sales?"

"No. Competition."

She smirks, extending her hand. "I'm Roisin. It's Irish. Ro-sheen. But it's spelled R-O-I-S-I-N. Confusing, I know."

Roisin. It's pretty. It suits her.

"I'm Lila," I mimic. "Lee-la. But it's spelled L-I-L-A, like Lie-la. Confusing, I know."

She giggles, and I almost think we could be friends.

"Well, Lila, it's lovely to meet you. Welcome to Luna Island's famous dress shop."

"*Famous* dress shop?"

"These aren't just any dresses. They're special. Magic, some would say." Her eyes twinkle as she pulls me over to a cluster of dresses hanging in one of the wardrobes. "You see, the silk is spun by the angels."

"Right . . . the angels." I study Roisin's ever-changing eyes, trying to decide if she's just teasing me.

She nods, leaning over and whispering, "They're alive as you and I."

A shiver slithers down my spine as I recall the voice at the dock. It's nothing. I've heard that voice my entire life. It isn't any different here than it was back home. Just my anxieties taunting me.

"You see, the dress you pick brings you good fortune. Whether it be for a first date, a meeting with your lover's family, or even a new beginning." Roisin tugs my wrist, whisking me away to another aisle of gowns.

The dresses are all floor-length and full, with bows that tie in the back and sweep into trains of ribbon. The more I study the ruffled sleeves and embroidered bustiers, the more otherworldly they appear. There's lace so dainty it would require a needle as thin as a hair to weave. Bows so small, they must have taken the nimble fingers of a fairy to tie. Or, perhaps, an angel. They remind me of the hopefulness of playing princess, and for a moment, I want to believe in Roisin's myths and magic.

I need something to believe in after I stopped believing in myself.

I'm deserving of gentle things, I silently affirm, indulging in the softness of the silks beneath my fingertips. Breath catches in my throat as I embrace the chiffon-spun flowers. I repeat my meditation like a mantra. *I can be good. I can behave.* I will not crumple the fabric with my fists, or puncture holes in it with my nails.

My eyes bloom as I meet a silk as smooth as water. It shines like a pool of opals. The connection is tender and romantic, like how the feeling of summer swelled up within Romeo when he first laid eyes on Juliet. She was beautiful, as fair as their beloved Verona. And here, this dress reminds me of all the loveliness of Luna Island.

It's hand dyed soft colors—blush and blue, lilac and lemon—like a sunset sky above island waters. A blue sash cinches the waist, and the bow in the back fans out into multiple ribbons, each one a color featured on the dress. Labyrinthine embroidery coils into roselike shapes, and the ruffled sleeves remind me of cream puff shells. I check the price tag, confirming it's within the budget Laina left me with.

"I'll take this one," I say.

"Oh, I just adore this dress." Roisin hums. "Good choice."

My nails tap against the counter as I wait to pay, *tik, tik, tik,* filling the silence between my burgeoning questions. I can't help but ask, "Where do these myths about the angels come from?" They seem like an important part of the island's culture, and I'd be naive to move here without learning more.

She giggles, folding my dress between thin layers of perfumed tissue paper. "They're not myths, silly."

"What do you mean?"

"It's our little secret on the island." She winks, handing me a floral shopping bag.

Secret. My stomach drops. Whether the angels are a myth or not, Luna Island is a paradise, and I don't belong here after what I've done. I look around the shimmering dress shop. It's too good to be true. Getting sent here was supposed to be my punishment, not some whimsical island getaway.

I take the shopping bag, but before I leave, I find the courage to ask, "What does the Angel of the Sea win anyway? I mean, why do you guys care about it so much?"

She tilts her head to the side. "Why does anyone care about winning, Lila? It's an honor, isn't it?"

I swallow a breath, holding back what I really want to say. It slips out anyway. "Winning isn't all it's cut out to be. Good luck though."

I push through the door, letting the bell drown out her response.

Clouds roll in as I leave, washing pale blue undertones across my skin, as if I too am fading. The pain lingering in my palms returns, a phantom sting that never quite wanes, reminding me of who I am. I did something wicked, and I'm not sure how much longer I can hide it. The ocean sings to me, echoing back and forth, calling me to embrace where I truly belong.

Come to me, Lila, it says. *Come to me.*

It's intrinsic. Feral. Like an animalistic urge I can't tame. Is it in my head, or is it real? It's a game my mind likes to play. All I know is I can't resist it. The water taunts me in the distance, begging me to cross the cobblestone street and white sands to reunite.

Come to me.

I run.

The wind mangles my hair and my true colors unfold with the tide, revealing how dangerous the waters can really be. How dangerous I can really be. My heartbeat quickens.

I want to fit in.

I want to be good.

I hold my breath, counting to ten as the waves retreat. My knuckles turn white as I clench the handle of the floral-print shopping bag from Luna's Love Shack. Bile crawls up my throat, remembering that the delicate gown cradled between the pink tissue is nothing more than a disguise to make me feel lovely while my own beauty fades.

I exhale, dropping the shopping bag into the sand, and run towards the wild sea. The brine welcomes me, each breath awakening my senses, as if the sea is entering the chambers of my heart and filling me with life. Salt water laps against my ankles, reclaiming me as its own. I close my eyes and embrace the rush of the waves.

A splash of colors explodes behind my eyelids—violet, magenta, and deep blood red—a memory of my violence. My feelings have always shown up like paintings, but this piece of art is harder to dissect. Or maybe it's just my mind protecting me from the pain of remembering.

With a deep exhale, I give myself to the sea.

I relevé, bringing my arms over my head as I rise off the ground. The waves thrash, but I adore them when they're mad. The water is up to my thighs, and when the ocean plummets into me, I don't collapse. I can't be overthrown. I throw my arms back, lifting my chest towards the setting sun. The colors pulsate, mixing and mingling.

Violet, magenta, deep blood red.

Passion, violence, destruction.

I rise from my arch, flowing into a series of pirouettes, swinging my body against the tide. I gather the fragments of shattered stained glass, stitching them into the scene of that night. When the waves roll away, I lunge into an arabesque. I see it faintly—

My mother struggling for breath on the ground.

They say the body never forgets trauma. The sensation still runs through me now. All I remember, the only part too heavy to black out, was how it felt to break the fruit—the summer pear grown in my mother's garden. My rage was building. Building and building, cascading and building, until hot stars burst in my blood. It escaped from my fingertips first, digging into the delicate fruit and dividing its flesh, destroying its purity and all my mother's collected love. A scream within me rasped, ripping through my throat and echoing an unbecoming sound. It was a fantasia of screeches and shrieks, a crescendo of a twisted violin, growing and growing until I began clawing at my mother's throat.

I collide with a nova of a wave, throwing my body into a pirouette. The colors come faster now, changing tone. *Stark bright blue, seafoam green, the palest lilac.* The color of a slow-changing bruise. I inhale sharply, remembering her shallow breathing.

All at once, it was silent and it was over.

Picking up the slivers of pear, I was hollow, as if I should cry but had nothing left to give. I stole a glance of my reflection in the window, unable to recognize the girl staring back. Instead, I saw a devil, crippling a fruit harvested with love, given with love, served with love on a porcelain plate—which too—I had shattered.

Another wave hurls at me and I fight it with my port de bras, my arms slicing through the icy waters as it knocks me over. I stumble, plummeting straight into the sand.

"No!" I curse, smacking my palms into the cold, wet ground.

Maybe, if I were a better ballerina, my parents would've wanted to keep me.

Maybe, if I worked harder, I could have earned their love.

That night, I realized I would never be the person my parents wanted me to be. And so, I would pretend. With my hands still covered in blood and tears and nectar, I swore from the pit of my heart to keep my demons buried, trapped within the bottom of my inner ocean forever. I would be an angel—the beauty everyone so fondly recognized from afar—but my father would never forget the devil within my eyes.

"*You were born this way,*" he whimpered beneath his breath.

My heart shattered. The next thing I knew, I was here.

A tear slips down my cheek. "I can be good . . . I can behave," I say to the sea.

It laughs back, echoing its otherworldly overtone—not quite human, mocking me. As the waves vibrate with the song of the deep, I see the ocean for what it really is.

My undoing.

My fingers sink into the sand, clawing for something stable to steady my racing heart. The icy waters shackle my wrists, coaxing me forward as the tide dwindles. But, when the sparkling sea-foam retreats, it spits out a broken body.

I scream.

She looks just like me.

Chapter
TWO

✦

Her sprawling limbs bring me to my feet. I rush over, hunching down to examine her crooked figure.

"Hello?" I shake her. "Are you okay?"

Tears gloss my eyes, blurring the twin image of myself. A serpentine coil of raven tresses cling to her sienna skin. Although I'm fairer, our similarities are uncanny. Same rose-shaped lips, a perfect bud when pinched, no wider than the width of my nose when relaxed. Dark lashes kiss her cheekbones like black feathers. They don't dare to flutter open.

Something is deeply wrong.

Despite her being as beautiful as Snow White under glass, silver scales plague her body. They travel from her temples, down her neck, across her chest, and over her arms, casting rainbow reflections like a mirrorball. Hints of crimson fissure between the mutations. *Blood*. It's as if the scales are piercing her from the inside out.

My breath wavers as I brush the sticky hair away from her face. The heat of her blushed-brown skin sears like salt spilling into an open wound. A tear slips down my cheek, landing like a dewdrop against her brow. I wonder if she can feel my racing pulse against her back or recognize the scent of perfume on my skin. She doesn't move.

What has the sea done to her? I look at the waves. It's not the friend I mistake it as.

"You're okay . . . it's going to be okay," I tell the girl. Or maybe I just tell myself.

And then I yelp.

Her eyes roll back as her head lolls, revealing twin white moons instead of irises. Her mouth gapes open, fighting for air with angler-sharp teeth. I scurry to my feet, shrieking as the Sleeping Beauty awakes.

"What the—" I scamper back. "Help! Somebody help."

I grab my shopping bag from Luna's Love Shack and break down the beach, not daring to turn around, not even as she starts to heave. It's unlovely and broken, like something dying that's trying to come back to life. My feet sink into the sand with every furious step, as if the island is pulling me back, begging me to stay.

Come to me, it says. *Come to me.*

"No!" I shout, heading towards the closest cottage on the shore.

It's a pale blue gray with white gardenias sprawling up the walls and over the sage-green windowpane.

"Hey!" My voice strains as I pound on the door. "Help! Please, someone help me."

A few seconds pass before a woman with tight coils of red hair answers the door. She pulls the robe around her body tighter, crossing her arms. "Sweetie, what's wrong?" she says in a gentle voice, scanning me up and down. "Have we met before?"

"I— There's a girl. On the beach. I think she's dying. Or at least badly hurt."

"Oh my god." The woman steps past me, snaking around to the back of the cottage to get a better view of the shore.

I follow her, muttering as I struggle to catch my breath. "She—she has these scales. And her eyes. They're white. When she opened her mouth—"

"Darling," she interrupts. "There's nothing there."

My jaw slackens. "What?" I push past her. "She was just—"

The sea laughs back. There's nothing but the endless white-sand beach. Did I just imagine the entire thing?

"I swear . . ." My voice hangs lifeless in the air.

"Dear Luna," the woman mutters. "You're new here, right? I know the island is a lot to take in, but it isn't something that should frighten you."

"But, I'm not—"

She places a hand to my back, ushering me forward. "You're overwhelmed. I get it. You should go home. Get some rest."

I hesitate, taking a breath. I know what I saw. I held her. She was real. But there isn't any use fighting.

"Sorry for bothering you," I finally say, turning to leave.

As I make my way back to Laina's cottage, I'm careful to take the streets, unwilling to test my fate on the beach.

✦

Back at home, I slip into a milky bath perfumed with chamomile and honey. Lemon slices and flower petals float on the surface of the water. The steam relieves my pores, turning my skin supple and dewy. I light a rose-scented candle, allowing the sweet fragrance to mingle with the herbal steam.

If I weren't so afraid to be alone, I'd lock myself in my room and never come out. But there's no hope in sleeping beside the sound of the sea or with the ocean lingering right outside my window.

The voice drifts back into my mind.

Before coming here, I only ever heard that voice in my dreams. It's the same every time.

The sea calls to me, echoing my name in a lilting voice that teases like a friend, coaxing me forward. I laugh with her, following her spirit into a sea-foam trap that binds me by the ankles. It starts gentle, like feathers and petals, telling me it's safe. I can trust it. And so I go.

Waves collide with my body like bursting stars. I struggle forward, water punching at my stomach, flooding up my nose, and sweeping me into the sand. It traps me like a puppet being strung along by a thread. I sink, blissful and intoxicated—*down, down, down*—aloof and entranced.

It's always beautiful, coating my skin with a natural grit, both crystal and grime. The sea is incandescent. A mirror of the sun, dividing her beauty into golden fractals, the house of trea-sures and pearly mysteries. She is a natural wonder, a goddess of the earth. But she is not just beauty. She has never been tamed. She is tsunamis. She is hurricanes and cyclones and wrath—free to envelop the shores, free to destroy worlds. Unapologetic. Unbreakable. Unforgiving.

Suddenly, frost bites into my veins, awakening chills like needle pricks. My eyes spring open. The water forms a gradient with aquamarine at the top, trickling into teal, into cobalt, into navy, and into midnight. It's an ombré of an ocean, flecked with golden stardust. It's different here.

The otherworld.

I reach out—hopeful and determined. My arms collapse against the waves, chopping away at me as I struggle to surface. It's no use. The tide is too strong, holding me back, cutting off my breath.

But before I sink into the abyss, a sculpture of muscles entan-gles my waist, hoisting me towards the aquamarine glimmer in the distance. *An angel?* I'm lifeless, like a rag doll dragged through the tide. Within a blink, I emerge from the sea in a rasping gasp.

Only to find myself still stuck on Luna Island.

Being here is like something of my dreamworld. Or rather, my nightmares.

I exhale a deep sigh, brushing away the image of the girl on the beach as I finish getting ready. I can't help but imagine her silver scales eating away at me like a parasite. I touch my pale skin, glass-like from the pearl highlight dusted across my cheeks. Did I really just imagine her? I wouldn't put it past me. It's not the first time stress has gotten to me like this. Especially with all the sleepless nights I've been having.

After perfuming my neck with lychee and fig oil, I touch up my barrel curls and apply a fresh coat of lip gloss. As I stare at my reflection, I almost believe I'm the angel I masquerade as.

My skin shines like opals, the iridescence catching the fullness of my lips and the high points of my cheeks. Coalescing down to my waist are ribbons of black hair, perhaps my favorite feature about myself. Though my mother has always loved my eyes the most—upturned and narrow, blooming with feathered lashes. I, for one, have always been frightened by them. Some would mistake their red-honey color for brown. But in the light, they glint with a tint of ruby. Like devil eyes. I shut them.

No more ocean of a girl.

At least not tonight.

✦

Just like Laina instructed, I'm at the dock by eight.

A bustle of perfumed girls giggles past me, sharing secrets with their rose-stained lips and linking arms as they board the boat. Sweet scents assault my nose—basil and nectarine, hibiscus and orange blossom, jasmine and ylang-ylang—a bouquet of summer wrapped up in amber notes. I sway as the fruity gourmand stings my sinuses.

The sea breeze fills my lungs as I take a deep breath. Despite its haunting echo, the ocean is mesmerizing—dancing with the setting sun and cradling reflections of gold. Light fractals as the waves crash, like fireworks settling into sparkles. I shut my eyes. *The sea is a friend*, I tell myself. *She won't hurt you.*

"Lila," a honeyed voice pours out. "There you are! I'm so glad you made it."

"Laina." I spin around, meeting my aunt with a hug. A sudden relief overcomes me for just a moment. It disappears too soon.

"Come on, let's go inside." She tugs me along.

The boat glows like a giant pearl, but I barely have a chance to admire it as Laina ushers me on board. I yelp as I enter the ballroom, nearly slipping on the dark wood floor. It's so polished, I can faintly see my reflection beneath the chandelier light. Laina laughs as I steady myself against the wall, but it isn't funny. All I think about is how I fell onstage and how history missed repeating itself tonight by a mere step.

Heads snap in my direction, and my lashes flutter to the ground, studying the bows on my heels to distract myself from their stares.

I almost fell.

Oh my god. I almost fell.

When I was a ballerina, I lived for the spotlight. But now, when I'm raw and real and me, I don't want to be seen. Not after what I've done. Shame comes rushing back like the slam of a wave. I wonder if the crowd can see right through me—a sad, lost girl, banished here on her birthday because her parents didn't want her.

If only there were someone familiar in the crowd. I scan the ballroom as a band comes alive with the medley of a saxophone, bass, and piano. The diamond chandelier casts a warm glow across the shimmering silk dresses, spinning into romantic colors.

Rich bright gold, soft blush, and glittering champagne.

Women bring cocktails to their lips with perfectly manicured fingers, clinking glasses with dashing men—sophisticated from their slicked hair down to their polished leather shoes.

I adjust the ribbons on my dress, and when I glance up, a young man sends me a wink. I turn away to hide my flush, but to my left, another group of boys leers at me. I stumble back before running into the crowd, dashing past the ruffles and frills. My throat closes as the bright fairy lights strung across the room pulsate. *Oh, dear.* A waiter offers me a flute of champagne. I down it, then grab another before pushing my way through the room of strangers. The bittersweet bubbles turn me heady. My heart pounds as the dancers melt into wisps, strobes of colors entwining too quickly to comprehend. I wipe the cold sweat from my forehead. Perhaps some air would be good.

I find the exit, seeking relief on the top deck. The sky is strewn with streaks of fuchsia woven between peachy clouds. Wind whips my face, relaxing my curls into waves. I lean against the metal railing, looking down at the endless sea.

"It's you and me again." I sigh.

Luna Island taunts me in the distance. Its crescent shape dwindles the farther we drift away, twinkling like a half-moon in the water. I gnaw at my bottom lip, hatred blooming for how perfect it all is. Its sparkle never fades, just like the dazzling people who live here. Maybe Roisin is right. Maybe they really are all angels. I shut my eyes, forcing away the island's glimmer.

I wish the boat wouldn't return so that I could fade away from here entirely. I'll never fit in, as hard as I try. The truth is bound to catch up to me eventually.

My eyes spring open as a cry rings out.

It's faint and distant, coming from the island. I pounce forward, hovering over the railing. There's something there. Wind whips my face as I lean farther, trying to get a better look. A bird?

Only it's too big to be a bird. I wince in disbelief. It's a monstrous thing with black wings on the shore. The dark feathers spread wide, looming over something. Or rather, *someone.*

"Oh my god." I blink, skittering back.

No.

There she is again on the shore. The girl I saw earlier today on the beach. The creature sinks to its knees beside her, enveloping her in a cocoon of wings, like an angel of death performing its reaping.

Angel.

Angel.

A scream rattles my throat.

It isn't real.

I'm imagining things again.

The mirage drifts away as the sea puts distance between us. Then, suddenly, it's gone. I look back up, double-checking it was ever really there at all, but it's all a blur now. I'm alone with the ocean again.

Lila, it hums. *Come to me.*

My knuckles turn white as I grip the metal rail. I squeeze my eyes shut as breaths rush out from my lungs as uncontrollable as the tide. It's mocking me.

Go, it says. *Jump.*

"No!" I push away from the edge of the boat and race back inside.

The warm, champagne-scented air envelops me in a balmy trance. I stumble, colliding with a picture frame as my fingers graze the velvet wall. I claw at its plush surface, desperate to hold on to something real. Instead, I sink to the floor, huddling into a corner and pulling my knees to my chest.

"Lila?" A familiar voice chimes. I don't look up, but her shadow engulfs me. "Lila, are you okay?" I'm forced to make eye contact as she sinks to the ground.

Roisin.

Soft curls woven with full-bloomed roses fall around her doll-like face. She grabs my hand, stilling my breath. At first, it startles me. I'm not used to being touched. But quickly, I find comfort in her palm and relax. Her warmth spills over me, and she offers a reassuring smile.

"I've been looking for you. My mother told me what happened earlier. I wanted to make sure you're okay."

"Your mother?"

She nods. "That cottage on the beach you ran to, it was mine." She squeezes my hand. "Look, I don't know what you saw, but you're not crazy."

I hesitate, paralyzed by her hazel irises. "I don't know what you're talking about."

She wraps a lock of hair around her finger, tugging. "You don't have to pretend. I know you're scared."

"What?"

Her fingers trail over the coral ruffles of her dress, as if grazing a bed of flowers. She's so calm. I admire her composure. It eases my nerves, just a little. "You really want to know why we're here at the Midsummer Ball, six years too soon?"

I don't say anything. I don't have to.

"The island is stealing from us. Nothing is in balance anymore."

Chills sprout across my arms. *Balance?* She says it as if the island is alive. Like, it has wants and needs in order to survive. "I don't understand."

Her mask drops, and I see her sorrow, like a sweet plum turning rotten. "It wasn't supposed to be this way."

I tilt my head to the side. "Well, how was it supposed to be?"

She sighs. "The Angel of the Sea isn't just a beauty pageant. It's a competition to seek a new High Priestess for the angels' commune in the center of the forest. Only, last time, things didn't really go as planned."

"Wait, what?" My heartbeat quickens. She makes it seem like some type of cult.

"Now you see why we keep this a secret from outsiders. They wouldn't understand."

Maybe she's right. But I'm not an outsider anymore, and I deserve to know the truth. "Why do the angels need a High Priestess?"

She leans in closer, whispering, "That's how they source their power. Before the angels came to Luna Island, we were a failing fishing village. The angels blessed us with abundance. Not only that but *magic*. Why do you think Luna Island is so charming?"

"I don't know, tourism?" A chuckle escapes beneath my breath, since I'm still in denial that any of this could be real. It's a joke. I'm the new girl—vulnerable and naive—the perfect victim for the beautiful girls of Luna Island to torment as they become bored with their idyllic paradise.

Dimples well in her cheeks as she laughs. She plucks a rose from her hair, placing it behind my ear. "If you haven't noticed, we don't get many tourists around here."

My tension softens, eased by her wistful smile. There's an innocence to her voice that suggests sincerity. Perhaps I'm the real vulture. She, on the other hand, has all the sweetness of a dove. "I'm sorry. It's just a little hard to believe."

"Is it?" She studies me, as if she knows what I've seen. I look away, in case she can steal the image burned into the gloss reflection of my eyes. I can't admit it. Not to myself. Not to her.

"What happened to the last High Priestess?" I ask nervously.

Roisin relaxes against the wall, releasing my hand from hers. She sighs, staring off at the ceiling. "For whatever reason, she wasn't enough. The Angel of the Sea is supposed to last seven years. Nadine only lasted one."

"Nadine?"

"Yeah." Her voice drops. "My girlfriend. Well, *was*."

"Oh, I'm—"

"You don't have to say it."

Her abruptness startles me. It's clear I've struck a nerve. I look away, tapping my nails on the floor to fill the silence. "Do you miss her?" I eventually ask.

"Of course." Her gaze is glazed as she twirls one of the flowers that fell from her hair.

I scoot closer, careful not to startle her. A question hangs from my lips until it grows heavy. I can't keep it from dropping. "What do you think happened?"

Her eyes snap to mine, suddenly cold and piercing. "What?"

I skitter back. I've asked too much. "I—I mean, how does this whole thing work? The High Priestess."

"Well"—her voice mellows as the subject shifts—"the angels work through the goddess Luna. You know, the moon?"

My nose scrunches. "The moon?"

She nods. "The angels are fallen stars and Luna is their goddess. They need a vessel to channel her power, hence the High Priestess. And, after her time is served . . . she ascends to the sky." Her gaze drifts upwards, gleaming and heavy, trying to keep tears from spilling over.

"Only Nadine never ascended," I assume.

"Perhaps." Her voice drops to a whisper. She looks at me, a softness glinting in her eyes. "Something's going on. And I'm going to figure it out."

"How do you plan on doing that?"

She lifts a brow. "By winning."

"Roisin!" I snap. I don't know her, but she's more of a friend than I've had in a while. "Why would you compete after knowing what happened to Nadine?"

"That's exactly why I have to. It's my only chance to learn the truth." She hesitates. "Besides, what if it was just some fluke? Maybe Nadine couldn't handle it."

I press up from against the wall, the realization clicking. "Oh my god. You still believe it could be you."

"Excuse me?"

"The High Priestess. You still don't believe the pageant is bullshit."

"It's not that simple," she bites out, folding her arms across her chest. "You haven't lived here long enough to understand."

"Then humor me." It's the least anyone can do around here.

She pauses, smoothing out her dress. "This is our culture, Lila. We were raised to believe in Luna, in the High Priestess. It's the greatest honor anyone can earn—being crowned as the most angelic of them all—revered for beauty, faith, and grace."

It doesn't take long for me to understand. She wants to be adored. Don't we all?

My shoulders slump as my muscles ease. I scoot closer, inhaling her sweet pea-and-vanilla scent. "I get it. You don't know me yet, but I think we're alike, you and I."

"Oh, Lila. I could read you the second we met. Game recognizes game."

I frown. "I don't want to compete against you, Roisin." I finally found someone who could maybe be my friend. I can't risk screwing it up.

"Then don't compete against me. Compete *with* me."

"Why would you want that?" I wince. "Like those girls at Luna's Love Shack said, I'm just one less bit of competition in your way."

"Yeah, but I could use a friend right now. And I think you could too."

Heat swells in my cheeks, embarrassed that she could see right through me. She doesn't need to know how desperate I am to finally call somewhere my home. I scoot back, putting distance between us. "I—I don't know. It's not really my place. Besides, I'm not even versed in your lore."

She laughs. "Well, that can change."

I sit up taller, meeting her eye to eye. "You mean, you'll tell me about the angels?"

She nods. "I'll tell you."

✦

Once upon a time, in the Kingdom of Luna, where all the stars shine, there lived an angel named Lucifer with lust in his eyes. From above the clouds, he gleamed, as angels do, guiding humans to their happily ever afters, their second chances, their new beginnings. Ever faithful was he in serving the goddess Luna—the Pearl of the Heavens—whom mortals worshiped and wished upon. Oh, how she was adored, especially by her angels, whom she granted the power to shine brighter with each mortal prayer.

But Lucifer didn't want to shine.

He wanted to feel.

For angels could not live for themselves. They existed only to serve, to be the hope in someone else's sky.

Thus, one day, against his goddess's will, Lucifer dove into the sea, and he came alive! A mere touch of the water transformed him into a soul with a beating heart. Like the humans, he experienced life in color, in multitudes. He settled on a nearby island and lived amongst the mortals. Though his love for Luna never faded, and he dedicated his new home in her name—Luna Island. As Lucifer bloomed in the wake of his freedom, the other angels envied him.

Like rainfall, more and more stars dove into the sea.

As her sky dimmed, Luna wailed at this betrayal. She commanded the tide, imprisoning her fallen angels in the sea they'd left her for. They bent over the waves like temple dancers—sparkling and colliding, bursting into nebulas to the push and pull of her command. Until, just like that, the fallen stars became nothing more than the shimmer of the sea.

Lucifer glimpsed the light from his island home and recognized the fallen stars as his brothers and sisters. He rushed into the waves to save them. Only, the tide pulled him under too. Coiled in the sea's firm grasp, Lucifer channeled his strength into grabbing hold of the angels and whisking them onto land. He could not return them to the sky, but a life onshore would suffice. With the last of his breath, he hoisted his kin onto Luna Island, before the sea swallowed him whole. Trapped at the bottom of the ocean—deep below the abyss and amongst the sea fires of Hell—Lucifer bloomed into something known to all as the Devil.

The angels on Luna Island mourned their fallen brother, wishing to repay his sacrifice with the love he showed them. But the Devil's rage only burgeoned, plaguing Luna Island with natural disasters from the sea. Hurricanes. Tsunamis. Cyclones. And so, to protect their beloved home, the angels channel Luna through their vessel—the most angelic girl on Luna Island—whose lovelight culls the ocean's wrath.

✦

The room spirals, beating to the tempo of my throbbing pulse.

The most angelic girl on Luna Island.

I can hear my father laughing now. My parents knew this would be my true undoing. A competition to finally prove that I'm not angelic. Is this why they sent me here? To mock me?

You were born this way. Father's voice echoes back.

No.

I pounce to my feet, stumbling as I rise.

"Lila?" Roisin stands to meet me. "Are you alright?"

My parents' voices are the only ones I hear now.

Not pretty enough.

Not special enough.

Not worthy enough.

"I—I'm sorry. I have to go."

"Lila—" She reaches out.

"Stop. Don't follow me."

"Hey, wait." Roisin grabs my arm, but I tear away.

I race across the dance floor, darting past the people who blur like watercolor. The jazz band turns into a piercing swarm of buzzing bees, and the floral garland strung between the ceiling beams coils into an aromatic noose. All that glitters dwindles as I break through the double doors and find myself on deck again.

The vicious sea breeze wraps me in a whirlwind of numbness, but I welcome the chill. The night air feeds the chaos brewing inside me, and I scream to the stars and sea, darting towards the front of the ship and pressing my palms into the metal railing.

My hands turn taut, clenching, as anger culminates in my palms. *No more good girl. No more nice girl.* I was never meant to be the perfect daughter my parents dreamt of. That's why they sent me away. I berate the metal, cursing, hissing, slamming into it until—

The screws come loose, and I waver, shrieking, trying to catch my balance but instead grab for air. I flail, reaching for safety, but my foot slips, and I plummet towards the sea.

I slam my eyes shut to brace myself for the rush of water, only there isn't any splash. I scream, louder this time, and open my eyes. An apparition appears before me—a beautiful man, glowing gold like a young Adonis. He's only there for a second before blinking into a cradle of glitter.

The sparkling waves gather me, holding me like a baby. My heartbeat settles as the ocean carries me back to safety. Before I know it, the sea spits me out onto the shore. I cough, clinging to the life I almost lost.

What the hell? My nails sink into the damp sand, collecting tiny grains beneath my fingertips. I heave as the sea-foam laps at me, trying to press upwards, but I'm too weak to stand. Instead, I rest my cheek against the ground, drinking in a faint trail of golden glitter leading all the way from the beach into the forest.

The same forest where the angels dwell.

Chapter
THREE

✦

I follow the trail but hesitate before the entrance of the forest. Roisin warned me of what's beyond here. An angel commune, where one of the lucky girls on Luna Island gets to live out her days as a High Priestess to their goddess, Luna.

But what if there's something more?

Something is haunting the island. Or maybe, it's just haunting *me*. The girl with the scales. The winged creature on the shore. The man who faded into a glimmer of the sea. Is it all just in my head? I hold myself, desperate to stay intact. *Keep it together, Lila.*

The starlight leading into the forest taunts me. For a second, I debate turning around, heading back to Laina's cottage, drying off, and going to sleep. That would be the smart thing to do. But I need to figure out what's going on before it's too late. Otherwise, I can kiss whatever chance I had at a fresh start goodbye.

With a deep breath, I make my way into the forest, following the shimmering trail. An evanescent breeze tangles my hair, and I shiver, alone between the looming trees that twist like fingers reaching for the sky. Their overgrown leaves block out any moonlight. If it weren't for the glowing path, I imagine I'd be left in total darkness. The thought of it makes me pick up speed, praying that the starlight won't burn out and leave me vulnerable to whatever lurks between the brambles. Twigs snap beneath my feet, and my heartbeat quickens. I don't like being here—lost to the void that swallows me.

Just as I'm about to surrender and turn around, something glimmers far in the distance. A trace of civilization? If I listen closely, I can hear a faint twinkle coming from where the light is. *Music.* It's sweet and romantic—harps and wind chimes . . . fluttering strums from a Spanish guitar . . . the shrill whistles of a flute. I run towards it, lured by the golden haze. Warm light engulfs me. I'm closer now. Dozens of chandeliers hang from above, threaded between the branches, dripping in opals and pearls. I race forward, following the string of lights.

A gasp cuts off my breath as I nearly fall. I waver, steadying my balance against a tree. I was so distracted by the blinding chandeliers that I didn't notice the trail I followed slopes off into a clearing. Beneath me is a glade, opening up into the otherworld.

"No way." I duck behind the tree that caught my fall. My chest stills against the rugged bark, and I press my fingers into the wood, before carefully peering over the edge.

Angels waltz around like in one of my daydreams, glitter-dusted as the faeries I was warned about as a child. They're mystic, with spindly limbs and gossamer hair and skin that glows. Their wings unfurl behind them, some gilded and others adorned with pale pink shimmer. They flutter across the flower-filled glade, twirling like falling feathers. A few of the angels thread starlight into garlands or coax the flowers to bloom. A train of them braid baby's breath into one another's hair. Others lay fruit in front of what look like shrines—seashells brimming with water and floating petals that gleam with reflections of the moon.

It's like something out of a storybook. Lanterns are strung between the evergreens, casting their light over a long table. On top of a silk tablecloth, candelabras drip with wax and flowers are strewn about—cerise roses, vibrant marigolds, velvet violets, and pale bluebells. Fresh fruit spills out of a giant shell like a cornucopia—mangoes, peaches, and guavas, champagne grapes and deep red cherries. Dark wine fills crystal cups. Rose-jam tarts with wild raspberries and hibiscus petals pile alongside tea cakes piped with custard and sugared primroses. In the center of the feast is a roasted duck glazed with honey and decorated with slices of pineapple. The smell of buttered potatoes lingers in the air, fragrant with hints of rosemary and garlic. All I can think of is faerie food, and how the stories warned me not to indulge.

It's a trap.

"I'm dreaming." I slam my palm against the tree. "Wake up, Lila!"

A cry cuts through the night, rupturing the dulcet music. Everything stills, like a nightmare that's stolen my will to move or even breathe. The reveling stops as a girl is carried forward towards a marble altar at the edge of the glade. She kicks and screams, fighting the two angels who bind her. She sounds like she's in pain, and from the way her body rasps against the angels, I know she is. They lay her upon the altar, across a bed of moonflowers and white lilies. It's morbid, like a funeral. Only she isn't dead.

Her shrieks ring out into the night, and she reaches towards the moon, as if its light could save her. She's a monster trying to come back to her human self. But the more she fights the pain, the more it changes her. Her legs are fusing, flesh morphing into a silver-blue tail. A thin iridescent film webs her fingers together, her nails turning clawlike at the tips. The angels gather around her, chanting to the beat of a drum.

Gratias ago, amabo te, me paenitet. Ambo te ignosce me.

It's her. The girl from the beach.

I try to scream. I try to run. My stomach tightens and I hunch over.

The angels light a fire behind her, and the flames ascend high into the sky. She wails, her spine splitting as her back arches towards the moon. The snapping of her bones shatters me. I break with her unlovely moans, desperate to stitch her together again. Her snakelike tongue slithers out, and she hisses, clawing at the marble surface beneath her as her chest rises and falls to the beat of the drum.

My nails dig into the tree bark. Amongst the crowd, I spot the angel from the beach—the one with black wings. He sticks out like a dying rose in a field of flowers, falling to his knees and pressing his face to the ground. It almost looks like . . . he's crying.

He's the only one who is, besides me. Besides her.

There's no humanity here. The angels are unfeeling, silent observers, chanting like she's part of a ritual and not a person at all. I pick apart her shallow sobs, moments where her voice breaks—mourning for her girlhood, her beauty, her life. *I recognize you*, I silently grieve. *You were real.*

She's just a girl.

Just like me.

My acknowledgment does nothing. Her body surrenders to the parasitic scales that eat away her brown skin, turning her silver as her curves dwindle away into a skeletal figure. She claws at her torso, trying to pick apart the scales, shrieking as her blood stains the white marble.

Nobody helps her.

The angels stay pressed with their faces to the ground, bowing as they chant their prayers. Some toss white flowers as she bleeds out on the altar—roses, gardenias, and jasmines—singing their hymns and leaving fruit at her feet, as if peaches and nectarines could make amends.

She wails, her insides spilling, back snapping, limbs breaking apart and fusing into something monstrous. They continue watching like she's a spectacle. Though all I see is *me*. Bleeding, screaming, terrified, as the crowd just watches and applauds. A sharp gasp rattles my throat. I clench my mouth in case someone hears.

This is what dancing made me.

This is what my parents made me.

I squeeze my eyes shut. "This isn't real!" I'm losing my mind again. Just like I did under the pressure.

No.

My vision eddies as the glow of the flames blurs everything into a blushing haze. The flowers melt into the colors of the fruit, the starlights fade into the trees, and the angels become one with the fire.

The flames grow higher, licking my flesh and breaking me into a sweat. Before it can claim me too, I dart into the forest as fast as I can. The light becomes violet as I run faster, farther, until I no longer see the brilliant glow of the fire. I don't even care what darkness comes to claim me now. I let myself roar. The island is just like the sea, just like me. Beauty, with an undercurrent of darkness. Don't get too close, or you might drown. My shins splinter while I push forward as quickly as possible, testing my limits until I'm met with an abrupt collision.

"Ow! What the hell?" I glance up. "Holy shit. It's you."

Chapter
FOUR

✦

"You." I pant, angrily slamming into his body. His unwavering figure makes me seem like a child lashing out. "Who are you?"

I try to piece his jagged edges together in the twilight. His face is fae-written like the rest, with sharp-carved bones that make his jaw and cheeks stand out like sculpted marble. His white-blonde hair paints his pale complexion sullen, almost ghostly, juxtaposed with his looming black wings.

"You're—you're real!" I twirl. "No, this is all wrong."

He grabs my arm, yanking me close. "What are you doing here?" His voice is hushed and raspy. "Humans aren't allowed in the forest without an invitation."

Gee. I wonder why. "What are you talking about? You led me here. All I did was follow the trail of starlight that *you* left behind."

His grip around me slackens. "Huh?"

I point to the glitter trail. "You left that behind after you pulled me out of the sea."

From the confusion on his face, I gather it wasn't intentional. Rather, he shed his starlight the same way humans shed droplets of water after a bath.

"You didn't have to follow." He looks behind his shoulder, as if someone could be watching. "You need to leave. Now."

I stand up taller on my toes, meeting him nose to nose. "Not until you tell me who you are. Why were you there at sea?" Could it be? Is he the voice?

In my recurring dreams of drowning, I'm always rescued by an angel. Just like how I was rescued by him tonight. Did he call me towards the sea on purpose? Is it all a trap? Or am I still dreaming, even now? It's like I never woke up. The world should've turned back to normal the second I reached land. Instead, I wound up in a living, breathing fairytale. Perhaps it's my fragile, tired mind, turning lucid and running wild. Alice stuck in Wonderland. Wendy cursed with Peter.

Wake up, Lila.

Wake up!

The angel's shoulders relax, his wings softening around him. He sighs. "I was trying to protect you . . . like, how I couldn't protect *her*."

Her. My nightmare deepens as her scale-ridden face and gutted stomach on the altar resurfaces. "Who is she?"

He looks away. "Just someone I used to know."

Someone I used to know.

I wonder if people will talk about me like that one day too.

She wasn't just a vanishing, dwindling *thing* that will fade into a memory. She was real. She *is* real. Her heart still beats. I bet she still dreams—still loves and grieves and *feels* the same way I do. Yet the angels treated her like a spectacle, a body to toss flowers at while she holds their attention for a glimmering moment. She's much more than that though. I know it from how the angel winces when he speaks of her, how his fist balls up and clenches, revealing the twisting veins in his wrist.

Only something real can cause such visceral pain.

I step closer, brushing my hand against his the way Roisin did with mine. I'm not very good at being there for anyone besides myself, but I try in the same way she showed me. He doesn't move as our fingers meet. "What happened to her? What did the angels do?"

"It's not the angels who are responsible for this," he bites out, flinging away my hand. He won't look at me. His jaw is tight, turning his throat taut and strained. "They were only trying to help, but it's too late."

It's too late. My flickering hope dies. Were the flowers, the fruit, and the song designed to strengthen her life, not diminish it? *Of course.* How could something so saccharine kill? How could beauty make one bleed? Though what else could have done this? More importantly, why? When I first found her washed up on the shore with white eyes and silver scales, it was as if the water had changed her. *Infected* her, somehow.

"It's the ocean, isn't it?" What else is so uncontrollable, so unfeeling, that it could cause this kind of evil?

His eyes snap to mine. They're golden in the moonlight, scintillating with a greenish sheen like beetle shells. "You can hear it, can't you?"

"Excuse me?"

"I saw you earlier. On the beach."

I stumble, backing into a tree. "Are you watching me?"

"Yes. I mean—" He shakes his head. "Not like that. I just wanted to make sure you were safe."

Safe.

My shoulders relax. Sometimes, I run so much, I forget what safety feels like. There's no hearth to warm me in the night, no castle to shield me as I lose battle after battle. I'm tired. *God*, I am tired. Who would want to protect *me* after what I've done? Even if it is just a fantasy, that desperate part of me yearns to pretend for just a moment.

My fingers graze his black wings, as if their softness could turn him gentle. There's a deep blue hue to them. Not just darkness, but a glimmer of something more. He doesn't move, like an animal I've gained the trust of through my touch.

"What, are you some sort of guardian angel?"

"Something like that." His eyes shut, tension creasing between his brows.

I step closer, tracing his sharp nose and upturned features. He's like my dreams fleshed out and made real, sent to me as if the universe knew I was drowning and needed saving. Have I been teetering so close to the otherworld that I needed an angel to shield me from it? Why am I even surprised? I haven't been careful with the sea's call. Every day it grows more tempting.

It terrifies me.

"Why did you help me?" I mutter.

"Because." He pauses, pushing the hair away from his face. "That's what angels are meant to do." He says it flatly, disappointed.

I understand why he wept now. The girl on the altar was his to save, and he couldn't. *Great.* How the hell is he supposed to save me?

"What are you protecting me from?" My voice quivers. I draw my shaking hand behind my back, tugging at one of the ribbons of my dress. If the sea is calling me, that must mean I'm next. It's only a matter of time before I end up on the marble, my dancer's legs robbed for good as I turn into a prisoner of the sea.

His mouth parts, but he doesn't reply.

"There's something haunting the island, isn't there?" My breathing deepens as the wind rustles the trees. "What is it?"

He turns his back towards me. "I shouldn't be talking about this with you."

"Please," I press. "I—I think it's after me too."

He tenses at my touch. "I told you—you shouldn't be here. And neither should I."

I yelp as he tugs away, breaking into the forest.

"Hey!" I call out. "Come back."

I snake between the trees, hunting him through the darkness. The glow of the chandeliers strung high casts vibrant strobes the closer we get to the ball. I wince, my eyelids shuttering, but I never stop running. That is, until the island yanks me back. I shriek, tripping over a tree root. Blood drips down my leg, and a whimper escapes my lips.

The angel halts, his wings slumping. "For Luna's sake."

"Ow," I whisper to the wound as blood seeps through the silk of my dress.

He approaches slowly and crouches beside me. "Are you alright?"

Tears pucker at the edges of my eyes. I try to hold them back, but I burst. "No! I'm not alright. In fact, I've probably just had the worst night of my life. Not to mention it's my birthday and my parents didn't even call to say hello. You know why? Because they sent me to this damn island to die!"

He jerks back. "What are you talking about?"

"I deserve it." My shrill breath breaks. "I don't even blame them."

With a sigh, he takes a seat beside me. "Look, I don't know what happened, but you don't deserve to die because of it."

I press my knees to my chest, embarrassed by my outburst. "You don't get it. . . you don't know the things I've done."

He leans against a tree, shutting his eyes. "Trust me, no one is as angelic as you think. We're all just doing the best we can."

Like how he tried to save the girl on the altar but couldn't. Like how I fell in front of everyone I wanted—*needed*—to love me. *What a disappointment.* Maybe we're not so different. Maybe we've both spun ourselves into defining goals as delicate as glass. And, if we can't achieve them, we shatter.

"Whatever happened to her," I whisper, "it wasn't your fault." I'm not even sure if that's true, but I feel like he needs to hear it. I wish I could hear it too.

Tears gloss his eyes, pooling like molten gold. I hold my breath, waiting for them to fall. Instead, he's tense, keeping it together—just barely. If only I could be that strong.

"I'm no angel," he says.

"Neither am I."

We don't look at each other. The distant murmur of the ball spills over the silence.

"The girl," I finally ask, "is that what will happen to me if I don't get off this island?"

He doesn't say anything.

I turn to him, crossing my arms. "Fine. Don't respond. But can you at least tell me whose voice is calling me from the water?"

His eyes flick over me, glowing with their feral sheen. "You ask too many questions."

"Forgive me, but being here isn't really my choice." *It's my punishment*, I remind myself. And it's coming for me.

He sighs. "Look, there's only one thing you need to know—if we don't find the next High Priestess soon, that girl you saw won't be the only one he'll reap."

"He?"

The angel shrugs, waving his hand, as if the answer should be obvious. The feathers on his wings ripple with the motion. "The Devil."

A shallow gasp parts my lips as my fingers clench the cool earth beneath me. *The Devil.* I squeeze my eyes shut, as if that could make the truth disappear. It only pierces deeper the more I try to force it out. When at last I look at the angel again, I know from the sternness on his face that it must be true. After all, if the angel is real, then the Devil must be too.

Of course he is. He follows me like a shadow, haunting the crooks of my mind and saying hello in my dreams. His darkness lingers, woven through my hair like smoke, weighing me down with every breath I take.

He's the voice that always calls.

The voice begging me to join him in the otherworld.

No.

"I'm sorry," the angel whispers, placing a hand on my knee. "I didn't mean to frighten you."

I force myself to be strong the same way he does. Though my voice wavers when I speak. "This is why you do it, then."

"What?"

"The pageant. If you don't find a High Priestess, then the Devil will take from the island. Like a tithe."

His hand drops from where it's rested, hesitating before he admits, "I tried to stop him."

I understand now. The island needs the angels—the angels need the priestess. That's what Roisin was saying at the ball. Everything is out of balance, and this angel was trying to fix it.

"Look," he says, rising. "I've had a long night. It seems like you have too. How about something to take your mind off things?"

"What?"

He turns, gesturing to the trees full of sparkling fruit. He picks one out. It's rose gold, the shape of a mango. Under the chandeliers it bursts with scarlet and amber, kissed with a magenta sheen.

"Do you know what this is?" he asks.

I shake my head. "No."

"Angel Fruit. The sweetest nectar to ever entwine with the tongue. To a human, one might call it . . . um, how do you say . . . a *psychedelic?*"

I tilt my head, studying it, thinking of the feast at the ball and how it reminded me of faerie food. Someone smarter would know not to indulge at all, but my curiosity spikes. "Why are you showing me this?"

"Because it helps you forget—to the point where all you feel is euphoria."

I'd be lying if I said that didn't sound inviting. Like Cinderella in the garden, bewitched by her fairy godmother before the ball. Me, with my bloodstained dress, my saltwater hair, my dirt-covered arms . . . my nightmares, my visions, the voices. I just want it all to disappear.

I reach for the fruit, but he pulls it away.

"I will let you have a bite. But there is a price."

Of course. Magic always comes with one. "What do you want?"

"First, I would like your name."

Predictable. Names hold power. I should know better than to give him mine. And yet that desperate part of me urges me to say, "Lila. Lila Rose Li."

He grins. "Very good."

"And you are?"

"None of your concern."

"Hey!" I stamp my foot. "That's not fair."

He laughs. "If you're good, perhaps you'll earn my name."

I roll my eyes. Ugh. He's painfully annoying. Just like human boys, he seems to like playing games. "Fine. What else, *my lord*?"

He smirks. "I want you to dance with me."

"What?" I wince, stumbling back. That was the last thing I expected. "Thank you for the offer, but you can keep your little fruit." I turn around, ready to take off into the forest. I can't dance again. Not for him. Not ever.

"Hey." He grabs my wrist. "I'm sorry. I didn't mean to offend you. It's just a dance."

I spin around, my voice thrumming. "It's not just a dance! I—I can't dance again."

"Why not?"

My body stiffens and I clench my fist, taking a deep breath. "Dancing is what got me sent to Luna Island."

"How could a dance do that?"

"Well, it wasn't just the dance," I admit. "It was what the dance made me do." I would stop at nothing to prove I was the best. Even if it meant putting myself at risk. Even if it meant hurting others. I can't go back to what it did to me.

He sighs. Perhaps pitying me. "Look, you don't have to tell me what happened. But if you take a bite, you can forget it all for just a moment and enjoy yourself." He lifts the fruit before my eyes, the magenta glow radiating off his pupils.

I hesitate, wondering why the angel could possibly want to share the fruit with me. Temptation paints my logic thin. I want an escape more than anything. "Really?"

"Yes, really."

I guess if I'm going to forget everything, what's the worst that could happen?

"Okay . . ." I say with caution.

"Are you sure now?"

I nod, and he smirks.

"Then cheers, Lila," he says, before taking a bite himself.

He draws the fruit towards my mouth, the nectar spilling over his hand. My lips part as I go to take a bite. The honey-sweet juice coats my tongue with a satisfying tang. My head falls back as I indulge, nectar dripping down my neck. The flesh of the fruit is radiant. It shimmers like the angel's skin. His skin. I realize I'm touching his skin. Velvet and dripping in juice. Velvet and full of heat. Smooth. Shimmering and smooth. Firecracker freckles burst on his flesh, bumps of chills and shivers, yet he's still warm. Velvet and cashmere and heat.

The euphoria has already begun.

My eyelids turn heavy, and my lashes flutter like butterfly kisses. He steadies me as I sway. "Lila, are you alright?"

I look up and he's a haze, all fuzzy edges and glowing. "I feel like heaven."

He laughs. I throw my head back and pull him into the clearing before us. My hand slips away as I twirl, my feet kissing the damp grass as I sway with the wind. Faint music from the ball trickles in like wind chimes, falling over me in a pixie-dust shower. My vision comes in waves, the light rippling around us. Everything is breathing. Everything has an aura. His is emerald, chartreuse, and gold. For a second, I think I see daisies sprout from where my toes meet the earth. I assume it's just the Angel Fruit muddling my mind.

"Come on, angel," I lilt. "I thought you wanted to share a dance?"

"Lila, you don't—"

"Come on!" I pull him forward before he has a chance to answer, howling, as we spin around the forest.

We turn weightless as we weave between the trees, all movement effortless as if we're floating. Pink and lilac light radiates off my body, tingling as his skin meets mine. I drape my arms around his neck. He's lovely, brimming with an unnatural brightness— radiant—like an angel. I smile.

He stumbles back, a crooked look on his face shattering the moment. My heartbeat quickens. "What's wrong?"

"Lila, are you doing this?"

"Doing what?"

He spins me around. "*This.*"

Gold-kissed magnolias blossom on the trees, multiplying before my eyes. Bright pink roses and coral-colored dahlias sprout from the ground. The buds hum faintly, a sweet sound that swirls around us in glitter. The roses blossom until they're full and round, shimmering with a faint iridescence.

I don't say anything. I can't.

"Lila." He taps me on the shoulder. "Are you alright?"

I open my mouth to speak, but everything goes black.

Chapter
FIVE

✦

A frigid chill nips my nose, waking me to the coastal breeze. The clouds break with a blood-orange sunrise. Goose bumps spread across my skin, and I nestle deeper into the grass—as if *that* could keep me warm. Shivering, I attempt to lift my body, but the cold paralyzes me. Where am I? *Shit.* Laina must be worried sick. I wipe the cold sweat from my forehead, the memory of last night a blur.

All I remember is a strangely vivid dream. An angel saved me from a death at sea. He gave me a fruit, and the world around me bloomed. There were bright pink flowers that sparkled and sang, gold-tipped petals and shimmering light. All spun by me.

My body.

My dance.

A pounding explodes in my temples as I force myself to rise. A note falls from my lap. That's odd. I unfold the paper and read.

Dear Lila,

Last night was magical. I must say, you truly are a lovely dancer. I have to see you again. Meet me in the forest at sunset for another dance. Follow the trail of starlight I've left behind.

—Your Guardian Angel,

Damien

My guardian angel.

Damien.

The angel who saved me in my dreams.

Only it wasn't a dream. It was real. My breaths come in snatches, too quick for me to catch. I read the letter three times over. I met an angel. I danced with him. And he was real. *Oh my god, he was real!* I gasp, wrinkling the note in my hand. If the angel was real, that means everything else is real too.

Luna.

The Devil.

The High Priestess.

But there's something more. Something I shouldn't have seen. I remember running through the forest. That's how I met the angel. But what was I running *from*? My temples throb the harder I try to recall. There was a fire, painting its rose-blushed glow across white flowers. But it wasn't a campfire, and it wasn't candles. It was not an inviting flame, even if it was beautiful. Rather, it was something ritualistic. A sacrifice? A cleansing? It comes in flashes—glimmers of gold, pearlescent sheens, incandescent reflections of light. My chest tightened at the sight of it. I was sweating, panting. That's when I ran. . . . The memory ends there.

I need to talk to Roisin. Oh gosh, I need to talk to Laina!

I push to my feet despite the aching in my muscles, gather the skirts of my dirt-stained dress, and run as fast as I can back to the cottage.

✦

"Laina?" I burst through the entryway in a pant. The door collides with a coatrack, toppling it over and knocking down several picture frames. *Oops.*

Laina jumps from an armchair and flings off a blanket. To my surprise, she isn't alone. Roisin is asleep on the living room couch. She rolls onto the floor with a thud.

"Lila!" Laina cries. "Where were you? We were worried sick. The police are looking for you everywhere. We were up until six in the morning praying for good news until we dozed off."

Roisin rushes forward, wrapping me in a hug. "Oh, Lila! There were boats all over searching for your body. When we found the broken railing, we thought—um, we thought—"

"You thought I was dead." My tone leaves a silence in the air.

"Oh, sweetie," Laina says. "Thank Luna a million times over, you're safe. Are you hurt? What happened? Oh gosh. I'm a terrible aunt. I can't believe I let this happen."

"No," Roisin cuts in. "This is my fault. If I hadn't sprung so much onto you, you would've never freaked out."

I look between them both. "Stop. This isn't anyone's fault but mine. Both of you have been nothing but kind since I arrived."

"Regardless, I should've been there." Roisin takes my hand. "As your new friend, it's my job to keep an eye on you. Girls are supposed to stick together."

I smile slightly, fidgeting with the frayed silk of my dress. "I can take care of myself just fine." She doesn't owe me anything, but she's sweet.

"That doesn't mean you have to do it alone," she says. Laina nods.

I don't know what to say. It's hard to believe them when I've never really had anyone to confide in before. Maybe things will actually be different this time.

Laina leads me towards the couch and drapes a blanket across my lap. "Roisin, why don't you make some tea. I'll draw Lila a bath."

"Thank you," I manage to say. "For everything."

"Of course, Peaches," she says with a coo. "While we wait, do you care to tell us what happened? How are you—"

"Alive?" She doesn't have to say it. I can read it on her face.

"Um, yes."

"Well"—I tug at the locket around my neck—"I met an angel . . . and he kind of saved my life."

Roisin shrieks, dropping a ceramic mug in her hand that shatters across the kitchen floor.

Laina squeals. "Dear Luna. You've been blessed."

✦

A steaming blend of lavender and chamomile warms my throat as I take a sip of tea. Ocean mist kisses my freshly washed face as I join Roisin on the bench-swing outside, surrounded by pink azaleas. The sea glimmers beneath the morning sun, illuminating her peachy skin.

"So," she says, kicking her feet back and forth as we sway. "How are you feeling?"

I steady a hand on the swing's rope, grazing the coarse twine to calm my racing nerves. "Do you really want me to answer that?"

Her shoulders slouch as she tilts her head to the side. "Lila, you met an angel. How are you not jumping over the moon?"

"Maybe because I didn't want to believe they were real in the first place." If the angels are real, it only means everything else about the island is true too. Including the Devil.

"I understand, but this is a good thing. The angels only show themselves if they want to be seen. And now that you've met one, it means you're one step ahead in the pageant."

The pageant. I almost forgot about the stupid pageant.

Competing will only destroy any chance I have at a new beginning. This is what my parents wanted—for me never to be content. I twist my hair to the side, tugging on the ends. "I told you, I'm not competing."

"Why not? You've been blessed! Most of us never even see an angel within our lifetime."

"Wait, what?"

She nods. "The angels are fickle. Like I said before, you never know who might be one. Which is why we always have to be on our best behavior."

"I don't understand. If you never see the angels, how do you compete in their pageant?"

"Well, the pageant is run by the commune's matriarch, Mother Marguerite. She's a villager who lives in the forest to help keep things in balance, but rumor has it she's really an angel."

"It's not obvious? What about her wings?"

"That's exactly what I mean," she says with a smirk. "A beggar on the street who asks you for a loaf of bread could really be an angel in disguise. They'll bring you sweet dreams, lost items, good fortunes, or even grant you a wish for your kindness."

I look off at the sea, painting the image of my angel in the ripples of the water, just like how he came to me as a glimmer in the waves. "You've really never seen one before? Like, in their true form?" It's hard to believe, given that I ran into one after merely a day here.

She laughs. "I wouldn't say 'never,' exactly. There is the Starlit Ball."

"What's that?"

"At the end of pageant season, the angels throw a ball where the final competition is held and they crown the Angel of the Sea. Everyone who attends has to take a bite of Angel Fruit. It all just fades into a dream after. Everything is hazy, details are blurred."

Angel Fruit. That's what the angel gave me last night in the forest. He was trying to blur my memory of meeting him. Or rather, he was trying to hide something from me. *The fire, the flowers, the golden light*—it's all just a haze now. No wonder he gave me the fruit so easily. He *needed* me to have it, even if it meant not fulfilling his barter. He was never trying to help me. He was trying to drug me.

It's best if I stay away from the angels entirely. That includes participating in their pageant. "I met that angel by mistake, Roisin. It means nothing. I'm not one step closer in the pageant. And even if I were, like I said, I'm not competing."

"What? Lila, why?" she whines. "It's a beloved tradition. We wait our whole lives for a chance to compete! Not even everyone gets the opportunity since the pageant only happens every seven years, and you have to be at least eighteen to be eligible."

I sigh, tired of her pressing. Even if there were no angels involved, I still wouldn't participate. "I'm not cut out for the pageant. Besides, I left competing behind in San Francisco."

Her gaze drops to her sandals, and she rocks the bench back and forth. "I just don't see why you'd want to pass up an opportunity like this. We may never get another chance again."

I shut my eyes, closing my fist around the swing's rope. I like Roisin, and I want her to stay my friend. That may not happen if I start competing with her—or with anyone for that matter. Not to mention, I'm not angelic. My parents know it. I know it. I can't let Roisin and Laina know it too.

"I just don't have a good feeling about it," I confess.

"Look," she says, scooting closer. "I know you're new here, and I understand this is a lot. But being chosen is an honor."

"So I've heard."

"Why don't you believe me?"

"It's not that I don't. It's just . . . my parents sent me here for a reason. To keep me away from competition." I don't tell her the full truth, what I actually did to get sent away. "I have a feeling they wouldn't want me to get involved." Or rather, they *do* want me to compete, only to prove that they were right and I was wrong. I'll never be the angel I pretend to be. But I also won't give them the satisfaction of my failure.

She rests her hand on mine. "But what if this is your chance to redeem yourself?"

Redeem myself. There's no way. "You don't understand what it did to me."

I think back to that night, that incident.

I had the role of my dreams in the San Francisco Ballet's preprofessional program—Aurora in *Sleeping Beauty*, just like my idol Misa Kuranaga. Growing up, girls who looked like us were never the princess, the love interest, the star. We didn't fit into that narrative. This was my moment to prove myself, to show my family I was worthy of their investment in my dream.

My parents were there in the front row with a bouquet of roses ready for me. I wanted to make them proud. Especially my mother. She was always challenging me, even when I was at my weakest. I nearly injured myself rehearsing. I couldn't get her voice out of my head.

You're looking soft. Have you been going to your Pilates class?

Don't forget to put concealer on. Your bags are huge.

Pretty girls don't stay out partying. You need to get more sleep.

You need to study harder.

Just because you're a ballerina doesn't mean you can fail tests.

We spend so much on your education.

You better be something.

Do something.

You better shine.

If you don't, then you're a waste.

This is all a waste.

I focused on the bruises pinched between my pointe shoes to cull her voice. My palms were already cut with scars and calluses. The other girls were beginning to notice and whisper.

She'll never last.

Her turns are off.

Did you see, her partner dropped her yesterday!

Oh my god, I would die.

She must be binging again.

How embarrassing.

I thought Sleeping Beauty was supposed to be beautiful.

She looks like a ghost.

No, a corpse.

A corpse.

I saw my hands and feet, bloodied and bruised, and screamed. I *was* a corpse. But I had worked too hard for this. I was meant to be a star.

Perfect.

Perfect.

Perfect.

I pushed myself to keep going. I should've stopped while I could. I stumbled in the studio, my pointe shoes slipping against the polished wood, nearly twisting my ankle. It happened several times that week. When catching my balance, I pulled a muscle in my calf that shot all the way up my thigh. My physical therapist said I wasn't in any condition to perform. My director threatened to replace me with my understudy, but I fought back. He should have done it anyway.

I choked.

I ruined everything that night.

A tear slips down my cheek.

"Lila." Roisin jumps. "Did I say something wrong?"

"No, it's— My whole life is wrong! I could've been recruited to dance in New York or London, even Paris if I didn't screw things up."

"What do you mean? You were a dancer?"

I sigh. "A ballerina."

"A ballerina?" Her face softens. "Why, isn't that just romantic. I bet you were a real fairy."

I smile half-heartedly. I suppose I was a fairy. Maybe for just a moment. All I ever wanted was to be a ballerina. Performing gave me such a high. I loved to be seen. Not for how I looked, but for what I was capable of. There's so much beauty in what the human body can do. But nothing I did was ever enough for my parents. I broke myself into pieces trying to hone my craft. Yet, for some reason, I still love it more than anything in the world.

"Performing was the only time I could release all the recklessness inside of me and still be something beautiful." A hand flutters to my mouth, in disbelief I admitted that aloud.

Roisin, however, stares at me with admiration in her eyes. "What do you mean?"

"You really want to know?"

She nods. I take a deep breath, and recall the magic of it all.

"Well, with every pirouette, we entrust the weight of our bodies on the tips of our toes, with the promise of them delivering us in cyclones. Our arms, always elegant it may appear, struggle beneath the heaviness our muscles battle to stay fluid. It looks effortless—every allongé, every piqué as simple as the natural flow of water. But every dance, every move our bodies make, is a war against itself. It's magnificently dangerous. Like . . . blooming into an ocean. That's what it feels like. An ocean. Deep and rich and all-encompassing, drowning out everyone in our presence. They sink into the moment, succumb to every movement, and simply just admire."

"Oh, Lila." Roisin swoons. "You have to perform for the angels. You have to!"

"I'm sorry?"

"That's the whole point of the pageant. 'Beauty, faith, and grace.' The last round is Grace. They want to see you dance."

My stomach clenches. I can't dance again. I won't. Not for me, not for the pageant, not for anyone. I graze the letter the angel left for me, tucked within my pocket. As much as I don't want to believe it's true, I can't deny I met him. And, for some reason, he's taken interest in my dance. Which is exactly why I can never see him again.

"Perhaps one of them already does," I say, tossing her the letter.

"Hm?" It lands beside her thigh, and she opens it, gasping as she reads. "Dear Luna! He asked you to dance with him? Do you even realize how lucky you are?"

"Apparently not. Because I'm not going."

She sits up taller, and the lilt in her voice disappears. "Lila, I simply won't let you pass this up. This angel might be able to protect you from whatever's haunting the island . . . you know, whatever caused Nadine to fall so soon."

I take the letter back, crumpling it in my fist. The wind whips my face, catching strands of hair in my lip gloss. I don't pull them away. I had almost forgotten. The angel saved me. He's protecting me from the voice—the Devil. If I'm not careful, he'll drag me to Hell any day now.

"Roisin." I tread with caution. "Have there been any other disappearances similar to Nadine's?"

The sea holds my gaze. It's so beautiful, I nearly forget what it's capable of. Part of me wonders if what I saw in the forest last night has to do with the voice that calls to me. I debate telling her the truth about what I can hear. But what if she thinks I'm cursed—an outsider plaguing her oasis? She wouldn't want anything to do with me. Or even worse, what if she thinks I'm crazy? Perhaps I am. Is this merely madness? A hallucination of some sort?

Roisin shakes her head. "Not that I'm aware of. Why?"

I tug my cardigan around me tighter as pinpricks nip my skin. "I was just curious."

One thing's for sure. My parents sent me here as a punishment. They know exactly where my demons hide. Deep below, past the abyss, amongst the sea fires of Hell. The Devil's coming for me. And if I don't find a way to protect myself, I'll end up as his.

But with the angel's help, maybe I really could be safe. Perhaps I could even call this place my home. Besides, where else would I go, if not here? I have no other family, no one who could grow to love me. My only hope is on this island. Which is the only reason for what I say next.

"Do you really think seeing the angel again is a good idea?"

"Yes!" she gushes. "I'll even take you to Luna's Love Shack and get you ready for the evening myself. Please, it would be my pleasure to do something kind after what happened yesterday."

I shrug, giving in. "If you insist." Damien is my best chance at survival. I have to see him again. Even if it means confronting the magic that terrifies me. Even if it means I have to dance.

Roisin claps her hands with a squeal. "Looks like you got yourself a date with an angel!"

Chapter
SIX

✦

The scent of orange blossom and rose entwine with notes of cocoa as I enter Luna's Love Shack, emanating from the handmade soaps at the front of the store. Beams of sunlight filter through the window, bringing the pastel dresses to life—peach, pistachio, and lilac. As much as I try to deny it, there's no escaping the glimmer of magic coursing through Luna Island. Everything here is more enchanting, even simple soaps and ribbons.

Roisin is at the back of the dress shop when I arrive. I make my way towards a whitewashed vanity, set up with glittering perfume bottles, glass makeup cases, and fluffy brushes. Beside it is a wedding dress with thin layers of chiffon cascading around one another like spilled cream. Luna's Love Shack apparently offers makeovers for weddings, balls, and other special events. Including, I guess, secret rendezvous with angels.

"Lila!" Roisin wraps me in a hug. "Come, make yourself comfortable." She ushers me to sit on a pale pink cushion.

I take a seat, smoothing out my dress. "How's your morning been?"

"Ugh," she groans, tying up her rose-gold curls. "We've been swamped with fittings for the pageant all day. But don't worry, no one should be bothering us now."

"Why not?"

She shrugs and begins brushing my hair. "Everyone has other preparations they need to tend to."

"Oh." The lull in the shop seems rather convenient, given how fussy the girls around here are about what they're wearing. Though I suppose it doesn't concern me. I'm not competing anyway.

I brush off Roisin's elusiveness and tell her what happened after she left Laina's cottage. We took a stroll to the bakery and had a breakfast of almond croissants and cinnamon-mocha lattes. Then I helped her wait tables at the tea shop, and we met an elderly couple who told me I look like a young Elizabeth Taylor. Roisin laughs, and I shield the flush swelling in my cheeks. It was quite peaceful working at the tea shop, with ladies gushing over mini cakes and bonding over herbal blends. I liked getting to know the islanders. I liked getting to know Laina.

The more I'm charmed by Luna Island—by my aunt, by Roisin—the more I want to fit in and really call this place my home. That can only happen if I figure out what's wrong with it.

Roisin notices me fidgeting with my locket and puts a hand on my shoulder. "Is everything alright?"

"Yeah, I'm fine."

She puts the brush down. "Are you sure? You can talk to me if something's wrong."

"It's nothing."

She lifts my chin to meet her gaze. "Is this about the angel? Please, you have nothing to worry about. Especially after I'm done with your makeover. You're already so beautiful, he'll go wild."

I sigh, unable to match her smile. "It's not that."

"Well, then what?"

My fingers trace a heart-shaped compact in front of me. "What if—what if I can't do it? What if I ruin my dance or say the wrong thing?"

"You won't."

My hand slips, piercing the vanity with my nails. I cover the shallow wells in the paint, praying Roisin doesn't notice. Memories of my failure flash in color—*ruby, scarlet, and vermillion*. The pain of falling onstage pulses through me, like a tattoo of my humiliation, embedded forever.

"No. You don't understand."

Everything bloomed into a cacophony when I collapsed—the ringing in my ears, the heat of the lights, the shocked whispers of the audience. I sat there like a broken doll, with hundreds of eyes suddenly deciding I was worthless. And, like any broken doll, I was discarded. I couldn't give them a show. I couldn't create effortless magic on the tips of my toes. In that moment, I boiled down to one simple thing—a failure. But it wasn't the shock of my failure that stung. It was the promise that I had never been enough all along.

Not strong enough.

Not graceful enough.

Not talented enough.

I knew I could never be anything more. My time was up after that one missed step. I slipped, collapsed, fainted—no matter how you spin it, it will always be tragic. I withered beneath those pitiful gasps, and my worth disintegrated with me. I've been small ever since. I'll never forget the word that fell from my father's lips.

Defective.

He never let me forget the horror of how I came into this world. I was born in a tangle of my own umbilical cord, a violent descent down a strangling canal, with a narrow chance at life. I wasn't supposed to live. My aunties—the superstitious ones at least—spread rumors that I didn't survive at all, that I am a ghost of a girl, my mother's barely breathing enigma. Father took one look at me, bloodied and purple, and muttered the word *defective*. The aunties thought I was an omen, and so did he.

Especially after I fell.

Defective.

Ballerinas don't fall onstage.

Purple babies don't survive.

Perfect daughters don't throw tantrums.

I steady myself against the vanity, knocking over two tubes of lip gloss.

Roisin shakes her head. "If you think negatively, you'll manifest negatively. If you believe you'll fail, then you will. But I know you won't slip up. I'm confident you'll come out of this with grace."

It's not that simple. "The dancer I was died when I fell onstage. There's no bringing her back."

"Don't say that! Dancing is a part of you. I could tell by the way you lit up when you spoke about it. Don't reject what makes you special because of one little mistake. You're greater than the past you're holding on to, and you'll never grow into your higher self if you don't move forward."

"Stop!" I thrum, smacking the vanity with my palm. "There is no 'higher me.' There's just me, and I wish you would accept that."

"I simply won't. You have a passion for dance, and the only person holding you back is yourself."

"You don't get it. I did embrace it, and I lost everything. My parents even sent me away because of it."

I don't tell her the whole truth—that the real reason I was banished is because of how I lashed out. My parents hurt me, and I wanted to hurt them back. I bite my tongue, cursing my impulsive nature. Why couldn't I just be a good girl?

Perfect daughters don't throw tantrums.

I shut my eyes. "There's no use fighting about it."

"I know, I *just*— You have a really special opportunity here. We can't give up on it."

"*We?*" My eyes spring open. I search for anywhere to release my rising anger besides the mirror in front of me. "Why do you care about me so much anyway? You just met me! And you don't understand what I've been through."

Heat pulses beneath my skin, prickling my cheeks as my throat tightens. I reprimand myself for my tone the second the words come out. *Shit.* I know she's only trying to be nice, and of course, I found a way to mess that up too. But Roisin doesn't flinch. She doesn't even frown. Instead, she brushes a piece of hair away from my face. Her touch is tender, a bit unnerving.

"I apologize if I came on too strong. It's just . . . you remind me so much of *her*."

Her? Who's her?

Oh. I catch the gloss reflection in her eyes.

Her.

"You mean Nadine?"

She studies me through the mirror. "You look like her. Dark hair, dark eyes."

My gaze softens. I place my hand on hers. "You really loved her, didn't you?"

"Yeah." Her voice shrinks down to barely a whisper, and she turns away. I give her a moment to process before I speak.

"I'm sorry."

She doesn't have to say it for me to know. My friendship reminds her of the girl she lost. But I'm not Nadine. I'm something worse. A reminder. Befriending me won't bring her back.

Roisin brushes away a tear. "If you want to know the truth, it's been lonely since I lost her. She was my best friend, and without her . . . the other girls whisper. I'm sure you understand."

I tilt my head to the side. "What do you mean?"

"When we found out the pageant was happening again, no one would shut up about what could have happened to Nadine. They asked me if I knew anything, but we'd broken up during the pageant, and I didn't have any leads. They said my vanity was to blame for the breakup—that the competition came between us.

Some even went as far to accuse me of sabotaging her for High Priestess." Her voice wavers. "I would never hurt her, Lila. You have to know that."

I rise without a word and wrap her in a hug.

She jolts back, releasing a startled breath. "What was that for?"

"We could all use a friend sometimes. Including me. And I'm grateful to be yours."

I never had many friends back home. She's right—I know what it's like for people to talk, for everyone to assume the worst of you. I could never imagine one of the other girls in ballet doing my hair and makeup before a show. I'm lucky to have Roisin here.

She leans deeper into the hug. "Of course, Lila. I'm grateful for you too."

Warmth pours over me like glitter. It tickles. I'm not used to it. I pull away, taking my place back on the vanity stool. "Thank you for helping me get ready to meet the angel."

"The pleasure's mine."

We share a smile, but beneath mine is an unspoken fear. I can't mess this up. I'll be good. I'll behave. Someone deserving of a friend like Roisin.

No more ocean of a girl.

And so I sit back, and for once, give in to someone else's kindness.

When she's done, my skin shimmers like the angels' does. I release a shallow breath as I catch my reflection in the rose-vine mirror. This evening, I wear a dress Roisin was kind enough to gift me. It's made of delicate angel's silk, so fine, I mistake it for chiffon. Airy puff sleeves hang off my arms, elegantly exposing my bare shoulders. The pale blue-and-pink rose pattern blends together like watercolor. From far away, one might mistake the design for sunset clouds.

Roisin fastens two pearl studs to my ears, whispering, "You're stunning."

I take another breath, running my hands down the dress. I look like I belong here, like one of the angelic girls born to the island. And maybe, in time, I really could be deserving of Luna's blessings.

"Come on," Roisin says. "I'll walk you to the forest."

"Wait." I pause. "I thought humans weren't allowed in the forest without an invitation?"

"Well, this is kind of an exception." A mischievous grin sweeps her face. I don't like the look of it.

"What do you mean?"

"You'll see."

◆

I follow Roisin through the forest. During the day, it's not so scary. The towering trees remind me of the redwoods I love from California. I pocket the comfort of home as we stroll down a winding trail, considering who could have paved this path since the forest is typically forbidden. Was it the angels, carving out a passage into town? I wonder how often they visit or why they'd want to bridge our worlds at all. Perhaps they're just as fascinated with us as we are with them.

The trail opens into a clearing surrounded by willow trees and bright flowers. There are nearly a dozen other girls there when we arrive, all dolled up in ball gowns and fussing to touch up one another's hair and makeup.

"Ow!" one of them screeches, swatting away her friend—a petite brunette in sage-green tulle ornamented with golden butterflies. "I said pin it to my hair, not my scalp."

"Sorry, Amelia," she apologizes in a whisper.

"Genevieve, move." Another girl bumps her out of the way—a strawberry blonde in pink silk layered with Chantilly lace. "Here, I got it." She hums, fastening the rose into her friend's pale buttercup ringlets.

"Thanks, Yvette," Amelia chimes, beaming a wide smile. Her fuchsia lipstick perfectly matches the layered chiffon draped across her tanned figure. "*Someone* could learn a thing or two."

Genevieve crosses her arms. One of the jasmine buds slips out of her braid. "It was an accident."

"There's no room for accidents!" Amelia snaps. "Don't you know the angels are always watching? We have to be perfect at all times. No. Room. For failure."

"Seriously, Gen." Yvette rolls her eyes. "You'll never make it past round one if you're not on guard."

I glare at Roisin. "What the hell did you bring me to?"

"Surprise," she cheers sheepishly. "Welcome to your pledge!"

"Excuse me?"

I take in my surroundings. The girls are lined up in front of a temple of some sort. Large columns of Calacatta Gold marble are ringed in carvings of angels tangled in a wreath of sea-foam. Canary diamonds encrust the sculptures like stars, adding a glint to the monument. Moonflowers snake up the pillars and pink bougainvillea drapes overhead as if this were the Hanging Gardens of Babylon. Hundreds of offerings litter the polished steps—lush bouquets, baskets of ripe stone fruit, and sparkling trinkets. Two guards are posted at the entrance with spears in their hands. They don't move. They don't blink. Their only purpose, I assume, is to protect the temple.

"What is this place?" I ask Roisin.

"This is Luna's Temple. It's where the High Priestess lives."

"You mean, Nadine is inside there somewhere?"

She shakes her head, her gaze drifting to the willow trees that rustle in the wind. "I—I don't know."

"Couldn't someone just go look?"

"No one's allowed inside. The temple is heavily guarded at all times. We don't speak to her, we don't see her. Townsfolk can leave offerings and prayers on her steps, but the only ones who interact with the High Priestess are the angels."

"Sounds like a pretty lonely life." I'm already sick enough of living in my isolated corner of the world—my loved ones fearing me, my peers hating me. The only thing possibly worse is being locked up behind a stone wall like that.

"Oh, it's far from sad." Roisin swoons. "The Angel of the Sea is adored by everyone. She receives offerings daily, wears dresses spun by the angels themselves, eats the rarest fruits in the forest, has feasts beyond imagination. The angels are in her servitude for the rest of her lifetime. You wouldn't have to lift a finger as High Priestess. They treat you as if you're their goddess incarnate. It's what every girl dreams of."

"Is it?" I indulge in Roisin's fantasy for just a moment. All I've ever wanted was to be loved. It feels so out of reach now, when I'm here on Luna Island. What if my parents never ask me back home? Will I be stuck here forever?

Or maybe, one day, they'll hear their daughter was crowned as High Priestess and that she ascended to the stars. I would be untouchable then. Perhaps, they'll finally miss me once I'm a star. After all, people love anything that shines. Maybe Roisin is right. What if it's better to be worshiped than to be loved?

Her dreamlike gaze never parts with the temple. "We'd leave this life behind and step into the otherworld. Finally, all of the angels' secrets would be our own, and they'd cherish us until we burn out. I'd trade it all to know the truth behind those walls."

And I'd trade it all to be adored—to finally know that I'm worthy, for once in my life.

Perhaps, in the temple, I'd actually be content. No more nightmares. No more parasitic hauntings eating away at my mind. I'd be pampered by angels, guarded from the Devil, and beloved like Luna herself. Maybe, just maybe, Roisin is right. Being crowned as High Priestess is an honor. An honor that just might solve every last one of my problems.

"But what about Nadine?" I recall, remembering there's a chance I could be chosen but still not be enough. What then?

"That's what we all wonder," she says softly. "This year's different. Not only does one of us have to win, but we also need to figure out what happened to Nadine and make sure it doesn't happen again."

I think back to the voice, wondering if it could be related somehow. But I can't bring myself to tell her about it. Speaking it out loud will only make my delusions real, and that's not a reality I'm ready to face yet.

I have to join the pageant. There's no other choice if I want to protect myself. As long as we're competing, the angels will have their eyes on me. Which means the Devil has less chance of hurting me. Not to mention, if I actually win, I'll be untouchable.

"Okay," I finally say. "I'll join the pageant with you."

She smiles, squeezing my hand to express her gratitude. I don't need her to admit she's relieved to have my companionship. Despite her enthusiasm about the potential of being crowned High Priestess, the pageant *is* different this year. We'll need each other's strengths not just to learn the truth, but to survive.

"What are *you* doing here?" A mousy voice squeaks from behind us.

I turn around, overwhelmed by a wave of hibiscus and rose perfume. Amelia towers over me with a manicured hand on her hip. Her tennis bracelet sparkles just as brightly as her smile.

"I guess I'm pledging for the pageant like the rest of you."

"What?" Yvette scoffs. "We wait our entire lives for this, and you just happen to show up right during pageant season? You know nothing about our culture. There's no way the angels will let you compete."

"*Let* me?" I wince.

Amelia rolls her eyes. "See. She doesn't even know how to pledge. Since when did we start letting outsiders compete in the pageant?"

Roisin cuts in. "Actually, Lila's not an outsider. She was born here. She's Laina Li's niece. So I would say competing is her birthright, the same as ours."

"Wait," Genevieve chimes in, "if you were born here, how come we've never seen you visit the island before?"

"Well, I—" My parents never made an effort to visit Luna Island. I always assumed something happened between my father and Laina and that's why they left. But after meeting my aunt, I can't imagine why anyone would harbor resentment towards her. There's so much they've kept me in the dark about. "I guess it's complicated."

I grab the mother-of-pearl locket between my collarbones, running my fingers across the smooth surface. My mother wanted me to have a piece of the place where I was born, believing our spirit is connected to the land where we took our first breath. There's a picture of my parents inside. My mother said to wear it so I'd always know they're nearby. It was meant to be a talisman to bring me strength. It just reminds me of my failure now, and how the island has only ever been a mystery to me, not a home.

"You may have been born here," Amelia sneers, "but you don't stand a chance."

"Yeah, we've been training our entire lives for this," Yvette adds.

Roisin drapes her arm around me. "Well, good thing she has me to help her through it."

Amelia scoffs. "Good luck with that alliance. We all know how the last one ended."

Roisin parts her mouth, but she's too late. The girls giggle as they leave, and she hangs there like wilting wisteria, holding back a sob. I catch the waver in her throat and squeeze her hand. Losing Nadine was never her fault.

"Don't let them get to you," I say. "We're going to win this. You and me."

"You and me." She smiles faintly.

I get why it's important for her to have a friend in the competition now. I'll do my best to not let her down.

"Okay, but Amelia's right. I don't know the first thing about pledging. How does this work?"

"Right." She nods, gesturing to the temple. "Pick a rose from the garden out front, then walk up the steps. Be careful not to fall. If you trip, you're out. When you get to the top, there's a bowl of moon water. Leave an offering in the bowl and pierce your finger on the rose's thorn to draw blood. It only takes one drop in the water for the ritual to work. If the water turns gold, it means the angels have accepted you. If it's pink, you're rejected. Simple enough?"

"Wait, I—I didn't come prepared with anything as an offering. I didn't even know we were coming here."

"Exactly," she says. "The offering should be something personal—something that can be given up at any moment to prove how badly you really want this. So, how badly do you want it, Lila? What are you willing to give?"

I grab my locket again, the last remaining connection to my mother. It was a gift from the island, then to me, now to the angels. I'm willing to sacrifice the last piece of my parents' love for a chance at worship. If I can pull this off, I won't need a token of their affection. I'll prove that I'm angelic—beautiful, faithful, graceful—and that I was always worthy of being loved.

"I know what I have to do," I say to Roisin.

The rose bushes surrounding the temple are something out of a wonderland, all fully blossomed with velvet petals in shades of crimson, blush, and magenta. I pluck the brightest pink. Its fragrance casts a dreamspell over me, guiding me up the marble steps in a trance. I remove my heels, pressing my bare feet to the cold tiles so that I don't slip. I'm careful in my ascension, like I'm floating to the Heavens. The breeze combs through my hair, anointing me like a blessing and settling my nerves.

Finally, I reach the top and kneel before the bowl. It's made of polished moonstone, flashing with a blue and violet iridescence. The water is fragrant with the scent of jasmine and rose. Petals float on the surface from the other girls' flowers. Inside, offerings sink to the bottom of the bowl—a sapphire ring, a rose quartz stone, a vial of perfume, and a pair of ruby earrings.

I remove my locket, admiring its pearlescent surface one last time. It reflects lilac, pink, and green beneath the sunlight. I press it to my heart, as if the image of my mother and father inside could hear its final beating. With a kiss to the token, I drop it into the bowl.

"Goodbye, Mom. Goodbye, Dad." I trade their love for a higher glory.

When I prick my finger on the rose thorn, my drop of blood turns the water gold.

Chapter
SEVEN

◆

The angels' validation awakens something feral in me—an animalistic urge to survive. No, to win. It tremors, pulsing through my bloodstream, a fever dream I thought I'd long forgotten. The truth is, I've never felt more alive. A simple taste of glory spills over my tongue like honey, leaving a ravenous hunger for more. It electrifies and terrifies me all at once.

I run.

The dew-damp grass coaxes the fire thrumming through me while I race barefoot through the forest. I follow the trail of starlight the angel left behind the other night—the same trail he requested I follow in his letter. It glimmers faintly, like a string of gold leading me closer and closer to my heart's desire. Clutching my chest, I slow for a moment, holding on to the thrill. It's this liminal space before diving in headfirst that I crave—the promise of something special waiting for me—mine to take, so long as I don't let it slip out of reach.

Sunlight breaks through the fractals of leaves, casting mosaics of golden rays on my skin. My eyes fall shut, just for a moment, imagining basking in the angels' glow. They applaud for me in the way I live for, in the way that makes me full. It settles like glitter falling over my skin, twinkling, sparkling. I smile. They love me. I made it. I'll never hurt again.

"Lila." A deep voice unfurls in the silence. "You came."

I startle, spinning around, the illusion shattered. My heartbeat quickens as the nerves rush back. Damien's shadow steals the sunlight, reminding me of the truth. Winning isn't guaranteed. And, I'll have to dance again if I even want a chance at redemption.

"Damien." I speak his name for the first time. It tastes forbidden, like an enchantment from a fairytale I shouldn't mutter.

He's even more mesmerizing in the light, haloed with the soft glowing edges of a blurred oil painting. A pearl shimmer dazzles his skin, sharpening his bones as the sun hits them.

"My apologies, I didn't mean to frighten you," he says.

"I—I'm not frightened," I stammer, betrayed by the tremble in my voice.

He smirks. "Please, I'm not going to hurt you."

"I told you, I'm fine." I'm not scared, just intimidated. His viridescent eyes glaze over me, as if examining every stray hair and flaw.

"You must know," he says, taking my hand, "last night was special. I'm glad to see you again."

Although his tone is sweet, perhaps even sincere, I'm apprehensive to agree. After all, he fed me Angel Fruit to muddle my mind. For all I know, he could still be deceiving me now. I break our tether, drawing my hand behind my back. "Whatever you think you saw, it was the fruit, not me."

He laughs. "Really now? Care to take a look at what you left behind?"

I hesitate, stumbling into the brambles. "What?"

"Come, I'll show you."

He guides us back to the glade where we shared our dance. I don't want to believe it, but it's even more beautiful than I remember. Iridescent rainbows cast strobes of pastel light onto the trees. Rose petals sparkle, as if preserved in crystalized sugar. Magnolias hang like treasures, soft white petals gilded gold.

"I couldn't possibly have done this," I whisper in an airy rush of breath.

"Well, you did. I saw you."

"It must've been a side effect of the fruit." There's no way I'm capable of such magic.

"If it were just the fruit, then all of this would have disappeared by now."

"You're lying."

He shakes his head. "You're different." He pauses, studying me as I tug at the ribbon of my dress. "Don't you want to know what you are?"

I jerk back, his words cutting into an open wound—reminding me of how I never quite fit in and how I don't really belong here at all. "I'm just me." Nothing more, nothing less.

"Please, I didn't mean to offend you." He steps forward, bridging the gap between us. "But you must be curious. Even just a little."

Of course I'm curious. Who wouldn't be? But it's all too much. Just last night, I believed none of this could be real.

"Don't you want to see if you can do it again?" Damien presses.

I bite the inside of my cheek, my insides churning with a muddled mess of color I can't pick apart. If I please him, I'll be one step ahead in the pageant. But at what cost? I can't go back to what dancing made me. That twisted perfectionist would only push away everyone I just started to care about. And for what? Just so I can fail again?

The glitter feeling coursing through me turns to dust as the promise of something more settles back into reality. The truth is, I may have been accepted into the angels' competition, but I'm far from being a winner.

"I can't dance with you, angel," I finally say. "I'm sorry. I shouldn't have wasted your time."

"Wait." He grabs my wrist as I turn to leave. "Don't go."

My breath hitches. His eyes scintillate with a golden sheen, bewitching me to stay.

"What you have is special. You weren't even dancing to perform last night and look what happened. Just imagine what you could do if you were actually trying." Before I can respond, he adds, "Don't dance for me. Dance for yourself."

Dance for yourself.

It's foreign, a thought I never even considered. Something within the angel changes too, like ice melting down. His glimmering eyes reflect a yearning beneath the surface—as if he's fighting pain, and just for a moment, hopes to indulge in a temporary relief. Could my dance do just that? After all, the angels are mesmerized by beauty. Why else would they have us compete in a pageant?

Even so, I can't help but ask, "Why are you so infatuated by my dance? You're an angel. I'm sure you experience magic every day."

"Not like this. You created a fantasy without even trying. Don't you see? You don't have to be perfect to be something great."

"I—" I don't know what to say. No one has ever looked at me the way the angel does. Like I'm the star of the show without even trying. His hopeful gaze taunts me, tempting me to perform once more. I take a breath. "I'm not even warmed up yet. Besides, I've been out of training for far too long. My technique is sloppy."

"It doesn't matter." He shrugs. "You don't have to prove anything to me. I just want to see you dance."

Stiletto nails sink into my palms to cull my racing pulse. I've never been worthy of my parents' love, no matter how hard I tried to be the best. What if I'm not worthy enough of the angel either? I can't fail again like I did before. "What if the magic doesn't work this time?"

"Trust me, it will."

"How do you know?"

"Because I believe in you. Perhaps it's time you start believing in yourself too."

His words twist like a knife. Is this really who I've become? A doubtful shell of who I used to be? I was the best in my class before my fall. And maybe, deep down, that version of me is still alive somewhere.

I cross my arms. "Okay. You want to see me dance? I'll dance." But then I pause. "There's no music."

"I can fix that." With a flick of his wrist, the roses and dahlias come alive with song.

I nearly laugh—or rather, scoff. *Ugh.* Of course he can do that.

"Fine, angel." He wins.

It's now or never. I better put on a good show.

With a deep breath, I extend my arms, beginning with an adagio, syncing with the melody of the flowers. When I find comfort in the rhythm, I dip into a cambré, sweeping my body into a whirlpool as I rise. I hesitate as plumes of color emerge from the ground, encompassing me in a veil of fuchsia, amber, and gold. The colors gather me, and I move with them like the language of fire—hot, quick steps, languid and elegant.

The forest begins to change, and my eyes widen. When I begin my bourrée steps, foxgloves sprout like lace-crafted trumpets, marrying the sound of blooming hibiscuses, rattling like tambourines. With every step I take, more flowers grow, kissing the earth with their velvet lips. I almost swear I hear the ground sing back, harmonizing with the forest's song.

I guess the angel was right.

With a glimmer of confidence, I burst into a grand jeté, and golden hummingbirds mimic me, tracing my every move as I dive into a piqué manège. Damien's eyes glisten, and it fills my spirit. With every chassé, the forest unravels in color.

Fireflies come to life and kiss my cheeks, circling my body in a lattice as I pirouette. New colors rise from the ground—topaz, lazuli, and chartreuse—dancing with me like my own ensemble. I transition into my fouettés, leaning into an arabesque, as if to touch the rising moon.

I lose all sense of self, leaping into the air. My body transcends into a wind-like creature, moving wildly with mild grace. New life sprouts, as if this world belongs to me and not the angels. Tiny stars emerge in a trail behind my feet, and I climb them like stairs. Damien smiles. I reach for his hand and lift him onto the steps.

His hands wrap around my waist, and together we spin higher into the sky. My grip around his shoulders tenses as we rise closer and closer to the Heavens. I can feel Luna radiating over me. Here, I'm in command. Here, I'm free. I wish I could hold on to this moment forever. If only my parents could see me now.

My parents.

My parents who sent me away.

They could never love you, Lila, the wind sings back. *You're just a failure.*

"No!"

My eyes spring open. I shriek as the stars disappear beneath us. We plummet towards the ground, and Damien's grip on me tightens. He expands his wings so we glide instead of fall. Damp earth kisses my cheek as I meet the ground and sink my nails into the dirt.

The world explodes in color—*ruby, scarlet, and vermillion*—just like when I fell onstage. My breaths rush out like the restless sea.

My ankles were too weak.

I wasn't strong enough.

My technique was flawed.

My mother's words come flooding back.

You didn't try hard enough.

What a disappointment.

We gave up everything so you could follow your dream.

I hiss, pulling grass out from the ground and releasing a cry. When I do, the world I created falls apart. I inhale sharply as every flower withers. Their worth decays, just like mine. Hot tears spring to my eyes, and the sky darkens to gray. *What's going on?* When my tears fall, the sky thunders and rain starts to pour. I choke on my breaths, frightened and confused as the rivulets fall faster, sharper, turning to hail. All of the beauty fades just as quickly as I created it.

I knew it was too good to be true.

I could never be something special.

Did my parents know I could do this? Is this why they pushed me so hard for all those years? Were they disappointed because my magic never manifested? There's only one thing I know for sure. They didn't love me because I failed them, and I don't want to go back to what my parents made me now.

"Lila," Damien hovers over me. "Are you alright?"

I glance up. His brows are furrowed with what I assume is disappointment. A sob breaks as my lips part. "Get off me!"

He could never want me now. Not after I proved how defective I am, just like my parents said. I ruined whatever magic was thrumming through me. And just like that, the one thing that made me special disappears.

"Please, I just want to make sure you're okay."

"Well, I'm not." I stumble to my feet, gather my dress, and run as fast as I can.

"Lila!" the angel calls, but I just keep running.

Chapter
EIGHT

✦

The frosted windowpane numbs my cheek as rivulets of rain trickle down the glass. Waves thrash from beyond my bedroom window, as if lashing out. *This is all my fault.* I burrow into the oversized cardigan I stole from Laina's closet, curling my legs towards my chest. The pink lace at the top of my knee-high socks reminds me of the innocence of being a little girl, when ballet was just a fairytale. Sometimes, I wish that's all ballet ever was—a dreamlike wonder, untouched by any darkness. Instead, it's my living nightmare.

"Lila." Roisin bursts through the door, startling me out of position. "I came as soon as I saw your call. What happened?"

I try to speak, but I can't. Instead, I bury my face in her shoulder as she embraces me.

"Hey." She holds me close. "You're okay. It's going to be okay."

I pull away, sinking into the violet cushion beneath me. "No, it's not. Everything is ruined." The angel could never want me now. I proved once again that all I'll ever be is a disgrace.

She rests a hand on my shoulder. "Whatever happened, I'm sure it's not that bad."

I shake my head. "You don't understand."

I don't tell her the truth about my dance, the magic it created before it fell apart. My body trembles, and I hold myself tighter. I would only hate myself more if Roisin saw me the way I do.

"It's okay," she says, gathering my hair to the side. "You don't have to tell me what happened. Let's get you taken care of first." She undoes the bow holding back her ponytail and ties my curls away from my face with it.

I rub my rubicund cheeks, taut from saltwater tears. Roisin rises, moving like a ghost through the moonlit room—blue hues spilling over my gauzy canopy and lace curtains. She flicks on a lamp and lights a candle, illuminating the floral wallpaper. Tumbles of seafoam-colored flowers sprawl across the wall— roses in a wreath of coral and starfish—an ode to Luna Island's seaside charm. The scent of orchid and lily perfumes the air, marrying with the brine that sneaks in from outside.

"You're shivering," she says, draping a blanket over my shoulders and shutting the window. "Where's Laina? Does she know what happened to you?"

"No. She's having dinner with her friends from the pageant committee. Please don't call her. I don't want her to worry." I'm already enough trouble as it is.

Roisin nods. "Don't worry. I got you."

The tension eases in my shoulders, and I allow her to take my hand and lead me into the kitchen.

"Wow," Roisin says, opening the cupboard. "Living with the owner of Petals Tea Shop comes with a ton of perks. Is she okay if we use this stuff?"

I shrug. "Laina said her home is mine. But don't go crazy."

She winks. "I won't."

"For some reason, I don't believe you."

She throws her head back and laughs, her persimmon hair tumbling down her back. "Lila, you can't have a girls' night without baking. It's criminal. And I'm going to make sure you have the best damn girls' night of your life. Catch!" she says, tossing a bag of flour to me.

A small smile breaks across my face as it lands in my arms. Just a bit.

There's comfort in the simple task of baking. I follow Roisin's lead, whisking, pouring, and kneading—falling into a rhythm that fills the silence and distracts my racing mind. One egg. A half teaspoon of salt. A quarter cup of water. It's nice knowing that, for once, everything will turn out perfect, so long as I follow the rules.

"Isn't everything cuter heart-shaped?" Roisin asks, gesturing towards the homemade pizza we constructed. She chose to be creative, selecting a pesto base, topped with lavender goat cheese and grilled peaches.

Something about her playfulness relaxes me. There's an innocence as she sprinkles shredded cheese into her mouth and leaves handprints on the counter with her powdered palms. It reminds me of being a kid, when things weren't so scary and we could just have fun. That time in my life hadn't lasted long. I always wanted to please my parents. They made sure everything I did was done with heart, and I was cautious not to disappoint them. But being with Roisin reminds me we can still create something while having fun.

"You know," I say, "I think heart-shaped cookies would be extra cute with this heart-shaped pizza. Don't you think?"

She squeals. "Oh, I love that idea!"

In between licking the spoon and adding extra teaspoons of vanilla, I draw kitten whiskers on Roisin's face with the flour. She tosses a handful of powder at me, and I squeal when it hits me in the face. We laugh, sinking onto the hardwood floor. I lean my head against her shoulder as the smell of cinnamon intensifies. We relax for a moment beneath the hot sweet air.

"Thank you," I say in a whisper—an expression of gratitude I try to keep hidden from the rest of Luna Island. I don't want them to know how much she means to me. They can take anything else, just not her.

"Of course," she chimes. "That's what friends are for."

Friends. My insides sweeten like the sugar enveloping us. I hold myself tighter, not wanting to let go of this comfort. I paint her in my mind, the rose-gold angel on my kitchen floor, teaching me to live again, teaching me to breathe. I hope she never disappears. When she's beside me, there's no darkness. I beg the universe to let me keep her.

"Mmm . . . I think the cookies are just about done." Roisin rises, making her way towards the oven. I catch the notes of sweet pea and vanilla tangled up in her hair, holding on to it as she walks away. It's familiar now, just like her.

We decorate the heart-shaped snickerdoodles in pink and lilac frosting, topping each one with a tiny rosebud. Roisin brews a pot of passion fruit tea, sweetening it with honey before pouring it over a glass of ice and coconut milk. It turns a cloudy purple color.

"This is a specialty at Petals Tea Shop," Roisin says. "Your auntie Laina named it the Midnight Rose Garden. It's one of my favorites."

"It's wonderful," I say, taking a sip.

It reminds me of family trips I used to take to Hawaii. My parents always said I was such a happy kid and didn't know what went wrong as I grew up. The passion fruit spilling over my tongue transports me back to placid waters—ones that never whispered. The kind of waves that turtles call home and coral reefs burn bright. The same waves that culled my sunburnt shoulders, kissing my welted flesh and telling me I was okay. I was safe here. The water was safe.

With Roisin, I am safe.

Dinner is served in the dining room. During the day, the large windows paint the lemon-colored walls with sunlight. Tonight, they reveal the starlit sea. Roisin sets the table with a floral tablecloth and tall taper candles hand painted with tiny bows. The rosy glow flickers against the hydrangeas in the center of the table.

"Look," she says, pointing outside. "It stopped raining."

She's right. The pitter-patter against the window has disappeared, and the waves settle into a mellow lapping. "It did."

Roisin made the storm clear. My rose-gold angel. Out of all the treasures on Luna Island, she's the most precious one. I wish I could tell her what she means to me, but I don't want to jinx it. Instead, I pick at the calluses on my palm, praying the storms stay calm.

"It's getting late," she says, after we finish eating. "I should get going. We have an early morning tomorrow with the first round of the pageant."

"Actually." I stop her as she rises. "Could you stay a while longer?" I'm afraid of what will happen once she leaves. Will the storm come back? Will the Devil call my name and drag me out to sea? I don't want to risk it. I don't want her to go.

"Of course, Lila," she says, setting down her purse. "How about I get you to bed?"

"Oh." I hesitate. She's right. It *is* getting late, and I'm sure she's tired. I shouldn't burden her any more than I have. "You know what? I'll be fine. You should go."

"No, I insist. How about I stay until you fall asleep? Or at least until Laina gets back."

"Roisin—"

"Shhh. It's fine. Like I said, it's what friends are for."

"But—"

"Come on," she says, leading me back down the hall.

She perfumes my pillow with a rose-scented mist before undoing the ribbon holding back my hair. Her fingers run through my tresses, and the sensation causes shivers. Soon, my eyelids turn heavy as the lapping waves lull me to sleep.

✦

Sea-foam tumbles onto the shore, claiming me gently in the way I've always craved. The ocean gathers me, carrying me over the surface like Cleopatra—and I, every ounce as lovely as her and Aphrodite combined. Bit by bit the water swallows me, gently nipping at my skin until I dissolve into an aquatic spirit. Only then do I understand the language of angelfish and squid, and I move just as languidly. The sirens gape at me with their jewel-bright eyes and try to steal me as their own. But before I can be taken by those curious witches, I rise to the surface again.

Everything glimmers here.

I embrace the dusk with a hopeful smile. The sky blends into a watercolor of pastels and ambrosial stars. It's an aurora borealis of magenta and lavender, tempting me into the forest and away from the safety of the shore.

Something's in the wind. I can feel it—like the twinkling stars will finally lead me to the love I desire. I want it more than anything. The thought of it turns me feral, like a vampiress thirsty for a drop of blood. I dart through the forest, trailing a path of golden light. Past the evergreens and pines, underneath the moon, I become wild and free.

Sweet summer fruit grows from trees, ripe and sparkling. With every cautious step I take, the flowers blossom. But they don't just grow. They *glow*. Ultraviolet irises, sugar-dusted peonies, and iridescent rosebuds unravel beneath my feet. Foxgloves bloom like trumpets, playing a regal procession beside twinkling bluebells. As I journey deeper into the forest, fireflies circle me, illuminating my path.

And then I see him.

I blink. He's awfully familiar, but I can't place my finger on who he is. He's beautiful. A boy with white-blonde hair and viridescent eyes. Where have I seen him before?

"Hello, Lila," he says.

I stumble back. "How do you know my name?"

He's peculiar. So unbelievably enchanting, I'm enthralled by the sound of his voice alone.

"Don't be scared. You're safe here. I wanted to bring you somewhere special. Somewhere where you can make the forest beautiful with your dance."

My dance.

Of course, my dance.

Witchlight flickers in his eyes. This world is meant for me. A gift wrapped up in velvet petals and sweet perfumes.

"It's marvelous," I say with a sigh.

The boy extends a hand. "Come, dance with me. We can make the world bloom."

I hesitate to place my palm in his. "But I—I don't even know your name. Who are you?"

"I'm your angel."

My angel. The same angel who saved me when I fell into the sea. I remember now. I take his hand, and he lures me away. We sweep through a brush of willow trees, and I gasp when we reach the other side. It's a pond with shimmering aquamarine water.

"Lila, will you dance with me?"

I stare into his familiar eyes. There's something safe within them. I don't dance with others often, but an impulse calls me forward, as if I've done this with him once before. I take his hand.

"Yes, I will."

The angel guides me onto the water, twirling me in the star-bright pond as the lilies unleash their dulcet perfume. The scent dances with us, and I laugh. He sings to me under the moon, and the trees turn gold. Beneath the starlight, he whispers how he loves the thin wisps of my eyelashes and the raven color of my hair. As he speaks poetry of my eyes, white doves flutter around us.

He draws my body over the ripples, incandescent and glowing. My long hair clings to the curves beneath my gown. He holds me there, a girl beneath glass, preserved and everlasting. "You're magic, you know that?"

I run my fingers down the side of his face—his temple, his cheekbone, his lips—drinking in his ethereal being. "So are you."

He trembles, and his grip on me slackens.

My muscles constrict. Something isn't right. But before I have the chance to break away, he draws me closer, gently taking my face, and presses a kiss to my lips. For a moment, I forget about everything—pain, anger, even breathing. My mouth dissolves into petals, and the forest bursts into a kaleidoscope of colors. It only lasts for a second before the illusion shatters.

Our world crumbles like fractals of stained glass. I yelp as the cold metal of a knife slits my throat. My blood spills into the pond, turning the waters black. All at once, the colors of the forest dim, slowly rusting into decay. The leaves fall from the trees, flowers hanging like rotting corpses, and the branches become gray, curving into grotesque fingers. They reach for me, grabbing, trying to steal me as their own.

I jump out of bed, screaming.

Roisin is gone, and the candles are blown out. I pant, grabbing for my chest. Only when my hand meets my collarbone, a cold brush of metal sends chills through my fingertips. I look down, and find my locket suffocating me like a noose. The same locket I sacrificed to the angels as my token to enter the pageant.

What the hell?

My fingers tremble as I stroke the gold-rimmed heart. Goosebumps rise on my skin as the canopy above my bed brushes my arms, swept up by the sea breeze. I could have sworn we closed the window before bed. I rush towards the roaring sea and slam it shut. I must've forgotten. That, I can believe. But there's no way my locket would've been returned to me unless the angels wanted to send a sign. Is this my warning? Have I been cut from the pageant?

I stumble towards the mirror, colliding with a nightstand in the dark. Cold sweats dampen my forehead as I clamor for the light. My reflection pales as I tug on the mother-of-pearl pendant, the smooth surface warm from the heat of my palm.

"Shit!" I hiss, my nails digging into my skin as I clench the locket.

I had one chance, and I blew it. Damien must have told the rest of the angels about my failure, and they decided I was unfit to be their priestess. Just a couple of hours ago, I would have agreed. But something bloomed inside me when I woke from my dream.

Anger.

Damien saw me at my weakest, and just like my parents, he decided I wasn't worthy of a chance at glory. He discarded me, just like they did. But I won't let him dismiss me so easily. I *can't*. Not when the Devil is after me. And, for whatever reason, it's personal. He must know what I did to get sent to Luna Island.

I need to win if I want to survive.

With the angels' permission or not, I'm competing. I can make it. I can win. I'll show them all it was a mistake to ever second-guess me.

Chapter
NINE

✦

There are four parts to the Angel of the Sea pageant—Beauty, Faith in Luna, Strength of Will, and lastly, Grace. This first round should come easy. At least, that's what I tell myself.

Laina fits me into a lilac dress with an opalescent sheen. The angel-spun silk shifts with flashes of champagne beneath the light, and the puff-sleeves fall off the shoulders like swaths of mascarpone. While the entire dress is spectacular, my favorite detail is the ruffle that sweeps across the sweetheart neckline.

Laina surprised me with the gown from Luna's Love Shack. Though, I was reluctant to accept it after seeing the price tag. No one mentioned how expensive pageant season would be. If I had known, I wouldn't have told Laina I pledged. It's bad enough that I've ruined every other dress someone's gifted me. Perhaps it's an omen. But if I do this right, if I at least pass this first round of the competition, maybe my luck will change. I just need to prove I'm as deserving of being here as the rest of the girls.

"Oh, Lila," Laina squeals, as she pins fully bloomed peonies into my hair. "I'm so glad you decided to pledge. You're going to have the most marvelous time."

A hot flush swells in my cheeks. I don't have the courage to tell her about my locket being returned or how I believe it was Damien who did it—warning me that I'm no longer eligible to compete. It's buried deep within my jewelry box now. No one can know the truth. Not if I want to prove the angels wrong.

I take a deep breath and place a hand to my corseted rib cage, examining my reflection. Laina added a few touches of Luna Island to my look. Lush flowers to crown my head like a halo. A ribbon to match the color of my dress, threaded between the peonies and tied in the back with a bow. A string of dainty pearls with a golden mollusk-shell pendant, clasped around my neck.

A shaky breath parts my lips. I look every bit like an Angel of the Sea.

Will it be enough to convince the angels?

Laina kisses me on the cheek, bringing me in for a hug. Her lemon-and-gingerbread scent eases my nerves, just slightly. "You look beautiful, darling. There's no doubt you'll wow the angels."

I untangle from her embrace and turn to face the mirror again. "Do you really think so?"

She smiles, placing a hand on my shoulder. "I couldn't have picked a better dress. The color suits you perfectly."

"Thanks." My voice dwindles. "It's my favorite color, actually."

Laina winks through the reflection. "I remembered. I kept every thank-you card you sent as a kid. You tied each of them with a bow in this exact shade." She hesitates, staring at me for a little too long. "It's a shame I never got more time with you growing up."

I turn around. A wrinkle creases between her brows, withering her gentle features. "Why did my parents keep us apart? I mean, Luna Island is where I was born. It doesn't make sense that we wouldn't visit."

Her hand falls to the side. "It's complicated."

"Of course." Nothing with my parents is ever simple.

"I know you never got a chance to meet your grandparents," she continues, "but they sacrificed a lot for us to be here."

"You mean on Luna Island?"

"No. America."

"Oh." I hadn't thought much about the privilege of where I grew up. I've always just accepted this is the life I was born into.

"After your grandparents passed, your father developed this . . . grief. Or rather, guilt."

"Guilt?"

She nods. "Your grandparents immigrated here from China after their village was pillaged. They came here with nothing, created a humble life selling crabs, and worked to provide us with everything we had. Your father didn't want their labor of love to be in vain. He wanted to make something for himself, give you a better life than the simple one I have right here."

I open my mouth to speak, but I don't know what to say. Most of the time, it's hard to imagine my father's love taking shape at all. But if what Laina says is true, moving away from Luna Island was an act of love itself. Is that why he pushed me so hard my whole life? His disappointment feels so much like hatred. I never considered it may have manifested from guilt.

"Why did you stay?" I ask Laina. No one else did. Not my father. Not any of my aunties. Just her.

She rests her fingertips against the window, looking out at the sea. "Sometimes, we run so much, we forget there's a home right here." Loose curls fall from her messy bun as she shakes her head. "I never felt the need to prove anything the way my siblings did. You see, Lila, life is what you make it. And I like my life just the way it is. I have my tea shop. I have my cottage. And now, I have you."

Her hand brushes my cheek, drinking me in as if I were the daughter she never had. I look back at her, and for the first time, I see family. "Thank you." My voice wavers. "For taking me in."

Dimples well in her cheeks. "You know, Lila, you can stay as long as you want. I'm happy to have you here."

I turn my back on the mirror, facing the window instead. Maybe Luna Island really could be my home one day. But not until I earn my place. It's clear the island knows I don't belong, and the Devil will only haunt me until I'm his. I'm what he wants, and I'm what the island will feed to satiate him.

"Let's just see how the pageant goes first," I mutter beneath my breath.

"Honey." Laina grabs my hand. "I don't want you to be so hard on yourself. Pageant or not, I still love you."

I shut my eyes, refusing to turn around. She can't know how much the promise of her affection kills me. I wish I could believe her. I wish I didn't have to prove myself worthy of her love. But that's never been a reality for me.

"We need to go," I say, heading for the door. "I don't want to be late."

✦

The townsfolk of Luna Island gather around the temple, which seems to be the only part of the forest humans are allowed in without an invitation. Florists wheel carts and carry boxes full of bouquets, selling them like peanuts at a stadium. Laina tugs my arm, ushering me through the crowd.

"They're for the people's favorite pledge," she whispers. "Humans don't get to vote on who ends up as High Priestess, but they do love getting involved with the pageantry. If they like you, they toss flowers. You may even receive bouquets on our doorstep."

I look over my shoulder as she pulls me forward, fixated on the carnations, tulips, and anemones wrapped in brown paper and tied with a bow. With ballet, I always measured my worth by how many flowers I received after a show, displaying them in my dressing room like trophies. There's no chance I'll be anyone's favorite now. Not when I'm an outsider to the girls who grew up here. I'm sure their families, teachers, and neighbors have already decided who they're rooting for. And yet, part of me still hopes I receive even one.

We shimmy through the sea of people wearing large sun hats wreathed in satin bows and fresh flowers, fanning their necks with hand-painted fans. Other vendors pitch sales for blood-orange mimosas, lavender lemonade, and different blends of iced tea. Ladies bring glasses to their lips with lace-gloved hands. The strange antiquity reminds me of being at a derby—the kind only rich people attend.

Laina ushers me to a long table with different desserts and charcuterie, where the other girls participating in the pageant mingle. I immediately recognize Serena and Ophelia from Luna's Love Shack. Serena's golden ringlets cascade over her shoulder, pinned in an intricate half updo with orchids threaded through. A big bright pink rose ornaments the center of her magenta gown, made from a simple satin trimmed with lace. Tiny springs of baby's breath nestle between the plaits of Ophelia's braid-crown, the rest of her honey-brown waves falling past her waist. She shoots me daggers, her lashes flicking up and down as she scans my outfit. Her dress is the same shade as mine, which doesn't seem to make her happy.

"Are you alright if I leave you here?" Laina asks. "I need to go check in with the pageant committee."

I fold my arms across my chest, shivering as goosebumps sprout across my skin. The last thing I need is the pressure of the other girls preying on me like sharks. I scan the crowd for Roisin, but she hasn't arrived yet. *Great.*

"I'll be fine," I say to Laina, forcing a smile.

She nods, squeezing me in one last hug before turning to leave. "You're going to do amazing. Remember, Lila, no matter what happens, I love you."

I love you.

Her perfume lingers as she walks away. I hold on to it like a memory. My mom and dad said they'd always love me too. And yet, somehow, they still sent me here. I know better than to trust that love is unconditional. But as I latch on to her scent, at least I have evidence of another person who cares for me. I won't let her down. Not like how I let my parents down. This time things will be different. I'll be different.

Amelia rolls her eyes when I turn around, whispering something to Yvette. She throws her head back, laughing, and a couple of pink petals fall from her strawberry-blonde hair. It'd be easier to hate them, pick apart every imaginary flaw I project, but I don't. There isn't a point in making anyone else feel small.

The truth is, Yvette's seafoam-colored dress complements her beautifully, fanning into full layers of lace and tulle. And, as bitter as Amelia is, her tan glows against the fuchsia she's spotted in again—which, I assume, must be her signature color. Rather than goddess-esque like the first dress she wore, this one matches Yvette's ball gown silhouette, with huge roses strewn together to make up the fullness of her skirt. Even from across the table, she smells like a fresh bouquet.

I try to remain composed, my nails digging into my palms as I make my way to where they stand. The only way to build resilience is to face my fears head-on. I figure, if I'm nice, what's the worst they can actually whisper about? They have no reason to hate me despite being seen as their competition, and I have no reason to hate them either. At the end of the day, we all want to shine. And just because they do, it doesn't mean that I can't.

They're still huddled in a whisper as I arrive. But this time, they're not talking about me. In fact, they don't even flinch as I approach. No. Their eyes are fixed on Roisin.

She's stunning.

Townsfolk hand her bouquets and sprinkle petals over her head. She waves as she enters, pressing a hand to her heart as she accepts compliments from everyone on her dress. The pale pink tulle accentuates her rose-gold hair and is scalloped at the top like mermaid scales, sparkling with diamond detailing. Her skirt falls into a train of chiffon-spun roses, following her like a fairy garden. She's mesmerizing, with a tiara dazzling the top of her head.

Amelia scoffs, tossing back her blonde ringlets. "Who does she think she is? Already wearing a crown like she's won. How tacky."

I mind my business, ladling a glass of punch from the crystal bowl on the table. Pansies and peach slices float to the surface. A very Luna Island touch.

A dark-haired girl next to us chuckles. Her chartreuse mermaid gown is bedazzled with tiny crystals, making her olive skin seem luminous. "Please," she says, "you're just jealous because her dress looks exactly like yours. Seems like the town already decided who wore it best though." She pops a mozzarella ball into her mouth before walking away.

Yvette squeaks, flittering a hand to her glossy lips. "Carmella's right. Roisin's dress is almost identical."

Amelia's grip around her glass tightens. I almost think it's about to shatter. "As if. That pink is so pale, it's nearly white. And her skirt isn't even made with fresh flowers! Besides, I don't know what's more tasteless, wearing artificial roses or wearing a crown to a pageant."

"Hey guys, what did I miss?" Genevieve cuts in, piling her plate with honeydew and strawberries. Although she doesn't wear butterfly clips in her hair this time, the mint-green dress she chose has a delicate butterfly organza layered on top of the chiffon.

Yvette rolls her eyes. "Amelia's freaking out because Roisin's getting more attention than her." Her gaze shifts to Amelia. "Don't give her the satisfaction of knowing she already won."

"I never said she won!" Amelia flails, jingling the charm bracelet on her wrist.

"Well, duh." Genevieve twirls a curl around her finger. "But first impressions are everything. Looks to me, Roisin's already made her statement as the front runner."

"Not again," Yvette groans.

"What do you mean, 'again'?" I find the courage to ask.

Their heads snap in my direction.

Genevieve is the only one who smiles. "Everyone knows Nadine and Roisin were head-to-head for Angel of the Sea last year. If it wasn't Nadine, it would've been Roisin."

"Yeah," Yvette adds. "We're pretty sure it's what broke them up."

My stiletto nails bite into my palms. I flex my hand as soon as I notice. They don't know Roisin the way I do. It's hard to believe she'd let competition get between her and someone she loves. At least I hope so. Though, it's me I'm worried about, not her. If I'm not careful, I could end up exiled just like Nadine.

Amelia pours a glass of punch into one of the crystal chalices, whispering in my ear, "Careful, Lila. I wouldn't want you to become collateral."

"Huh?"

Before I know it, she's beelined straight for Roisin.

"Amelia, wait!" the girls call after her, scampering behind.

Oh, shit.

I jog after Amelia, but it's too late. Roisin reels out a gas-leak shriek as red punch splashes across her powder-pink dress. It stains like blood.

"Oops, I'm *so* sorry, Roisin. I—I tripped!"

Her eyes widen. "You did that on purpose. *And* you ruined my dress."

"Why would I do that?" Amelia's high-pitched voice pierces.

Tears bud in Roisin's eyes. "You know Angel of the Sea means everything to me."

"It means everything to all of us," Amelia snaps. "Don't think you're special just because you were last year's runner-up."

"I never said I was!"

"Oh, yeah? Then what's the tiara all about?"

Yvette cuts in. "Amelia, that's enough."

"Y-yeah, seriously," Genevieve stutters, "you're causing a scene."

"No. I don't think Roisin's had enough yet. Have you?"

Amelia plucks the tiara right from Roisin's head and throws it onto the forest floor. Genevieve and Yvette gasp.

"Let's get one thing straight. You're no one's queen."

Flashes of my past life blink before me, remembering my defeat and how everyone smiled behind my back after I slipped onstage. They were happy about my downfall, happy I left ballet. Condensation fogs my glass. I don't have to see my reflection in it to notice the sea of red spreading across my face. A burning zing swells within me, churning and rising with my blood— spreading up my neck and down my arms and to my hands. They're shaking. Reminding me of how it felt to break the fruit. The pear. The pear I shredded with my feral hands. The feral hands I wrung around my mother's throat. I glance at the bright red liquid in my glass now.

No.

The old me would have thrown my drink right back in Amelia's face. But I'm not that girl anymore. At least, I don't want to be. Instead, I grab Roisin's arm, tugging her towards the willow tree looming over the refreshments table. She sniffles, hiding her tears as we shuffle through the crowd.

My grip around her tightens. "Stop, you're going to ruin your makeup."

"Who cares! My entire outfit is already wrecked."

I whip around, cleaning under her eyes with my fingers. "I think I have some mascara in my bag."

"It doesn't matter, Lila. Amelia already sabotaged me, and it's only the first round."

"No, she didn't," I say, powdering her face. "Because you're going to switch outfits with me."

"What? I can't let you do that."

"Switch with me," I say again.

She crosses her arms. "No."

"I have a plan," I plead. "Do you trust me?"

Her shoulders slump. Reluctantly, she lures us behind a bush. "I trust you."

A moment later, Roisin is in lilac, and I'm in pink. It's odd seeing us in the opposite colors. The blue-toned lilac doesn't complement Roisin's complexion nearly as well as her signature pink does. And I'm pretty sure her dress washes me out. It's too close to my skin tone. Regardless, she's still beautiful. Even in the wrong shade, she's fairy birthed and angel kissed. I wonder if anything could dim her sparkle.

"What now?" she says, as all of the contestants are lining up for the competition to start.

I take a deep breath, praying I don't regret what I'm about to do. "Like I said, just trust me."

I make my way back over to the refreshments table, and with shaky hands, I lift the punch bowl in the air. My eyes squeeze shut as I pour its contents over my dress, staining it red like Carrie White's or Jennifer Check's on prom night. Gasps break out at the sound of the splash. Punch seeps into the pale pink fabric, darkening the chiffon roses. The spill feathers out in fissures, bleeding out like blooming tie-dye.

"Lila!" Roisin cries.

Amelia throws her head back, laughing. "Wow! A plot twist. The outsider is also a total freak."

I lower the bowl, steadying my breath. One stain is considered an imperfection. An entire spill is artwork. Persephone didn't become less lovely just because she was dragged to Hell. Carrie was still prom queen. And Jennifer . . . well, Jennifer was still Megan Fox. The point is, it's not about the dress we wear. It's about how we carry ourselves in it.

I only hope I stand out in the right way.

I take my place with the rest of the girls. Roisin tugs on my arm, hiss-whispering as I fall in line beside her. "Are you *trying* to get yourself disqualified?"

"Relax. I know what I'm doing."

She scoffs. "You better hope so."

We're ushered away from the glade to a hidden path behind the trees by someone on the pageant committee. When we arrive, we're greeted by a beautiful woman in white. Her floor-length gown glimmers as if woven entirely of stardust. The trumpet sleeves encompassing her arms move like plumes of smoke, and in her lovely pale gold locks are summer flowers in different shades of pink and purple. She's stunning. Like a fairy godmother brought to life before my eyes.

"Hello, darlings!" She claps, beaming a smile. "My, don't you all look so beautiful."

I hide behind Roisin, careful not to draw too much attention to myself. "Is that—"

"Mother Marguerite?" she finishes. "The one and only."

I understand what she meant now. Mother Marguerite is either an angel, or she's been blessed by one. I wonder if the High Priestess has a shimmering haze about her too.

"Welcome to this year's Angel of the Sea Pageant." There's a lyrical vibrato to her voice that sounds like music when she speaks. "As you know, things are a bit . . . different this year. Seeing as most of you have already participated, congratulations on your second chance. Not many are as lucky as you."

Every girl radiates with a smile. As much as I despise Amelia's petty animosity, part of me also understands her. Just a year ago, every girl here thought her chance of becoming High Priestess had slipped away for good. No wonder they're threatened by me, by Roisin too. She's the girl they're most likely to pick. I'm the girl who has the potential to surprise them all.

"For those of you who are new, I will reiterate the rules. There are four parts to the pageant. Beauty, Faith in Luna, Strength of Will, and Grace. To start off the season, you will descend the temple staircase in your best dress, presenting yourself to the town and the angels. Remember, beauty isn't about how you look—it's about how you carry yourself. You are all gorgeous, my little chickadees. No matter what the angels decide."

I try to hide the smile tugging at the corners of my lips. Amelia may think I've already thrown the competition, but I was always one step ahead.

"After all of you have descended, the angels will vote on which of you will continue, and I will announce the results. Easy enough?"

The girls nod, and we make our way up the temple steps.

From up here, the people look like a basketful of pastel Easter eggs—a sprawl of yellows, pinks, and blues. I scan the crowd for any sign of angels, but there isn't a wing to be seen. Maybe they're disguised in the audience. Perhaps they're hidden behind the trees. Or what if they're amongst us right now on the steps, watching closely without our knowledge? A shiver slithers down my spine at the thought. I flex my shaky hands.

Don't mess up, Lila, I say to myself. *All you have to do is make sure you don't fall.*

The girls descend the steps one by one, introduced by Mother Marguerite. There are a couple of names I don't recognize yet.

Isadora Ivy.

Celine Amarosa.

Giselle Buchannan.

My nerves creep up as each girl floats away. Roisin spins around before her turn, squeezing my hand one last time. "You got this, Lila. All you have to do is smile. Oh, and don't fall."

"Yeah." I wince. "I know."

"Good luck." She blows me a kiss before she descends.

Even though she's in my dress, the crowd adores Roisin, tossing flowers at the staircase while she smiles and waves. My point is proven—it was never about the dress, the makeup, or the hair. It's about the girl beneath it. I smile. No one deserves the praise more than her.

"Lila Rose Li," Mother Marguerite announces.

Shit. Before I know it, it's my turn.

I smooth my hands over the punch-stained ruffles, taking a deep breath. *Persephone is still Persephone even in the winter,* I remind myself. *And I am still Lila even though my dress is stained. Even though I fell onstage. Even though I was banished because of it. I am still Lila.*

And as Lila, I descend.

The crowd erupts in a roar. They holler and cheer and throw just as many flowers as they did for Roisin. Roses, marigolds, and violets hit the glossy marble steps like confetti. Their applause floods me, turning me full, just like it did when I took my final bows onstage after a show. I throw on my best smile, waving like the pageant queen I pretend to be. Roisin howls, screaming my name with the crowd. The praise goes to my head. It's like I'm the Queen of Hell, like Persephone herself. And, as I reach the final step, I re-emerge into spring.

Roisin thrusts her arms around me, and the townsfolk swarm us like we're royalty. Even as they shove their bouquets at us and scream our names, I never break our embrace. That's when I realize—being celebrated is more rewarding when the person you love is winning with you. Our joy is collective. Her bliss is mine. It's then I know, even if Roisin wins, I'd be just as happy as if it were me.

"You did it, Lila!" she squeals.

"No, we did it together." I doubt I would've made half the impression without her dress.

But like any dream on Luna Island, it doesn't stay sparkling for long. Over Roisin's shoulder, I spot my dying rose in a field of flowers—looming black feathers in a field of pastel.

Damien.

I jerk away and stumble back. He turns around as soon as our eyes lock, taking off into the forest.

"Hey, what's wrong?" Roisin brushes a fallen curl away from my face.

"Will you excuse me for a moment?" I mutter, pushing past her and breaking into the crowd.

"Lila! Where are you going?"

Her voice drowns out as I shove past the flowers and frills, slipping between the trees and following Damien's path.

"Hey! Stop," I shout after him, never breaking my tether to his black wings. I hound him like a huntress, ignoring the burning in my calves as I press forward. "You can't avoid me forever. I know you told the angels about last night."

I know you're trying to sabotage my chances of winning.

"Damien!"

He disappears behind the tall grass-like bushes. The sudden sound of shattered bone makes me jump. My heart stills, twisting and dropping into my stomach. I sink my nails into my palms to stay calm as my hands tense.

Cautiously, I part the drooping leaves and clasp a hand to my mouth. Damien isn't alone. He's on his knees, blood dripping from his lips to his chin. He presses his forehead to a leather boot. It belongs to another angel. An angel with wings just as black as his.

"I told you not to get involved," the angel says with a thrum that sends pinpricks over my skin. His tone is too familiar. It reminds me of my father.

My teeth break the tender skin of my lower lip as I force myself to remain silent. Suddenly, our cat-and-mouse chase is no longer a game. Not when one of us is really getting hurt. I resist the urge to dart through the bushes and gather him the way I wish someone would have done for me in my pain, in my humiliation. We may be different, but he doesn't deserve this. None of us do.

"You don't understand," Damien pleads. "You didn't see what she could do."

"Exactly," the angel above him spits. "You don't get to decide who is or isn't worthy. You haven't earned the right."

I knew it. Damien *was* the one who returned my locket.

"But, Father, I—"

"What are you doing?" A voice rings from behind me.

I startle and spin around, clenching the chiffon flowers on my dress like they're my last tether to reality. The voice belongs to an angel. And not one hidden or disguised like Roisin warned me about. Her lush, feathered wings fan out behind her like a swan queen. Ringlets of white-gold hair tumble over her shoulders, emanating a soft glow. Her eyes are eerily familiar. The same beetle-shell green gold as Damien's. Only hers are large and doe-like.

"You shouldn't be here," she says quietly. Her voice is ambrosial and languid. She takes a step closer, and golden freckles flash across her face like stardust.

"I—I'm sorry," I stammer. "I'll go."

"Wait." She grabs my wrist. "Stop by Heaven Divine later. I have something for you."

I reel back, shocked by her icy touch. "You do?"

She nods, pursing her lips together in a closed-mouth smile. "Consider it a gift."

A gift? "For what?"

Her eyes flick over me up and down. "If you ask another question, I may change my mind."

"Okay, okay." I back away. "I'm sorry. I'll go now."

"And don't come back here unless you're invited," she says, voice echoing.

I never look back.

◆

When I emerge from the forest, the winners of the first round are announced.

Amelia Everhart.

Carmella Valentine.

Celine Amarosa.

Genevieve Brentwood.

Giselle Buchannan.

Isadora Ivy.

Ophelia Hawthorne.

Roisin Kelly.

Serena Beaumont.

Yvette Montgomery.

And Lila Rose Li.

Chapter
TEN

✦

When I was younger, my parents used to take me to our local diner after ballet recitals. It was my favorite tradition because I was rewarded with fries and a milkshake—which I was typically denied any other day. On Luna Island, after a competition, all of the girls go to Petals Tea Shop.

I recognize Carmella, Celine, and Isadora from the pageant earlier today. They're huddled around a floral-print table, sharing a Princess Cake with green fondant and pink roses. Celine's white-blonde hair snakes down her back with hints of golden tinsel. She braids it to the side before taking another bite of cake, showing off her cheekbones that flash with an iridescent shimmer. Carmella sweeps her dark brown locks into a French twist, before helping Isadora collect the seashell charms woven through her golden curls. The three of them sport matching

Luna Island sweatshirts in different colors—pale yellow, teal, and lilac.

Another one of my favorite post-performance rituals is the relief of slipping out of costume while still holding on to a bit of magic from the stage. Meaning full hair and makeup, minus some frizz and sweat. Instead of our dresses, everyone wears comfortable clothes. Even Amelia, Genevieve, and Yvette are spotted in matching velour sets as they enjoy their afternoon teas and scones.

Roisin has changed into a peach-colored waffle knit paired with black leggings. I've never seen her dress so casually before, but she still wears a ribbon in her hair. I've thrown on my favorite oversized sweatshirt—a pale blue crewneck from Monterey—paired with shorts and flip-flops.

A hostess donning a strawberry-print apron seats us at a booth by the window, framed by lace curtains tied back with bows. Waves crash against the jagged rocks, and a bit of sea spray splashes the glass. Roisin squeals as an otter pops its head up from the water. She snaps a picture with her phone before placing it face down on the gingham tablecloth.

"Well, isn't this a treat," she chirps, holding up a blush-hued menu.

I nod, scanning the swirly cursive on mine. All of it jumbles together like a mess of threads. This moment was supposed to be happy. We should be toasting to our victory, grateful to see another day in the competition. Instead, my stomach twists in knots.

Roisin slouches, placing the menu down. "Okay. You wouldn't tell me what happened last night, and then you just ran off into

the forest again without a word. Now you're barely talking to me."
She crosses her arms. "What gives?"

I concentrate on the menu to avoid her gaze, taking a deep
breath. All of the tea titles read like something out of a fever dream.
I'm too exhausted to decipher the fine print that describes each one.

Breakfast at Luna's
Fairy Milk
Sunset Sweet Pea
Love in the Afternoon
Siren Tears
Velvet Honeymoon

"Lila," she snaps. "You can't avoid me forever."

I squeeze my eyes shut, as if this were all just a bad dream I
could make disappear. I may be on Luna Island, but my past is
following me. Just like back home, the audience adores me, but
it isn't enough to fill the void of what I really crave. *Worthiness.*
Though, this time, the validation I seek is from Damien, not my
parents. He's the one who stole my locket back from the angels.
He's the one who tried to get me removed from the pageant.
He's the one who wanted me gone so badly, he defied his own
father because of it. Damien was supposed to be my edge in the
competition. But, of course, I screwed it up. And now he'll stop at
nothing to sabotage me.

"I—"

"What can I get ya?" Our waitress cuts in. Her name tag reads
Betty, and she wears a high ponytail that sways when she talks.

Her winged eyeliner and pinup-style fringe remind me of the models on the vintage postcards I used to collect.

"I'll get the—um." My finger lands on a random title. "I'll get the Midsummer Moondrop."

"I'll have the Aphrodite's Ambrosia," Roisin decides, sliding the menu forward.

"You got it," Betty says, taking our menus and flashing a smile lined with cherry lipstick. Her blonde ponytail swishes as she walks away.

Roisin grabs my hand as soon as she's gone. "Come on, Lila. What happened?"

I lean back in my seat. "Can we at least wait for the tea first?"

She lifts her hand from mine, taking a deep breath. "Fine."

Despite her annoyance, I know she isn't mad. She's worried about me, and I understand why. Something out there got to Nadine. And that something could be after me too if I'm not careful.

Betty returns in a couple of minutes, setting down our pots of tea and two towers of treats. There are small tea cakes dressed as mini presents, tarts in the shape of flowers, chocolate-covered strawberries sprinkled with edible pearls, macarons decorated with pressed violets, and a tray of scones accompanied by tiny finger sandwiches. She explains each tea before leaving us to indulge.

Aphrodite's Ambrosia—a blend of caramel, rose hips, white chocolate, and raspberry.

Midsummer Moondrop—a confection of violets, butterfly pea flower, and sugar plums.

I lift the porcelain cup to my lips, hand painted with tiny cornflowers and gold leaf. The sweet, dark blend relaxes my muscles like a dreamspell.

"Okay," Roisin mutters, stuffing a dainty raspberry custard into her mouth. "You have your tea. Now spill."

I sigh, warming my hands against the cup. "Well, as you can probably guess, things didn't exactly go as planned yesterday. And now I'm afraid I've ruined everything."

She licks a bit of custard from her thumb. "I'm sure it wasn't that bad. Things always seem way worse in our heads."

I refrain from telling her how horrifyingly my dance really ended. Nobody else needs to know about my power—or, my inability to control it—other than the angel. I slip a bite-size tiramisu onto my tongue, hoping the bittersweet taste will settle the bile threatening to crawl up my throat. "I fell."

"Oh, Lila! I'm so sorry."

Her apology feels like needles to my skin. *How pathetic.* "You don't have to feel sorry for me. In fact, it's the last thing I want right now."

Her shoulders slump. "I just want you to feel supported. That's all."

"I know you do, and I appreciate it."

We share a brief smile before I groan again, burying my face in my hands. "It was awful. I—I'm worried he'll tell the other angels. What if I'm cut from the pageant?"

I shovel two more cubes of sugar into my tea to cull the nerves. Damien already decided I'm not worthy of my gifts, just like my parents. It's only a matter of time before the other angels realize I'm a fraud too.

Roisin shakes her head. "This is what you've been so stressed about? I promise, the angels aren't going to remove you from the pageant just because of one little mistake."

Only, it wasn't just one little mistake. I summoned a storm in a perfect paradise. There isn't so much as a gray cloud on Luna Island any other day. My face falls, and I trace constellations between the crumbs on my plate. "It was a disaster."

She grabs a scone before cutting it in half and smothering it with lemon curd. "Well, what exactly happened after you fell?"

I clink my spoon against the teacup as I stir in a dash of cream. "I think the angel visited me while I was asleep. He's taunting me."

"Whoa, what do you mean he's taunting you?" She nearly chokes on her bite. "You saw the angel again after I left?"

"Well, not exactly. The window was wide open when I woke up, which I know we closed. And then . . ." I pause, running my fingers over the pearlescent finish of the teacup. "I—I woke up with my locket around my neck. The same one I sacrificed to pledge."

"Wait, what?" she shouts, rattling the table. Heads snap in our direction, and she hunches down. "Oops. Sorry."

"See." I lean in closer. "He has it out for me. This is why I was scared to tell you." I proved I'm not some sparkling, magic *thing*, and just like my parents, he's ready to discard me.

"This doesn't make any sense. Why would the angel try to prevent you from competing? I mean, he could've just not extended his blessing. But returning your locket? That's not for him to decide. The Angel of the Sea is a collective vote."

That's what his father said. Only, Damien is right. His father didn't see what I could do. It was bad enough for him to want me out of the pageant. And perhaps bad enough to want me off Luna Island altogether.

"I don't know, but something else came up while I was in the forest earlier too."

"What is it?" Roisin's doe eyes widen.

"I—I—" I set my teacup down, steadying my shaky hands. "I met another angel. And she asked me to meet her at some place called . . . Heaven Divine?"

Roisin gasps. "Lila! Do you know what this means? You didn't screw things up at all. The angels are offering you a blessing. You must've really stood out to them today."

"Wait, seriously?" Was my stunt with the punch bowl actually enough to set me apart from the rest of the girls?

"Yes!" she gushes. "Heaven Divine is a perfumery on Main Street. And let's just say their fragrances are known to do more than just make you smell nice."

"I don't understand."

"It's like Luna's Love Shack. The perfumes are made by the angels. If you're gifted one by an angel themself, it's usually an enchantment of some sort."

"An enchantment?" What kind of enchantment could the angels possibly want to share with me?

She nods. "Yeah. Like sleeping spells, love potions, glamours . . . you have to go, Lila! This is a good thing."

I guess. I clench the frayed sleeve of my sweatshirt, rubbing the worn fabric for comfort. Damien might have it out for me, but perhaps with a blessing from the angels, I won't just be safe, I'll be one step ahead in the pageant after all.

"Okay," I say, before downing my last sip of tea. "Let's go."

She stops me from rising. "I'll walk you to the store, but you have to go in alone."

"What?"

"I can't go with you, Lila. This is your honor. The angels only show themselves when they want to be seen. And this one chose you."

Great. I just pray the attention on me is a good thing. Guess there's only one way to find out.

✦

Roisin squeezes my hand before releasing me in front of Heaven Divine. Overgrown ivy sprawls from the base of the stone-built cottage all the way to the roof. I hesitate to step inside. Although this isn't my first encounter with an angel, she's still an *angel*. And I'm not sure what she could possibly want with me.

"Go on," Roisin nudges me. "I'll be waiting right across the street on the bench beneath the azaleas."

I follow her pointed finger to the streetlamp wreathed with bright pink flowers.

"Don't worry," she affirms. "Everything will be fine."

"Okay." It's now or never. I sigh, finally pushing my way through the door.

A bell chimes as I enter Heaven Divine. French music fills the warm yellow room, illuminated by an antique chandelier.

The shop reminds me of the perfumeries I once visited in Paris. Glass bottles line the shelves, sparkling like crystals and casting rainbow reflections on the walls.

"Oh good. You made it."

I whip around, and the door clicks shut the second I turn my back. The angel flashes her fickle smile. Her wings are hidden, but even in her human form, she's lovely. White-blonde ringlets cascade around her heart-shaped face. Instead of stardust freckles, blush sweeps across her cheeks and button nose. Although she no longer glows, she has a gentle aura about her. Soft mint-green eyes. Milky, rose-kissed skin. Full pale pink lips. Her puff-sleeve dress suggests her innocence, but her devious smile warns me to proceed with caution.

She makes her way forward, slow and catlike, her hips swaying with every step. Her movements are so graceful, it's almost like she's floating. She doesn't stop until I can feel her breath on mine. I shudder, uncomfortable with how close she is.

She takes a lock of my hair, twirling it around her finger. "My, you're even more beautiful up close."

I lean back from her embrace. "Thank you?"

She circles me like a snake, and I, her prey. My throat tightens as her eyes flick up and down. "He didn't tell me how lovely you are."

"He?"

She lifts a brow. "Damien."

Damien. Of course. I knew he'd already spread word of what happened to the other angels. "Why did you ask me here if you know what I did?"

She folds her arms across her chest. "Why did you compete if you were already warned not to?"

Fair. "I—I guess I just wanted to prove him wrong."

Her devilish smirk returns. "You and me both."

"Wait, what?"

Her hand sliding to my face cuts me off. She tucks a weft of hair behind my ear, tracing her fingers down my cheek as she studies me more closely. "You must have been blessed by Luna," she finally says.

I inch back. "There's no way." Why would Luna choose me?

She shrugs. "I can't explain it, but if I had to place my bet on who's going to win the pageant, it's you."

"Really?" For a moment, everything disappears. *Pain. Confusion. Longing.* All that's left is that glittering, tingly bliss.

"Mm-hm." She nods. "Which is why I'm going to help you earn a second chance."

My brows knit inward. "How?"

She saunters behind the glass counter, and I follow her, scanning the bottles as her fingers trace each one in the case. Some are dainty, with long crystal stoppers, sharp at the tip, a signature design from the 1920s. Others are full and round, with pastel puff atomizers at the end. My favorites are the jewel-toned bottles with intricate glass-blown flowers at the top.

She finally picks one shaped like a star with rough crystal edges. It sparkles beneath the chandelier's light. "Jasmine, to put you to sleep. Gardenia, to open up the garden of your mind. And roses, because angels just love the scent. Put this behind your ears before you sleep, and your angel will come to you in your dreams."

"My dreams?"

She removes the crystal stopper and pulls out a single strand of white-blonde hair from her pocket. It still glows, and when she drops it into the bottle, the liquid shimmers gold.

"There." Her voice is pillow soft. "Now he's sure to come back."

"What do you mean?"

Her eyes narrow at my ignorance. "It's infused with Damien's essence so that he can enter the garden of your mind."

The garden of my mind? I step back, as if to distance myself from the thought. It sounds so invasive, welcoming someone into a space that's only ever been for me. "What am I supposed to do once he's there?"

"You'll know." She slows her words, closing her fist around my hand as she places the bottle in my palm.

I accept the perfume, inspecting the swirling incandescent liquid. "Why are you giving me this?" This has to be about more than just Damien. It doesn't make sense why she'd go out of her way just to sway another angel's opinion of me.

She shrugs. "Like I said, consider it a gift."

"But I—I don't even know your name."

She lifts her pearly nose in the air. Even as a human, she still has a faerie-like charm to her. "I'm Aurora."

"Aurora," I echo back. Like something from a storybook.

"Sweet dreams, Lila. I do hope you enjoy."

Anxiety wells in the pit of my stomach, fluttering through my arms, up my neck, and to the blush of my cheeks. Something about the way she says my name is unsettling. I've never given her that part of me, but she knows it anyway. She's been watching. Have they all been?

I stumble out of the perfumery, clenching the star-shaped bottle in my hand. Its strange glow taunts me—ever moving, as if alive.

"Lila!" Roisin calls my name from across the cobblestones, jogging over to meet me. "How did it go? What did she say?"

"Well, she gave me this weird perfume." I toggle it between my hands. "She said to wear it behind my ears before I go to bed, and it'll bring Damien back."

Roisin gasps. "It's a summoning. We'll have to prepare you."

"Prepare me? What, like a ritual or something?"

She shrugs. "Something like that."

✦

At night, Roisin helps ready me for the angel.

She motions me to lie down, lighting candles around the room that flicker in the dark. Rose petals kiss the tops of my pillows and tangle with my hair. Roisin says it's common to present oneself like an offering when summoning the angels, which is why she brushes a hint of rouge across my lips and a shimmer on the tops of my cheeks.

She cracks open the window, placing an offering on the sill— half an oyster shell with celestite, selenite, and aquamarine— tokens for the angels. Finally, she spritzes the perfume from Heaven Divine behind my ears, anointing me with the blessing.

"Sweet dreams, Lila," she whispers, creaking the door shut.

I only pray that this time, they really are.

Chapter
ELEVEN

✦

My mind unfurls in a tumble of flowers—roses, jasmines, and gardenias—all white and perfumed. The warm, sweet air is heavy, like something sticky clinging to me. I fall subject to its honeytrap, and move slowly through the world.

Above me is a galaxy of aqua blue, navy, and lilac, glittering with diamond-white stars. Something about the void is unsettling. Perhaps, it's that the sky doesn't seem to have a beginning or an end, and I'm victim to its vastness.

I'm small here. Tall hedges surround me—a maze built from crystalline white flowers. I pause, fixated on the fullness of a rose. It's unnaturally perfect, huge and round with velvet petals that shimmer with silver sparkles. Each symmetrical bud is identical to the next, too manicured to be real. I step closer and caress one of the petals. The rose shivers beneath my fingertips, shedding its glitter. The vines start to slither like a slow-moving snake. I reel back, but I'm too late. I shriek as the demon plant snaps around my wrist, its thorns cutting into my flesh.

I lurch back, but the vines pull me forward. The coils tighten around my arm, drawing blood. As it spills over the glittering flowers, they tremble awake and hiss, snapping like angry animals and suffocating me with their saccharine scent. I reach forward, trying to break free, but the vines crack against my rib cage, squeezing my waist. I yelp, but the air is cut from my lungs as the plant restricts me.

"What the hell!" I heave, attempting to pry myself away. The more I struggle, the more it tightens, drawing me farther and farther into the hedge.

"Lila!" A familiar voice shouts.

I glance up, narrowing my eyes on the angel of death himself. *Damien.*

"You! You did this. You set me up!"

"I swear, I didn't," he pleads.

My nails sink into the coarse vines. "Get me out of here."

He freezes, gaping at me. "Who gave you the glamour that brought you here?"

"I don't know." I pant. "Some angel I met in the forest. Aurora?"

"Aurora." He wavers, steadying his balance against the hedge. It doesn't move or overtake him like it does to me.

"You know her?"

His viridescent eyes meet mine. "That's my sister."

"Your sister?" I yelp. *The angels are fickle,* Roisin warned. I should have never tested them by participating in the pageant against their will. "What the hell does your sister want with me?"

Damien shakes his head, running his fingers through his hair. "*Devil's Teeth.* I told her not to get involved."

"I knew it. You guys have been after me since I arrived." Of course, she didn't mean to help me. Of course, she didn't think I'd win. Of course, I was never blessed by Luna.

I've been damned from the start.

"Lila," Damien says softly. "I need you to stay calm. Listen to me, okay?"

Tears spring to my eyes, blurring his face. My lower lip trembles at my defeat. I have no other choice but to trust him. "Fine."

"Do you know where we are?"

"No." I wince, biting back the quiver in my voice.

"We're in the garden of your mind. All of these flowers are secrets you've kept inside. They've blossomed into this labyrinth. When you come face-to-face with one of the hedges, you have to confront a fear you've hidden in order to release yourself from its hold."

"What?"

Before Damien can answer, the snapping and hissing smoothens into a voice. A voice I recognize all too well—the one that calls to me in the ocean, the one that's haunted me all my life. It unravels in an overtone, one high, one low.

Lila Rose Li. What a pretty name for a pretty girl. The world could have known that name. You could have been a star. But what happened, little rose? Your petals fell and you came undone. Now you're nothing but a worn-out stem. Thrown out and unloved.

I screech, sinking my stiletto nails into my palms. My throat strains as I hold back my temper. My voice roars out anyway, spilling the truth I've suppressed since arriving here. "It wasn't my fault! My mother doubted me from the start. She's the reason I fell on that stage. She got what was coming to her. You can't blame me."

The vines release their hold, and I drop to the floor. Hunching over, I drink in the hot, nectar air. Hair tumbles over my face, shielding the tears that slip down my cheeks and the shame that comes with it. I've been avoiding how a part of me relished my mother's pain. Part of me even felt like she deserved it. She hurt me, and I wanted to hurt her back. All this time I've told myself I didn't mean it, but I did. And I hate myself for it.

"Lila," Damien whispers, leaning down and touching my shoulder. "Are you okay?"

I don't look at him. I can't. My blood boils at his touch. "Get off me!"

I stumble to my feet, pouncing through the labyrinth. I need to find my way out of here. *Wake up, Lila.* I say to myself. *It's just a dream.*

Wake up.

Wake up.

Wake up!

It's no use. I press forward, clawing through the brambles that close in, snapping branches and smashing petals as the labyrinth tries to claim me again.

"Ahh!" I wail, tripping over a vine. It wraps around my ankles and pulls me towards a hedge of gardenias. I claw through the dirt, scratching the garden floor as it collects me.

Don't think I forgot about that blue-and-purple bruise. The one around your throat that you try so hard to conceal. What did you do to earn that beauty mark, little rose? We always thought you were your father's favorite flower. Well, that is until you wilted, and he saw the real you.

My throat stretches taut as a screech reels from the center of my chest. The world around me shakes. "If I weren't so fragile, I would've won that battle! I was never scared of him, no matter how much he barked at me like I was a dog. I fought back. Don't think I didn't. I would've slit his throat if he hadn't sent me away."

My eyes fall shut as the vines release me. I bury my face in the dirt as I whisper a cry into the cool, wet earth. The gardenias crumple beneath my body, a delicate reminder of my father's fragile love. I made excuses every time he lost his temper—saying he never meant it, that I forced his hand, that I scared him because he saw himself in me. The truth is he turned me cruel, and it frightens me the same way I frighten him.

"Lila." Damien reaches for me again, but I push him back, and he collides with one of the hedges. "Stop," he says. "You don't have to do this. I can take us away from here."

But it's too late for that. My rage is building, just as it did when I broke the fruit that started my downfall. *Building and building, cascading and building.* I ride it like a wave until anger engulfs me, carrying me through the world—reality suspended at its crest.

I continue swelling forward, the garden nurturing the beast inside me with its poisonous nectar. Veins pulse pale blue and violet beneath my arms, throbbing as if there were a demon within me, ready to cut through my human body. I don't fight the garden anymore. Instead, I surrender to the jasmines in front of me. They don't gather me. They don't have to. We face one another in a final battle.

No one is there to love you now, little rose. You lost that chance when you turned everyone to ash. You're a wildfire, not an ocean. You belong with the Devil, and with the Devil you shall go.

My voice unravels like tendrils of burbling fire. "I'll bring myself to the grave before I let that monster have me. In fact, I'd like to see him try. Don't believe me? Ask my mother. I will never—and I mean never—surrender."

I reach for a fist of jasmines, crumbling the buds in my hand, and the entire garden wilts. One by one, the pristine white buds lose their sparkle, turning brown and shriveling to nothing. The leaves from the hedges fall away with the wind, leaving nothing but their brittle branches, which shrink and disappear into dust. It's relief and loss all at once—a heaviness that's lifted, throwing me off-balance. I sink to my knees, choking on the tears that follow.

Damien sweeps down to where I lie, his feathered wings cradling me. They're silk smooth, reminiscent of the angel-spun dresses at Luna's Love Shack. I give in, shaking as he gathers me.

"Hey, it's okay. I got you," he says. "And I'm not going to let anything hurt you."

I bury my face in the crook of his neck, muffling the cries that rush out of me. His wings stroke my back. The feeling is too soft. Part of me wants to shake him off, put distance between our beating hearts. But I can't move. I can't breathe. He holds me closer, tighter.

"Why are you still here, angel? Please, just go." I don't deserve his kindness or his pity.

I understand Aurora now. She wanted to show me the truth—that I'll never be angelic. I shouldn't have competed in the pageant in the first place. If I ever were worthy of Luna's glory, the garden of my mind wouldn't have betrayed me. I know it. Aurora knows it. And now Damien knows it too.

I'm a monster, and I belong in Hell.

"I'm not afraid of you." Damien confesses.

I shake my head. "You don't have to lie. I know it was you who tried to remove me from the pageant."

"Lila." He brushes the hair away from my face, caressing my chin and tilting my gaze towards his. "I was trying to protect you. The same way I have since you arrived to Luna Island."

"I don't—I don't understand. Why would you protect me after knowing what I've done? The Devil noticed me the moment I arrived. He's trying to drag me to Hell, and you should let him." Maybe then the island would know peace. Roisin would be safe. Laina would be content. Everyone would move on with their lives as they should.

His icy hand grazes the inside of my wrist, sending pinpricks up my arm. "I don't fear you because I recognize you."

"What?" I hesitate, paralyzed by his golden gaze.

His thumb presses into my skin, rubbing my tender pulse. My hand relaxes into his. "Let's just say I know what it's like to disappoint the people you love . . . I also know how hard it is to breathe, no matter how much you try to come up for air."

"Huh?" I can't help but wonder . . . *The dreams I have so often. The reflections of light in the distance, trailing into the otherworld.*

The hand that reaches for me while I'm drowning, that gives me a second chance at life . . . Has Damien been here before, in the corners of my mind, protecting me from my thoughts of being called to the sea? Perhaps when I fell from the boat, that wasn't the first time Damien saved me.

"You *have* been watching me," I say. "Why?"

A smile breaks across his face, softening his jagged features. He tucks my hair behind my ear, combing through my raven locks, before looking up at the galaxy painted by my mind. "Do you know where the angels come from, Lila?"

I follow his gaze. "You're all stars."

"Right. And what do stars do?"

"Shine?"

"They light up the dark." There's a wistfulness in his voice, a glimmer of hope and longing. "You see, the angels were never supposed to be here. The island changed us. Stars are meant to be guardians of lost souls. But when my ancestors fell from Luna's grace, we suffered like humans do—experienced hate, anger, and sorrow—like humans do. And now I'm afraid I'm just as lost as the mortals we were meant to guide." He's fragile when he speaks, as if he'll shatter at any moment.

I place my hand to his beating heart. He looks down, grazing my fingertips across his chest. It rises and falls with his breath, a reminder that he's as human as I, and that humans were never meant to be perfect.

He looks back up at the sky. "All I've ever wanted is to return to the stars, away from this human mess. The Devil dove from the Heavens to gain free will, but he never anticipated the wildness of the world."

I frown, thinking of how something so perfect, so untainted, could learn pain the same way we do. It reminds me of my childhood and how we all start out innocent. Just like my innocence, his is lost, and he sees that emptiness in me. I'm not special. I'm just a mirror of his pain. He chose me because I'm as broken as he is. I can't save him, but perhaps together, we'd be less alone.

"What happened to you, angel?" I find the courage to ask.

"Let's just say you're not the only one who feels like a disappointment to their family." He turns his back to me. "You see my wings? Did you notice how they're black instead of white?"

I study them, raven feathers with a subtle iridescence, blue beneath the light. "Yes."

"The angels call it an honor. I consider it a branding."

"A branding?"

His voice shrinks into a whisper. "My father said to wear them with pride, but all I see is a reminder of everything I'll never amount to."

He doesn't have to explain for me to understand—he's playing a role he never wanted. The same way I was forced to play a princess while I was only becoming a corpse.

"I'm sorry," I manage to say, placing a hand against the feathers so he knows that it's alright. He recoils, and I take a step closer, until we're breath to breath. "I understand what it's like to disappoint your parents. I also know what it's like to be punished for it." He looks at me, his gaze surprisingly tender. "All I ever wanted was for my parents to love me too," I confess.

"In their own way, they do," he mutters. "Or they must, deep down."

"Maybe," I ponder aloud. "But you don't know my parents, and you don't know me." The angel's eyes expand, as if to learn me. I look away, intimidated by the intensity of his gaze. "I'm not as gentle as you think."

I return to the moment that got me sent away—the tender flesh of the pear and how I crushed it between my palms. I threw the plate at the wall, and it shattered. Tears sprung to my mother's eyes, though she'd probably say it was because of the pear, not the porcelain.

In my culture, mothers show their love with a plate of fresh cut fruit—grown with love, selected with care, washed until pure, perfectly sliced, and arranged into a flower. I destroyed the love she offered because to me, her American daughter, a plate of fruit was never enough. I shut my eyes, allowing my tears to fall.

I wanted her to say *I love you*. I wanted to hear it. I wanted her to mean it.

I took the pear for granted. Now I'll never earn back her love—with my dance, with my apologies, with anything.

I take a deep breath. "You know how I dance, angel?"

"Of course."

I almost laugh. "I used to love it. Dancing was the only thing that ever made me feel like me. But my parents said if I wanted to be a ballerina, I would have to prove myself."

Only, I never did. I never earned their love.

When I started taking dancing seriously, so did my mother. She told me if I wanted to pursue it, I would have to be the best. Otherwise, it was just a waste.

"I exhausted myself every day, perfecting every piqué, every arabesque. All for them."

It was never enough.

I was never enough.

"I'm sorry," Damien whispers his condolences.

The memory of my outburst turns me heady. I hold on to my frame as if it could keep me together. My father wanted to kill me for what I did to my mother, and if he hadn't sent me away, I think he just might have. I don't dare tell Damien the full story—what I actually did to get sent here. He's already heard too much.

Damien pushes a piece of hair away from my face, tucking it behind my ear. His touch is too gentle, too kind. I don't want him to pity me. I'm not as weak as I've been letting on.

"They wanted me to be something, to bring honor to our family. But what they didn't know is that I was *always* going to be something great." I glance at the vast constellations of stars above us, grazing the space between my collarbones where my locket used to rest. My parents never saw people who looked like us onstage. I was going to prove that I could be seen. No matter what the cost.

"What do you mean?"

"Look at me." I don't ask, I command. "Have you ever seen anyone like me around Luna Island before?"

My reflection gleams back in the iridescent sky, reminding me of where I come from. I'm from Oceania, birthed from the Pacific Seas, just as much as I'm from the Okinawan shores of Japan and the Guangzhou River in China.

He pauses for a second, shaking his head. "No."

"Girls like me don't show up in fairytales. I wanted to prove that no matter what you look like, you can still be the star."

When I was six, I took my first trip to the ballet. It was *The Nutcracker*, and to my surprise, the dancer playing the Sugar Plum Fairy looked just like me—she was Asian. When I was that young, I thought it was normal to be admired the way she was. But as I grew up, I realized that's not the case and that the world will always be against people who look like me.

"I wanted to be recognized in the stories I loved so badly. With ballet, it doesn't matter where you come from. It matters how good you are."

"That's why you trained so hard."

"Yes, but it wasn't just that." Before things were bad, my mother used to ask why I was so drawn to the sea. I told her that although the sea is dangerous beneath the surface, people still find beauty in it from above. It's still something to be adored, even if it is usually only ever loved at a distance. That's why I loved performing. For a moment, I could just be admired. Not a danger to everyone around me.

Like the sea, I have a tendency to destroy things. Beautiful things. Sacred things. The sea takes things she loves—like coral or shells—and obliterates them to sand. I've always told myself she doesn't mean to; it's just the way she is. She can't choose when the hurricanes roll in or when the tsunamis rise. They flow out of her as they should. Maybe even in ways she doesn't understand.

Ballet makes me feel like the ocean—silently unfurling with all the rage I've buried deep down, yet still manifesting in something beautiful. For those few moments, with all eyes on me, I'm heard. Ballet tells stories, and this is how I tell mine.

But that's not all. I look away, for the real truth is selfish. "I wanted to feel beautiful more than anything. I wanted to belong. Instead, they called me vain."

"You're not—"

"They thought I was superficial."

"Lila—"

"Is it so much to want to be seen?"

He hesitates, before saying, "I notice you. And you shouldn't be ashamed for wanting the spotlight. It's already yours."

As much as I don't want to condone the cliché poetry of his words, I can't help but smile.

"You're enough." His voice is sharp when he says it. "Don't ever forget it."

I meet his eyes, and to my surprise, I do feel seen.

Something within me softens, turning my cheeks warm. Maybe it's my glacier of a heart melting down. I untangle my folded arms, welcoming Damien closer. His fingers stroke my throat, rousing a shaky breath.

I lean closer, and his lips part wider. The whole world stills, all thoughts fading as I graze the wetness of his bottom lip. My eyes nearly shut, until he stumbles back. I follow his gaze over my shoulder.

"What's wrong?" Blood rushes from my face towards my fingertips, puncturing my calloused palms.

"Lila—"

"What's going on?"

"I'm sorry," he mutters.

Everything goes black.

I gasp, shooting out of bed.

Stars flood my eyes in a flurried daze. As my vision adjusts to the dark, moonlight spills into my room through an open window, sweeping the lace curtains into a dance with the sea breeze.

The angel is gone.

Chapter
TWELVE

◆

It was only a dream. The angel was a figment of my imagination. I didn't almost kiss him. *Shit.* I almost kissed him. What was I thinking? I tug my curls, knotted from a restless night.

I trusted him too easily.

I opened up too quickly.

I made myself vulnerable.

Ugh! This is all my fault.

The hissing shower faucet masks a scream as I welcome the water pressure against my face. Which is worse—almost kissing the angel or revealing my past? I sink my nails into a bar of soap, desperately wanting to break something. Instead, I scrub my hands against my eyes, as if to remove the memory of last night rather than my stubborn makeup. The blush and black water streaming down my torso reminds me how pathetic I am. *I wasn't enough.* My acrylic nail slices my jaw, adding another color to the water.

Red.

Fury. Humiliation. Desire.

How could I have let my guard down so easily? No one was supposed to know the real me when I moved here. This was my chance at a fresh start. And somehow, I managed to screw that up too.

I force the shower faucet off and tie up my hair with a towel before returning to my room. As much as I wish my anger could kill off the heartache, it doesn't. I bring my knees towards my chest, swaddling myself within the softness of a robe. The waves tumble onto the shore, slamming into the sand and spraying sea-foam that faintly mists my window. I wish I were as unapologetic as the sea, not afraid to let it all roar. But I can't go back to being my mother's ocean of a girl. And I can't chase Damien anymore.

I won't.

The flutters in my stomach turn to bile creeping up my throat. He left for a reason, just like I knew he would, and there's no use dwelling on it. Maybe, just maybe, if I can actually win the pageant, everyone will finally see me as something special. Something worthy. Something they won't leave. So I'll do what I always do—pretend to be perfect, and hope whoever's watching might just fall in love.

✦

Pageant season is in full swing on Luna Island. Blooming Bella's Salon is bursting with business as girls try out different hairstyles and add fresh highlights to their locks. Soft butterscotch, straw-berry blonde, and white gold kiss loose waves. I recognize two girls from the pageant—Giselle and Celine—one with a classic blowout, the other with vintage pin curls.

Mothers bicker with their daughters in front of Luna's Love Shack—some debating the outrageous prices, others arguing about what style and color would look best. I shudder, remem-bering my days being fit into ballet costumes. *No one likes a stage mom.* That, I definitely don't miss.

A saleswoman in a candy-striped dress twirls across the cobblestones, puffing perfume into the air to entice girls to find their perfect fragrance for the Starlit Ball. *Ugh.* I wave my hand in front of my nose, fending off the strong apple-and-peony blend. Though, I don't need a heady fragrance to keep me far away from Heaven Divine. After what happened in my dream, I won't be back anytime soon.

"Lila!" Roisin waves from across the street beneath a chipped wooden sign that reads *Aurelia's Antiques* in Luna Island's signa-ture hand-painted cursive.

A breath of relief rushes from my lungs at the sight of a familiar face. *Thank god.* "Roisin." I embrace her. "It's good to see you."

"My." She examines my outfit, twirling me around. "You're really starting to fit in here, aren't you?"

I grin, tugging at the end of my braid. "I'm trying."

I've been studying how everyone dresses here and doing my best to fit in. Today, I chose a white puff-sleeve top from Luna's Love Shack, with blue flowers and crescent moons embroidered across the fabric. Normally, in California, I'd pair it with some jeans. But on Luna Island, I decided to match it with a long lace skirt with tulle ruffles that fan out when I spin. I even fastened my braid to the side with a bow, just like Roisin does.

She smiles. "See, you do belong here."

Belong. Maybe I really could. If I ever did become the next High Priestess, perhaps I'd miss this place. I'd miss Roisin. That, I know. I'd come back for her after I'd proven my point, if the Heavens allowed it.

"Come on," she says. "Aurelia's has the best dresses."

A bell chimes as we enter the shop. Aurelia's Antiques is like a treasure chest of the decades. Chipped aqua paint peels off the walls, which are decorated with glittering seashell ornaments and yellow-stained love letters. Some date back all the way back to the 1800s, revealing secret rendezvous, romantic poems, and valentines.

Crackling music streams out of a record player, and I follow the sound deeper into the shop. Milk glass trinkets, lace gloves, and pearl necklaces nestle between the shelves. I swoon at the array of different vintage dresses. A poofy pale pink confection, probably for prom in the 1950s. A beaded seafoam flapper dress, reminiscent of a sparkling mermaid tail. A cream satin night-gown, with lace trim and a bow that dips between a sweetheart neckline, fit for an angel.

"These are gorgeous."

"I know, right." Roisin tears through the racks of gowns. "Everyone's going to be wearing something from Luna's Love Shack at the Starlit Ball. But if we want to stand out, we'll need something one of a kind."

"You're a genius," I say, pulling a light-blue gown off the rack. The white lace layered over the tulle reminds me of falling snowflakes.

"So." She bumps her hip to mine. "What do you think your angel would like to see you in?"

"Oh." I turn down the aisle, resting my hand on the metal railing. "About that. I don't think I'm going to see him again."

"What?" She flings a dress over her shoulder. "What happened now?"

I sigh, making my way over to a pair of vintage Mary Janes, examining the polished red leather. "He almost kissed me."

"He what?" she nearly shouts.

"Shhh." I press a finger to my lips, as two ladies snap their heads in our direction.

"Sorry," she whispers. "What do you mean, he tried to kiss you?"

I cross my arms, pressing the ball gown close to me. "Well, things kinda escalated last night. Maybe I was the only one who wanted it." My eyes fall shut, tingles shooting up my veins as I recall his breath against mine. "He pulled away. And then he disappeared."

"Oh, Lila. I'm sure he wanted to. Maybe he's just shy."

"Yeah, or maybe it was a mistake."

She jumps at the bite in my tone, scurrying to keep up as I drift between the racks. "Don't think like that. It's just in your head."

"No. It's better to just forget about it. Besides, I have a whole village of angels to win over. I should be more focused on that."

"Whatever you say." She shrugs. "If we're going to blow the angels away, we're going to need something breathtaking. Oooh!"

Her eyes light up as she flitters over to the other side of the room. "Something like that."

I follow her pointed finger to a mannequin wearing a wedding dress made for a goddess of the sea. As I get a closer look, the thin white fabric reflects a golden sheen, layered with an organza decorated with chiffon-spun jasmines stitched to the bottom that trail upwards into evanescence. A mosaic of pearls glistens across the bustier, pale pink and green in the light. My fingers dance across them.

"It's stunning."

"Lila, you need to try it on. It's a dream."

I shake my head, stepping back. "I can't. You saw it first."

"It's really not my color." She glances down at the gowns in her arms—an array of pink, coral, and red. "At least see if it fits."

I hesitate, studying the jasmine buds that shift with iridescence in the light.

"Go on," Roisin presses.

"I guess it wouldn't hurt."

I make my way over to the fitting room with cold feet, as if I really am getting married. Besides ballet, calling someone my forever has always been a dream of mine. But the thought of knowing that, no matter what, someone will always love me exactly as I am is a fantasy. I can hardly picture it happening now, which makes slipping into the gown all the more painful. Just like any dress, it becomes another costume.

I step out from behind the curtain.

Roisin gasps. "I've never seen a dress so beautiful."

I turn to the full-length mirror ornamented with intricate golden appliqué. The bodice contours my body wonderfully, its sheer fabric extenuating my every arch and dip, with pearls perfectly concealing the parts of me otherwise indecent to expose. Jasmine blossoms ascend the skirt and billowing sleeves, which are as thin as water. I feel like a princess of the sea, held in the most delicate curl of sea-foam.

I slowly run my hands down the pearl detailing, imagining a version of myself worth loving—me as a bride before I say *I do*, the moment heaven is promised forever. Only when I look up at the mirror, it's not me I see at all. Over my shoulder, gold eyes beam back like twin suns, and black wings expand as if to steal me away to Hell where I belong.

Damien?

I gasp, spinning around. Nothing is there. No angel. No Damien. Am I losing it again? My blood turns hot, bubbling beneath the surface. I stumble away from the mirror, my hands flying to the zipper. I need to get out of this thing.

"Roisin, help me. I can't breathe."

"What's wrong?"

I heave, tripping forward as the heat of my body undoes me in a sweat. Roisin's hands fly to the zipper, tugging, but it won't budge. "It's—it's stuck."

"No!" My lungs expand, catching my balance on a wooden chair as a bell chimes above the door. The coastal breeze rushes in, nipping my flushed cheeks. From outside the window, I see him running.

"Oh no, you don't, angel." There's no more hiding. Whatever he has to say, he can say it now. I gather my skirts, sprinting out of the shop barefoot.

"Hey!" a woman calls. "You have to pay for that."

"Lila—" Roisin's voice echoes.

I don't slow down.

He's in the distance, making his way towards the beach. But instead of meeting the sand, he races up a bluff. I huff as I hound his path up the steep hill, and my braid comes undone with the wind. He picks up speed, darting to the cliff's edge. Is he going to jump?

"Damien!" I call out.

He halts at the sound of my voice. Though he doesn't turn around, as if he's ashamed to face me. I catch my breath and jog the rest of the way to meet him.

"What are you doing?" I pant. "Are you trying to hurt yourself?"

He scoffs, waving me off. "Did you forget that angels know how to fly?"

"That's not funny." I smack him against the arm. My cheeks burn with flush. It's so obvious I care. But why should I after he abandoned me last night?

He looks at me, and the furrow between his brows softens. "I'm sorry."

"For what? Scaring me just now or leaving me hanging in the garden of my mind?"

"Both." He sighs, running his fingers through his hair. His eyes glimmer like starlight on water. He's frightened. "I'm sorry

I left you last night. I couldn't stay. But I—I also couldn't stop thinking of you."

Wait, really? I cross my arms. "Didn't seem like it to me."

"Well, it's true," he snaps. The harshness of his voice lingers.

I frown and step forward cautiously, gesturing for him to meet my gaze. "What happened?"

He looks behind his shoulder, as if checking for someone, then leans in and whispers, "I saw her in your dream—Aurora."

"What—"

"Shhh!" He holds a finger to his lips.

"I don't understand." I knew Aurora wanted to expose me, but why is Damien so afraid of her? She's his sister.

"I can't be seen with you," he admits.

We're so close, I can feel his heart beating against mine. "Why not?" I ask, my breath shuddering.

"The angels wouldn't like it." His jaw tightens, and he looks out at the sea, avoiding my gaze.

A flutter skips in my chest. "What?"

I want to be good.

I want to behave.

I've been on my best behavior since arriving. Or at least I've tried.

He exhales, taking a seat and dangling his legs over the cliff's edge. I join him, staring down at the ocean beneath us, which glitters with reflections of the sun.

"My family thinks you're a distraction. I should be more focused on my duty rather than protecting someone. I'm not a guardian angel . . . not when I'm here."

"Your duty?" I never put much thought into what Damien's life must be like in the commune or how different it must be from mine.

He turns to face me. "Last night, I mentioned my wings are considered an honor. But I never told you why." He hesitates, words catching in his throat. It must be hard for him to talk about.

I place my hand on his, letting him know it's safe. "You can tell me."

He takes a breath. "My black wings mean I'm responsible for leading the commune one day. That's why my father is so hard on me."

"Your father—"

"I know you saw what happened in the forest." The words rush out like a wave.

I look away, ashamed of what I witnessed. No one deserves to be hit like that. I don't know what to say that could make up for it.

"I'm sorry," he says.

"Don't apologize."

He nods, smiling just a little. Though, I know he only does it to ease the tension.

"Is that what you want?" I say after a moment. "To lead the commune one day?"

A sound of annoyance escapes beneath his breath, and he chucks a pebble into the ocean. "I'd rather see what's out there."

"Where?" I look off into the distance. The vastness of the ocean swallows me. It stretches for as far as the eye can see. Birds disappear from my line of sight as they sweep across the infinite waves. I wonder if that's how Damien wishes he could be too.

"Anywhere but here." His voice is flat and bitter.

"Then why don't you just leave?"

"It's not that simple."

Of course not. "I get it." Nothing with our parents could ever be easy. I squeeze his hand in mine, to let him know I'm here, that I understand. His feathers ruffle at my touch, and a blush rushes to his cheeks. I mask a giggle. "Guess you're stuck here with me."

"Things could be worse." His shoulders relax, and a dimple wells in the corner of his cheek. Although it's only half a smile, I'll take it.

We sit there in silence for a while longer, looking off at the horizon. There isn't a need to speak. With each other, there's no need to run, no need to explain. Instead we honor one another with our presences.

"Lila."

A burning blooms in my chest when he finally says my name, catching in my throat and cutting off my breath. "Yes?"

He tucks my hair behind my ear and gently traces the edge of my cheek as his hand slips away. "Please believe me when I say I never wanted to leave you last night."

"I know." It was just a misunderstanding.

He moves in closer, grazing the bottom of my chin with his thumb. My heartbeat flutters. "Then I hope you'll also trust me when I tell you it's not safe here."

"What?" I lean back, pressing my fingertips to his chest. Of course there's something off about Luna Island, but the abrupt change in conversation startles me. And his confirmation only makes the danger real.

"Quit the pageant," he commands. "I'll protect you, and we'll run away from this place together."

My heartbeat quickens. Just like in my nightmare, the illusion of our solace shatters. I should have known. Nothing good is ever mine to keep. I shake free from his grasp and leap to my feet. "Of course this was too good to be true."

"Huh?"

Humiliation courses through me, reminding me of how I fell before him and how much he saw in the garden of my mind. He returned my locket for a reason—a threat to get me to quit. Clearly, his feelings haven't changed. "You're still trying to get me to throw the competition. You don't think I can do it."

You don't think I'm worthy.

"Lila, I—" He rises to meet me.

"No! I'm going to win, whether you like it or not."

"Lila!" he calls after me.

But I gather my dress and run, never looking back.

Chapter
THIRTEEN

✦

"Roisin, I am so, so sorry for ditching you at the antique shop yesterday," I plead, shoving two hundred-dollar bills into her hand, taken from the savings box kept under my bed. It should be enough to cover the dress. "I feel awful for leaving you hanging."

She shakes her head, squeezing my hand as she accepts the offer. "Lila, I have no problem bailing you out. I just want to make sure you're okay."

I groan, scrunching the pale green satin of the dress I threw on for this morning's flower market. The pink-and-purple floral pattern wilts as I reprimand myself. *No more ocean of a girl*, I said. Yet I ruined another dress—one I pretty much stole. I left my closest friend on the island to worry. And I made a fool of myself by nearly trusting the angel. *Again*.

The dulcet florals fill my lungs, reminding me of the garden of my mind. I take a deep breath, selecting a bundle of sterling roses and placing them into my woven shopping basket. Their silvery-lilac shade complements the maroon buds I've also picked out. I try to be thoughtful when it comes to aesthetics, knowing how much the angels value beauty. I'll need to stand out again in this next round of the pageant—Faith in Luna—where we build shrines at her temple.

"Hey." Roisin places a hand on my shoulder. "Talk to me."

I sigh, glancing at the peonies to the left. "I just don't want to let you down anymore. I'm sorry."

"You already said that. Stop apologizing." She swings her hip to the side, shifting her weight. "You're not letting me down. You're not letting *anyone* down. Where is this coming from?"

I sweep forward, losing myself between an aisle of lilies and sunflowers. The ruffled awning overhead bathes me with the cool relief of shade.

"I let the angels down," I confess, choking on my words as they come out. I try to be strong, I try to hold myself together. But my shoulders tense, and a sob breaks through my throat. My grip on the basket tightens, and Roisin rushes to my side.

"Hey," she coaxes, gathering the hair away from my face. "What happened?"

I swallow a breath, shaking. "The angels. They're trying to get me to throw the pageant. They don't—they don't think I'm fit."

They don't think I'm worthy.

Roisin rubs my shoulder. The warmth of her skin on mine eases the tension, just a bit. "I don't understand. I thought Damien wanted to protect you?"

I brush a tear away with the back of my hand. "Yeah, well, the angels are fickle, like you said."

She pauses. The wind ruffles her blouse, but she doesn't wrap her arms around her body to ease the chill or pry away the strands of hair clinging to her face like static. "You don't—you don't think he's trying to protect you from the competition, do you?"

I wince. "What?"

"Yeah." She lowers her voice into a whisper. "I mean, we still don't have answers about Nadine. What if the angels know something we don't?"

I hesitate, locking eyes with her. All this time, I've been so obsessed with winning the pageant, I forgot about the fate of its last winner. She has a point, but I refuse to admit it.

"No." I shake off the thought, turning the corner down a path of hyacinths and violets. This pageant is all I have to validate my worth. And if I quit now, I'm scared this gaping defeat in my chest will swallow me until I'm nothing. "I need to win, and I won't let the angels stop me. I'll prove them wrong."

"But, Lila . . ." She trails after me. "This angel has been watching over you. Don't you think it'd be wise to heed his warning?"

"Just stop," I snap. She jumps at the bark in my tone. "I—I'm—"

"If you say you're sorry again, I swear."

I hang my head, defeated. "There's just been a lot of pressure on me lately."

She lifts my chin, smiling, as if urging me to grin as well. "Hey, it's okay. Pageant season is supposed to be fun. Don't worry about winning. Let's just—" She plucks a hyacinth from the stand. "Let's just worry about building the most beautiful shrine possible. Easy enough?"

I nod, gathering a couple of violets.

We make our way to the farmers market, where we collect different fruits to appease Luna. Roisin told me the goddess tends to favor the sweetest fruit possible, so I gather some stone fruits since they're in season. My basket swells with blushing peaches, deep damson plums, and bright red cherries. Before we leave, I hesitate, plucking a pomegranate too. Something sour to offset the sweetness—another surprise to help me stand out from the rest of the girls.

"Okay," Roisin says, pulling me in for a hug. "I'll see you tonight. Best of luck."

I fall into her embrace, inhaling her sweet pea and vanilla perfume, and remind myself of everything I have to lose—her kindness, her warmth, her loyalty. I'll be good tonight. I'll make things right, and she will love me. The angels will love me.

They'll all love me.

"Goodbye," I whisper. The next time we meet, I'll be a better version of myself. A tender, poised version of myself, who everyone might actually adore.

✦

"Oh, I just love this part of the pageant." Laina hums, carrying a large white box into my bedroom. It's tied with a huge satin bow.

I turn away from my vanity, rising to meet her. "What's that?" I gesture to the box.

She squeals, handing it to me. "Open it."

I take the package, slowly pulling back the ribbon. Inside is a dark green velvet cloak, almost black, unless it hits the light. I lift it from the box. It's heavy.

"It's for tonight," Laina explains. "You're supposed to wear the hood over your head so that your identity is kept secret."

"Secret?"

She nods. "This part of the pageant is all about the grandeur of your offerings, not your beauty. Your face must be kept hidden."

"Oh." I tremble, glancing at my basket of flowers, praying the seashells, pearls, and candles I have too will be enough.

"Don't worry, sweetheart." Laina squeezes my hand. "You're going to do great."

I fake a smile, nodding, and drape the cloak over my shoulders. The weight of the velvet cushions me like a hug. A bit of relief settles over me. I hope that my hidden identity will earn me passage through this part of the competition. If the angels don't know which shrine is mine, then there's more of a chance my work will speak for itself. I only hope it's enough.

I pull the hood over my head, hanging its edge over my line of sight. The world becomes darker, shadowed, waking a chill as I brush against the velvet. Laina takes my hand and leads me out the door.

We're silent as I'm chaperoned through the forest by a horse-drawn carriage. The hooves clacking against the cobblestones drown out my pre-competition anxieties. Just a few weeks ago, I'd find this mode of transportation outlandish, but dozens of carriages trot through the streets of Luna Island daily—another part of the island's strange charm and antiquity.

My nerves creep up as the forest swallows the remaining daylight. Suddenly, this part of the competition becomes less like a game and more like a ritual. A climbing orange fire in the distance is the only light, painting the temple in flickering shadows. My heart races, falling in rhythm with the clicking hooves.

Don't mess this up, Lila.

Safety is yours as long as you behave.

"We're here," Laina finally announces.

I do my best to breathe as she helps me out of the carriage, before guiding me to the base of Luna's temple. The other girls gather in a half circle around Mother Marguerite, bathed in a citrine glow by the fire. She smiles brightly. Long strings of pearls hang from her elegant neck, and her dress glitters with silver sparkles, dancing like reflections on water.

I can't make out any of the other girls' faces, not even Roisin's. Everyone's hair is tucked beneath their velvet hoods. I turn around to glance a familiar face and ease my nerves, but Laina is already gone. *Shit.* My pulse races, and I clench my basket tighter, the coarse twine biting into my fingers.

"Welcome." Mother Marguerite beams, throwing her arms open wide. Her overwhelming cheer offsets the eeriness of the hooded figures. "Congratulations on making it to the second round of the pageant—Faith in Luna."

She pauses, as if waiting for a response, but all that rings back are the crickets and crackling fire. Everyone is so still, it's like they've been turned to stone. Perhaps they're just as nervous as me. Or maybe this is their way of honoring Luna—the same way I used to honor God at church.

"For this part of the competition," Mother Marguerite continues, "you will build a shrine to Luna, a time-honored tradition on the island during full moons. If Luna accepts your offering, your shrine will glitter gold in the morning. However, if she rejects your gifts, your shrine will remain as it is, and you will be cut from the pageant. Does everyone understand?"

"*Yes, Mother Marguerite,*" they chant back in unison.

The echo is chilling, reminding me that this is a ritual these girls have done once before. Not only that, but they build shrines every full moon. I, on the other hand, don't even know where to start.

"Now." Mother Marguerite claps. "You may begin."

My cloak pools around me as I sink to the forest floor in a rush of breaths, huddled over my basket. From my periphery, I notice the girls don't hesitate to get started like I do. They build their shrines intrinsically. I stare back at the fruits and flowers and trinkets, selecting a handheld mirror with shaky hands.

It's oval shaped, with ornate gold detailing curling around the glass like sea-foam. I stand it up by its base, tilting the frame slightly so that the reflection captures the stars and moon. What better way to honor Luna than by reminding her of her own beauty? *Great.* At least we have a start.

A few petals scatter across the ground, broken from the sterling and maroon roses I gather with shaky hands. *Shit.* I try to sweep away the imperfections, collecting the petals and placing them into two clamshells I set on either side of the mirror. On top of the petals, I leave some of my favorite crystals—jagged rose quartz, pale blue celestite, raw aquamarine, and glowing opalite. *Looking better.*

Sweat drips from my forehead as I notice some girls are already finishing up. I turn from side to side, panicked, as I become aware of my growing isolation in the forest. I glance around the glade, and Mother Marguerite is nowhere to be found. I had assumed she'd stay to the end, that they all would. But this is not a sisterhood, I remind myself. We are not a coven. *Each woman for herself.*

My breath wavers as I remember the last time I was alone in the forest. *The Angel Fruit.* Damien gave it to me to muddle my memory. As the other girls slip away one by one, my panic rises. I shouldn't be here. There's something lurking that the angels don't want me to see. I look down at the flowers, and it triggers something . . . a girl lying on an altar, similar to the shrine I'm building now. There were white peaches and nectarines . . . white roses too . . . and gardenias . . . and jasmines.

Oh my god.

Did I dream her? Was she in the garden of my mind? Or were the flowers from *her* garden of the mind? The white buds are too convenient to be a coincidence. I'm next. I must be. My heartbeat quickens and I pick up speed, desperate to not be left here alone.

I take out two long taper candles and place them into crystal holders. The warm candlelight illuminates the romantic tones of my offerings. It still needs something more. I drape a string of pearls around the mirror before setting out more shells of different shapes and sizes. To sweeten Luna's mood, I place a small vial of my favorite perfume right in front of the mirror—lychee and fig oil.

Finally, I set out the fruits, laying the peaches, plums, and cherries before the shrine. The air around me is still. I look up, realizing I'm the last one here. *Great.* I bite my tongue in an attempt to stay calm, then reach for the pomegranate at the bottom of my basket—my final item. Just one more touch, and I can get the hell out of here.

All I have to do is cut the pomegranate and sprawl its seeds. *Easy.* Or so I tell myself. I reach for the knife I brought, the silver blade glistening in the moonlight. My hand trembles when I meet it.

Don't mess up, Lila.

Don't mess up.

I go to cut the pomegranate, releasing a shrill cry as the knife slips, nicking my finger.

"Ahh!" I ring as blood gushes from my hand, mixing with the fruit's juice.

No.

No, no, no.

This is all wrong.

I glare at the blood dripping over my shrine, and I finally remember.

The girl on the altar's scream rings back. Her back was arched, and she clawed at the marble beneath her. Her body was changing—no—*transforming*. She was in pain. There was blood. Her brown skin turned silver, and her curves whittled to bone. Scales overtook her body like parasites. Eating her. Becoming her.

A rustling in the bushes jostles my balance, and I spring to my feet, dropping the pomegranate carelessly across the altar. *Someone's coming.* A burgeoning fear swells in my chest, and I hide behind the trees, abandoning my disheveled mess.

"Fuck," I curse beneath my breath, pressing down on my finger to clot the blood. A familiar voice distracts me from the stinging pain, and my eyes snap up.

"What the hell, Damien!" she sneers. "It's like you don't care about this family at all."

Aurora.

They don't make their way into the glade, but I'm struck with fear anyway, as if I've already been caught. I stay huddled behind the tree, careful not to make a sound.

"I've told you a million times—stay out of it," Damien snaps.

"And I warned *you*. We all remember what happened last time."

"Is that a threat? What are you really saying, Aurora?"

"All I mean is that Father will be thrilled to hear about the progress you've made. You wouldn't want to disappoint him again. Would you?"

"Watch your tongue," he says through gritted teeth.

"Tigers don't play with their food," she snaps back. "That's for kitty-cats. And if you don't act soon, I will."

There's a pause. I crane my head around the tree to get a better view. Damien winces, shaking his head. "What's gotten into you? You're starting to sound like Father."

Aurora's brow arches, and she swings her hip to the side. "I grew up, Damien. And maybe you should too. We're not twelve anymore. If you want to be a man and fulfill your duty, you better start acting like one now."

"I am a man!" His voice echoes.

This startles her. She shrinks back, folding her arms across her chest. "I'll see you at home." The chill in her tone hangs heavy in the air.

Damien scoffs as she turns to leave. But he doesn't follow her.

Instead, he makes his way into the glade. My hand jumps to my mouth, holding back a startled sound. *What is he doing?* He circles the shrines, scanning each of them.

There's one made in exclusively soft shades of pink, with a bouquet of blush roses at the center. It's surrounded by oysters, each one nestling a pearl. Smooth, heart-shaped rose quartz surrounds the perimeter in a perfect circle. Sliced guava reveals its rosy flesh, next to clamshells full of cherry blossoms.

Another is built from a large shell in the center, filled with water that reflects the moon. White magnolias float on the surface, along with golden glitter that sparkles like starlight. Oranges with long stems and blossoms surround the shell, paired with sliced mango drizzled with honey.

I swear I know who some of these belong to. The one with green grapes and pears decorated with golden butterfly appliqué must be Genevieve's. Beside it is one crafted from fuchsia carnations and obnoxiously large peonies, with different berries in porcelain dishes painted with bright pink flowers. So obviously Amelia's.

But then Damien stops in front of one that's so obviously mine.

Anxiety shivers through my fingertips, and I clench my fists. He hesitates, tilting his head as he studies the messy string of pearls and tumbles of pomegranate seeds sprawled out on the forest floor like a crime scene. *Don't look too closely*, I beg, but he squats down, examining it further. My eyes squeeze shut. *Shit.* He reaches down, touching the pomegranate beads. *No, no, no.* He lifts his fingers to his nose, wincing. *Blood.* It takes everything in me not to scream. That is, until he lights a match, hovering the flame above my shrine.

He's going to burn it.

"No!" I pounce from behind the tree, slamming into Damien's body and tackling him to the ground. He yelps, his eyes wide as I pin him to the forest floor. We tumble across the dirt as he throws my body over, rolling closer to the fire. The dancing flames paint his jagged face in shadows.

"Get off of me!" he demands.

I dig my palms deeper into his shoulders, holding him down. "What are you doing here?"

"What are *you* doing here?"

"*I* am participating in the pageant. The same pageant *you* keep trying to ruin for me." I sink my nails into his skin, and he grimaces. Using all my dancer's strength, I lock him between my thighs.

"Why must you insist that I'm against you? All I've done since meeting you is save your life over and over again."

This strikes a nerve. I bend down, putting us nose to nose. "I don't need saving, angel. Just stay out of my way."

"No." He throws my body over, pinning me down instead. My breath cuts off with a shriek. He softens at the terror in my eyes before brushing the stray hairs away from my face. His thumb is gentle as it moves down my cheek, wiping away a tear. He leans down, speaking softly in nearly a whisper. "It's not safe here, Lila. We need to go."

"Wh-what?" I stutter. My hands tremble as they always do when my anxiety strikes.

Damien gets up and pulls me to my feet. He stands close, his wings surrounding me, as if to shield me from the forest and the creatures lurking in it. "Please understand, I'm only trying to help. The pageant—it's not what you think. You're in danger."

Danger. The unsettledness that's followed me like a haunting since arriving—a reminder that there will never be peace. The Devil's voice. The garden of my mind. *The girl on the altar.* Coming to Luna Island was always a punishment. Tears spring to my eyes.

"Come with me," Damien says. "We'll run away to the stars."

I shrink back, creating distance between us. This is too much. Too foreign. Just words without meaning, like a fairytale in a language I don't speak. "What?"

"Your dance," he says. "That first day in the forest, you began building a staircase to the stars. But something startled you and it slipped away. Dance with me, and I'll help you tame your power until we reach the Heavens."

I wince, spinning around. "No!"

Is this why he's been following me, trying to get me to leave the pageant? He wants my power all to himself to help him escape Luna Island. My lashes flutter as I blink. Suddenly, my anger softens, and I remember we're both running.

The wrinkle between my brows settles. "What are we running away from?"

"Come," is all he says.

Chapter
FOURTEEN

◆

Damien leads us out of the forest and onto the beach. The sky is clouded, the ocean lacking its usual luster. Instead of the sparkling ripples I'm used to seeing on Luna Island, it's an endless black void. The fog blurs Luna's moonlight, swallowing us as we make our way closer to the water.

"What are we doing here?" I ask, tugging my cloak around me tighter as the sea-foam nips my ankles.

He gestures to the sea. "We're at your favorite place. I brought you here to strengthen your magic."

"I don't understand."

"When you're happy, you create beauty. When you're scared, the world crumbles."

I glance at the water, finding solace in its breaking waves. My feelings have always felt too big—unpredictable, like the ocean. Only, here on Luna Island, they manifest with my dance.

"My magic has something to do with you, doesn't it?" I finally ask. "I can do it only when I'm with you. Like, you have some sort of spell over me."

"I'm not doing anything. When are you going to admit that maybe when you're dancing with me, you actually feel safe? And maybe that's why your magic creates wonders whenever we're together."

I open my mouth, but I can't find anything to say. What if he's right? What if I *need* Damien to control my dance? I hate the idea of depending on another person for anything, let alone my own power. My eyes shut as my muscles tense. "Be honest, are you just trying to get me to quit the pageant because you don't think I can win?"

Do you want me off the island like Aurora?

Do all of the angels feel the same?

His brows furrow, and he caresses my arm. The feeling makes me shiver. "Lila, I think you're sensational. I wouldn't be asking you to reach the stars if I didn't think you could do it."

"You're wrong." My anxiety rises, building in my chest and crawling up my throat. Reaching the stars is hopeless when I can't predict how I'll react next. As much as I try, all I'll ever be is a threat to everyone around me. "I can't control my dance."

"Well, I can help you. It seems like your magic manifests through your feelings. If you want to control your dance, then you'll need to master your emotions, and I'll support you."

"Just stop. You saw what happened the last time." My voice dwindles, losing its defensiveness. I can't hurt him. I won't. As much as I try to deny it, there's no doubt I care about Damien deep down.

"What if I dance with you? When the storms come, I'll protect you, and we can transform all the scary feelings into good ones."

Sea-foam breaks around my ankles, leaving pearly bubbles on the shore—reminding me of the ocean's duality. It's a dangerous kind of wonder . . . just like my dancing. Maybe Damien can't tame the sea. But perhaps he can help me find the beauty in it.

"You want to dance with me? Like, a pas de deux?"

"A pas de what?"

"A pas de deux. A dance for two. It takes years to perfect. What if you drop me? Or what if I hurt you?"

"You won't." He steps closer, closing the distance between us. "You just have to trust me."

Trust me. My eyes fall shut. I've never relied on anyone but myself before, and if I start now, if I let him get close, he'll turn into collateral. I turn away, facing the cottages that line the shore. "I'm sorry, angel."

"Lila." He grabs my wrist, grazing that tender spot above my pulse that makes me falter. "Just try."

Everything in me screams to run, but my legs don't move. His fingers trail the inside of my forearm, causing my breath to shudder.

"Dance with me," he whispers. "We can run away to the stars."

I pull away, breaking our tether. "What makes you so sure I'm willing to run away with you?" He won't even tell me what I should be running *from.* "I'm not dancing unless you tell me what's going on."

He sighs. "Fine. What do you want to know?"

"Why is the Devil really after me?" I find the courage to ask. "What does he want?"

Damien hesitates, before asking, "Do you remember anything from that night in the forest when we first met?"

All of it. The girl on the altar—bleeding out, bones snapping, claws carving out her own flesh. "No thanks to you. I know you gave me that fruit to muddle my mind."

He looks away, silent and ashamed. "And yet, you remember?"

"It came back to me when I was building my shrine. . . . It was like the altar she was on."

Damien tenses as the memory of her surfaces. He curls his fist, the same way he did the first time he spoke of her. "What you saw was the birth of one of the Devil's sirens. The angels were trying to save her. Only it was too late."

Sirens? That would explain the scales, the claws, her angler-sharp teeth, and lifeless white eyes. "Why does the Devil have sirens?"

"Because." Damien grimaces. "He needs something beautiful to make his kingdom shine."

"Something beautiful? You mean, like—"

"Like you."

A sharp breath escapes my lips. I grab my arms, roused with pinpricks. "That's why the Devil wants me? So he can turn me into a *siren*?"

Damien looks off at the ocean. "That's what he does."

No. I refuse to be some glittering *thing* that lights up the Devil's halls. I'm better than that. I'm *more*. I see now why Damien wants to help me reach my full potential. He's always believed in me. Perhaps it's finally time I start believing in myself.

I'm not saying I'll run away with him, but I am curious to see what he can help me do. After he's helped me master my powers, I'll decide how I use them.

"Look, I'm not committing to anything, but if you really think I can do this, I'll try."

"Really?"

I turn my back to him. "I said I'll try—not that I actually will."

He sweeps through the water to meet my gaze. "Well, that's a start." When I don't match his enthusiasm, his smile disappears. "Hey, there's nothing to worry about when you're here with me. If this is going to work, I need you to trust me. I promise I'll be right here to watch over you."

Even the toughest things have a delicate spot. I break again, turning soft like the waves shattering into sea-foam. Regardless of the secrets Damien's kept, he's always believed in me, and don't holy things need faith to shine? I doubt Luna would be as bright if she weren't worshiped. Look at how she's blessed the island in return. She refuses to stretch her magic to any other corner of the world. Maybe, like Luna, I'll lean into Damien's faith, and for a moment, I'll finally shine.

"Okay." I give in. "Show me what we can do."

His lips twist into a grin, and he presents his palm like an offering. "Take my hand."

When I do, moonlight radiates from my body, encompassing me in a glow. When the light fades, I'm dressed in a ballerina costume. The bodice is made of shimmering sea-foam, with iridescent opals adorning the bust. Golden stardust twinkles across the fullness of my rosebud skirt, which fans out with layers of lush petals.

It all rushes back.

The thrill, the bliss, the freedom. I once loved this part of myself more than anything in the world. And maybe, deep down, I still do. At least for this moment, I don't fight it. This is who I am. This is what I'm best at. I want to honor that. Not for Damien. Not for my parents. Not to escape or run or prove a point. But for myself.

"I don't—I don't really know what I'm doing," Damien confesses.

I get it. Ballet is my world, not his.

I take a deep breath. The pas de deux takes years to perfect—requiring trust, strength, and foundation. It's the greatest test of faith two dancers can extend to one another. Although I know Damien isn't a dancer, he *does* have faith in me. That's enough for me to try.

"That's okay. Can you follow my lead?"

He nods. "I'll do my best."

"How about you start across from me?" I point down the shore.

Damien nods, taking his respective side. I center myself, easing my breath and aligning with the music that unravels from the sea—a glamour I imagine Damien has cast, the same way he did with the flowers in the forest. The twinkling harp melds with the crashing waves. Water laps at my ankles, but I don't mind. This is where I feel most at home.

Fanning my arms to the side, I draw my pointe shoe forward. As I make my way towards the sea, more twinkles of music unfurl with each step, adding to the present melody. I take a breath, mustering the courage to walk on water. An aquamarine ripple flecked with golden stardust flickers to life beneath me, glowing brightly. I drag my other foot forward. The ocean sparkles, as if accepting the magic I offer.

When I find comfort on the water, I relevé—bringing myself onto pointe. My arms extend in a port de bras, and I begin a series of quick bourrée steps. A ribbon of stardust unravels from my feet, kissing the ocean with that glittering aqua glow. I embrace the beauty I've created, tilting into an arabesque. When I send my arm into the sky, the night illuminates. Stars explode like a shimmering tapestry woven from my body. I smile—proudly owning the stage—or in this case, the sea.

I ignite the ocean with a piqué manège before leaping into a grand jeté, sending shooting stars as I fly. When I land, I fall into a series of chaîné turns before transitioning into more bourrée steps. Every move leads me closer and closer to Damien.

The emptiness between us disappears as I leap into his arms. He lifts me towards the sky, moonlight showering us, before I fall into a fish dive—my face towards the sea and my legs swept into the air. I glide my fingertips through the water, painting even more color into the night. The ocean radiates with undernotes of jade and lavender, shimmers of bright cyan and pearl.

He gently places me down, guiding me into a pirouette. I tether my vision to his as the symphony of the sea blooms into a crescendo. Together, we burst into an allegro—our own medley of fast, brisk movement.

I surrender to his familiar hands around my waist, feeling weightless as he lifts me, as if I'm becoming an angel myself. Damien gives me wings, and I fly across the ocean. The once-black waves have transformed entirely. Plumes of stardust swirl like milk in water, feathering out into a soft iridescence.

With a newfound freedom, I chassé across the sea, bursting into several jetés and whipping the water with my fouettés. Damien runs to me, and I leap into his arms. He catches me and lifts me with grace. My back bends over his hand almost effortlessly.

We run to opposite ends of the sea as the waves rise, grand enough to envelop us. They crash as we rush into each other, sea spray showering overhead. I sink into the water and come undone with laughter.

Damien swims to me slowly before cradling my body, sending twinkles up my veins. "It's true," he says. "You really are magic."

A warm glow rouses in my cheeks. The ocean glimmers like a reflection of the Milky Way. I study Damien's face in the twilight. No one's ever believed in me the way he does. When I'm with him, he resurrects a version of myself I thought was dead. With a kiss, I'm confident I could lift the stars from the sea, ascending the illusion as our own stairway to the sky. I feel the power running through me, as if my magic is multiplying. It wouldn't take much to transcend this tapestry to the Heavens.

I drape my arms around his neck, a breath away from his lips. As much as a part of me wants to indulge, something stops me. My fingertips trail down his chest, pushing back and creating space between us. "Tell me the truth. Why do you really want me to run away with you to the stars and throw the competition?"

It's clear the Devil is after me, but there's something more. Something that has to do with the angels and the pageant. Why else would Damien try to sabotage my shrine tonight? I'm not leaving Roisin here on her own. Especially when knowing something happened to Nadine after she won.

"Lila, I—I—" he stutters.

"Tell me the truth, and I'll make the world bloom. I'll take us away from here, to the stars, anywhere you want. All you have to do is be honest." I plead, begging him to give in and be the man I want him to be—someone I can actually trust.

"I—I'm sorry," he says, "I can't."

His answer kills off the hope burgeoning in my heart. I can feel myself turning small again as my magic shrinks, and suddenly, my tether around the glamour dissolves completely. The world stills as my power disappears, and everything fades back to darkness. If I don't leave now, I'll cry. He can't see me like that again.

"I knew I couldn't trust you." I slam my fists in the water as I rise, sending up splashes that make him skitter back. He knows the pageant isn't safe. He knows the angels did something, that they're still conspiring, even now. Most of all, he's still protecting them.

I turn my back, trudging onto the shore.

"Lila—"

"Don't!" It's the last time I turn around. "We're done."

It takes everything in me to leave him behind.

Chapter
FIFTEEN

♦

It's raining again.

I can't tell if it's because of me, but I wouldn't be surprised. This time, I don't call Roisin. I don't even greet Laina when I get home. I can't risk worrying anyone or giving them a reason to trace Luna Island's strange weather back to me—as unbelievable as it seems. It's typically gorgeous here, the perfect, idyllic paradise. Even at night, the air is brisk, but it never storms.

I'm only lying to myself.

Of course the rain is my fault.

Soft candlelight holds me in a cocoon of warm sugar and vanilla, and I wrap my sheepskin blanket around me tighter. It's no use. The more I try to force the comfort, the harder it becomes to achieve. My arms rouse with goosebumps from the gust of wind sweeping through the cracked window.

Begrudgingly, I pull myself out of bed to shut it, but stumble back with a gasp. Pressed against my window is a single white rose, just like the ones from the garden of my mind. Its velvet petals splay against the glass, contorted like broken limbs but ever sparkling like in my dreams.

"What the hell?"

I move closer, cautious when I approach, as if it'll spring alive at any moment and hiss curses in my ear, reminding me of what I've done and how I'll pay. Instead, the downpour crumples the bud until it withers. I press my fingers to the glass, frosted by my shaky breath. The flower falls the second my fingers meet it.

I scream, skittering back when I see where it lands.

Beneath my window, more glittering white flowers form a trail leading straight to the ocean—roses, gardenias, and jasmines. I don't need a reminder of where they come from. I fall to the floor, fighting for breath, as I'm returned to the garden of my mind. A screech reels from my throat. It's too much, too loud. I'm trapped by my own cries, a prisoner to my mind.

Lila, it calls. *Come to me. Come to me where you belong.*

My eyes spring open. "No!"

Everything stops, vibrating as it settles. The room spins, and a ringing blooms in my ears. I wrap my arms around my shaking body and slowly rise from the ground.

"Hello?" I tremble, calling out into the night.

Only the wind sings back.

When I look back out the window again, the flowers are gone.

✦

I couldn't sleep all night. As much as I tried to force myself to, all that came of it was endless tossing and turning until the sun came up.

A wave of relief washes over me as I welcome the light, letting it tangle in my hair and bathe me in its glow. I lie there with my limbs sprawled out, woven between blankets. My hands and feet tremor with the aftermath of my outburst, a reminder that the anxiety has settled but is still present. I know it'll last for a few more hours, but I'm thankful for this sensation. It means the worst is over.

I tell myself to move, to bathe, to eat, to drink water, but it's like nothing's working anymore—as if I'm a doll that needs to be wound up in order to function. It would be easier if I had someone to dress me, walk me through the motions of my life like a Barbie. But I'm a real girl. I'm eighteen now. And the only person capable of moving me forward is myself.

Which is the only reason I hoist myself out of bed and get into the shower.

It's a new day, and just like the water from the faucet, it washes me clean. My entire life, I've always made choices to please others—my parents, the audience, the angels. And when I was broken, I stayed broken. But not this time.

This time I have something to fight for.

I have myself. I have Roisin and Laina and the island. In the short time I've been here, they've become my family. Instead of winning for my pride, I need to win to protect this life I've built. It's obvious the Devil wants something, and I've always known it's me. But I have a feeling his reapings won't stop after I'm gone. He could target every girl in the pageant until our shores wash up of blooming beauties for him to collect like treasures.

I need to make sure that never happens.

Before the rest of the island wakes, I make my way back to the temple to visit the shrines.

✦

Dawn settles as I find myself back at the glade. Golden light filters through the leaves, drawing fissures of sun across my arms. It claims our shrines like a wash of sea-foam, and to my surprise, they all glitter back.

Including mine.

"No fucking way," I mutter beneath my breath.

It's as if they've been fairy dusted in the night, cascading with rivers of shimmering starlight. My pomegranate lies sprawled out across the floor, with sticky pearls scattered across the rose petals. However, under closer inspection, my blood gleams back rose gold instead of red.

"Are you impressed?"

The voice startles me, and I jump, spinning around.

"M-Mother Marguerite," I stammer.

She towers over me like a goddess herself, smiling brightly with her arms wide open like someone awaiting a hug. Though she never closes in. Instead, she's composed, taking in the sunlight that highlights her sparkle. Faint wrinkles pucker at the sides of her eyes, revealing an ancient sort of charm—a crack of her age beneath her ever-preserved youth. I see right through it, wondering what sort of enchantment the angels have cast over her to keep her looking young.

"I apologize if I frightened you, dearest." Her voice is mellow, like honey spilling into tea. I can't help but want to drink it more and more.

"You didn't. I was just surprised."

"By me, or by your blood?"

"What?"

Her grin widens, and she takes my face in her hands, examining me closely. She brushes her thumb over the corner of my eye, perhaps examining its faint reddish hue. "Oh, you think I don't know? Magic courses through you. It's right there on your shrine."

I stumble away from her embrace. "I don't know what you're talking about."

She laughs. It comes out coquettish and soft, like playful music. "Stop fighting it, Lila. You're only fooling yourself."

My heartbeat quickens. I crumple my nightgown to calm my racing pulse. "How do you know?"

"Well, of course, the angels talk, my dear."

"Sure they do." My gaze falls onto my shimmering blood. I wonder what they've said about me now.

"All good things, all good things," she reassures.

"Wait." I hesitate. "Really?"

"Why, of course. It's as if you've been blessed by Luna herself. The angels are intrigued."

"They are?" All this time, I thought my powers were putting a target on my back—exposing me as the danger that I am, and how I belong with the Devil. I didn't realize they were actually helping me.

Mother Marguerite nods. "A part of Luna lives within you. It's evident in the blood you shed last night. Be thankful, Lila. You're more capable than you think."

I don't know what to say. Ever since I learned about my power, I've seen it as an unpredictable danger, terrified of the attention it could attract. But my magic has always been *mine*. Something good. Something to grow and nurture. Not to run away to the stars with or to impress the angels, but a part of me that I want to love.

"What do you know about my magic?" I ask.

She laughs. Sunlight catches the shimmer in her gossamer sleeves, moving like smoke as she taps me on the nose. "Some things are better left unsaid."

"But, Mother, I—"

"That's enough." She waves a hand in front of my face. "You better get back to the village and prepare for the Blood Moon."

"The Blood Moon?"

She snickers, as if I should know better. "Yes, it's tonight. How else do you think we perform the Strength of Will trial?"

"I don't understand." As much as I pretend to belong here, this is all still new to me.

"Oh, but you will." She gathers my hair, draping it over my chest. Shivers sprout across my neck as her fingers pull away. It's all wrong. Too invasive. I look up at her, and she's smiling.

"Run along now, Lila. There's a lot to do before tonight."

I turn around, unsettled by her Stepford charm. I can still feel her staring at me from behind—smiling, probably, like a creepy doll on one of the shelves at Aurelia's Antiques. There's no use fighting her for answers. At least not yet, if I want to play my cards right. Defeated, I make my way back to the village.

✦

"Roisin!" I pound on her cottage door. Gardenia petals fall overhead as I knock harder. The sprawling vines of the white blossoms framing her doorway make me queasy. I used to love these flowers. Now the sight and scent of them just reminds me of the garden of my mind.

My nerves dwindle the second Roisin opens the door.

"Lila," she says with a yawn, undoing her messy bun and letting her red hair spill over her shoulders. "What are you doing here so early?"

"I—I'm sorry. I didn't mean to wake you."

"No, it's fine." She steps outside, wrapping her satin robe around her tighter as the sea breeze tangles her curls. "What's up? Is everything okay?"

"Well, yes and no."

She nods, squinting as her eyes adjust to the morning sun. "Good news first."

"Okay, the good news is that all of our shrines made it to the next round."

"Oh, yay!" she squeals, clapping her hands. "What's the bad news?"

"Um, well, something about a Blood Moon?"

She shrieks, grasping the porch banister. "*Devil's Teeth!* You're right. The Blood Moon is today."

"What the hell is the Blood Moon?"

She leans against a whitewashed pillar covered in ivy, steadying her balance. "Isadora's family already left last night, and she decided to go with them. Which means there's one less girl in the competition now."

"Wait, slow down. What do you mean Isadora left?"

"Her mom is pregnant," she blurts.

"What?"

"On the day of the Blood Moon, no life can be created. If Isadora's mom gave birth tonight, the baby would die. The family couldn't risk it, so they left."

I shudder. "The baby would *die*? That seems pretty extreme."

"It is! That's why we need to prepare for it. Come on, we need to make a list."

We run into her bedroom, decorated in a yellow wallpaper with tiny pink flowers. Audrey Hepburn posters mount the walls. I recognize iconic scenes from *Breakfast at Tiffany's* and *Roman Holiday*, some of my favorites too. There's a vanity with peeling paint next to her vinyl record player, both probably from Aurelia's Antiques. Heaps of dresses litter the floor in a mess of colors and textures—jade silk, powder blue velvet, pink ruffles, white lace, and lavender chiffon.

She rummages through her drawers until she finds a journal, then plops onto the frilly pink duvet and clicks her pen to write.

I sit beside her, sinking into the mattress. "Are you going to tell me what's going on yet?"

"Sorry." She pushes back her hair. "I'm just . . . flustered."

"It's okay." I take the pen from her, closing the journal. "Just breathe."

She sits up, inhaling and exhaling.

"Are you back to your regular self yet?"

"Getting there," she says, turning on an oil diffuser. A puff of lavender mist streams out and fills the room. "The Devil's Blood Moon is a day of mourning on Luna Island, when the moon beams bright red—claimed by the Devil's flames. It happens annually, to symbolize the day the Devil was claimed by Luna's tide."

I grab the teddy bear on her bed and squeeze it for comfort. If the Devil has enough power to scorch Luna, then he has enough power to hurt me here on the island. No one's safe today, especially not me.

I assumed he'd have to seduce me out to the sea if he wanted to claim me as one of his sirens, but anything can happen now. No wonder I saw those petals outside my window last night. That must be why Aurora wanted to open the garden of my mind. The Devil and I are connected now. He knows exactly where and how to find me.

Shit.

"I don't understand. How does the Devil even have the power to reach Luna? Shouldn't he be trapped in Hell?"

Roisin takes the teddy bear from me and gives it a hug of her own. "During the Blood Moon, the Devil's rage burgeons into uncontrollable fires, reaching magnificent heights. The air turns stale with grief, and no life can flourish. It causes fear within the people. Bad omens happen. Everyone is far more superstitious than usual. Anxieties surface, confrontations bubble—arguments, breakups, delays! You name it."

"Gee, isn't that great." As if my life weren't already complicated enough.

"Yes!" Roisin flips open the journal. "Which is exactly why we need to prepare for tonight."

Tonight. The next round of the pageant is tonight too. Mother Marguerite called it a trial. No more waltzing down the steps in pretty dresses or crafting shrines to honor the moon. *No.* This test is meant to measure our strength of will.

"Wait." I stop her. "What exactly *happens* tonight? We have to compete in the next round of the pageant."

She nods. "Traditionally, this is the hardest round—like, a threshold before the finish line."

"Oh, how delightful." If it were up to me, I'd lock myself in the cottage and never come out. It's the only way to guarantee my safety. So much for that plan. "What do we have to do?"

She shuts her eyes, before hesitantly explaining, "The Strength of Will means exactly what you think. We test our faith in Luna while she's at her weakest."

From the worry on her face, I have a feeling this trial won't be easy. "And that means?"

She sighs. "That means diving off a cliff under the Blood Moon and swimming to safety at Seal Rock."

"Roisin!" I spring from the bed. "We could die." The sea isn't safe for me right now. And with the Devil's power at its peak, who knows what he'll do.

"Exactly!" she screeches. "Which is why our strength of will needs to be strong enough to save us."

"This doesn't seem ethical," I protest. "I mean, what if one of us *actually* dies?"

"Lila, don't worry." She takes my hand, lowering me back onto the bed. "I know it's scary, but no one has ever died from this portion of the pageant before. There will be boats nearby on the lookout if something seriously goes wrong. And the whole town will be there too, so if anything happens to you, there are dozens of people who will rush to your rescue."

My breath slows, settling. At least there are precautions. That doesn't make it any less dangerous though. Roisin said nobody's ever died from the Strength of Will before, but they also weren't being hunted as one of the Devil's sirens. The sea is the most dangerous place I could be right now.

If what Mother Marguerite said about a part of Luna living in me is true, it could mean two things—either I will be at my weakest when Luna is at her weakest, or I will be able to channel her power as my own.

I only pray that will be enough to save me.

"Hey, I know you're scared," Roisin says. "And I get it. This is a lot. But there are things we can do to prepare."

"Like what?"

She clicks her pen and begins to write.

1) *Hang a wreath of moonflowers on your front door to ward off evil.*
2) *Sage your body and your home to cleanse any negative energy.*

3) *Anoint yourself with moon water to ensure Luna's protection.*

4) *Wear moonstone jewelry to call on Luna's strength (bonus points if the jewelry has been blessed).*

5) *Avoid any seafood to prevent the Devil's poison from entering your body.*

6) *Drink tons of moon water to purge yourself of toxins.*

7) *Leave a gift on a neighbor's doorstep to encourage comradery.*

8) *Dress in white to stand in solidarity with Luna.*

9) *Take a salt bath before bed for an extra cleanse.*

10) *Sleep with moonstone under your pillow or moon-flowers in your hair.*

"Wow." I take it all in. "That's a lot." I knew Luna Island was superstitious, but I never truly felt how much until now.

"I know!" She tosses up the journal. It lands in her pile of clothes. "Which is why we need to begin *now*."

We immediately fall into the motions of preparing for the Blood Moon. Roisin lends me several pieces of moonstone jewelry from her collection—a crescent-shaped pendant, dangling tear-drop earrings, and a beaded bracelet. Their blue aura flashes with a violet iridescence beneath the light. I complete the ceremonial dressing by slipping into a floor-length white gown, lace crafted with a simple satin ribbon tied beneath the bust.

Roisin drapes a long white robe with enormous ruffled sleeves over her outfit, which reminds me of jellyfish tentacles in the way they cascade down her arms. The sheer fabric tastefully pairs with her lace bustier and silk trousers. Before we leave, she ties a white velvet choker around her neck with an oval moonstone in the center and braids tiny moonstone gems throughout her hair.

Main Street is bustling with islanders frantically boarding the ferry or standing outside of Violet Haze Apothecary to get their Blood Moon essentials. Dozens of townsfolk leave with tapered bottles tied with white ribbon—moon water blessed by Luna.

Street stalls offer their own varieties of essentials—moon water, sage, crystals, moonflowers, jewelry, and bath salts. Roisin and I stop by a couple of them to beat the line at Violet Haze.

The bath salts I choose are perfumed with lavender and bergamot, and tiny petals are peppered throughout them like confetti. I pick up an extra bundle of sage for Laina and a moonflower wreath for our door in case we still need one. My bottle of moon water comes in a tiny jam jar with golden moon and star charms dangling in the front, tied together with twine. The vendor even threw in some complimentary crystals for the occasion—a moonstone, as well as a piece of labradorite, selenite, and clear quartz. Although the vendor prices are a bit higher than what we'd find at the apothecary, Roisin and I are both relieved to have our protections rather than be stranded without them for even a second longer.

The entire town comes together in comradery for the Blood Moon, with most shops giving away free gifts to everyone who passes by. Clair De Lune Bakery passes out lychee mooncakes, reminding me of my childhood celebrating the Lunar New Year. Petals Tea Shop hands out sachets of white peony tea and jasmine blossoms. Luna's Love Shack tosses free ribbons out at the front of the store, embroidered with metallic stars and moonflowers. A French restaurant, La Vie en Rose, offers moon water in polished wine glasses to anyone who stops to look at their menu. Some flower stands even hand out moonflowers for free instead of selling them.

Everywhere we turn, people are dressed in white. Not an ounce of color bleeds into the streets of Luna Island besides the pastel buildings. The panic doesn't excuse the pageantry either, as all of the girls I recognize are still in their best dresses. Carmella waltzes down the street in a satin cami flared with a ruffle at the bottom, fanning into a floor-length tiered-lace skirt. Serena and Ophelia flutter by locking arms, both wearing puff-sleeve dresses. Serena's is long, the airy fabric hitting just above her ankles and revealing white strappy sandals with tiny rosettes threaded between the crisscrosses. Ophelia's is short and full like a cupcake, ornamented with an oversized bow tied to the side of her waist. Hints of moonstone glint in their hair and around their wrists and necks. None of them wear any seashell jewelry—typically a staple of Luna Island's seaside charm. But not today.

All the seafood restaurants are closed—Sam's Chowder House, Ula's Mediterranean Dining, the Halibut Hut. The surfing school is empty too, as no one dares to step foot onto the beach. Even all the fishing boats remain docked.

We exit the bustle of town, making our way back to the cottages. Every doorstep overflows with different gifts from neighbors—wreaths, bouquets, homemade sweets, fresh-baked bread, mason jars full of soup, different crystals, letters sealed with wax.

The scent of sage hangs heavy in the air, so overwhelming that it almost outshines the sea's brine. Roisin and I fall into our rituals, becoming silent in meditation until nightfall.

Once the sun sets, scarlet bleeds across the sky, and Luna Island burns.

Chapter
SIXTEEN

✦

Sunlight flickers across the sea like dancing ribbons, a bright blood orange that bleeds into the water. The rays taint the clouds with peachy halos, blurring with the pinkish glow that spills over the land. Everything is still. The air is stale, with not even a whisper of sea breeze to ruffle the flowers or tangle our hair. Luna emerges in the sky, full and red like a ruby mirrorball casting a rose tint over us.

No one speaks. There isn't room for it when sorrow creeps into the crooks of our hearts and rots them from the inside out. I can barely explain it, other than an immeasurable wave of empti-ness. It's different from my normal anxiety, when everything is too much at once—coming in colors, ringing in my ears, trem-bling through my entire body. Instead, I'm numb. Is this what a mother feels like when she loses a child? All I know is this is how it felt for Luna to lose the Devil.

Could it be, this is how it felt for my mother to lose me too?

Grief swells in my chest, building and building until it culminates in tears. No matter how strained our relationship was, I was her and she was me. How cruel must it be for your own flesh to spill your blood? Maybe that's why it was so hard for us to get along. She saw herself reflected in my being—a version of herself she could not tame, one who wanted freedom from her control. The same way the Devil wanted freedom too.

At first, I desired nothing but to make her proud. I *needed* to make her proud. But when I couldn't, I snapped, abandoning every tether that made me her own. When everything fell apart, I no longer cared about her approval. It turned me feral, and I only craved revenge.

Revenge for trying to mold me.

Revenge for pushing me when I had enough.

Revenge for never loving me as I am.

I don't want it to harden me the way it hardened the Devil. To be someone who hurts in a cycle as a reminder of how broken I am. Is this why my parents hurt me too? Are they just as unhealed as he is? We all have our demons. Not everyone is lucky enough to have theirs buried at the bottom of the sea.

If I don't forgive myself now, there's no telling what I'll become. I told myself I'd create a fresh start. That, although this is my punishment, I'd find a way to make it my own. Luna Island is my home now. Roisin and Laina are people I love. I would never want to burn them with my wildfires. I made mistakes—I know that. But I also know they don't define me. I can't go back and undo the damage, but I can move forward and vow to never repeat the past.

"Lila," Laina whispers in a soft hum. "It's time to get ready now."

I nod, backing away from the window. We don't turn on any lights as the darkness settles in. Instead, we light white candles throughout the house. There's a heaviness to my body, weighing me down. Every inch is tender, the same way I feel when I bleed each month. I wish I could hold myself here, under the covers, by the fire, in a warm bath. Instead, shivers course through me as Laina strips my robe.

I fold my arms across my chest as she presents me with another gown. It hangs from a satin hanger like a ghost in the red-hued night. Long sleeves gather at the wrist, cinched by a ruffle of lace. It's simple, white with a bow tied at the waist—more of a nightgown than a dress.

"Wait, don't I get a wet suit or something?" I know Luna Island is enchanted, but even the angels have their limits. The ocean is freezing.

She shakes her head. "Strength of Will is about testing your limits in every aspect—mind, body, and soul. You will have to bare your most vulnerable self tonight as part of the trial."

Great.

I slip into the nightgown and feeling reenters my body. Though, not in a good way. The air is cold, weakening me to the point where everything hurts. Even a simple chill is enough for me to want to hunch over and disappear.

"It's okay," Laina says. "I'll have a pot of tea waiting for you when you return. We received tons of gifts today for you to enjoy once you're back. Rosemary focaccia, potato-leek soup, apple-hazelnut cinnamon rolls. We can heat up a meal before your salt bath. It'll be great."

She smiles, and I nod. I don't have it in me to tell her there's a chance I won't return.

Dear Luna, I pray, *may your power be enough to save me.*

Laina takes a final measure of precaution before we leave, performing a smoke cleansing and anointing my body in moon water one last time. The cloak of sage falls over me like a blessing, burrowing in the curls of my hair and clinging to my nightgown. She rubs the moon water behind my ears and on my wrist like a perfume. It smells like jasmine and rose.

When we're ready, she takes my hand and leads me out into the night. It's too quiet, too still, like we're walking through a bloodstained painting. Laina's heels on the cobblestones make the only sound that rings back. *Click, clack. Click, clack.* It's as solemn as a funeral procession. There's no corner safe of the Devil's mark as everything is claimed in shades of red. The cottages. The cobblestones. My dress. My hair. My flesh.

No.

I rub the beads of my moonstone bracelet between my thumb, praying on each one. *I won't be his. I will never be his.* As much as the Devil tries to take me as his own, he can't. He won't. I have Luna's magic thrumming through my blood. If there's anything he should be scared of, it's her. After all, Luna is the reason the Devil is trapped at the bottom of the sea, and it's clear he hasn't forgotten it. I have my faith, and that's enough. At least, I hope so.

"Good luck," Laina whispers, dropping me off at the edge of the cliff where the other girls competing in the pageant reside. "I'll be waiting for you down at the beach with the rest of the town."

I squeeze her hand before she departs, unable to offer a final farewell. Not when silence shrouds us. All of the girls face the sea, not a hair moving on their heads, not even their lungs rising as they breathe. Each one is dressed identically in a gown just like mine, with long white sleeves and chiffon that hits above their ankles. They loom over the cliff like a band of swans, ready to jump as soon as I take my place in line. I freeze, my breath hitching as I hesitate to join them.

Amelia turns at the sound. To my surprise, she doesn't scowl. Her gaze is empty, as hollow as this night. "We can't start until everyone is here."

I nod, taking my place beside her.

"You made it."

I wasn't expecting her to speak again. I clench the soft fabric of my nightgown, startled, peering over the edge of the cliff. The waves break into white peaks down below. I can't gauge the strength of the undertow from here. We're so high up that the ocean looks gentle.

I glance at Amelia, realizing just how pretty she is. The freckles across her sloping nose remind me of Aurora's fae-like charm, but her upturned eyes are reminiscent of a siren's. Like everything on Luna Island, she's enchanting. Though, her soft blush and the blonde curls framing her face offer a breath of innocence, and I see her for what she really is. Just a girl, just like me. And, like me, she's scared.

"Yeah," I say after a moment. "I guess we both made it."

"If I'm being honest, I wasn't expecting you to get this far."

"I know." If anyone second-guessed me, it's myself. Amelia is just a ripple in comparison to my tide.

"I'm sorry for earlier," she confesses to the sea.

"You—you are?"

She's unmoving, her gaze fixed on the waves. "I shouldn't have doubted you. I mean, you showed up here tonight. It couldn't have been easy."

"It wasn't." Although nobody has died from this event before, the waters lapping against the jagged cliffside suggest otherwise.

"It's not fair, is it?"

"What?"

Her blue eyes float up as she breaks her stoic tether to the water. "We train our entire lives for this. Looking pretty. Being poised. Always trying to be the perfect girl. Even risking our lives. And for what? Just so the angels will like us?"

I stare back, unflinching. I don't know what to say. The last thing I expected tonight was Amelia becoming . . . real. "Yeah. It sucks."

It fucking sucks.

For as long as I can remember, there's been an unspoken war between girls. Who's more talented? Who's prettier? More popular? Smarter? Skinnier? Funnier? *Better.*

We all just want to be loved at the end of the day.

"You know, I was wrong before," Amelia continues. "You do belong here."

"I'm sorry?"

"You've earned it."

You've earned it. "Did I?"

She shrugs. "No matter how hard it gets, you continue to show up. Not just that, but you surprise us. What you did for Roisin that day . . . I don't know anyone who would've done the same."

"Oh," I say to the white peaks of sea-foam down below. "It was nothing."

"I'm serious." She practically grits through her teeth. "Regardless of what happens tonight. . . . You stick up for your friends. You show up for every ritual, no matter if it's strange to you. Shit, you're standing right here, willing to risk your life for us."

"I—thank you." She's right.

I made a home for myself here. I toughed it out, I stepped up when I had to, and I was there. For myself. For Roisin. For the island. And for once, I don't need anyone else's approval. I'm enough for me. I'm enough to be here. And I'll do what I need to do to stay.

"Welcome." A voice behind us bellows.

I'm the only one who turns around to acknowledge Mother Marguerite. When I notice the other girls don't move, I fall back in line, looking down at the beach. The islanders light up the shore like fireflies with their candlelight, which eases my nerves just a bit. Two boats are stationed on either side of Seal Rock, ready to haul anyone to safety if needed. I take a deep breath.

It's fine.

I'm going to be fine.

"Thank you all for being here during this year's Blood Moon," Mother Marguerite says with a vibrato. "The angels are grateful for your attendance and humbled by your dedication to their goddess, Luna. You have all exercised a notable amount of resilience by showing up for this test of will. Tonight, you will prove just how strong your faith in Luna is by swimming out to Seal Rock, trusting that her light is enough to guide you to safety. When you hear the gunshot, you will jump into the sea and begin."

Normally, Mother Marguerite would ask us for our confirmation that we understand the rules. But not tonight. Everyone is as poised as a marble carving of themselves. Amelia's breath shudders. It's the only sound that breaks. I turn to her, and she's trembling. I grab her hand and squeeze. She looks down but doesn't protest.

"Good luck," I whisper.

She squeezes back tighter.

The gunshot rings in the air.

I close my eyes, fix my grasp on Amelia, and jump.

The fall happens too fast.

A rush of water floods my nostrils, spilling into my lungs. The sharp cold paralyzes me for a moment, like a thousand knives cutting into my skin. I kick and flail as the undertow jerks me. A flurry of bubbles unravels from my mouth as I let go of my held breath.

It's Amelia who pulls me to the surface.

"Swim!" she yells.

Everything is a haze, pouncing like a dancing red aura. It takes me a moment to process where I even am. Salt water laps at me, hitting my face and leaking into my throat. I cough, spitting up the brine. Seal Rock is in the distance, but it feels like a mile away.

"Lila," Amelia snaps. "You have to swim!"

I blink, swaying back and forth before taking a deep breath and going back under. The tide is choppy, working against me with every stroke. I bob for air more frequently than I should, trying to catch sight of the other girls in the distance. They're so far ahead, like montages of white in the scarlet sea. Roisin blends in with the rest of them, each bathed in red-toned moonlight. It's impossible to pick out her fire-bright hair.

I press forward, harder, faster, trying to keep up. Everything hurts. My muscles strain as I fight the current, channeling everything in me to push forward. Tonight, the sea is not the friend I mistake it as. It's the Devil's ocean now. Maybe it always has been.

"Ahh!" I cry as my calf constricts. The pain shoots all the way up my thigh. I falter, and the salt water slaps me in the face as I struggle to stay afloat.

Something strikes me when I'm at my weakest.

I scream as a hand pulls me under, and I see her for a second as her skin bites into mine. A flash of gold. A whisper of white feathers. *Aurora?* The vision disappears into the movement of the sea, the same way Damien did the first night he saved me from falling off the boat.

I claw for the surface, but the more I reach, the more I suffer. Suddenly, I'm captured by a whirlpool, coiling my body in a dense ribbon of water. It punctures my ribs and constricts my lungs. I open my mouth without thinking, as if to gather air. Only a mouthful of bubbles trails out, gleaming gold.

What the hell?

The sea's hold weakens me, but I don't lose breath. Everything is wrong, like it's draining me of my magic. No, draining me of *Luna*. My entire body electrifies, glowing and igniting the sea. I shriek, jerking back as the water before me melds into the shape of a demon. His face is god-like, large enough to swallow me whole. The apparition is horned, with a pointed chin and a serpent's tongue.

Lila. Come to me.

Come to me where you belong.

The overtone harmony rattles me, and my muscles contract. My body is not my own anymore, and I can't control it from snapping back. The tide pulls me, and like a puppet, it makes me dance. My limbs work like brushstrokes, spilling my magic into the sea and painting tendrils of gold into the water. With every arabesque and allongé it forces me into, neon flowers sprout from my fingertips—chartreuse, magenta, and aqua blue—blooming and multiplying like a kaleidoscope. They fan out, doubling and doubling and doubling.

Until everything goes black.

Something slams into my stomach, wrapping around me and pulling me to the surface. I heave, fighting for breath as I break from the water. I throw my arms around my rescuer as soon as I can breathe. The relief overwhelms me, and I sob into their chest. As pathetic as it is, I can't stop myself from falling apart.

"What the fuck!" My voice strains out. Their unwavering body keeps me afloat as my tired legs continue to kick.

"It's okay. It's going to be okay," my savior says to me.

Once I realize I'm no longer at risk of drowning, I relax. My gaze snaps up, meeting a head of slicked blonde hair and black wings. "Damien?"

Before I know it, he's gone.

"Lila!" The girls on the rock scream my name. I'm too disoriented to pick out who the voices belong to. It all fades into a singular ringing.

I paddle forward as the ocean beneath me propels me to safety. Though I know it isn't Luna helping me. It's Damien.

"Lila," Roisin cries, bending down and extending her arm. "Take my hand."

To my surprise, Amelia falls beside Roisin and offers her support in unison. I lurch towards them, and they hoist me onto Seal Rock.

"Oh my god, Lila!" Roisin throws herself into me. I fall into her embrace, and we tumble onto the jagged stone. "Are you okay?" She pants. "You were under for so long."

"She's fine," Amelia says, hovering above us. "She's breathing, isn't she?"

Roisin's breath slows. She looks up at Amelia. "Thank you," she manages to say.

Amelia kneels, whispering in my ear. "Congrats."

She drifts away before I can respond and takes a seat beside Yvette.

I look around, scanning the sea for any more traces of white. Only a handful of girls are here. *Amelia. Yvette. Carmella. Serena. Roisin.*

"Where are the others?" I ask, shaking, as Roisin holds me close to her chest. Our shared body heat is my only warmth.

"On the boats." She gestures. "They didn't make it. It's just us now."

It's just us.

I did it. I made it. Only at what cost?

Damien was right.

The pageant isn't what it seems.

Chapter
SEVENTEEN

✦

"Lila," Laina says in nearly a whisper. "Are you sure you're okay? You've hardly touched your food. It's going to get cold."

"I'm not hungry," I say to the bowl of potato-leek soup.

Aromatic garlic and thyme flood the candlelit room. I break off a corner of the rosemary focaccia on the table, still warm from the oven, attempting to stomach even a crumb. It's not enjoyable like it should be. On any other day, this would've been the perfect meal to come home to after a swim at sea. But since I returned, I've only been able to go through the motions. My limbs are heavy, not fully my own. I can only move when the sea wants me to move. I peer over the honey wood table and fixate on a single divot. Droplets of water from my freshly washed hair collect in a puddle beneath me.

It's a surprise Laina and Roisin got me into the bath at all. I've hardly spoken since coming face-to-face with the Devil. My submission is a mystery to even myself. Perhaps I'm merely preparing for my inevitable fate. I tuck my legs close to me beneath a large knit sweater, as if to remind myself I still belong to me, at least for this moment.

"These cinnamon rolls are divine," Roisin gushes, breaking off another bite with her fork. Sticky tumbles of brown sugar and glazed apples spill onto her plate. She wipes a bit of icing from the corner of her lip. "Are you sure you don't want one, Lila?"

"Like I said"—I push back my bowl—"I'm not hungry."

Roisin and Laina look at each other, and everything inside of me tightens. I know what that means. They're worried, and I hate it.

"I'm going to bed." The chair screeches against the floor as I stand.

"I'll come with you." Roisin rises.

"No, it's fine."

"Lila—"

I round the corner and shut my door before she has a chance to protest. I'm unable to help myself from sinking onto the floor and shaking with a sob. I curl inwards, allowing my tears to fall. The second my magic became my own, something I yearned to learn and love, the Devil tried to take it from me too. Nothing about me is sacred anymore. Everything hurts, like a part of me has been extracted by the sea and feathered into nothing. What if I'm never the same again?

This is what the Devil wants though. To weaken me, break my spirit, take parts of me I've kept private. And when I'm nothing, when I've lost the strength to fight, it'll be easier for him to make me his.

Wind sweeps my curtains into ghostly figures. The brisk air nips at my skin, steam-cleansed and tender from the bath. It bites the tip of my nose, taming the rubicund blush in my cheeks. *That's odd.* The air has been still ever since the Devil painted the moon with blood.

I rush over to the window, peering over the beach. The shores are still red and the waters are still thrashing. The Blood Moon isn't over yet. So why did the sea breeze return? With shaky hands, I go to light the candles around my room to cleanse the space.

Lila. The second I turn my back, the wind whispers my name.

I freeze, dropping the box of matches. They scatter across the floor.

No.

Lila.

A shiver tremors through me, my hands shaking as the flicker of the candle comes to life. The glow of the flame triggers a pounding in my temples. I steady myself against the nightstand, knocking over a lamp. Everything goes dark, and I slump onto the bed.

✦

Within the darkness there is a light. It calls me forward, begging to be kindled. I slowly tread through blackened waters, closer and closer to the flickering flame. It's familiar, like I've loved this light all my life. I want to harbor it, bury it in my chest. I'd slit my own throat to protect this light. I'd eat my own tongue and forever be speechless. But, of course, only if the light wanted me to.

It shelters me, until all that's left is warmth. The candlelight blooms like a flower, spilling out a song that anoints me in a gentle balmy bliss. All fear melts away, creating a happiness so warm, I transcend to an otherworldly state. The light fractals into a kaleidoscope of rose-gold glass, consuming me from every angle, like a honeycomb nestling a bee.

But then the music stops and the prisms shatter.

Lila.

The sound of my name startles me awake. It's a dull whisper, not quite human—the same voice from the song in my dream. It followed me from my mind to the outer world. Or maybe I'm still dreaming. It's night when I awake, my room bathed in ruby tones. I grasp the sheets as I rise, reminding myself of something tangible.

This is real.

I am real.

Wind sweeps into my room from the open window. I slowly make my way forward to shut it, but before I can, the ocean sings back.

Lila.

I shudder.

It's not one voice, but two—one high, one low—an overtone of the other. Something otherworldly. Like in my dream, the sound bewitches me forward. I follow it, believing it'll lead me to that gentle balmy light. Like a silk thread, it pulls me out of my room, out of the kitchen, out of the house.

Lila, it calls.

The voice lures me towards the scarlet sea. Rising and roaring, it welcomes me home as my feet meet the edge. I continue out until the water swallows my torso. Here, I'm free.

Come to me, the waters whisper.

I submit, lovelight bathing me as I float away from the shore.

"Lila!" A familiar voice yelps. Only, I can't make out where I recognize it from. "Don't listen to that voice—listen to mine. Come back right now."

His cry is but a whisper compared to the invitation of the ocean.

Come to me, Lila.

Come to me.

I continue forward, surrendering to the call. My muscles relax, and I sink into the waves.

"Lila!"

Cold water kisses my skin and combs through my hair, flowing up my nose and down my throat, becoming one with me entirely. I give myself to the sea, my body bending elegantly as I drift farther and farther into the deep.

That's it . . . Come to me.

Come to me where you belong.

My eyes shut, the lullaby of the sea bringing me to placidity. *I will. I will.*

It's like a whisper in my ears, a feather on my skin. It prickles my flesh, igniting an unbecoming sensation. I crave it. I need it. Deeper and deeper I go, closer and closer to the voice that calls.

"Lila!" A muffled cry from above startles me, and my eyes spring open.

Huh?

Something shatters the water and lunges towards me in a flash of gold. Wings spread wide, sweeping through the sea.

Damien?

Damien!

I scream, swallowing a mouthful of the ocean. My arms are weak against the undertow, pulling me away from his reach. I struggle to clamber to the surface, channeling all my strength, but my muscles strain. I cry, releasing a flurry of bubbles.

His arms find their way around my torso. He fights the tide as it grows more vicious, thrashing and kicking. By some miracle, I'm pulled to the surface. I heave, clenching Damien's body as he carries me through the water.

"Damien," I croak.

"It's okay. It's going to be okay."

It's the last thing I hear before my eyes fall shut.

✦

Crooning seagulls rattle me awake. I wince, shadowing my vision from the faint orange glow rising in the sky. Wet hair sticks to my face, and sand cakes my skin. I'm back in bed, crusted with a saltwater film as if I never showered off last night. The window is wide open, and it all comes back to me in flashes.

The dream.

The light.

The voice.

Holy fucking shit.

I sit up and scream, surrounded by dozens of sparkling white flowers—roses, gardenias, and jasmines. They're tangled in the curls of my hair, scattered across my pillow, overflowing beneath the covers, sprawling across my duvet.

My heart races, and I clench my fist, realizing there's a note tucked within my palm. I unfold it and read.

Lila,
We must escape to the stars as soon as possible. It is not safe on Luna Island. Meet me back on the beach tonight and we'll run away.

Yours Truly,
Damien

Chapter
EIGHTEEN

✦

"Lila." Someone knocks at the door. "Is everything okay?"

I freeze, paralyzed by the garden of my mind, brought to life and made real. My pulse quickens, causing my chest to flutter. I leap out of bed and sweep the flowers onto the floor. Their fragrance lingers, clinging to the cotton.

"Lila." She knocks again.

"Give me a minute."

Panicking, I shove the buds beneath my bed and rush to open the door. Roisin glares back as I greet her with short breath.

"Roisin. What are you still doing here?"

"I—I asked Laina if I could spend the night on the couch. I was worried about you."

I sigh, leaning against the doorframe. She's trying to be a good friend, but I wish she'd returned home for a proper recovery after the Strength of Will trial. She must be exhausted.

"You didn't have to do that," I say after a moment.

"Of course I did. I'm the one who made you join the pageant in the first place. If it weren't for me, you wouldn't—"

"Stop." I grab her hand. Her shoulders relax, and she takes a breath. "Nothing is your fault, okay? I joined the pageant because I wanted to. I jumped off the cliff by choice. And I made it back safely, so there's nothing to worry about."

"For some reason, I don't believe you."

Of course she doesn't. I fake a smile. "I was just exhausted last night. The Blood Moon really drained me."

She nods. "I get it. It was your first Blood Moon, on top of the Strength of Will. I should have prepared you more or set up better aftercare. I could have—"

"Roisin," I say gently.

"Sorry." She shakes her head. "I just hate to think any of this could be my fault."

I pull her in for a hug, and her body relaxes. "You couldn't harm a hair on my head." If anything, Roisin is the reason I'm still here, fighting to make Luna Island my home as much as it rejects me. I don't want to leave this place. I don't want to leave her.

She pulls back, smiling. "Laina and I were talking, and we think you could use a break."

"A break?"

"Yeah, you know. Just some girl time. You've been so stressed lately. She has something special planned for you this evening, and I thought I'd get you out of the house in the meantime. We can start preparing for the Starlit Ball."

The Starlit Ball.

I think back to Damien's letter. *Luna Island isn't safe.* He's right. The flowers on my bed are only a confirmation. But just for a while, one more day, I can pretend like none of it exists. If I'm forced to leave Luna Island, I want to make the most of it with the people I've grown to love. Which is the only reason I say—

"Okay."

I'll pretend everything is fine. Like the Starlit Ball is something I still have to look forward to. That the Devil didn't try to drown me last night. And that the pageant is as innocent as it seems. For just a moment longer, I'll hold on to the magic of it all. And maybe, just maybe, if I dream hard enough, I'll make it real.

✦

Life on Luna Island has resumed as normal, as if the Blood Moon never impacted us at all. Families scatter across the beach, sending kites up in the air and building sandcastles with their children. The fishing boats return to sea, and all the seafood restaurants reopen too. Islanders lunch on bowls of clam chowder, oysters, and lobster rolls. There's a line outside of Ula's waiting for them to open, and Sam's Chowder House is so busy, even the tables out front are occupied despite the morning's chilly breeze.

Nearly every girl on Luna Island floods the shops on Main Street, fluttering between Luna's Love Shack, Heaven Divine, and other boutiques I've yet to visit—Siren's Cove, Moon River, the Pink Seashell. Each one of them has pastel shopping bags fluffed with tissue paper hanging from their arms.

"What, is there a huge sale after the Blood Moon or something?" I ask Roisin, assuming it must be similar to Black Friday or other post-holiday discounts.

"No, silly." She rolls her eyes. "The Strength of Will is over now, which means everyone's preparing for the Starlit Ball, even those who didn't make it to the next round or weren't participating in the pageant. It's the biggest holiday on Luna Island."

Of course. I notice Isadora has returned. She links arms with Carmella as they stop to examine a champagne-colored gown in Moon River's window. They're wearing matching seashell necklaces. Girls accessorize with starfish clips in their hair, puka shells around their wrists, and sea glass on their fingers. Even Roisin has replaced her moonstone choker with a string of pearls.

It's as if the town transformed overnight, turning from solemn to celebratory. Genevieve happily squeals while window-shopping for jewelry with Amelia and Yvette. Serena and Ophelia step out of the salon, admiring their new manicures. Roisin is right. It doesn't matter if someone didn't make the final cut of the pageant. They're just as excited as if it were prom.

Luna Island blooms with color, a stark contrast to yesterday's whiteout. All of the moonflower wreaths are gone, replaced by bright pink and purple blossoms tied with large bows. They're hanging on the doors of every storefront, and the same vibrant buds are used to decorate the streetlamps, carriages, and the fountain at the center of Main Street.

Fairy lights are strung everywhere—crisscrossed above the cobblestone streets, woven between the rose bushes, up the tree trunks, in the windows of each shop, and hanging from the roof of every cottage. I imagine that at night, the entire town glows. I wonder if you can see it from the mainland.

"Come on," Roisin says, leading us into Dulce de Leche, the local tanning salon.

The excitement of playing princess sets in, and for a while, I allow myself to focus on feeling beautiful while celebrating this milestone. The Starlit Ball marks a rite of passage. Like Amelia said, I showed up. It didn't matter how uncomfortable it was. Despite everything, I made it through each challenge. The Devil wants to break me, take away my newfound home. But how can I leave now that I've earned my place?

"You ready?" Roisin asks.

I nod, following her into the tanning room.

The spray tans on Luna Island are different from the ones I'm used to. Instead of simply bronzing my skin, the machine coats me in a veil of golden glitter, like I'm an angel myself. My complexion gleams back in a shade of mellow honey, sparkling from every angle.

After, we head over to Blooming Bella's Salon to get blowouts and mani-pedis. The staff offers us virgin Bellinis while we wait. We relax as our rollers set, watching *Splash* on the flat-screen TV, a popular mermaid movie from the 1980s. Roisin's red hair falls in ringlets like tight coils of ribbons. I fluff out my bouncy barrel curls, which gleam back glossy beneath the light. We're ushered to another room to get our nails done after. Roisin goes for a classic French manicure, and I choose a pearlescent polish for my stiletto acrylics. We both decide on a matching pink shade for our toes and admire the pastel shade in the sun once we step outside.

The day wouldn't be complete without shopping. We stop by some of the boutiques I haven't been to before. Although we should be finding a gown for the Starlit Ball, I can't help but pick out a slip from the Pink Seashell. It's lilac, my favorite color, with pale pink flowers embroidered onto the silk. It's figure hugging and sleek, with a bit of lace detailing running along the sweetheart neckline.

"It's lovely." Roisin swoons. "You should wear it tonight."

"Tonight?"

"Duh! Did you forget Laina has a surprise waiting for you at home?"

Warmth floods my cheeks, and I turn away to hide my flush. I don't know what to say. This *is* my family. People who love me enough to make sure that I'm okay. Maybe if I can accept their love, the nightmares might end. The voices will settle. Darkness will stop following me. And finally, I can grow up. Have a normal life. Be a regular girl.

"Let's go," Roisin says, linking her arm in mine and leading us back to Laina's cottage.

✦

"Hey, girls!" Laina chimes, inviting us inside. "You're just in time."

The dining room has been transformed into a fairy garden this evening. Flowers are strewn across the long table—magnolias, anemones, and roses—paired with hydrangea-and-peony centerpieces. Long taper candles flicker over the display, complemented by the remaining sunlight. A feast sprawls out from one end of the table to the other, a medley of some of my favorites—crab cioppino with bright tomatoes and red wine, garlic bread flecked with parsley, linguine and clams swimming in broth, seared abalone presented in its opalescent shell, fresh oysters on a bed of ice.

"Laina, this is incredible. You did all of this for me?"

"Of course." She throws her arms open with a grin. "We have a whole birthday to make up for."

"Birthday?"

"Surprise!" Roisin sweeps into the room with a heart-shaped cake, decorated with frosting piped in scalloped edges. *Happy Birthday Lila* is written in cursive.

Eighteen candles cast a glow across my face. "Oh my gosh. You guys didn't have to do this."

"Of course we did," Laina gushes. "If anything, we should've done it when you first arrived. There was just so much going on with the ball and the pageant—you know. But better late than never, right?"

"Oh, Laina. Really, this is too much."

"Nonsense." She waves me off.

"Make a wish," Roisin presses, bouncing on her tiptoes.

I blow out the candles, but I don't make a wish. Everything I could ever want is right here. Laina and Roisin giggle, clapping as candle smoke tangles in our hair. They embrace me, sandwiching me in the middle of their affection.

We come together for our meal, and Laina even lets Roisin and I have a glass of pink champagne. Everything becomes funny as the bubbles rise to our heads. The coastal breeze drifts in through the window, offering a cool relief to our blushing cheeks.

If only I could preserve this moment forever.

Laina clears her throat, gathering our attention. "So, there's actually another reason I wanted to get us together tonight. Lila, I should've given this to you sooner."

I blink, sitting taller in my seat. I had hoped this moment wasn't too good to be true, but from the glances Laina and Roisin exchange, something's wrong. "What is it?"

Laina reaches over to the seat next to her and picks up a parcel. "Your mother sent this."

My mother.

The world stills, bringing me back to the last time we were together. Her face was tear stained and twisted. Her nails bit into my wrists, resisting me. I was a mirror of her, a product of everything she hated, all wrapped up into one raging teenage girl. If her insecurities couldn't kill her, I would. Her living, breathing disappointment. I read her name and recoil from the package.

Midori Li.

There's no mistake. It's from her.

I look up at Laina. "Why are you giving me this?"

"Don't you want to know what she has to say?" Her voice is mellow, as if she's afraid I'll startle easily.

"No!" I fling the package back, rising. "I don't want anything to do with her." Or maybe, I just don't want anything to do with the person she remembers me as.

"Come on, Lila," Roisin urges. "She wouldn't write to you if she didn't still care."

Why would she care after everything I've done? Besides, Laina and Roisin can't know me the way she does. She's like a ghost from my past showing up to haunt me. I'm different now. I'm *better.*

"You're on her side?" I snap at Roisin.

"I'm not on anyone's side. I—I just think you're lucky to hear from someone you used to love."

I sink back into my seat, realizing I've been insensitive. Roisin lost Nadine, and despite what happened between them, they loved each other. It's not possible for them to make amends when none of us know what happened to Nadine in the first place.

"You're right. I'm sorry," I say. "I'll open the package. But if it's alright with you, I'd like to be alone."

"Understood." Laina rises. "I'll get started on the dishes."

Roisin nods. "I'll help too."

The two of them disappear into the kitchen, leaving me alone with the parcel. It taunts me, like a ticking bomb waiting to explode. I debate throwing it in the trash or hiding it deep within my closet. Maybe, I could even send it off to sea. It can't hurt me if I don't let it. At least that's what I tell myself. But the truth is, what happened between me and my mother is always going to hurt. And if I don't face her now, whatever she has to say will only turn into another haunting. I can't handle that. I'm already too fragile.

With a deep breath, I tear the package open, bracing myself for whatever is inside.

It's a crisp white envelope pressed with a golden seal. There's also a small box tied with a pale blue ribbon—my favorite chocolate as a kid—sea-salt orchid with a lychee center. I stopped eating these a long time ago. It's odd my mother would send some now. What could she possibly want? I break the seal and read.

Dear Lila,

I should've said this to you sooner, but these things are always difficult to put into words. I understand how I've hurt you, and I paid for my mistakes when you lashed out. I don't blame you for what you did. After all, I am your mother. You are who you are because of me, and I regret placing my burdens onto you. Coming here, I struggled in more ways than you know to have the life I do now. I never wanted you to suffer the way I did just to feel like you have a place in this world. That's why your father and I are so hard on you. We love you, Lila. We want you to be the best so you never know what it feels like to have nothing. I forgive you for your mistakes, and I hope one day, you can forgive me for mine.

Love Always,
Mom

My tears fall across the page, smudging the ink and turning my mother's words blurry. Everything within me trembles, shaking with a furious need for movement. Only, I'm locked to my seat. I can't stand, can't breathe.

It all comes in flashes.

Scarlet cuts against her white skin.

Blood dried beneath my fingertips.

My father roaring as he tore my body from what I assumed was her corpse.

I don't deserve her forgiveness. I don't deserve any of this.

An unwarranted scream crawls up my throat, and my tears rush out without consent—ugly and heavy in a way that makes my chest rasp.

"Lila?" Laina calls from the kitchen. "Are you okay?"

Her nearing shadow forces me to rise. She can't see me like this, especially after everything she's done to make sure that I'm okay. Disappointing her by being this upset would only make me more ashamed. My heart pounds fiercely as I exit through the back door. The sea breeze whips my face as I run down the beach. I'm so angry that I can't feel anything else at all, not even the sand beneath my feet or the strain that should be in my calves.

I fall before the ocean, heaving as the sea-foam breaks around my wrists. The water claims my mother's letter and turns the paper soft. It doesn't take me much to shred it, dissolving her words as they're claimed by the tide.

I'm left with numbness as my breath settles. After any outburst, I can almost laugh at the drama. Why does it make me so furious to feel my mother's love? Why can't I just accept her apology?

Whatever the reason is, I'm sorry.

I want to be good.

I want to behave.

Just as I'm about to rise, a shadow steals the remaining sunlight. A shrill gasp parts my lips as I glance up. Dark wings sprawl above me. *Damien.* He's like a reaper, cutting my time on Luna Island too short.

I leap to my feet. "What are you doing here?"

"Lila." He grabs my hand. "Are you alright?"

I reel back, breaking our tether. "Leave me alone."

"You're crying."

"What?" I wipe my face, wishing he would disappear. I don't want him to see me like this again. "I have to go." I brush past him, racing farther down the beach.

"Hey." He speeds after me. "What's wrong? Lila—"

"Stop!" I spin around. "Just stop." Dark clouds form overhead. The waves thrash as my voice thrums.

Damien closes the distance between us despite my protest. "We can't stay here," he says. "We have to go. Now."

"Wait—" I yelp, as he pulls me forward. "Damien!"

Before we can even run off, the beach is swallowed by a scarlet glow, breaking through the clouds like fire.

I scream, my neck snapping back and my throat stretched taut. My heart pounds with a furious explosion. I claw at my chest, ripping the silk of my dress, my nails cutting my own flesh. I want to squeeze my heart. I want to carve it out and throw it into the sea. It burns, bringing me to the sand.

"Lila!" Damien falls to his knees beside me.

The waves rise to monstrous heights, hovering over us as if to swallow the island whole. My lungs seethe, begging for me to scream, but I don't have the breath left to do it. Swaths of sea-foam meld into a god-like face, the same one I saw during the Strength of Will.

This can't be real. It's another nightmare, spiraling out of control. I squeeze my eyes shut, trying to vanquish the vision. Only, it never folds.

"My little moon, my Lunalie," the apparition says with a

vibrato. "I've been waiting to meet you." His voice is an other-worldly overtone, just like the one that's been following me.

The Devil.

"How do you know who I am?" I snap.

"Why, I've known you all your life, my dear." His voice is too calm to trust. "Why do you think you've always felt so called to the sea? It was me you were following all along."

"No." The sea is my friend, my place of comfort. "You're lying."

"How else would I know exactly where to find you? Did you enjoy my song last night? I can't wait for you to join me in Hell."

Hell. I've always known it. My parents sent me to Luna Island for a reason—to make sure I wound up in Hell where I belong. I've felt the darkness haunting me since the day I arrived, but I refuse to give my parents that satisfaction. I shove off Damien, finding the strength within me to stand.

"This is not my fate."

The Devil laughs. "You don't belong here. I know what you can do."

What I can do. I falter. "You mean, with my dance?"

"What else?"

Of course my power has something to do with the Devil. My throat strains against the urge to cry. "What did you do to me?"

"I did nothing," he says with infuriating ease. "You have Luna to thank for that."

"Luna?"

Pressure swells in my head, causing a ringing in my ears. My feelings come in colors, swirling like a whirlpool—none of which I can grasp.

Violet, magenta, deep blood red.

I don't recall what they mean, other than the pain attached to them. The more I try to decipher them, the angrier I become. I curse myself, I hate myself, for not being able to tame it.

"You will never have me." I reel back.

The desire to scream is relentless—clawing, rising, welling—filling all of me. My throat begs for the release. I reach towards the sky, my arms straining as if I could escape it. With my command, the clouds thunder and rain pours over the island.

"It's destiny," he says with relish. "There's no place for a girl like you here."

"What are you talking about?"

"You're a threat. Just like me."

"I could never be like you." I beg, I plead, to make the words true. We both know I'm only lying.

"Oh, really?" he taunts. "You were willing to kill when someone didn't love you enough. You slit the flesh that gave you life when you felt unpretty, unworthy, unspecial. You're a vain, twisted girl. Wrathful. Vengeful. Chaos Incarnate."

No.

The dark, evil part of me I hate begs to come out. It burns. My breaths come in snatches, the fire inside of me dancing as my flesh burbles with an intense desire for movement. My nails sink into my palms until ribbons of blood trickle down my arms. I wail, my throat burning raw as all my tendons strain. The sea crescendos, shattering the Devil's apparition and slamming back into its natural state. The waves splatter everywhere, soaking Damien and me in salt water.

I sink to the ground.

"Lila!" Damien sprints forward.

Tremors rack my body as I examine the blood on my hands, ashamed of the girl I've become. She is the demon that almost killed her mother—the demon the Devil knows me to be. I will never be the angelic thing I masquerade as. I am uncontrollably, irrevocably, undeniably wicked. And that is why no one can ever love me. I press my forehead to the sand.

"I'm sorry," I whisper to the earth.

"I've got you." Damien sinks to his knees, and I lean into his embrace, crying into his chest. His dark wings wrap me in a cocoon of soft feathers.

I press into him harder. "I'm scared," I confess.

"It's okay. The Devil can't hurt you now."

"Not of the Devil." I'm scared of *me*.

I'm scared no one will ever love me.

I'm scared I don't deserve love at all.

Not when I was born a monster.

"Look at me," he commands. "You're sensational. You were born sensational. The Devil can't take that away from you, and you shouldn't let him. I vow to protect you. Wherever you go, whatever you do, I'll be there to watch over you. I'm your guardian angel, from here on out, forevermore."

We breathe in sync, our bodies entwined, his chest beating against mine. His vow of protection seeps into my heart, and I don't fight it. I'm too tired. And so, I say, "Take me away from here, angel."

Chapter
NINETEEN

✦

We don't escape to the stars. I'm too weak for that. My body goes limp in Damien's arms as he carries me through the forest. On another day, I'd be ashamed of my inability to stand on my own. But I don't fight it. My pride has already been lost.

We break through a clearing as the trees give way to the angels' village. Golden light and chimney smoke cast the illusion of comfort. Instead of staying in the village, Damien heads towards the tallest tree at the edge of the commune. Tangled in the branches above us is a sanctuary of some sort. He sets me down before tugging on a dangling vine. A ladder unravels as a result.

"What is this place?"

"Come. Let me show you."

My limbs tremble as I find my footing. Using whatever strength I have left, I follow Damien up the ladder.

To my surprise, it's larger than my bedroom. I would barely call it a tree house. It's more like a cottage in the sky. There's a small kitchen in the corner with a fireplace and a cupboard. It's so spacious, there's even a dining table and enough room for a bed.

"This place is huge." I swoon.

Damien chuckles, lighting a few oil lamps and candles to illuminate the room. With a flick of his wrist, starlights come alive, strung across the ceiling like a string of pearls. The warm glow casts a golden sheen over foiled books and overgrown plants. Leaves creep in through the windows and wrap the room up like a present. I peek inside the cupboard, but the shelves are empty.

"Sorry," he says. "I wasn't expecting company. I usually only come here when I want to get away."

"You don't live here?" I ask, inspecting the bed in the corner of the room. It's nestled in a honey wood frame, perfectly made with white cotton sheets and a crocheted blanket.

"No. It's more like an escape for me when the world becomes too big."

"Oh." This is his safe haven, I realize.

Suddenly, being here seems invasive. My fingers graze a watercolor painting of sunflowers pinned to the wall, the parchment wrinkled from the brush being too wet. There's a youthfulness to this place that reminds me of being a kid, when I'd pretend tree houses were castles and happily ever afters really did exist. But now I know the world isn't built for us to be happy. At least not forever. No matter what, it always fades. I sink onto the bed, and Damien follows me.

"Are you okay?" he asks, taking a seat beside me.

"Didn't you see what happened?" There's no running from it anymore. My mother's apology was full of shit. This is why she sent me here. She may play it off to ease her conscience, but I know the truth.

"Lila—"

"Tell me." My voice falters. "What's really happening on Luna Island? Why do we have to leave, and why are you running too?" I know it's more than just the Devil. The angels have been hiding something, and it's about time I know the truth.

"I—I can't talk about this." He looks away, and his eyes fall away from mine.

"Damien, please," I plead.

He sighs, pushing back his saltwater-matted hair. "I'm sorry."

My eyes shut, causing a swell of tears to fall. It's not fair. None of it is fair. I hold myself the way I wish he'd hold me, trying my best to keep it together. If I'm being honest, I'm not as tough as I pretend to be. I'm tired of running. I'm tired of fighting.

Damien wraps his wing around my shoulder. I relax beneath the feathery embrace.

"Please understand," he says. "My family is already furious with me for interfering."

"Interfering with me, you mean?"

"With you, with the pageant. They'd punish me severely if I told you anything more."

I pause, remembering how his father hit him that day in the forest. He hit him because of *me*. Damien was trying to protect me all this time, and he got in trouble for it. I was right. Everyone I care about will only get hurt as long as I'm here. I won't force him to betray his commune's trust. Damien has already done enough. Any answers I find will have to be on my own.

"I'm sorry," I confess.

"What do you have to be sorry for?"

"Everything." All of it. I was always my parents' mistake. If I weren't here, then no one around me would suffer. No wonder they sent me away. "My parents wanted this to happen."

"Deep down you know they would never hurt you. Not like this."

"No. What the Devil said is true." I was made for him. I know it. My parents know it. The angels know it too. I don't deserve anyone besides him.

Damien scoots closer. His voice comes out in a whisper. "That's just what he wants you to think. You can't give in to his lies."

The heat of his body seeps into mine, warming me. It's hard to breathe when he's so close. My chest tightens. "You don't even know what I really did to get sent here. Trust me, if you did, you'd never want anything to do with me."

I expect him to run. I *wish* he'd run. But he doesn't move. "Whatever you did, it's in the past now. You can't hold on to it forever."

Oh, but I can. "You don't understand."

I hate myself for what I did. My hair tumbles over my eyes as my face falls. It's better this way. I don't want him to see how much it hurts.

"Well, what happened?" he asks.

My nails sink into my palms, reminding me of how I spilled my mother's blood. If I tell him, then maybe he'll finally disappear.

I won't have to worry about hurting him anymore, and he'll be free from the burden I placed upon him.

"You can tell me," he presses. "I won't judge you."

"How can you say that?" There'll be nothing left to protect once the truth is out. Why would anyone want to save a monster?

"Because I know you now, and that's what matters. You aren't your worst moments, Lila. None of us are." He's patient, sincere, pleading for me to believe him.

How can I? "I'll always be haunted by my mistakes." They follow me everywhere I go, even here to Luna Island. I think I'll die with the ghost of them.

His eyes shut, and he sighs, sinking deeper into the mattress. "Believe me, I know how you feel."

"You do?" For a moment, I wonder if the grace Damien extends to me is what he also tells himself. *We aren't our worst moments.* He's my savior, my angel. Damien is good. Kind. Better than I'll ever be. Though, I guess none of us are ever truly perfect.

"We all have our demons, Lila. Perhaps, it's finally time to face yours."

I tug at the moonstone bracelet still on my wrist from the Blood Moon, before stopping on a single bead and rubbing it between my thumb. Maybe he's right. Maybe if I can admit it, I'll finally be free.

My breath wavers as my lips part. "I'll never forget the sensation of it . . . how my fingers trembled when it was over. Like, they were ashamed of what I made them do."

He brushes the hair away from my face, gentle with his touch. "What did you do?"

My eyes shut. I can't look at him when I say it. "I—I wrung my hands around my mother's throat." Clawing at her. Strangling her. But that wasn't enough. I wanted blood and I got it. I slit her flesh. The blood dried beneath my fingertips, and I cried when I washed it out. "All I wanted was for her to love me. She would never say it. And now I'm certain neither will my father. Not after witnessing what I did."

Shivers rack my body as I'm overcome by shame. They didn't understand. Who could ever? I didn't mean it. I hate myself for it. Everything just became too big, too much. All of their screaming, all of their voices . . . it built up inside me until I burst. They were determined to see the worst in me until I saw it too. I believed them—I was their perfect ballerina who fell from grace—no longer something precious to admire. I shattered, and they were just collateral. Their blood cloaked my broken shards, staining me, haunting me. No matter what I do, I can never wash them clean. It would be better for everyone if I just disappeared.

I smooth out my dress, rising. "I should go. I'm sorry."

"No." Damien grabs my wrist. I turn around. He studies me, placing a palm to my cheek that's still warm from tears. "Don't leave."

I hesitate. Our breath lingers, warm and wavering. Why would he want me to stay? My reflection gleams in a mirror across the room, tearstained and feral, a creature meant for the depths of Hell. I shove him back. "You should've let him take me."

The Devil is right. My own parents don't love me. And if they don't, no one will.

"Hey." He pulls me forward, and my breathing hitches. "I understand your anger, and I could never hate you for it."

"How can you say that?"

"Because, like you, I've done things I'm not proud of. I did what I could to earn my family's respect, and yet, it was never enough. It wasn't until I met you that I realized maybe we shouldn't have to fight for the love of those who don't give it freely. You are not unlovable just because someone else makes their love unobtainable."

We linger for a moment, both processing the idea, both trying to unlearn what we've been conditioned to believe. Everything is quiet, until I say, "Maybe you're right. But even then, I don't know if I'll ever stop feeling this way."

"Feeling what way?"

"Defective," I admit. "Like, I shouldn't be here at all." Maybe God made a mistake with me. The Devil's right. I'm too much for this world. *Wrathful. Vengeful. Chaos Incarnate.* No wonder I hurt every person I grow to love. There's too much rage in me that can't be tempered, no matter how hard I try.

Damien's hold around me tightens. "Why would you say that?"

"Because it's true. All I've ever wanted is to be loved. So why does everything always break whenever I'm near?" It's like the world is glass that will only stay intact when I'm on my tiptoes. The second I exhale, it shatters.

"Lila, you are not defective. Sure, you feel deeply, but it doesn't make you weak."

"I never said it makes me weak. It makes me dangerous."

He wrings his head from side to side, closing the distance between us. "You've made mistakes, but don't act like we all haven't. What matters is that you're sorry, and I forgive you. So why can't you forgive yourself?"

"Because it's not something that can be forgiven!" I snap. I just wish he would understand.

He doesn't jump when I raise my voice. Can anything scare him? "You keep telling yourself that. But do you really think it's a fault to experience the world as deeply as you do?"

"What?"

"You're ashamed because you let your emotions get the best of you, but the only reason they did is because they're powerful. That's not a bad thing. And I'm not saying what you did was okay. It's just more complicated than you think."

"I don't—I don't understand."

"You know what it's like to hurt, and you don't want anyone else to hurt the way you did. That's why you try so hard to protect everyone from yourself, isn't it?"

He isn't wrong, but I'm reluctant to admit it. I can't let myself off so easily. If I accept what Damien says, it could explain why everything around me is so delicate. I don't want to hurt anyone anymore. I don't want them to know what it's like to feel what I do. And so I keep it buried and it builds until it roars, washing over them like a tidal wave. Is this why Damien tried to tame me with my dance? Did he believe he could feather out the chaos instead of letting it culminate?

"This is why you chose to help me, isn't it?"

"What?"

"You wanted to see me turn my ocean into something beautiful." And I've been pushing him away ever since. If I let him in, if

I really gave this a chance, maybe I wouldn't be so destructive. But that's not a risk I'm willing to take. Not when he could still get hurt.

"It won't be easy," he says, "but I'll be there with you. Whatever you need, wherever you go, I want to be there too. I'll hold your hand when the waves turn rough and the rains run wild. If you'll have me, we can escape this place together, and you'll never be alone in this again."

"Escape with you . . ." The idea is tempting.

"Yes." He moves a step closer. "Let's run away to the stars."

I want to say yes. I want to trust that this could be something real. But how can it? Monsters aren't supposed to get their happily ever after. I'm what the hero slays to save humanity.

"I'm sorry, Damien. I don't deserve you." It's all I can manage to say.

"That's not true."

"Then why did my parents send me away? How do you explain that?"

"Listen." His grip around me tightens. "You are not undeserving of love just because you're imperfect. Maybe that's what your parents taught you, but that's not love. Love is never giving up on someone at their worst. Love is accepting all of a person, even the parts they hate."

I want to run.

I want to push him away.

I can't.

His hold around me is firm, and I fall into it, allowing myself to cry. I wish love were as tender as he spins it, that it weren't something used against me as a punishment. Maybe if I surrender, it can be. But where do I even start? I can't hide from the Devil any longer, and I'm not strong enough to reach the stars. Everything I feel comes in multitudes. We'd never get there with how unpredictable I am.

"There's no escaping this fate, Damien. You need to let me go. Even if I wanted to control my power, it's not safe to dance anymore. I feel so strongly that it overwhelms me." I'll never have a hold over it the way it does on me.

"What I see is a girl who knows her worth. You recognize how great you can be, and that's why you push yourself so hard. So why stop now? Especially when you have me."

You have me.

I place my fingers to his chest, drinking him in as something real. He's not a fantasy, or an illusion, or another one of my dreams. He didn't run. For once, someone stayed. He isn't scared of me. So why am I?

"Look at all we can do when we're together," he continues. "You can be that on your own. You don't need me to be great."

Maybe he's right. Maybe it's time I start believing in myself too. I was the one Luna blessed, not Damien. I don't know why it happened, but if it was a gift, it's only right that I treat it like one.

It's my *feelings* my powers are connected to, not my dance. That's what I have to nurture. That's what I have to learn to love. All I ever strived for was perfection on that stage. It never occurred to me that I was fighting for the wrong thing. I was always worthy. I just didn't love myself enough to see it. But with Damien's help, I do.

I need to forgive myself if I want to reach my full potential.

Like magic, the island gathers me, kissing my cheeks with its tender breeze. A buzz of glowing light flutters in through the window. A firefly. There's one. There's two. They take me by surprise, illuminating the space between Damien and I. My giggle lifts the mood as one of them lands on my nose.

"Would you like to see where they come from?" Damien asks. "We're just outside their pond."

"Really?" A childlike wonder blooms inside me as I'm brought back to the island's whimsy. This is my home, where I took my first breath of air. I belong here, and I won't let the Devil force me out.

"Come." Damien smiles. "Let's go."

He leads us outside, and the forest air nips my skin.

"Look!" I point at the pond. "Fireflies." There are dozens, illuminating the fuchsia lilies in the water.

"Dance with me." Damien takes my hand, guiding me forward.

"Right now?"

He nods. "Let's forget about the world for just a moment."

"Okay." I surrender, allowing myself to indulge in the one thing I love the most. Dancing is a part of me. Why should I deny it any longer?

Luna bathes us in lovelight as fireflies catch in my hair. I laugh as they tickle my neck. Damien pulls us into the water, and coolness washes over our ankles, relieving the pent-up tension lingering inside my body.

The pink lilies glow as we spin around the spellbound pond. Their nectar extracts from the blossoms at the command of my dance, the perfume materializing from the buds like ribbons as we twirl. They bow towards me as we glide through the water, as if the island is folding to my every move. With my quick bourrée steps, the twinkling fireflies change color—gold and green, pink and blue—fluttering around us like living music notes that burst with song. Fountains of water ascend as Damien sends me into a pirouette, and when I lift my arms into the air, the water spouts as if to kiss the moon.

I descend, and he holds me there. Something changes. Damien looks at me differently. His golden irises glow like halos around his pupils. He studies me, immortalizing this moment. Everything stills. It's just us. Me and him on Luna Island.

"Lila." He says my name like it's something sacred.

"Yes?"

"I love you."

"What?" It takes me by surprise.

"I love you," he says again. "I love the commanding tone of your voice and how it falls in gentle rhythms. I love how you dance like the waves and pull me in with your tide. You're every ounce as beautiful as the sea and every bit as wild. You have no idea the extent of how vibrantly you glow, but perhaps you're learning. And I love that. I love you."

A flutter in my chest multiplies, blooming and blooming and blooming, like the kaleidoscope in my dream. Only this time, it doesn't shatter. It holds me there in that rose-gold glow. I burst, but in a way that's expansive, not destructive.

I leap forward, pressing my lips to his, obliterated by the dew-damp softness.

His eyes widen as he pulls away.

I gape at him, flushed. "I—I'm sorry."

He hesitates, but then he pounces, drawing me towards his embrace and crushing into my open mouth. It happens so fast. He grabs me by the thighs, welling up my skirt as he carries me out of the water. My fingers curl through his hair, and novas explode as he slips his tongue onto mine. He holds me tighter, kissing me over and over again like repeating a melody. It's as natural as language, as wild as the roaring sea.

We fall to the ground, and a bed of flowers blossoms beneath us, pale pink and soft. The velvet petals tangle in my hair as he presses into me—skin on skin, blooming with wild heat. We fold into each other, our arms coiling like serpents, my fingers tracing his body.

He pulls away for just a moment, but only to study me like the rarest opal, admiring my every color and curve before kissing my lips—sweet and soft and slow. We repeat the motion in a ritual that's only our own.

I try to catch my thoughts, but they're all tangled up. Though, there's one thing I know for sure. Through my unsteady breathing, I whisper, "I love you too."

Despite what the Devil thinks, I am capable of love, and I won't let him win, not now. Damien and I collapse into the damp petals, surrendering to the night.

Chapter
TWENTY

◆

The whole world stills, and I hold us there in a painting preserved. Thousands of stars shimmer from above, watching over our sacred oasis of pink petals and warm breath. I curl into Damien's chest, cherishing the gentle rise and fall of his beating heart. He's already deep in slumber, but I fight the urge to drift off to the garden of my mind. Not when I'm here, and everything is so perfect. *I deserve this*, I say to myself. I won't give in.

I make the mistake anyway.

Smoke creeps into my lungs, awakening me. To my confusion, when my eyes open, the world is painted in a rose-hued tint. It's the smoke, claiming our clearing. It curls and tangles around me, heavy like a slow-weaving snake—slithering into my lungs and constricting until I'm weak. I spring up with a cough, bile creeping up my throat.

Shades of red spill over our holy ground. The vibrant hues come slowly. Pink-tinged fog, thick and blinding. A current of crimson. A ribbon of scarlet. Then, a burst of a sunrise flame. I scream as fire claims the trees and flowers.

Damien, I try to call out, but I make no sound.

Some unexplainable force holds me back, stitching me to the painting I preserved us in. I squirm against the magic that paralyzes me, the invisible restraint squeezing my body and tightening the more I try to break free. Panic turns me balmy, sweat seeping from every pore. Something's wrong. *Where's Damien?* I attempt to call his name again, but my throat strains.

A dark-winged figure emerges from the fire with glowing eyes. *Am I about to die?* My eyes water and I silently beg, pleading for my life. Only the creature doesn't make its way towards me. The smoke clears, and the monster towers over Damien.

Damien.

He's unmoving as the winged creature strikes him with a whip. The snapping sound makes my insides twist. Damien lets out a cry, but he's too weak to defend himself. He takes the lashing, his nails raking through the dirt as the hook of the whip tears into his back. My mouth stretches wide, but I can't scream. The demon strikes like a viper, over and over. My throat burns the more I try to call out. The whip mangles Damien's back, cutting into his muscle and tendon. His abuser doesn't offer any mercy. He only stops when Damien is barely breathing.

The hold over me breaks for a second, and I gasp for air. I thrust forward, but the vines spilling from the trees grab me by the wrist, pulling me back. Thorns bite into my skin as I wrench my limbs. I'm helpless, my voice still trapped in my throat.

This is all my fault. Damien said he would be punished for meddling with me. I'm sure our kiss has only made it worse. His father warned him he had no right to get involved. *His father.*

I blink through the smoke, attempting to get a clearer look. The creature attacking Damien isn't a demon at all. It's an *angel.* An angel with black wings, just like him. I see it now. They have the same strong bone structure and golden eyes, but his father is raven-haired instead of blonde. I remember him from that day in the forest.

My rage burgeons, swelling like an exorcism begging to come out. Although the angels' magic binds me, my spine arches and my chest rasps with rapid breaths. I pull on the constraints using all my strength, and in my fury, I finally snap the vines. I gasp. As I'm released from the glamour, Damien's father lifts him by the throat and slams his body into a tree. There's a crack before Damien slumps onto the forest floor.

"No!" I call out.

There's blood.

So much blood.

I roar, loud enough to shake the seafloor. *This happened because of me.* I look up at the sky, praying for the angels to take me instead. *Please, don't let him die.* When I finally glance back at Damien, his father is gone.

My body trembles as I take in our surroundings. Blood stains the pink petals that bloomed when Damien and I kissed, charred and blackened by the flames. I cut through the pink-hued smoke and sink to my knees as soon as I meet him. His wings loom over his body. Crimson blood trickles down his back, winding in ribbons across his flesh. My lungs tighten as I battle the strong copper scent.

"Damien." I gather him, propping his head onto my lap.

"Lila," he mutters. His voice is hoarse, barely a whisper. "You need to go."

"I'm not leaving you like this."

"Listen. You will only make things worse."

"Don't fight me." My voice wavers, brushing the matted hair away from his eyes.

He turns away. "Spare me this embarrassment."

Embarrassment? He's seen the darkest parts of me. Every part I hate, every part I've tried to hide. I can't abandon him now. "Swallow your pride."

His lids are heavy, struggling to stay open. "I don't deserve your help," he mutters.

"How could you say that?" Especially after everything we shared tonight. All he's done since meeting me is save me over and over again. From my nearly fatal fall at sea to the garden of my mind, Damien has always been there. It's my turn to help him now.

His body slackens in my embrace. He doesn't have the strength to say anything back.

"Stay with me." My heart races. I look to Luna shining through the leaves.

Luna. The Goddess of the Moon.

I have no idea if what the Devil said is true, but if Luna really is the one who blessed me with my power, I have no choice but to lean on her now. I rise, stepping into her light. All this time, I've been afraid of what I can do, allowing my chaos to overcome me.

But what would happen if I danced for love instead of fear? Could it heal instead of hurt?

In my desperation, I embrace the moonlight, collecting it and calling its power upon me. I come alive with a glow as we sink into harmony, like I'm a star in Luna's sky. With a deep breath, I center myself, beginning a series of piqués around Damien.

I spin around the glade, collecting the blood that stains our petals like rubies. It levitates, swirling in the air, the essence of Damien's breath and heart tangoing together. I lend it to the stars, making it shine. With fervent concentration, I use pirouettes to spin the rubies into bright ribbons. Lifting them to the moonlight, I offer them to Luna, and they glisten with a pink glow.

I stitch my love to each silk thread, my movement becoming a ritual—every allegro and adagio an act of worship. With master control, I dip into a cambré, and the ribbons pour into Damien's body, returning his spilled blood back to him. His back arches, and his jaw clenches taut as he bites back a scream. I try to make the process quick and gentle. He slumps to the ground as soon as it's over.

I fall to my knees, meeting him. "Are you okay?"

"Lila," he croaks. "Why did you do that?"

I wince. "If I hadn't, you would have died."

"You should have left me."

"Stop. How could I leave you after everything we've been through?" More importantly, how could he want me to? Didn't tonight mean something to him too?

"It was wrong for us to get this close."

What? My heart breaks as soon as it mends. "I don't understand. Why are you pushing me away?"

"You need to go. Now."

"No. I'm not leaving you."

"Now!" he shouts. It comes out cold and twisted, like my father's voice.

I shrink back, sinking into the broken petals. "You didn't have to yell."

"I told you to leave. Don't make me ask again."

Tears spring to my eyes. "Why are you doing this?"

"Because." His gaze narrows. "It's not safe here. Everything you've learned about Luna Island is a lie. The angels don't worship Luna—we worship the Devil."

"What?" I spring to my feet, stumbling back as my heartbeat quickens. "I don't believe you."

"I told you the truth. Now go!"

Shaking, I turn around and break into the woods. The dream of Luna Island was always a nightmare. I knew it from the beginning, but I didn't want it to be true. There's no protecting myself from the Devil now. Not when I've let the angels come so close to me. They know too much—about what I can do with my dance, about what I have done in my past. I'm vulnerable here, and I've always been a part of their game. I cry all the way back home.

✦

When morning comes, it takes hours before I'm finally able to rise. I press my pillow close to my chest as sunlight filters into the room, holding on to it as if it were Damien still in my arms.

Damien, my angel, who I love.

Damien, my angel, who loved me too.

Or was that just a part of the illusion? I'll never know now, when everything I've grown to believe is false. *The angels worship the Devil, not Luna.* It lingers like another haunting I try to outrun. I can't. Not when it's playing on an endless loop. It chases me in circles, dizzying me until I give out. And so, I lie here, with my pillow pressed to my chest, surrendering to the truth.

The pageant is a fucking scam.

I don't know what enrages me more, the fact the angels deceived me, or the fact they won't be my redemption after all. Or maybe, it's how I've been a pawn in their game this entire time. Clearly, Luna marked me, and it's turned me into a target. It's time to find out why.

Sweet air sweeps through the cottage, enticing me into the kitchen. The scents of maple bacon and blueberry pancakes waft around the room from the crackling griddle. Laina parts the lace curtains above the sink and opens a window to release the smoke before sweeping her hair into a French twist and tightening the bow around her yellow apron.

"Lila," she chirps. "Wonderful, you're awake."

"Good morning," I reply, taking a seat at the counter.

"You're just in time for breakfast," she says, setting down a plate in front of me.

Teal flowers decorate the edges of the cream porcelain, reminding me of brunch served at a fancy cafe. Instead of syrup, my pancakes are dressed with fresh berries and condensed milk. To my surprise, it's quite good. There's comfort in living to see another day of this—another day of Laina. All I have to do now is figure out how to best the Devil, and I can have this life forever.

"How are you?" Laina asks, taking a seat beside me and pouring herself a glass of orange juice. "I'm sorry the letter from your mom overwhelmed you so much yesterday. I should've thought about it more before springing it on you like that."

"Oh, don't worry about it." I brush it off, taking another bite. My mother is the least of my concerns right now. But Laina doesn't need to know that. I've already caused enough trouble during my time here.

"Are you sure, honey?" she asks, placing a hand to my back. "You ran away again last night, and I—I just want you to stop running. You can come to me, you know. I'm always here for you."

I smile, setting down my fork. "I know. I'm sorry. It's just—it's how I process things. But I don't want to run anymore either." I want to make this place my home, and I will.

She pulls me in for a hug, holding me close for a little too long. "If there's anything you need, you just ask."

"Actually." I lean back in my seat, untangling from her lemon-and-gingerbread scent. "There is something."

She tilts her head to the side. "What is it?"

"I—um, I was wondering if you'd be able to arrange a private meeting between me and Mother Marguerite at Petals Tea Shop."

"Mother Marguerite?" She scoots back. "Did something happen with the pageant?"

"No." I shake my head, placing my hand to hers to calm her rising panic. "It's just, the Starlit Ball is coming up soon, and I want to learn more about the angels before the big day."

"Well, what do you want to know? I can fill you in."

"I appreciate that, but I thought it would be cool to hear it right from Mother Marguerite. You know, since she lives in the commune."

"Um, well, I am on the pageant committee." She mulls it over. "I guess I could try to pull a few strings. But it's rare for Mother Marguerite to visit town. *If* I can make this happen, you'll have to wear your best dress. Oh, and don't forget to bring a gift."

My lips twist into a smirk. "Don't worry. I already have the perfect gift picked out for her."

"Okay." Laina nods. "I'll see what I can do, but no promises. Mother Marguerite is a very busy woman."

"I know." I smile sweetly. I also know she'll make an exception as soon as she knows the meeting is with me. After all, I'm the one the Devil wants, and I'm sure the angels will do whatever it takes to make him happy.

✦

Just as I had expected, Mother Marguerite agrees to my invitation.

"This is a *big* deal, Lila," Laina stresses, finishing up my French braid with a pale pink ribbon at the end. She pulls out a few face-framing pieces, making sure everything is just right. "If I'm being honest, I'm surprised she even agreed to this."

"I know. I'll be on my best behavior."

"Here, take this," she says, handing me a basket of treats. I peek beneath the gingham cloth, revealing a jar of honey, fresh chamomile flowers, and apricot scones.

"Laina, don't worry. I already have a gift prepared, remember?"

She stops messing with the ribbons on my dress and looks up. "You can never bring too much. It's better to be safe than sorry."

"I'll be fine," I say, backing away from her fussing hands.

I smooth out my dress, then take one more glance in the mirror before heading out. The eyelet halter falls to my ankles with blue cornflowers stitched across the lace. Laina pinned a large pink rose to the center with different ribbons falling down my torso—lilac, peach, and white. It adds a nice shabby-chic flair.

She finishes off the look with a string of pearls around my neck. "There. Now you're ready."

With her blessing and a hug goodbye, I make my way to Petals Tea Shop.

A bell chimes as I arrive. Mother Marguerite is already seated, and the table is set with a spread designed just for her. She's stoic as I approach, glitter-dusted and smiling while I sweep past the ditsy print and floral tablecloths. The mismatched patterns are extra noticeable without any pastel-dressed guests to fill the pink velvet seats.

Sparkling gossamer sleeves cloak Mother Marguerite's slender arms, and a wreath of summer flowers ornaments the top of her head. She looks like a fairy godmother beneath the seafoam chandelier, decorated with tiny pink rosettes.

"Lila," she says. "To what do I owe this pleasure?"

I sit down, placing the basket Laina gave me onto the table, and take in the spread before us. All of it is bright pink. Hibiscus and rose hip tea, Persian Love Cake with sugared petals and green pistachios, strawberries-and-cream finger sandwiches, peach macarons with raspberry jam, and guava shortbread.

"I have a present for you." Smiling, I extend the bouquet I brought with me—white roses, gardenias, and jasmines, tied up with a lilac ribbon. They glimmer beneath the sunlight, just as unnaturally as they appeared in the garden of my mind.

Mother Marguerite tilts her head to the side, examining the flowers. "Wherever did you find such lovely blooms?"

My smile drops, and I fling the bouquet onto the seat beside her. "You tell me."

A wrinkle creases between her brows as she feigns astonishment. "I don't know what you mean, dearest."

"Oh, spare me."

"I beg your pardon?"

"Please. I doubt the hostess of the pageant would go out of her way to meet with any of the other contestants. That would be considered cheating, wouldn't it?"

She stiffens, sitting taller in her seat. "What do you want, Lila?"

"Answers." I'm firm when I say it, refusing to leave with anything less.

Mother Marguerite laughs before bringing a floral teacup to her lips and taking a sip. "The angels' secrets are as precious as treasure. What makes you think I'd reveal anything to you?"

"Because," I bite out, sinking my nails into the plush velvet seat beneath me, "if you tell me what I want to know, I'll go to the Devil willingly, and you'll have exactly what you want."

Her brow quirks up, and she studies me, seeing if I'll crack. I don't fold. I'm honest when I say it. I'm sure she can tell. After all, she's an angel. If they have the power to manipulate my mind, I bet they can read it too.

She nods, popping a macaron into her mouth. "Fine. What do you want to know?"

I smirk, cutting a slice of cake. "I know you know about my magic. You weren't coy about it that day in the forest. And if that's true, then you can tell me where my powers come from."

She giggles, as if I'm cute. "You really don't remember me, Lila?"

My gaze narrows, scanning over her spirals of white-blonde hair and pale green eyes. "Why would I remember you?"

"My." She fans a hand to her heart. "I was there the day you were born."

My teacup rattles as it hits the saucer. "You—you were?"

"I delivered you." She shrugs. "If it weren't for me, you would have died."

My father was right. I wasn't supposed to be alive at all. Something saved me. *An angel.* "What did you do?"

Mother Marguerite looks at me sweetly, brushing my cheek as if I were a granddaughter she hadn't seen in ages—someone precious who she once loved. Only I know better than to trust the angels. She doesn't care about me, and she isn't on my side. "I blessed you, darling. I couldn't let you die."

Blessed me? "*You're* the one responsible for my magic?"

"Not exactly," she says, reaching for a shortbread cookie. Crumbs fall to her plate as she takes a bite. "You were born beneath a Blood Moon. You were never supposed to survive."

"What?" I know the lore. No life can flourish beneath a Blood Moon. I felt the heaviness myself. If what Mother Marguerite says is true, it means my life belongs to the Devil. No wonder he's been haunting me, waiting for my return. Coming to Luna Island only gave him the perfect chance to take what's rightfully his.

"You're very special, Lila." Mother Marguerite hums, pouring more tea into her cup. "Luna breathed life into your soul and saved you, making you a daughter of the island."

I blink, sinking into my chair. "That's why my dance can create things here." Though, it isn't the dance that does it alone. It's *me*. How I feel and how I express it. Dance is merely the tool I use to paint with.

Mother Marguerite takes a long sip of tea. "So, you see, this is why the Devil must have you. Aside from his anger that you're alive at all, you help the island thrive. He can't have that. You obstruct the balance."

"The balance." That's what Roisin said during the Midsummer Ball. Everything is out of balance, and that's why the island is taking from us. Only I know I'm not the first girl the Devil has targeted. "What happened to Nadine? The Devil took her too, didn't he?"

Mother Marguerite's lips purse. She leans forward, whispering, "All I'll tell you is that he grew restless. He wants *you*, and with your gifts, you'll keep the Kingdom of Hell beautiful forever. Finally, our bartering with him will end for good, and we'll be free."

"What?" The chair screeches against the hardwood as I rise.

Mother Marguerite stands, digging her nails into my skin as she grabs my arm. "You said you'd go to him if I told you the truth."

"I—I will." My voice trembles. I'm not so sure she believes me this time. Her grip tightens, sinking her nails deeper until I cry. "You're hurting me!"

"Promise me you'll go."

"I promise!"

It's not enough. She reaches for the cake knife on the table, and I scream. Before I can stop her, she cuts my palm, draining my blood into her teacup. The liquid turns gold as it settles.

"Now I have it in blood." She flings me away before gathering the basket and bouquet I left for her. "Thanks for the tea, Lila. It really was a pleasure. Ta-ta now." The bell chimes on her way out.

What did I just get myself into?

A yelp cuts off my breath as I turn around, met with Damien on the other side of the glass door.

Chapter
TWENTY-ONE

✦

I stumble across the tearoom, racing outside. I've never seen Damien without his wings before. It's like a fever dream. In his human guise, his fatigue is more noticeable. Without his glow, his complexion is sallow and his cheeks are sunken, like rice paper pulled taut over his bones. Blue circles form in the hollows beneath his eyes, probably from a lack of sleep. I don't even want to imagine what his back must look like beneath his blouse—all mangled and cut with scars.

"Damien. What are you doing here?"

It takes everything in me not to thrust myself into his embrace or scream from the relief that he's okay. But he's stoic, barely offering a smile in return.

He lends his gaze to the sea. "I know what you're doing. I told you to stay away."

"I did. I haven't set foot in the forest since last night." My heart breaks all over again, holding on to the feeling of his skin on mine and how we entwined above the petals just hours ago. I wish he would hold me now too. Like a ghost, he faded too soon, and now his phantom touch lingers all over. Is it even possible to miss someone standing right in front of me?

"I meant from the angels." His eyes scold me. "What were you doing with Mother Marguerite?"

My balance wavers, the bite in his tone taking me by surprise. "I—I was just—"

"Are you trying to get yourself hurt?"

"Hey." I press up on my tiptoes, shoving him back. "I'm doing what I can to survive, no thanks to you."

His defense shrinks, and he stutters. "Lila, I—I—"

"You knew about the Blood Moon, didn't you?"

He sighs, looking over his shoulder to make sure no one is watching. But I know better now. The angels are *always* watching. Nowhere is safe. Yet he pulls me past a candy-striped kettle corn stand and several booths selling sea-glass jewelry, leading me onto the beach as if it were any refuge. While the sea used to be my place of comfort, it mocks me now—a reminder of my fate below the depths.

"Mother Marguerite told you about the Blood Moon?"

"Someone had to."

"*Devil's Teeth*," he mutters beneath his breath.

"This is why you've been watching me since I got here, isn't it?" Although I should be mad, I'm not. Damien knew I'd been marked by Luna this entire time. He was trying to save me, be the guardian angel he could have been. I just wish he had been honest about his motivations from the start.

His gaze falls to the sand. "I couldn't betray them, Lila. You have to understand. You saw what my father did."

The memory surfaces, and I blink it away. It was awful. I close the distance between us, gently tracing his cheek. The blue beneath his right eye is not a dark circle like I thought. It's a bruise—plum hued and yellowing. I never wanted this. How many people are going to get hurt trying to protect me?

"I can't lose you." His voice wavers. It's unlovely and contorted, like something dying while struggling for breath.

I come undone, rushing into him like a wave, and lock him in my embrace. He surrenders, melting beneath my arms. We hold each other there, in the silence, in the stillness. This is my refuge. He is my safe haven, and I am his.

"I'm not going anywhere," I whisper. I wish it were true, but we both know our story could never end this way. Yet I lend a bit of hope for the sake of his peace.

He presses my head against his chest, combing his fingers through my hair. "Of course you're not. We're going to run away to the stars."

"Damien—"

"I told you," he snaps, "Luna Island isn't safe."

Words dissolve from my tongue. There's no way I'm leaving. Not when I have Roisin to think about. Or Laina. Or anyone on Luna Island for that matter. Mother Marguerite said the Devil has been growing restless, and he won't stop until he has me. I'm the only one who can end this all. If I don't, he'll reap every girl on Luna Island until there's no one left.

"Be honest. What actually happens to the winner of the pageant?"

Damien pulls away, letting the wind drown out the absence of his words. I know it's hard for him. I know he's scared. I brush the hair away from his eyes, tender with my touch, reminding him that with me, he's safe.

"The winner of the pageant doesn't become Luna's High Priestess." He pauses, his eyes shutting as he confesses the truth. "She becomes the Devil's Bride."

I stumble, my ankles sinking in the sand. "There's no way I'm leaving, Damien."

"Lila—"

"No! Who's going to be there when he takes Roisin, or Amelia, or any of them? I refuse to let them pay my tithe."

"And I refuse to let him take *you*." He grabs my wrist, attempting to reason with me. It's too late for that now. "Do you even know what he does with those girls who become his bride?"

"The sirens . . ." *Of course.* The girl on the altar transforming into a siren *was* Nadine. It all makes sense now. Somehow, the sea gave her back, and I discovered her on the beach. During the Midsummer Ball, when I was on the boat, Damien found her and brought her back to the angels' commune. They laid her on an altar as she transformed into a siren. The angels didn't save her. I know that now. They were aiding in her transformation. Back to Hell she went to keep the Devil's kingdom beautiful once the ritual was complete. "He's going to use me to make his palace shine."

Like I'm some pretty, sparkling *thing*. Not a person at all.

"It's worse than just being an ornament, Lila. You remember that night during the Strength of Will when I saved you?"

I fold my arms across my chest, ashamed that Damien was there to witness that. It had felt like all my will had been robbed and I was made a puppet for the Devil's amusement.

"Yes," I mutter. My cheeks burn from the humiliation.

"It's like that. But for you, it'll be eternity."

"What?"

"It's a sham! The whole pageant is a sham. None of it matters besides what happens at the Starlit Ball. It's your dance the Devil is after. And with your power from Luna, you'll never burn out like the other brides."

"Burn out . . ." Like how they burn out every seven years. That's why the pageant takes place every seven years—the brides can only last in Hell for so long. But it still doesn't fully make sense. "Why my dance?"

Damien turns and faces the sea, studying the waves. "What do you know about our lore?"

"Roisin told me everything."

"So then you'll know that when the stars fell from the sky, they became dancers enslaved to the sea, making it sparkle. That's what he'll do with you—paint his kingdom with your body. Only because of Luna's blessing, you'll never burn out. Is that what you want? Damned to Hell at eighteen?"

I tremble, holding myself. Tears cloud my vision. My dance has always been *mine*. As much as I hated it at times, as much as it nearly broke me, I wouldn't be me without it. Nothing sounds more violating than sacrificing the most intimate part of myself.

Then I remember, I wouldn't be the first.

"What really happened to Nadine?" I demand. "You were there. You watched her turn into a siren."

"I tried to stop it," Damien pleads. "You know I did."

"What about when it's me? Are you going to let that happen to me too?"

"No. Because you will never turn into a siren."

"What?"

"Nadine burned out before her seven years were up because she couldn't handle it. And once a bride burns out, she's turned into a siren and made a prisoner of Hell. But like I said, Lila, *you* will never burn out. Not with Luna's blessing."

My throat breaks with a sob. I remember Nadine so clearly, how her sienna skin turned silver, scale ridden instead of silk smooth . . . how her angler teeth and moon-white eyes beamed back soulless . . . how the angels tossed flowers at her feet while she carved her body out on the marble. She didn't deserve this. None of them do.

I'm the only one who can end it all.

"He could've just let her go." It's not fair. Nadine should have returned home to Luna Island, to her family, to Roisin. She had a life, just like me. Just like all of them before her too.

"That's the selfish thing about the Devil," Damien says through gritted teeth. "He likes to keep what he takes, even when he's done playing. He collects them like treasures—his sirens, keeping Hell beautiful for him to enjoy."

Sand scrapes my knees as I fall to the ground, surrendering to the ocean, my fated prison. I hate this. So much about girlhood isn't fair. Why do *we* have to pay for this? More importantly— "Why do the angels do this?"

"You think we want to? It's not our choice."

"Is it not?" I snap. "You guys are the ones who keep feeding the Devil's lust."

Damien sinks down to where I lie. His voice is gentle. He doesn't fight me. "If we don't, then we die. Not just the angels. All of Luna Island."

"What?" My anger dissipates. "Why?"

"The brides are the only way we can satiate the Devil enough to keep him from destroying Luna Island. It's the deal we made for him saving us at sea. If the Devil has to be trapped in Hell, then we make it beautiful for him."

"Yeah, you make it beautiful with innocent girls."

"Lila." He reaches for my hand. "I'm trying to help you. There's no returning to the Heavens for me, but with you—"

"No!" I cut him off. "I already know what you're going to say, and I'm not running away to the stars. I—I can't." Not when I have the island to think about. I made Luna Island my home, and it still will be even after I'm gone.

"Please," he whispers. "Just think about it."

My eyes shut as I cherish his hand in mine. It's warm, my place of comfort. I never want to let it go. "Fine." I'll at least give him that.

"You have until the Starlit Ball to decide."

"That's in two days."

He nods. "You better think about it hard."

We linger on the beach, silent and unmoving, as we stare off at the sea.

I have to make a choice.

Run away to the stars with Damien, or sacrifice myself to Hell.

Chapter
TWENTY-TWO

✦

It's the day before the Starlit Ball. I should be getting my hair done or trying out new makeup looks like the rest of the girls, but nothing can break my tether to the sea. The waves crash outside my window, a reminder of how they'll gather me, stitching me as one with their tide. I always imagined that our merging would be beautiful, something I've yearned for my entire life. But as lovely as the sea is, it was never something I should have aspired to be like.

Wrathful.

Vengeful.

Chaos Incarnate.

I press my legs close to my chest, nestling into the plush violet cushion beneath my window. In just one day, I'll lose everything. My dance won't belong to me anymore. I'll be as good as sea-foam. Will Laina remember my face? She barely had time to study it. Will Roisin come looking for me like she did for Nadine? Or will I be a blip to both of them?

Just someone they used to know.

Or I can run from it all, hiding between the stars—a universe apart from the Devil, somewhere he can never reach me. It wouldn't be perfect. I'd watch the island crumble from above, knowing everyone I'd grown to care about died because of me. I couldn't live with the guilt. Damien's love alone isn't enough to erase that sort of pain.

A knock on my door startles me out of my position.

"Lila?" Laina's muffled voice calls from behind the door. "There's someone here to see you."

"Tell Roisin I'm not feeling well. It's the nerves." She already begged me to come over to test out looks for tomorrow. But I can't fuss with the pageantry now. Not when I'd only be preparing for my wedding to the Devil. I don't even have a dress picked out yet. What does it matter if I'm going to burn in Hell?

"It's not Roisin," Laina responds.

What? I drape a cardigan over my nightgown, then open the door. "Who is it?" I don't have any friends besides her.

"Come on." Laina gestures me forward, and I follow her out front.

Beneath the sea-glass wind chimes wreathed with roses is Amelia. Bright blush sweeps across the bridge of her freckled nose, the perfect sun-kissed flush to her summer glow. Instead of wearing her signature fuchsia, she's in a simple white dress with a crown of vibrant hibiscuses in her hair. In her hand is another flower crown made of pink and purple hydrangeas.

"Amelia. What are you doing here?"

She extends the flower crown to me, its scent fresh and fragrant. "I wanted to offer an invitation to you. I decided to host a dinner for the remaining girls in the pageant before the Starlit Ball."

"You did?" I hesitate to take the flower crown. She was nice enough to me at the Strength of Will, but that's because she was scared. She needed someone to lean on, and I was there.

"Oh, isn't that just sweet!" Laina squeals. "One last hurrah before the big day."

I swallow a breath.

Amelia lowers the crown. "Look, you don't have to come. I know I haven't been the nicest to you and Roisin."

"Amelia—"

"She would love to!" Laina cuts in. "Wouldn't you, sweetheart?"

"I—" I look between the two of them, unsure of what to say. It's not that I'm unwilling to give Amelia a chance. It's just if I do, I worry it's going to be even harder to say goodbye. I already have Roisin to think about. That's as much as my heart can handle.

"Forget it," Amelia says. "It was a dumb idea."

"No," I yelp. She freezes. "It's not dumb. I'd love to come. Thank you for the invite."

"Really?" She wavers, half turned to leave.

"Yes." I know she's trying. Even more, I know what it feels like to want a fresh start. It takes a lot to make peace with your past, and I'm sure she swallowed a lot of pride to show up at my house like this. I won't be the one to shut the door in her face.

"Well, okay." She hands over the flower crown. "Meet me at the temple after sunset. And wear white."

"White?"

She nods. "Clean slate."

I smile. Maybe girlhood isn't dead after all.

✦

The sun descends as I make my way into the forest, sapphire hues painting the night like a jewel. Lanterns flicker in the distance, guiding me forward.

The spread Amelia has set up is illuminated by tall magenta candles bathing the table with a rosy glow. In the center, there's a tiered cake with vanilla frosting, decorated with pink pansies, marigolds, and violets. Beside it is a summer salad with juicy peaches, soft cheese, and pitted cherries—a perfect pairing to the bruschetta topped with diced tomatoes. Different fruits are scattered across the table, sliced open to show off their vibrant innards—blood oranges, figs, and plums.

Everyone is dressed in white with bright flowers crowning their heads. Carmella pours sangria into crystal cups while Yvette helps Amelia string more lights in the trees. Roisin is seated beside Serena, adding tiny braids into her hair and placing daisies between the plaits. She looks up as I arrive, smiling.

"Lila!" She springs forward, thrusting into me with a hug. "I knew you'd leave your room eventually. Come, sit with us."

She guides me to the table, and I take my place beside her. It takes everything in me not to cry as dimples well in her cheeks. At the same time, there's ease in her contentedness. She laughs as Serena bites into a berry, staining her lips and cheeks with juice.

This is how I'll remember her—welled up in bliss over the simplest of things. She won't need me. I trust she can create magic wherever she goes, with whoever she's with.

I'll just be someone she used to know.

"I'm surprised you came," I finally say to her. "I thought you and Amelia hated each other."

She shrugs, releasing a sigh reminiscent of Laina's wistful ease. "Life is too short. Amelia apologized, and that's all I can ask for. We're not our worst moments."

We're not our worst moments.

That's what Damien said too. How lucky am I to be in the presence of such grace? Life is more beautiful when we let go of the hate, the anger, the pain. It frees room for tenderness. And here, tonight, the girls collect it like a ritual bath they dive headfirst into. Finally, it washes us clean.

It's Amelia and Yvette, running through the grass as they chase fireflies. It's how Carmella sets the table with a rose on each plate, a special offering for each of us. It's the way Roisin and Serena devour fresh fruit, letting the juice drip down their chins and stain their white dresses as the sun disappears and crickets come alive. It's the butterfly that lands on the table. The slight breeze in the trees. How the world stills and all the girls smile. This is what I give to them with my sacrifice.

Their girlhood in exchange for mine.

Amelia and Yvette rush to the table in a swell of breaths, their curls loose and rustled by the summer breeze. Flyaway hairs stick to their dewy cheeks, golden from the flickering candlelight.

"Lila," Amelia says. "You came."

A smirk tugs the corner of my mouth. "I said I would, didn't I?"

She takes a seat beside Yvette. "And here I thought you were just being polite."

"No." I glance at the petals sprinkled across the tablecloth like confetti. It's too hard to look at her when I confess the truth. "I wanted to be here." I wanted to belong.

"Well, good." Serena pipes up. "Because we want you here too."

"You do?" They've barely spoken to me since I arrived on Luna Island. I was sure no one would even realize if I were gone.

Carmella nods. "Yeah. What you did for Roisin that first day of the pageant was totally cool."

Amelia rolls her eyes, and the girls laugh.

"Okay, I guess what you did was pretty cool," she admits. "Roisin is lucky to have a friend like you."

I smile, just a little. "It was nothing."

"The point is," Yvette chimes in, "we're happy to have you here. You really changed things once you arrived."

I bury a nervous laugh with a sip of sangria. "Did I?"

"Duh!" Roisin gushes. "Come on, Lila. I doubt any of us would be sitting at a table together if it weren't for you. What you did for me that day showed everyone what really matters. What's the point of winning if all we ever do is obsess, and fight, and hate one another? I mean, you risked your spot to save mine, and it reminded all of us that there's more to life than just winning."

"Yeah," I say, unable to look her in the eye. "Winning isn't always what it's cut out to be." I've known that since the day I arrived. And now, winning will lead to my undoing entirely.

She's right.

All I've ever wanted was to win. Be perfect. Have everyone love me. What I never realized is that I'm most adored when I'm just being *me*. My true self is not the girl with the crown, or the flowers, or even the applause. It's the girl in the ruined dress. That's the girl everyone admires. That's the girl they want to be around.

Only, it's too late.

They laugh and clink their glasses, taking bites of fruit and cheese and flicking frosting at each other that matts their glossy hair. *This* is girlhood. And I can't take it from them by running away. They deserve these moments, this tenderness, their chance to grow up. If I go, they can have that. Everyone will finally be at peace. The competition will be put to rest. And the angels will never have to barter with the Devil again. Luna Island will thrive. All I have to do is go.

Which is the only reason I decide to sacrifice myself.

"I'm sorry." My voice wavers as I rise. "I need to leave."

"Wait, what?" Roisin grazes my arm. "Why?"

"I—I think I ate something wrong. I should go lie down."

"Well, I'll come with you."

"No," I nearly bark. "I'll be fine. You have fun."

"Lila—"

"I said it's fine." I turn to leave, disappearing before she can further protest.

◆

I had hoped when I arrived back home that Laina would already be asleep and I wouldn't have to face her too. She usually heads to bed fairly early. But to my surprise, the lights are on and she's perched on the couch reading a book when I return.

"Lila." She looks up. "You're home early. Did you have fun?"

"I—I wasn't feeling well. I need to go to bed."

"Well, wait." She rises. "Maybe this will cheer you up."

"What?"

I follow her into the dining room, where a large box tied with a satin bow rests on the table. It's a light seafoam color, same as the island waters. A wreath of golden flowers encompasses hand-painted angels and sparkling waves. It flashes beneath the light when I finally have the courage to pick it up.

"Who brought this?"

Laina squeals. "It's a gift from Mother Marguerite. You must have really hit it off during tea. This is a huge honor, Lila."

Breath leaves my body. I try to fake a smile, but I can't. I know better now. Gifts from the angels are hardly what they seem. I hesitate, reluctant to discover what threat she's hidden inside.

"Well, go on." Laina nudges me. "Open it!"

With shaky hands, I pull back the ribbon and carefully lift the lid. My lungs tighten as a saccharine scent unravels with the tissue paper—jasmine, gardenia, and rose. *No.* I skitter back as one of the buds falls to the ground. It still sparkles, but they've all been stained bright red.

Tucked within the box is a dress fit for the Devil's Bride.

I lift it from its coffin, and it glitters in the light. It's a curve-hugging bodice, ombré from maroon to lilac and feathering into thin wisps of gossamer. The sweetheart bustier is bedazzled with thousands of dark rubies that sparkle like angels' blood. It tapers off into a bright red chiffon that fades into lilac tendrils, curling like plumes of smoke. The flowers from the garden of my mind drape across the gown, starting from the right shoulder and coiling around the figure like a cobra— *constricting, constricting, constricting.* I drop the dress with a shallow gasp, remembering how the flowers tightened around my body and cut off my breath.

"Lila, what's wrong?" Laina places a hand to my forehead. "Your temperature is high. Are you coming down with something?"

I shake my head, stumbling back and grasping the chair for balance. "I'm fine."

"Are you sure? You can barely stand. Look, you didn't even finish opening the rest of your gift."

"What?" I glance down and part the tissue paper. At the bottom of the box is a mask made of red lace and rubies.

"It's for the ball," Laina explains.

"It's masked?"

She nods. "It adds a bit of mystery for the Angel of the Night."

"The angel of the what?"

She laughs. "The Angel of the Night. They're the one who crowns the High Priestess. While the pageant is a collective vote, ultimately, the Angel of the Night has the final say. Kind of like an official stamp of approval."

I drop the mask back into the box. *Great.* I won't be able to enjoy a minute of the ball while constantly on the lookout for my reaper. "No one ever told me about that."

"Oh, sweetie." Laina strokes my hair. "Don't worry about the Angel of the Night. You're going to do just fine. Besides, I'm sure you've had more dance training than all the girls combined. The final challenge will be a slice of cake."

"Yeah," I manage to say. *Because they've already decided I've won.*

"Come on, Lila." Laina places her arm around me. "Let's get you to bed."

Only, I don't sleep at all.

How can I, when it's my last day of freedom?

Chapter
TWENTY-THREE

✦

"I can't believe the ball is finally here!" Roisin swoons. Her dress blooms around her like a jellyfish moving through water as she twirls around the room. The iridescent pink underlay catches the light beneath layers of pale peach tulle. Delicate magenta flowers cascade from her left shoulder, falling across the bodice.

I sink onto the bed, brushing the white fur blanket at the foot of it to ease my shaky hands. As much as I've tried to go about the motions of my day, the Devil has already made me his, and my body no longer feels like my own. It's like I'm broken, unable to do anything unless he winds me up and tells me to. *Get dressed. Do your hair. Put on makeup.* It's all a ritual, my duty. Nothing else matters besides this moment. One more chance to be beautiful, breathe air, create magic on the tips of my toes. And then I'll vanish, becoming one with the sea-foam.

"Lila." Roisin drifts over, leaning against the bedpost. "Is everything alright?"

I glance up at her hazel eyes—color changing like the glint of an opal. I wish I could pocket them like treasures and take a part of her with me to Hell. "Everything's fine."

She takes a seat beside me. "We both know that's not true. Something's been up with you ever since you got that letter from your mom. What gives?"

I squeeze my eyes shut, as if I could disappear from this moment. Sweat cuts through my powdered cheeks, and despite trying to maintain my composure, I unravel. A sharp cry escapes my throat, forcing me to steady my balance.

"Lila, what's wrong?"

My sob blooms into a ringing, until all I hear is my own pain echoed back. I think about telling her. I think about telling *anyone*. But how could I? They'd only try to stop me. They'd never understand. All I'd do is cause more worry, and they don't deserve that. I vow to hold on to my grief, harboring it in the depths of my heart until it swallows me.

Even if I wanted to tell her, I wouldn't know where to start. How do you tell someone you love that you were born to die? That the Devil has followed you your entire life, waiting for the perfect moment to steal your innocence?

Through my tears I paint her blurry figure. Her face is ever present in my mind—milk-rose skin dusted with freckles, tumbles of rose-gold hair, opal eyes. I don't need to see her to know I love her, and I would never put her through what I have to go through. I'll do it for her. I'll do it for all of them. If I leave this earth, at least I'll leave knowing one thing. I wasn't perfect, but I wasn't bad. I tried my best. I did the right thing when I had to.

I am not my worst moments.

Roisin takes my hand, but she doesn't say anything, allowing me the space I need. When I've collected myself, I say, "I'm just really going to miss you."

She inches back. "This is what you're worried about?"

"It's just—" I swallow a breath. "I may never see you again after tonight."

Without a word, she pulls me into a hug. I fold into her, clinging to her scent of sweet pea and vanilla. "Let me ask you something," she whispers. "Do you know what true love means?"

"What?"

"True love is the one spell that can never be broken. Not by anything—hate, anger, even being worlds apart can't take that from us. I love you, no matter where you go or what you do, you'll have me and I'll have you."

A tear falls down my cheek, given up like an offering. "What if I don't want to lose you though?"

She frowns, taking my hand and squeezing it. "We don't have to go through with this. We can drop out before the final competition. It's not too late."

"No," I bite. "The island won't be safe until we put to rest whatever happened to Nadine."

She looks out the window, staring off at the sea. It takes her a moment to finally say something. "If I'm chosen, I swear to you that I'll fight like hell to defeat whatever took her. And then, I'll come back for you once it's through. We can be safe. We can be happy."

I hesitate, dropping her hand. How could I have not seen it before? There's still a chance to fight. Just because the Devil takes me as his prisoner doesn't mean I have to be complacent. I'm the one with the power. I'm the one Luna blessed. Roisin is right. Nothing can come between true love. And I love her enough to put an end to the Devil for good.

"I love you," I confess. Just like with everything I've been through on Luna Island, Roisin helps me breathe. With her, I'm okay. I'll always be okay.

I'll fight the same way she'd fight for me.

She giggles, wiping the mascara away beneath my eyes. "Come on, princess. Let's get you ready for the ball."

I take a breath, turning to the mirror. Dark shadows haunt the creases beneath my eyes—bloodshot and strained. Usually, my favorite part of a spellbound evening is getting ready for the event itself—a sacred moment just for me to worship myself with tenderness. As a dancer, I'm rarely ever kind to my body. My feet are typically as bruised and bloody as my palms. But when preparing for a special night out, I like to take the time to nurture every cut and wound, as if to tell myself I'm sorry—that I'm deserving of feeling beautiful like the rest of the girls. I should have been drinking more water, catching up on sleep. I've been so consumed by my own anxiety that I've neglected any self-care. But I won't let the Devil take this from me too.

I look deeper into my reflection, and this time, there's a girl deserving of all the tenderness that surrounds me—Roisin's laughter and our afternoon teas, Laina's warm embrace and home-cooked meals, Damien's lips upon mine in the twilight, and all the secrets we confessed between the gardens and brambles.

They love me.

They love me because I deserve it. Because I'm a good person who deserves good things. Despite my anger and my chaos, they've been there, reminding me it's okay to bleed out on the altar—that eventually, the cheers and audience will fade, and I'll finally have the peace to heal.

And maybe, there's room for the Devil to heal as well.

It's then I realize, our anger is not innate. It's something birthed that festers until it becomes us. It took the collected love of those around me for me to accept my past. The Devil was once an angel, and I was once a simple girl—just a baby nestled in my mother's womb. The same mother who makes mistakes, who's human, who's angry too. If I can forgive her, then I can forgive myself. My story doesn't end here, and neither does the Devil's. I will be the one to end it all. Not because I'm his little dancer, but because I'll be the first bride to show him love.

When I look back at my dress in the mirror, I wear it with honor. It's a gift to be chosen, and I'll own it with pride. If there's anything I'm good at, it's proving people wrong. I'll show Mother Marguerite and all the angels—

I'm no one's tithe.

Lilac gossamer falls like mist over my legs, allowing me enough freedom to still dance. Floral organza reveals peeks of my skin beneath the red lace, with rubies dotting the bustier across my chest. The flowers from the garden of my mind snake around my torso, and I reclaim them like Eve taking back Eden. These flowers may have bloomed in darkness, but they're a part of me, and they're beautiful. I refuse to be ashamed of my grief any longer when it's what made me who I am.

Roisin brushes a wash of terra-cotta eye shadow across my lids to complement the red tones of my gown. She ties the look together with a lilac-tinted blush, scarlet lips, and a golden shimmer across the high points of my cheeks. I pin a few roses throughout her curls, and she adds some orchids to the back of mine. We spritz each other with a bit of perfume and add one last mist of glitter across our skin. I finish off with a pair of pointe shoes, which Laina hand dyed red and embellished with rubies to match my dress.

"You look enchanting," Roisin gushes. For a moment, I forget about the Devil, and just enjoy the excitement of attending a ball with my closest friend.

"Are you ready?" I ask, picking up my mask.

"You kidding?" She reaches for hers. It's a light peach color with a large peony decorating the side. "I've only waited for this my entire life."

We laugh, helping each other tie our masks before linking arms and heading outside.

Roisin wasn't joking when she said the Starlit Ball is the biggest event on Luna Island. People gather in front of their cottages—whispering to one another, snapping their heads in different directions, cooing as carriages trot down the street. Everyone gapes as girls step out in their best dresses.

Even though we all have masks on, I've become familiar enough with the girls on Luna Island to recognize them. There's

Amelia in her signature fuchsia, with glittering crystals and a huge bow tied across her chest. The bottom of her dress fans into ruffles crafted like calla lilies, each silk fold airbrushed with a pink ombré. Carmella dons a guava-hued chiffon, spilling off her bronzed shoulders like water. The gossamer ribbons of her gown dance with the breeze, and the sparkling pomegranate appliqués stitched to the fabric make her twinkle like a moonlit Persephone. Serena emerges with the essence of a faerie queen, cocooned in champagne organza with a garden of maroon flowers covering her bodice and gold bell sleeves that delicately fall over her arms. Dozens of flowers lace through their hair— woven between braids, pinned throughout cascading curls, and worn as flower crowns.

"Let's go," Roisin says, stepping into the carriage that arrives at the front of the house.

I follow her, sliding onto the plush velvet seat. Hooves clack against the cobblestones as the sun dips behind the trees and we enter the forest. Chandeliers dripping in strings of pearls illuminate our path forward. Although I've been to the angels' forest more than most people on Luna Island, it doesn't become any less enchanting.

We exit the carriage once we arrive at the angels' glade. The forest glimmers like a snow globe, with glitter kissing every surface. Pink roses and bright marigolds twinkle with iridescence that casts rainbows over us. Starlights and pearls hang from the trees like goddess-strung necklaces tossed from the Heavens. A feast of desserts stretches across a long table lit with tall candles. I note some of my favorites—marshmallow meringues with candied lemons, lattice-spun butter cookies as delicate as lace, tea cakes piped with custard and topped with sugared violets.

Mother Marguerite waits by the entrance to greet us. I expected my chest to tighten, but instead I carry myself tall, smiling. She can't break me. I made my promise in blood, and I have every intention to follow through.

"Lila," she greets. "Don't you look stunning. What a lovely dress."

"Thank you," I respond politely. Though, I wonder if she can catch the sneer beneath my mask. "It was a gift."

"And what a perfect fit it is." She extends a silver tray with golden fruit dipped in chocolate, garnished with jasmine petals. "Here, have a bite of Angel Fruit."

I recoil, remembering how it blurs the lines between dream and reality. "No thanks."

"It's mandatory," she insists. "No one can enter without it."

"It *is* tradition," Roisin adds. "Don't worry, we all have to do it. None of us can leave here with the secrets of the angels' commune."

"Fine." Whatever I have to do to get away from Mother Marguerite.

I pop a sliver of Angel Fruit into my mouth, and the honeyed taste coats my tongue. A shiver blooms from my chest, thrumming through my body. I forgot that Angel Fruit is also a hallucinogenic. I stumble forward and collide with the dessert table. The colors around me pounce, turning bright instead of pastel.

"Lila, are you okay?" Roisin asks, steadying me.

I shake my head as her aura comes alive—a sunset pink crowning her like a halo. I recall how the fruit altered me that first day in the forest. My magic multiplied, and I was more sensitive to everything around me. In that moment, all I felt was bliss, so flowers sprouted at my touch with ease. But now, a wave of anxiety burgeons. Not because of the Devil.

But because all of the angels' wings are black.

They twirl around the glade, clinking glasses and laughing. The vision swallows me. It's as if every angel had been burned in the night, but they carry on joyously, like everything is fine.

"What is this?"

Roisin turns her head to where I look. Every pair of wings is ornamented in shades of night. Some flash with an indigo opalescence beneath the light, and others are flecked with gold or silver stardust. They stand out like charred petals, juxtaposed with the shimmering dresses that sweep across the glade. Every angel and islander wears a mask decorated in swirling designs, bedazzled in jewels, stitched with lace, or blooming with flowers. Some have horns or look like animals—swans, deer, foxes. The masks meld into their faces, and their glares gleam back like a pack of wild creatures ready to strike.

"What do you mean?" Roisin tilts her head. "Is something wrong?"

"Their wings. They're all black."

She laughs. "Oh, they're fine. It's all a part of the pageantry. The angels paint their wings black so you don't know which one is the Angel of the Night."

"What?" I falter, catching my balance against the table.

"Yeah. The Angel of the Night has black wings."

Everything is spinning, blurring, breathing. The trees shiver awake, each leaf blinking like an eye. Watching. Waiting. Preying.

No.

My chest tightens. It's a trap. It was *always* a trap. I shove past the ruffles and wings, perfumes turning me heady in the sea of revelers. I need to find Damien. He'll tell me it's just some sort of mistake, that he was never the Angel of the Night all along. My heartbeat quickens. The masks leer at me like monsters with fangs—snapping, barking, hissing. Or am I imagining that too? I run, pressing through the crowd.

"Watch where you're going!" someone squeaks, spilling wine over the gossamer edges of my gown.

"Sorry." I push my way through, dodging feathery wings that flutter in my face.

"Villagers of Luna Island." Mother Marguerite's voice breaks overhead. The crowd goes still, turning to the center of the glade.

Shit.

"Thank you for gathering with us today for this time-honored tradition. We appreciate every one of you who has competed for the coveted title of Angel of the Sea. It is with great pride that we select our new High Priestess—crowned for her beauty, poise, and grace—to serve our goddess, Luna."

The audience applauds. I scan the crowd until I see him. *Damien.* Even with his black-feathered swan mask, I'd recognize my angel anywhere. Tonight, he's fitted into a dark velvet blazer with subtle golden stars embroidered throughout. His wings are gilded at the tips, and a crown of golden ivy ornaments his white-blonde hair.

"This evening, the remaining contestants of the pageant will perform a dance before us all, and our Angel of the Night will crown the next High Priestess. Please welcome to the stage Amelia Everhart, Carmella Valentine, Roisin Kelly, Serena Beaumont, Yvette Montgomery, and Lila Rose Li."

More applause rings out as the girls make their way to the center of the glade. I keep pressing forward to my angel.

"Lila," he says, as soon as he sees me. He lights up with a smile, pushing past the crowd. I wish I could say I was happy to see him too.

"When were you going to tell me that you're the Angel of the Night?"

His smile fades. "What?"

"I know it's you."

"Hey," he says in a whisper. "Can we talk?"

I glare back, grabbing him by the wrist and shoving through the crowd. From the corner of my eye, I see Amelia begin her dance. I should be up there too, but nothing is more important than getting answers. I drag us farther away until we're at the edge of the ball, tucked behind the trees. The chatter and music fade into a distant murmur.

"I'm so glad you found me." He closes the distance between us, as if this moment were romantic. "Now's the perfect time to run. Come, let's go to the stars."

I shake free from his embrace. He's not Romeo and I'm not Juliet. "We're not going anywhere."

He takes off his mask, attempting sincerity. "Is this about the Angel of the Night? You know I'd never hurt you."

I don't believe him. I don't believe anything anymore. My lungs tighten. I step back slowly, as if he might lurch towards me at any moment.

"Tell me the truth." My voice wavers. "Were you planning on dragging me to Hell this entire time?"

"Lila." He motions forward.

"Get away from me!"

He falters, backing away like I'm a wild animal. "You're just scared. But the Devil can't hurt you as long as you're with me. There's no more time to waste. Let's go right now."

"I'm not going anywhere with you." The stars were just a ruse. He's about to drag me to fucking Hell.

"Where is this coming from? I love you."

"No." My throat strains as I hold back tears. Love is about making sacrifices, not turning someone into one. It lives in Laina. It lives in Roisin. It even lives in my mother and my father. But it does not live here. I break away and take off my mask, letting my tears fall. Damien steps closer, and I offer one more chance. "Tell me it's all in my head."

"Lila—"

We're cut off by sudden footsteps. I turn around, and my breath is stolen by the dark figure that sweeps away the light. I look up at the angel with a stone-carved face and raven hair.

Damien's father.

"I'm sorry, princess, but it's true. Damien was only trying to get close enough for you to trust him. And it worked."

"Father—" Damien protests.

"Shut up!" His voice booms as he smacks Damien across the face.

Damien recoils, tending to his jaw where blood breaks. I can't move. I can't breathe. It's all too much, my feelings coming in colors, flashing like the evanescent love that bloomed into its own garden.

Emerald, gold, and black.

Black, so much black. It darkens. It's cruel, drinking me until I'm dry and shriveled. The feral part of me screams to fight, but I can't. Not when my heart concaves and I fold over. It's too late.

"You're lying." I was so quick to point my finger, but now I beg to take it back.

It's just a dream.

It's just a dream.

It's just a dream.

I never wake.

"Lila, I'm sorry," Damien admits in a whisper. He doesn't deny it. Finally, it becomes real.

"No." My body racks with shivers. I convulse, shaking, sobbing, ruining myself before the king who built me up on a pedestal of pink petals and starlight. It was all a sham. Just like the pageant. Just like *everything*.

How could I think someone could see my scars and still love them? How could I be stupid enough to believe he'd take one look at me and not want me damned to Hell? I was right. I'm a monster.

Wrathful.

Vengeful.

Chaos Incarnate.

"It was you! It was you all along." I shove him back. "You dragged Nadine to Hell, didn't you?" What cuts deeper is knowing I betrayed my closest friend. I fell in love with the Devil in disguise, the same one who led Nadine to bleed out on the altar.

"Lila, please—"

His father cuts in. "He was weak. He tried to save her, but it broke the spell and made her aware."

"What?" His confession catches me off guard.

The angel smirks. "But with you, nothing can break the Devil's tether. You were made for him, and to the Devil you shall go." His grip digs into my arm, and I yelp.

"Lila!" Damien cries out. It means nothing to me now.

"Come." His father pulls me forward. "The show must go on."

Chapter
TWENTY-FOUR

◆

"Get off me," I screech, as the angel drags me forward.

He's so strong, it's like I'm weightless—nothing more than a curl of smoke carried by the wind. Damien screams my name, but it's drowned out by the crowd. They laugh as their masks morph with their faces—scales fusing to their skin, feathers sprouting from their temples, horns growing from their heads. Everything is spinning, golden light turning chartreuse and poisonous, swallowing me in a sickening neon glow.

The angel drags me towards the center of the glade, where Roisin is finishing her ribbon dance. She paints the wind with scarlet silks, staining the night with blood. It streaks the air with scars, cutting into my fantasy until it drains every drop of its life source. The sky turns pink as it feathers out, and I see the world for what it is.

It was always the Devil's trap.

It has been since I got here.

The crowd applauds as Roisin takes her bow, tossing flowers at her feet the same way the angels did for Nadine. She's just another tribute to them, a body he'll steal the soul from and string up like a puppet. And like the rest, she'll dance. She'll spin beauty forever, because to him, that's all we're good for. Just another body.

I yelp as the angel shoves me to the ground.

"It's showtime." He grins.

My heart pounds as I rise in the center of the glade, stumbling back as demons and animal faces gawk at me. Their leering eyes hunt from every corner, ready to devour their long-awaited sacrifice. There's no music, just the pounding of my temples and the ringing in my ears, claiming me from the inside out.

I burst into furious movement to complete my final performance, my dance overtaking my every motion as if it's happening *to* me. A startled cry spews from my mouth as something sharp pierces my back. I hold myself, grazing the tender flesh as black feathers flake from my shoulder blades like scabs. I gasp as wings split my spine. My nails morph to claws, my teeth to fangs. Like Nadine, I fall to the ground, scratching at my neck, my chest, my stomach, as if to cut myself open and free myself from the demon I'm becoming. It's uncontrollable, my body racking with shivers until I bleed, red spilling down my arms and over my torso.

If anyone screams, I don't hear it. Instead, I paint the glade in shadows. They rise like waves from either side, crashing into the center where I lie and cloak the world in darkness. The shadows dance, like ghosts that shiver up from the forest floor and waltz to my swan song. The crowd encloses around me, unmoving and watching. Silently observing. Like I'm the girl on the altar—Nadine—bleeding out for their amusement. I continue to dance for their inevitable applause.

Are you happy yet? Am I everything you wanted? Do you love me now? Will you tell me that I'm perfect?

Perfect.

Perfect.

Perfect.

"Lila." Damien's voice breaks from the crowd.

He's the only one I see, the only one who matters.

My heart races as I stumble forward. "I trusted you!"

"You have it all wrong." His voice is shot and desperate. "My father had my back against the wall. It was my duty to end this tithe for good, and I failed him."

"So that's all I was to you? Another sacrifice?"

"Of course not. If you would just listen—"

"No! I gave you everything." My voice shoots like an arrow, piercing the memory of it. *The fireflies. The pond. The bed of roses and how they crumpled beneath our bodies.* Damien holds a piece of my heart, not because he took it, but because I gave it to him. And now, I can never get it back.

"I'm sorry." His apology hangs lifeless.

My back arches as I growl, and the earth tremors, forcing Damien to his knees. Everyone skitters back, either falling to the ground or running into the forest.

"Please, this isn't you," Damien's voice shrinks to a whisper. "I'm sorry it's what I made you, but this isn't who you are."

Oh, but this is who I've always been.

Fury pierces my chest like a red-hot needle, stringing up a scream through my strained, hoarse throat. The bellow crests and tumbles over the forest, blooming into a wildfire—my own natural disaster. Everything from the decadent feast to the sparkling chandeliers go up in flame. The fire takes sentience as my anger reels, twisting and contorting. Flames climb up the lush trees like serpents, snapping and hissing.

Eve reclaiming Eden.

No.

Eve destroying the place that damned her.

The leaves scintillate beneath the golden light, blurring like an oil spill, turning iridescent and heavy. *Drooping, swelling, blooming.* They burst into beetle wings, my insect army that flutters over the land, reminiscent of the plague that fell before the Red Sea parted. Their sweeping buzz vibrates with the simmer of my burbling rage, taunting the masked creatures to unravel back into their shameful human selves. These creatures can't hurt me anymore. Not when I unveil them for what they truly are—mortals at my mercy—and I, a goddess incarnate.

Cries break out, and my fists clench, resisting a second thunder. It sits at the back of my tongue, a poison ready to spew. I rack my head from side to side, fighting the urgency, fighting the *wrongness.* It swells until my temples pound and my veins stretch taut. *Building, building, building.* I start to cry. And, as my tears fall, I roar.

Luna Island bursts into flame as my scream ascends higher and higher, wider and vaster, reducing the Devil's honeytrap into ash. Fire spreads like waves, fanning and rippling in a red-gold dance. It flickers hauntingly in the still, black night—steady and impenetrable. There's no one left to extinguish my hurt. No one besides Damien.

He stays pressed to the ground. "Please." He trembles. "There are people here. People we both love."

Something snaps like a cord in the spell.

I falter as my anger dwindles. I hate it—this vulnerability, the reminder that I can love. Why love, when it's only ever hurt me? It's wrong, softening me in the ways I never want to feel again. Being tender has only ever ripened me for slaughter, like a lamb with her delicate underbelly exposed. I led his knife straight into my gut, and now, I cry. The sky rains down, but not in the gentle way we crave. It's a hurricane, turning to hail as my cries sharpen.

I sink my nails into the thin gossamer of my gown, shredding what remains of the fabric. My blood dances with an unwarranted kinetic energy. I want to hit something, I want to break something—

I want to kill.

Damien knew it all along. Just like my mother and father. I would always make the Devil's perfect bride. They wanted me damned, trapped, a prisoner of Hell.

"You thought I deserved this," I snap.

"No," he rings back.

It's all an act. I know the truth. "You thought I should burn in Hell."

"I don't." He continues with his persistence.

How could I have been so naive? "I should've known you could never love me."

"That's not true."

I hiss, wrenching my head from side to side. He hasn't seen the worst of it yet. There's no saving him if he pushes me, and fighting only makes it worse.

"Leave," I demand.

"I love you," Damien cries. "Please, believe me."

I stumble back as that vulnerable, human part of me wins for just a moment. I refuse to believe his lies. He'll only humiliate me again if I let him. My nails sink into my palms, drawing blood that coalesces down my wrists. Lightning pierces the sky. My chest pounds fiercely, causing my breaths to expel so chaotically fast, I want to rip my heart out and crush it in my hands.

I'm not worthy of being loved.

I never have been.

The sea rises over Luna Island, stretching over the forest and curling inward, sharpened at the peak.

"Damien, leave!" It's too late now. I couldn't stop it if I tried.

"No." His stubbornness cuts deeper.

I squeeze my eyes shut, anticipating my destruction before it happens. "Go!"

I beg and beg to hold it in.

I can't.

I'm weak.

I scream—my throat turning raw as all my tendons strain. The ocean becomes my weapon, thrashing out of control, a sea monster created from my own self-loathing. The waters lash at Damien, slashing his body fervently. He cries, over and over, berated by my insatiable hatred.

One whip for your lies.

One whip for your games.

One whip because I love you.

Suddenly, his wails bring me back to that moment at the tree house, where I was helpless as he lay there nearly dying. My angel, my love. The guardian who saved me from myself.

Through all the thunder and bewilderment, his screams are what calms the beast within me. It leaves my body like an exorcism, and I falter, sinking to the dirt where he lies.

I tremble, examining the blood on my hands. I am nothing of the me I know, the me who Laina protects and Roisin cares for. My lip quivers as I trail my fingers over my arms. I will never be the angelic thing I masquerade as. I am uncontrollably, irrevocably, undeniably wicked.

That is why Damien could never love me.

Damien.

The rain pours, and my tears get lost in between. I place a gentle kiss to his forehead.

"I'm sorry." My words can never make up for what I've done. The memory of this will haunt me, just like the memory of my mother. Her voice rings back—*You're a killer, Lila.*

Wrathful.

Vengeful.

Chaos Incarnate.

His eyes blink open, and he reaches for my face. "It's okay."

I can't bear his tender gaze. "No, it's not." My voice is small and lost. "It never will be."

He smiles, taking my hand. He's not angry, and I wonder if he could ever be. "We all have our demons, and I still love you, even with yours."

There it is. That word again. *Love.*

"Stop it."

"I love you, Lila."

"No."

The rain hails down, and I bow across his chest, pressing my forehead to his beating heart. Damien was right to try to sacrifice me. I belong in Hell. I think of my mother. I think of my father. I remember the lotus in their homeland, where all my ancestors come from. *Honesty, goodness, and beauty.* I knew all along I would never live up to their ideals.

I may be beautiful, but I'm not honest, and I've never been good.

The ocean rises inch by inch, climbing high into the sky until its shadow blocks out any moonlight. What a disgrace I must be to Luna. I command the waves to shield me with every breath. It's time to finish what I started.

"What are you doing?" Damien rasps, sitting up. "You're going to wipe out the island."

Of course I am.

Wrathful.

Vengeful.

Chaos Incarnate.

"You're right." My chest contracts. "The Devil wanted a bride, but it looks like he's going to get a Queen of Hell."

"Lila—"

Screams break out as my natural disasters consume the island, a tsunami and a hurricane dancing a pas de deux. The rain and sea entwine, cascading over the forest.

Damien slips out from my reach, washed away by the wave that brought Hell to Luna Island. I trudge through the flooded woods and race to the sea. The embers coursing through my blood multiply, popping with a firecracker sensation. The ringing in my ears drowns out Damien's voice, reaching for me like a faint whisper, but all I hold on to is that strenuous zing. I won't let him have me. I don't deserve him anymore. My heartbeat quickens as I break off into the darkness, engulfed in my destruction.

The Devil was right.

I'm not capable of love, or being loved. I never belonged to this world, nor can I indulge in the earthly pleasures of affection. But I would rather die loveless than to end up as the Devil's Bride. The Kingdom of Hell will be mine, my own haven beneath the sea to create the oasis I could never have here. Perhaps I'll fade into a legend—the girl who lives beneath the sea, the monster that guards the underworld with all the other women who were scorned. There, we'll hide. In the darkness. In our pain.

Nothing else can hurt us now.

My breaths rush out as I dash closer to the shore. Curse this stupid, wicked place. Curse these angels and devils and the people I mistakenly thought could love me. I break onto the beach, as if I could outrun the memory of how it felt for them to care. The Devil haunts me with every step.

You were willing to kill when someone didn't love you enough.

You slit the flesh that gave you life when you felt unpretty, unworthy, unspecial.

You're a vain, twisted girl.

I don't belong here. I never did. I will never be nurturing like Laina or compassionate like Roisin. I finally face the truth. My glory, my praise, meant more than the life of my own mother. Her blood on my fingertips haunts me, even now. I hate myself for who I've become. Or rather, who I've always been deep down.

Wrathful.

Vengeful.

Chaos Incarnate.

I rip my pointe shoes from my feet and welcome a cool rush of sea-foam. My hair spills over my face as I surrender to the sea, falling to my knees and pressing my face into the damp shore.

"I just wanted them to love me," I whisper.

The ocean veils me from the outside world. I hold my shivering body, as if to shrink into a shell of my own flesh and slip away.

Luna Island is destroyed.

All that's left is the ocean. My ocean. The one I possessed with my heartbreak. I weep into the sea, attempting to rid myself of the remaining pain. Only, the release never comes. I glance up, drowning in the nightmare I created. *I did this.* I curse myself, wishing I were normal, wishing my darkness were contained.

I imagine Luna now, looming down from her kingdom of starlight. The angels from above can't bear what I've done. They cry diamonds of water that mists my skin. My tears spill with theirs, as the Heavens shame me for losing my temper.

I am no Daughter of Luna.

I belong in Hell.

The waves dance to the melody of my racing heart, rising and crashing, pouncing like titans coming to reclaim the earth. It terrifies me—the power that I have to possess and command. Though, it doesn't drown the world this time. The civilization I knew is already destroyed.

Instead, the waves swallow me, drawing me into the mouth of the Devil.

Chapter
TWENTY-FIVE

◆

The sinking is evanescent, a cool rush of relief. My skin melts into the ocean as I slowly shed my human essence. Angelfish nip at me, their kisses eating away until I'm as weightless as a spirit pulled by the tide.

Come to me, the Devil says.

Come to me.

Finally, I do.

His seafoam fingertips coax me forward with their feathery touch. It's gentle, until it blooms with wild heat. My eyes spring open as I'm greeted by the sea fires of Hell.

A churning undertow pulls me towards wrought iron gates that part before a gilded castle. It's mystic, not sculpted with brick and stone. No. It spirals in organic tendrils, coral twisting like wildfire at the bottom of the sea. Flames paint everything in a rosy glow. Metallic laurel leaves and water lilies sprout from the tops of the glass-blown palace, moving to the push and pull of the tide. It's lit up like a lantern from the inside out, a faint glow emanating between the twists and coils of the coral.

It's nothing like I imagined it'd be.

In fact, it's beautiful.

As I enter, my heart swells with a love so fragile, it shatters as I exhale. Statues of half-dressed naiads hold candles in their palms, illuminating the blackened waters. Every inch shimmers gold, with dim candlelight painting the hollows in flickering shadows. Vines grow through the crevices, coiling around marble pillars like serpents.

It's more wonderful than any dream I could have orchestrated. Tall windows built from iridescent glass cast rainbows across the hall, accented with golden brocade, curving and coiling like ribbons around seashells sparkling with opals. Candelabras cast warm reflections in the mirrors crested with ivy, bathing me in sienna light.

To my surprise, I look like me—ruby eyes and raven hair, not a monster like I thought. Though, my dress is shredded, revealing only the lilac underlay that gleams nearly white. A thin stretch of floral organza barely conceals my chest, dotted with a few remaining crystals. Chantilly lace hugs my hips, tapering into faint-purple gossamer cascading over my legs.

A glimmer of laughter tickles my ears. I round the corner to a grotto. Aureoles of light fractal into veins on the cove, dancing to the beat of the waves. But even more beautiful are the creatures the haven harbors. Sirens at play, bathing beneath waterfalls with their breasts hidden by pearly shells. Honeyed music spills from their blossoming lips, calling me forward.

Mistress, they whisper. *Lie with us.*

I follow their call, entering the grotto. They frolic to me and offer gifts. The first is a veil, decorated with starlike appliqué, crowned to my head in a cluster of pearls. The next are makeups pressed in seashells that they brush across my face—blush and rouge and shimmers. The last gift steals my breath. A pearl ring that coils around my finger and up my wrist in a wreath of gilded laurel and lilies, just like the ones that ornament the castle. It shackles me like a promise.

The sirens pull me through a tunnel, and everything darkens. They hold my veil, and I float like a ghost to an empty ballroom. It's dark and simple, lacking the decadence of the rest of the palace.

"Lila, you made it."

I shudder, glancing up at the angel who appears at the top of the stairs.

No.

I blink, pinching my skin as I lose sense between dream and reality.

Damien?

My heartbeat quickens. I want to run to him, fill the space that separates us and fall to my knees, begging for forgiveness. But I hold it together, protecting my pride. He's so poised. As he emerges, I notice there's something different about him. His aura beams gold—dandelion hair and bronze skin. He concentrates on me with hauntingly verdant eyes, a deep dark green, not the lively viridescent I fondly recall. Yet, I'm bewitched by his dreamspell, and I fall for it the way I always do. *My angel. My love.*

I run to him.

"Damien." He gathers me, and I fall to pieces in his embrace. It's coming home. It's safety. My lungs relax, and I'm free from everything—loathing, guilt, and fear. "I thought I'd never see you again."

"Oh, Lila." He strokes the back of my head, running his fingers through my hair. "We were meant for each other. I could never leave you."

I press my head to his beating heart. He's alive, living and breathing and mine. I'm through fighting. All I need is right here.

"What is this place?" I ask.

"This is our oasis, my gift to you. As soon as we are wed, you will be my queen, and you can make anything you dream of here." He pulls me close, a breath away from my lips. "Here, we are safe from the outside world. No one can stop us. Nothing can hurt us."

I breathe a sigh of relief. All of it can end. It doesn't matter if I build or destroy. This is my playground. A perfect paradise just for me. "I don't know what to say."

"Then don't say anything. Just dance with me."

"What?"

"Dance with me," he commands. With a wave of his wrist, candelabras flicker to life with flames.

The sirens begin singing, gentle hums that harmonize into a vocal orchestra. It's haunting and beautiful, an overtone of voices, both high and low. It's like harps and whispers. Harps and whispers and feathers. Twinkles of stars, twinkles of high-pitched hiccups that float above their tongues. The lullaby awakens a euphoria I have never known. Damien's eyes twinkle, sparkling like emeralds.

"Of course I'll dance with you," I say. I'd slit my own throat for him. I'd eat my own tongue and forever be speechless. But, of course, only if he wanted me to.

He smiles.

I take his hand and melt into honey and heat. Honey and heat and rose-blushed cheeks, swelling from our fervent movement. We fit together like the sun and moon, twirling around our own sacred universe. In the rapture, we fade into a rush, a blur—a holographic vision, ever changing behind a veil of rose-gold glass.

I focus on the way my palm fits into his hand, a simple pleasure aroused within me. Maybe, that's where the magic comes from. His beating heart, his hand in mine. He twirls me around the ballroom, and I come alive like a mirrorball, radiating my glow across the dance floor.

I'm passive in his possession as he arches my back and sweeps me across the marble, like a wind-up doll in a music box that bends to his control. Nothing matters when I'm in his embrace. Not technique or form or grace. It overcomes me and it's intrinsic, my beauty spilling like blood in the form of golden light.

Blooming.

Blooming.

Blooming.

Until the world explodes in a kaleidoscope.

Sea-foam peaks spiral into pillars of a dulcet green glow veined with gold. Ocean flowers sprout from the ceiling, glass-like and glittering—white-plumed anemones, violet beach peas, blue water hyacinths. Golden laurel leaves fill the space in between the blossoms, curling into a chandelier that blooms into an iris. It's mesmerizing, artwork birthed from my body.

Suddenly, an expanding pressure swells in my chest and rushes to my head.

I waver, and Damien steadies me. "Is everything alright, my dear?"

My vision swirls into a glittering haze of soft gold and champagne. The flowers fractal into orbs of light, blue-green bubbles floating in slow motion. Damien's figure blurs, doubling in a mirage of chartreuse and emerald. The neon colors pulse to the rhythm of my pounding heart. *Blooming, blooming, blooming.* I release a cry as they burst into twinkles.

Everything snaps and I awaken, suddenly aware of the magic taken from me.

My beauty.

My power.

Whatever spell I was under shatters.

No.

It's just a dream. Just like everything. Nothing perfect is ever mine to keep. My heart races, and I see the Devil for who he is. He has all the beauty of an angel—a chiseled face and a faint glow. But there's something wrong about him. A rawness that never melted down. His smile is crooked, forged by a false sense of happiness. Though, he is undeniably enthralling. Golden hair and sharpened bones. Fox-like eyes that trail my body as if it's for show. Silently undressing me. Ready to pounce. In another world, I might have let him.

I smile, fawning naivety as he takes a step closer. His red lips part with a grin as he brushes a weft of hair over my shoulder. I shiver as he trails my bare skin. His touch is delicate, careful not to startle me as my breathing hitches. Slowly, his fingers trace the vulnerable part of my throat, grazing gently instead of drawing blood. He's careful in his movements, taking his time, awakening my senses until I let out a kitten cry. His hand perches beneath my chin. Our eyes lock, trapped in honeyed heat, as his thumb strokes the fullness of my bottom lip.

"You're immaculate," he says. His voice is lush and dark. I tense, trying not to tremble as his tether possesses me. It becomes harder when he whispers, "I have never seen such a beautiful girl."

Electric shivers rattle my bones. My knees slacken, and he stabilizes my balance.

I refuse to give him the upper hand.

I press my palm against his chest, grazing right where his blouse parts. My eyes turn doe-like with wonder, honoring his beauty and tending his fragile ego. "Are we to be married now? I can't wait a moment longer."

He grins. "Soon, coquette."

I move my hand up to his neck. Not slow and delicate like he was with me. But feral, delicious, wanting. "I need you." I nearly pant.

That's it. That's enough to make him tick. He drinks me in like nectar, a sweet ambrosia brewed just for him. "Come," he says, offering his arm.

We make our way through the ballroom before turning into a hall that reeks of decay. The mildew scent hangs heavy in the air. It's less beautiful here. Or maybe, it's a sign that the glamour has faded. Is this what this place truly is? Nadine's remaining magic wanes. It's more cave than castle now, with algae and sea growths sprouting in crevices and drooping from above. It's humid, like a wet, breathing tongue.

We enter the belly of the beast. A throne room of some sort? It sits upon a balcony. The cave-like walls trail into a domed stained glass ceiling. Citrine, ruby, and amber mosaics trap me in his doll-house. We stop before a velvet throne. There's an altar too. It's marble and overtaken by kelp. On top of it are two crowns nestled atop plush pillows. A tiara for me. A crown for him. I scan the other ritualistic objects, remembering that this is Hell. Of course, a wedding here is far from traditional. There's a single red rose with thorns. A crystal bowl filled with water. A vial of something golden.

I peer over the balcony the throne room sits on. Below us is a sea of red. Water? Blood? Lava? Whatever it is, the sirens won't go near it.

I look at the Devil. "Is there not a witness for the wedding?"

"No." He takes my hands. "This moment is sacred. We can't let the others see."

I swallow a breath, squeezing his palms to steady myself. It suddenly becomes intimate and less like a game.

"Of course." I offer my sweetest grin.

This pleases him. "You really are heaven's desire."

My lashes flutter. "Just for you."

He slowly gathers my hair, bringing it across my chest. His fingers comb my raven locks, savoring each curl. *His little doll.* A subtle gasp parts my lips. *You're mine*, he says with each caress. *All of you.*

I play my part, keeping my composure with a smile ever present on my face.

"Let's begin," he says.

The bowl, the water, the rose . . . it all reminds me so much of the ritual I partook in to enter the pageant. The angels were always grooming me for slaughter. And here, before the Devil, I'm the real sacrifice. Not the jewelry or the crystals or the petals we gave up. No.

My beauty.

My faith.

My grace.

Laid out before a king like an offering.

He takes the rose before pricking his thumb on the thorn and drawing blood into the water. It feathers out, turning pink. Without permission, he takes my hand and does the same.

"What does the water symbolize?" I ask.

"Your baptism."

"Pardon?" We're in Hell, after all.

"Your baptism into our oneness. I worship you and you worship me—each of us the divine master to the other's heart. You please me, and in return, I make you my queen." He leans closer, whispering, "Whatever your deepest desire is, no matter how wild, you can have it here."

I shudder. It's all a trap. The only magic here is mine. And if he steals my will, would it be enough to manipulate me into forgetting my power is my own? I won't let that happen. But it's too soon to strike. If I want the crown, we need to marry first.

And so, I nod. "How romantic."

He dips his bloodied thumb into the water and smears it across my forehead. It drips slowly, spilling over the bridge of my nose, my lashes, my cheeks. He motions for me to do the same to him. I almost think it's over once I do, but it doesn't end yet. He opens the golden vial, dripping the liquid onto his thumb, still red with blood.

"Open your mouth," he commands.

"Wh-what?"

"It's honey."

"Oh." My lips tense, swallowing hard before I part my mouth.

He draws it open wider, generously placing his thumb onto my tongue. I recoil as the sweetened blood hits my taste buds. It doesn't have an iron tinge like human blood. It's dark and heavy. Like a current of wine. Cigarette smoke. Bitter orange peel or unripe fruit. What disgusts me more is how much I want it. It possesses me, and I let his thumb linger. He grins.

I pull away, ashamed and blushing. His laughter almost eases me.

"Your turn," he says.

My hand shakes as I go to pour the honey. Not because I'm scared to have my finger in the Devil's *mouth*, but because it will be over soon. And once it is, there can only be one of us on that throne. I need to make sure it's me.

With a wicked smirk, I part the Devil's lips. He invites me eagerly with want, drinking me in like salted chocolate, savoring my blood on his tongue. He thinks he has me. My muscles tense when he weakens, my power growing as his desire burgeons.

It shifts too suddenly. I gasp as he grabs me by the waist, pulling me firmly against his body. His hand coils around my neck, lifting my lips to his. My eyes shut instinctually, tasting the blood and honey on his tongue. The taste deepens, layered like spiced sangria. I want more. I want it so much, it consumes me. I press into him harder. He's ravenous, squeezing me, threading his fingers through my hair, ruining my curls.

No.

My eyes burst open, but I don't shatter his fantasy. Not yet. I come up for breath as his lips find their way to my neck. I tilt my head back, glancing at the stained glass ceiling. The upper hand is mine again when I push him against the stone wall, furiously feeding him kisses to satiate his hunger. He grabs my leg, pulling it around his waist. I balance myself against the cave, and with my touch, crystals start to sprout.

Citrine, ruby, and amber.

They form into points, my own glittering weapons. Once they're long enough, I snap a piece off. The Devil mistakes my destruction as rapture. I play into it further. Grabbing him by the collar, I spin us away from the wall, continuing our tango over to the balcony. Wisps of my gossamer gown pool around my thighs as he explores me. My fingers twist into his hair, pulling, stringing up his appetite until he begs for more. And, once I have him truly at my mercy, I jab the crystal straight into his back.

He cries out, driving me back. I stumble, colliding into the altar. The bowl of blood and water spills onto the ground. I steady my balance, toppling over the tiara with a *clink*. The Devil roars, and in his rage, he tosses it over the balcony and into the red sea beneath us.

"What did you do?" He charges at me.

I yelp as my back meets the altar's stone. I spit, ridding his blood from my mouth. "You really didn't think I knew about your game? You've been playing me since I got to Luna Island."

His laugh is different now, drunk and poisoned. "What difference does it make? I've already won. Or did you forget about my tongue inside your mouth?"

I snarl, shoving him into the balcony. "Actually, this time you were playing *my* game."

His eyes widen. "What are you talking about?"

I tug on his collar, bringing us nose to nose. "Did you really think you'd win so easily? I was blessed by *Luna*. The same goddess who damned you to this place." I shriek as his fist meets my cheek.

"Don't say her name!" His voice is a lion's, so vociferous, his cold, wet teeth sink into my skin with every word.

But I don't break.

Instead, I laugh. I don't know what scares him more—my divinity, or the mirth that tumbles from my lips. He holds his fist close to my cheek. The heat is violent against my flesh, but I don't let him sense any fear. I force my eyes open, focused and unwavering. Though, behind my back, my hand quivers, wishing I had the power to unleash the fury welled beneath my fingertips. I imagine the freedom to send him into nebulas with my hands, so slender and glass-like compared to his. Though, my true strength is not my body.

He doesn't know that yet.

"Stop looking at me like that!" he wails.

I kick him back. "Sorry, I don't answer to those beneath me."

He snarls. "May I remind you who you're speaking to?"

"Or may I remind *you*?"

"Excuse me?"

"You wanted a Queen of Hell. So you're going to get one."

Before he understands, the crimson waters rise to the command of my voice, spouting to the ceiling and shattering the rose glass prison that holds me. My scream unravels in fire, scorching the tendrils of gilded lilies and laurels built around us like a cage. As my voice echoes throughout Hell, all that glitters slips away, shivering into stardust. We see this place for what it is—rock and stone, rotting decay, algae and fish bones.

Pathetic.

I nearly laugh at the irony. This is what everyone wanted. To see me burn in Hell. For the first time, I understand. Here, I'm finally free to be the me I always have been.

Wrathful. Vengeful. Chaos Incarnate.

The Devil cracks, falling to his knees as Hell trembles. It nearly hurts to see something so pretty break. Though, I remember he never cared when it was us—me, Nadine, the rest of his sirens.

"Why are you doing this?" he rasps.

I kneel to where he lies. Not to soothe him, but to pick up the golden crown resting on the floor. "Look around. Your kingdom would be nothing without me."

I only wish the other brides realized the power they had. We have always been in control. This was always our kingdom to take, our power to reclaim. This world bends to us and us alone. If I'm cursed here, I will not be damned. This is my kingdom now.

"Don't forget your place," the Devil hisses. "You are my *bride*."

I press his face farther into the ground with my foot. "I was born beneath your Blood Moon, blessed by Luna herself. Which also means I'm the most powerful bride you've ever had. So powerful, that I can take away this magic as easily as I can spin it. Is that what you want?"

He doesn't say anything.

I bend down, whispering in his ear. "Or do you want me to dance for you? If you obey, I'll make sure that every arabesque, every developpé brings beauty to this place. I'll paint color into your night and build you worlds within worlds."

He glares at me silently. It's almost a pity to see him lose when we were having so much fun.

I laugh. "So, you see, I am not your little bride. You can't string me up and make me dance. I choose when and how I use my body. I am your queen, and you bow to me. This is my kingdom. I make it beautiful. And I am the Queen of Hell!" My voice erupts, causing the sea fires to rise.

As the infernos bathe me in lovelight, I place the Devil's crown upon my head, taking a seat on his throne.

"Yes, Your Majesty." He kisses the floor in a bow.

I had it all wrong. I was never like the ocean. I was always fire. And now, I am the Queen of Hell.

Chapter
TWENTY-SIX

◆

"What now?" says the Devil at my feet.

I cross my legs, sitting taller in his throne. "Wait for me in our bedchamber. I'll come to you when I'm ready."

As handsome as he is, I have no intention of consummating my marriage with *the Devil*. I just need an excuse to be alone . . . one he'll actually obey without a fight.

He smirks. For a moment, I wonder if he likes this change in power. "And what do I get once you find me?"

I lean forward, slow with my words. "Anything you could dream of."

This pleases him. "As you wish," he whispers with a bow.

Once he's gone, I waltz forward to the balcony and look over the boulders that were buried beneath the red sea. It's quite startling, seeing this place for what it is—all brown and rugged, coated in film and decay. Thousands of barnacles cling to the stone. The heavy mildew scent is even more prominent now, mixing with the sea's brine and rotting fish.

I almost feel sorry for him. Banished here, alone beneath the rubble and rot. He was once a star in the sky, emanating with all the love of the moon. How did we both fall to such ruin? In the myth I know, all the Devil wanted was to live—taste freedom, be his own person. So what led him *here*, reduced to a lustful, hungry creature that bows before a bride for even a sliver of her offerings? He was never the monster I dreamt of. Not really. He's just . . . sad.

I press away from the balcony and explore the cave he led me through. My fingers graze the damp limestone, caressing the fissures of algae and grime. Perhaps, I could spin it into gilded fili-gree—like at the Palace of Versailles or the Palais Garnier. Maybe he would like that.

It seems wrong, suddenly wishing the Devil comfort. I wonder what it would be like if I had arrived sooner, by my own free will and not a tithe. I could have told him he wasn't alone. Because I understand. I know what it's like to push away the ones who love you the most. I recognize that desperate desire to feel whole. It's unbecoming, ripping your soul from your skin, your heart from your chest, all to finally be *free*. We're not bad for wanting to grow up. It's not wrong to hate the expectations we're confined to.

Sometimes, when you love something so much, you hold on to it too tightly. I wonder if that's what I've done—with ballet, with everyone around me—trying to shape it all until it fits my life the way I desire. The same way the Devil strings girls up to paint his paradise.

I pick at one of the barnacles. It could be an opal if I transformed it. Maybe even a pearl. I wish I'd been here sooner. Now, it's too late. Nothing can excuse his sins. Can anything excuse mine?

I drift back to the hollow ballroom we shared our dance in. My screams have reduced it to ruin. The glass flowers I spun loom from the ceiling in cracked and jagged pieces, and little shards rain over me like powdered snow. A fallen pillar has shattered the dance floor, now cracked and split in half. I drape across a sloping edge of the broken marble, smooth and cold to touch. I used to think the world around me was fragile, that I couldn't possess anything without breaking it. But what if I'm the one who's fragile?

I'm the one who falls apart too easily.

What no one tells you is that even queens cry. Winning is like an exile, polarizing you from the ones who brought you up. *Was it worth it?* They'll ask. The answer is no. That's the thing about power. Having it means putting yourself first, no matter what the cost. Just like when I wrung my mother's throat for a second of glory. Just like when I punished Damien too.

I know how it looks. No one else would understand. I've lied, convinced myself that if I earned their praise, it meant I was loved. But that isn't love. In fact, it was never love I needed. Not from my mother, not from Damien.

I needed to protect myself from the shame. The shame of falling. The shame of betrayal. The shame that I wasn't enough. I barked louder so that they wouldn't bite. It only pushed them all away. It finally dawns on me. It's not that my parents didn't love me. It's not Damien either.

I didn't love myself.

I finally let it go—all of the anger I've been holding on to. It feathers out into frustration at the world that failed me. Why was I taught to make enemies instead of friends? Why was I conditioned to believe there could be only one? *The prettiest, strongest, smartest.* Isn't it just enough to *be*? I gave my life for a crown, and all it's ever done is destroy me. Anger turns to hate, and hate turns to tears. They trickle into the water, transforming into pearls.

A ripple shivers into a current. I reel back. Something silver gleams in a wink. A sleek fish tail. One of the Devil's sirens. I gasp as she emerges, and duck behind the remnant of the fallen pillar. She laughs, prying herself over the marble edge.

To my surprise, she's beautiful. Dark lips like two halves of a plum, glittering skin, and a deep set of onyx eyes. Black hair clings to her skin, falling past her waist. She's not a monster at all.

I know her.

Like a twin image of myself, she nears, examining me like her own reflection.

"Nadine?" I ask.

"Hello, Your Majesty." She bows. "That was quite an entrance."

It's hard to look at her after knowing what I've done. Though, I owe it to her to honor her presence. If I stare closely enough, there's still a trace of the girl she used to be. Large, deep-set eyes that turn up in a point, feathered with dark lashes. Strong arched brows that frame her angular features. And yet, a tenderness in her lips that swells fully bloomed like a garden rose. She's still lovely. More importantly, she's still herself.

"What are you still doing here? I destroyed all of Hell. You can leave now."

She shakes her head, tracing her tail. "The sirens can't flee, even if we wanted to. The Devil cursed us with fish tails after we burned out, so we can never escape his ocean."

Of course he found a way to punish these women further. It isn't fair. Haven't they suffered enough?

"What? No. I—I need to get you back to Luna Island. I need to get you to Roisin." If I do anything good as Queen of Hell, it needs to be for her. My true failure would be denying them the happy ending they both deserve.

"It's okay." Nadine closes the distance between us. "I can't face her again anyway."

Huh? "But she loves you. She entered the pageant again just to find you. Why wouldn't you return home?"

She hums and gently runs her fingers through my hair, as if to calm me. "Oh, Lila. I've been watching you ever since the Devil realized you were here. I know as much as you that you wouldn't return to Luna Island if given a second chance either. And why is that? It's because you're ashamed."

Ashamed? The word sears, burning in my cheeks in a flush of humiliation. But she's right. We really are a mirror of each other, and it goes beyond our looks. Nadine knows what it's like to have a part of you taken against your will, and how even if it wasn't your fault, you'll blame yourself forever because you can never get it back. You'll never be the same. She's not the same Nadine, and I'm not the same Lila. How can I face everyone now?

"It's different for you though," I tell her. "Roisin adores you. She wouldn't judge you for what the Devil did to you. You guys share true love." I think back to what she told me before I left Luna Island. "It's the one spell that can never be broken. Not by anything—hate, anger, even worlds apart."

She laughs, tucking the hair she plays with behind my ear. "If it's so easy to believe in true love, then why don't you?"

"What?"

"You're so quick to dismiss the idea that anyone could still want you after all this. But take a look, Lila. They do. They all do. I've seen it myself just within the days of watching you. Your mom. Your dad. Laina. Roisin. Even Damien."

Damien.

His name is like a knife twisting in my gut, a reminder of what could have been if only I'd controlled my temper. Why couldn't I just hear him out? Instead, the worst clouded over me. *Blooming, blooming, blooming.* Just like my magic does when it multiplies and explodes. I needed to assume the worst so that I wouldn't be surprised when it turned out to be true. I ruined everything.

"I know what you think," she goes on. "But Damien isn't evil, and he wasn't trying to betray you. He had to do what was expected of him in order to survive."

"Look, I get that you're trying to help, but I'd rather not talk about Damien right now." Or ever. It's better to forget it even happened.

"No," she snaps, sitting taller. "You need to know the truth. Damien was always against this tithe, and it isn't his fault the responsibility fell on him. His oldest ancestor was marked with black wings when the Devil reached for shore, scorching him in his pursuit for land. That curse has been passed down for generations, marking Damien's family as the chosen ones to make things right—ease the Devil's broken heart, and stop him from destroying Luna Island. Only, when you showed up, the angels thought you'd be enough to end it all. With your blessing from Luna, they saw you had a power that might never burn out."

My eyes shut as I drink in her story. The saddest part is I knew the truth from the start. Damien never wanted this. He was always trying to escape to the stars. He tried to take me with him so we could both be free of this burden together. Only, I fucked it all up, and now I'm here.

I fold my legs close to my chest. I may hate myself forever for what I've done. Damien was just trying to meet his parents' expectations. I, if anyone, should know what that's like. He did what he had to do to avoid getting hurt, even if it's not what he wanted deep down. I can't hold that against him. The same way I know he'd never hold it against me.

"Is it true that Damien came back for you and that's why you burned out so soon?" I need to know it's real. That deep down, he really did show up when it mattered.

She nods, collecting my pearl tears from the water and stringing them into her hair. "Roisin and I got into a fight as the competition neared. I started seeking solace in an angel. Little did I know he was the Angel of the Night, and he was only speaking to me because the angels had already chosen me as the next bride. Regardless, we formed a friendship, and when I got to Hell, I thought the Devil was Damien. Just like you, I believed I was safe here with my new friend. Only, when the real Damien came to rescue me, the spell shattered, and I burned out."

I release a breath as the truth about the past comes to light. Damien tried. He always tried. He never wanted this. Not for me, not for Nadine. The same way my parents never wanted me to burn in Hell either. They were always trying to protect me—from my future, from my fate. It's now that I realize, sometimes love comes out in all the wrong ways if you never learn how to do it right. The same way my love unfurls in natural disasters. A shallow gasp parts my lips. I'm not broken. I'm not defective.

I'm just unhealed.

"Nadine, gather all of the sirens," I command.

I know what I have to do.

She leads me from the ballroom and through the tunnel to the sirens' grotto. For the most part, it stayed intact after the kingdom crumbled since it's made of stone—one of the only parts of Hell untouched by any glamour. Faint candlelight illuminates the crevice, flickering and casting shadows across the rugged rocks as dozens of sirens emerge from the obsidian water.

They're radiant, with ever-preserved beauty, despite their blackened eyes and scales. Dainty pearls dot their long hair, which I assume are from tears just like mine. It breaks my heart and turns me warm all at once. It's a symbol of their unity, a reminder that girlhood isn't dead, not even in Hell. It binds them, and they wear their sorrow like a badge, as if to send the message that they're together as one.

The flickering flames paint them in orange light, and their scales dance with holographic rainbows. They bow, and it's better than any applause I'd find onstage, because for the first time, I'm finally seen as me. Just a girl. Just like them. I collect their reverence like an offering, recognizing the experience we share. It's an honoring, woman to woman, acknowledging we're both bound to ruin, tainted by lost innocence, branded as demons. Suddenly, the darkness isn't so lonely. It becomes human. It becomes a woman.

I heave, collecting their pain, revering it as my own. I recognize the grief they carry as tenderly as my beating heart. None of them deserved to be damned for wanting to feel beautiful, wanting to be worthy, wanting to win. They were girls with dreams—dancers, just like me.

We're all so young, barely even adults. I wish we'd known that glory is never what it seems. A crown, being perfect . . . none of it compares to genuine love. What if we had worshiped ourselves instead of some false idea that a goddess's approval made us worthy? We're all deserving of being admired, feeling special. Competing only brought us to the darkness. Together, we're stronger. The Devil would have no kingdom at all if not for us. And, if I don't heal, the cycle of abuse will only repeat with me. I can't let that happen.

I was wrong. I'm not fire and I'm not Hell. I was always like the sea. Only, in ways I didn't realize before. I used to think the sea was a beauty to admire but not touch, that below the surface, there was only violence, destruction, and chaos. But that's not true. The sea is also a life source.

Instead of burning out, being made to feel like shells of ourselves emptied against our will, what if we took the pain and made it beautiful? We are art. Living, breathing art. Whatever makes us special still lives within us all. I just need to pull it out of the darkness and remind them.

I kneel, honoring the sirens like sisters. We sit there for a moment, in a prayer to one another. It's okay. Together, we're okay.

"My sirens." I finally speak. "I recognize the grief that haunts you, the same way it haunts me. You entered this kingdom believing your thorns would be plucked, that you'd finally be viewed as a rose. But instead, your wounds only deepened, and now all of us bleed. You deserve to heal. As your queen, I free you."

"Lila, what are you doing?" Nadine skitters through the water.

Before I can answer, my back arches and my lungs seethe. I try to collect the darkness within their hearts, but it consumes me instead—rising from them in tendrils of smoke and cascading over me like gossamer ribbons. The dark gray threads entangle with my own tainted heart, and I yelp. It stings, it burns, but I never sever the connection. I have to be strong for my sirens, my sisters. Rage rips through my throat as I collect their shame and loathing.

Then, all at once, there is numbness.

There is release.

I slump to the ground, my crown falling from my head with a *clink*.

"Lila!" Nadine screeches. Her figure doubles, glowing gold and pulsing. "Hold on," she says, squeezing my hand. "I'm going to get help."

I blink, catching the blurred faces of angels looming over me, before succumbing to the darkness I stole from them.

Chapter
TWENTY-SEVEN

✦

"Lila." A lyrical voice rings out.

My eyes begin to open, and her face comes alive before me like watercolor on the page. At first, it's nothing but a blur of ink and water—peach and persimmon—a blend of soft and vibrant tones. Bright blood orange tumbles over me in a wildfire, coming to claim me the same way I claimed the forest. Instead, it's gentle. She reaches out, touching my cheek. She looks so much like—

"Roisin?"

She laughs. "You can call me Saoirse."

My vision wanes, blurring golden light and curls of pale green as I look up and take in my surroundings. The colors entwine like something gentle meeting—gilded fingertips on silk chiffon—blooming and bending, falling over us like a veil. They float above fallen seraphs, beautiful women birthed from every color. Their bodies glow, emanating between the braids of translucent emerald.

I place a hand to my pounding temple. My throat is sore and strained. I'm barely able to sit upright. Twisting black veins trail over my limbs, spanning up my neck and, from what I can feel, to my face as well. "What happened?"

Saoirse frowns. "You don't remember?"

I wish I did. Everything went black.

"You saved us," she says when I don't respond.

"I did?"

She nods, stroking my head with a tender hand. "You took away our pain so that we no longer carry it. But now, it lives in you."

I blink, adjusting. *Yes.* The sirens float above me with sparkling gold tails. They're as lovely as mermaids now.

Like Angels of the Sea.

They twist between an overgrowth of seaweed. We're in a kelp forest of some sort, still within the confines of Hell. The laurels and lilies hang overhead, gilded and shimmering. It must be far from where my destruction took place. Everything seems untouched. The kelp is healthy, the flowers a bright yellow gold. Nothing is singed or tarnished. It's a haven, protecting us.

I push up, steadying my balance against Saoirse. "What are you all still doing here? I freed you." I slump forward as soon as the words are out. My dagger-point nails sink into the remains of my dress. It burns. The darkness travels through me, moving like twisting black tar over my skin.

Saoirse places a hand to my back, motioning me upright. "Are you hurt?"

"Please," I mutter, "you need to go."

She shakes her head, persistent. "I can't leave you here like this."

"I command you as your queen."

"No," she says again.

"Why are you so stubborn?"

Despite my frustration, she remains patient. "If you don't get better, then the Devil will reclaim Hell. That's why we took you here, to hide you. He knows you're weak."

"What?" My gut twists, threatening bile at the back of my throat.

She nods, combing her fingers through my hair. "We heard him calling for you. Every shadow made us scurry. It will be any minute before he finds you."

My breathing hitches. Without my power, I'm nothing. I have no defense, no control. Everything I've done will be in vain if the Devil finds us. My likelihood of surviving isn't high, but the sirens still have a chance. If they're free, the Devil will have no kingdom, no more beauties to possess like dolls. Just rocks and a dying bride. That's better than all of us being trapped here. I refuse to let them rot with me.

I turn to Saoirse. "I want you to be free. Find the people who still think of you, if there are any."

"Lila—"

"It's a blessing to be loved. Even if you are at the bottom of the sea."

Nobody will miss me now. Not after what I've done.

"Funny," a familiar voice lilts. "Because last I recalled, there's still someone above the shore who loves you too. No matter how deep beneath the sea you are."

He emerges between the twines of kelp, and my eyes widen, tracing his familiar shape and the details I prayed to never forget. Ivory-carved bones that glint when they hit the light. Moonlit hair more white than blonde. Viridescent eyes flecked with constellations. He twinkles like a fantasy. Like a dream.

Damien.

I freeze. Am I hallucinating? It's the darkness taking root, teasing my fragile heart, ready to break me while I'm at my most vulnerable. I skitter back as he nears, shutting my eyes and forcing the apparition away. *It's just a dream.* I tremble.

The memory of his screams still pierces my tender ears, cutting me from the inside out. When I see his pretty face, I'm reminded of the blood that stained it. The blood I drew. The blood still dried beneath my nails now.

"Lila, please." He bends down slowly, careful not to startle me further. I shiver as he touches me, reminding me it's safe. With him, it's always safe. "It's really me."

"Damien?" I give myself a second to pretend.

He brushes his thumb against my knee. "I'm here."

My heart swells, filling all of me until I nearly burst. If I look at him too long, I'll cry. Even if it is a dream, I hold on a while longer. "What are you doing here?"

He leans in closer, tightening his grip around my hand. "I made a vow to you that night in the forest. One I never intended to break. I want to hold your hand when the waves turn rough and the rains run wild. If you'll have me, you'll never be alone in this again. So here I am, Lila. I'm still holding your hand."

My voice catches in my throat. I squeeze his hand back tighter. After every monstrous thing I've done, he's still here. He's *really* here. "I never thought I'd see you again."

"Please believe me, I never intended for you to be here. It pained every ounce of me to lose you. So much so—" He turns his back.

I gasp. His flesh is strewn with scars, crisscrossed and mangled as if a creature ripped the wings right out from his back. The wounds are still young, bright red and tender.

"Damien! What did you do?"

"I severed my wings so that I'd never be bound to my fate as the Angel of the Night again. Don't you see? I chose you."

Me.

After every shameful thing I've done, he still chose me.

"You sacrificed your wings for me?"

He nods. "You made me realize that love isn't something that should be earned. And so, I severed myself from the people who held their love above my head. True love is loving all of a person, even the parts that terrify them, and especially the parts they hate. I love you, Lila, for all that you are."

A smile overcomes me effortlessly. Not because of the praise, but because he really sees me. As a beauty queen, as a ballerina, and as the Queen of Hell too. Despite my demons, Damien still loves me. He forgives me.

Maybe it's time I forgive myself.

Damien tucks my hair behind my ear in that familiar way I adore. I brush my fingers across his temple, right at the edge of his eye, studying the depths of his irises—a vibrant viridescence, undernotes of the sea, chartreuse aureoles, twinkling into novas when they look at me.

I lean forward, bringing my lips to his. We crash into each other like two seas meeting, as natural as nature, as wild as the tide. Everything fits so right. We click back into place like we were always meant to find each other, our mouths greeting one another in that secret language only we know. He shakes beneath my embrace, and I can tell we're both scared, both vulnerable. With every hopeless kiss, we fight for freedom. We long for light and find it on the tip of each other's tongues.

I break away, but only to say, "I love you too."

Damien's eyes squeeze shut. He cries out, stumbling back.

"Damien?" I lift his face towards mine. His lips are stained black from the darkness inside of me. It claims him too, black veins feathering across his pale skin, dimming his glow. "What's going on?"

He breathes heavily, coughing like there's smoke in his lungs. "I was trying to save you."

"What? You can't take this darkness from me. It was never meant for you."

"No, Lila."

I spin around. *Nadine.*

She drifts forward. "I brought Damien back here to help. If he didn't step in, you wouldn't survive, and the Devil would reclaim Hell."

At the sound of his name, full and heavy laughter blooms around us. Slowly, the Devil emerges through the kelp. Blood rushes from my face as his shadow swallows me.

"So this is where you've been hiding." His lips curl into a drunken smile. "Not even a day into our marriage, and you've already betrayed me."

I step in front of Damien, refusing to let him get hurt again because of me.

"Our marriage was never *real*. We both know it was just a game." I slow my breath, keeping my composure. But deep down, my heart pounds and my mouth goes dry.

"It was real when you drank my blood." His breath lingers across my face. I tense as he takes one of my curls between his fingers. "It was real when you kissed my lips . . . when I traced your body . . . when you purred in my—"

"That's enough!" Damien pounces. I yelp as he yanks me back.

The Devil grins. "You think you've won, angel. But it's her tongue on mine, my blood in her mouth."

"Damien!" I shriek, as his fist meets the Devil's jaw.

Blood drips out from the Devil's parted lips, and his eyes turn into obsidian voids.

I turn to Damien, furious. "What the hell did you just do?"

The Devil's chest rises with rasping breaths; his muscles multiplying in size as his anger becomes him. His figure towers over the kelp forest, and his skin turns red with twisting veins. Breath leaves my body as he transforms from the handsome fallen angel to a beast I've only ever imagined in folklore. Horns sprout from his bulging head, blood spilling from his eyes and mouth. He roars, and wings of fire expand across his back.

"You are my bride!" His voice unravels in a thundering overtone that shakes the ground beneath us.

Damien and I fall back. The sirens skitter away in a frenzy.

I find it in me to stand. "You don't own me. I am not some *thing* to possess. Besides, even if I did have a choice, it would always be Damien. Not you."

"Lila," Nadine bites. "Was that part really necessary?"

The Devil roars. Fire blossoms in the water. I gasp as the flames rise like a tidal wave, hissing and snapping. They take sentience the way my anger did in the forest, coming alive in the form of a dragon. Its jaw widens, and an inferno ruptures from its chest. I falter, inching back. I've seen how my own rage takes shape. I know how it feels—so uncontrollable, you have no power over it at all. Even if the Devil did desire me enough to preserve my beauty, let alone my *life*, he has no influence now.

"We need to go!"

I grab hold of Damien as the flames crescendo, attempting to find a way out of Hell. He heaves as I tug us through a cave, and Nadine gets lost in the frenzy. It's pure darkness. We tumble into jagged stones, clawing our way through rock and rubble with panicked breaths. Light only returns as the dragon hounds us, fire slithering up and down, ready to consume us like its prey. It growls, nearly scorching us. Somewhere in between, I lose Damien's hand.

No.

I'm weak against the undertow that drags me farther and farther away. My muscles strain, fighting the tide as it grows more vicious, thrashing and kicking in pitch black. The current pulls me, sweeping me forward. I yelp, colliding with the rugged stone. A pathetic whimper cuts the silence as I start to cry. It's so dark, there's no hope in finding him now.

Just when I think it's too late, a body slams into mine. I scream as I'm swiftly pulled through the current. *Damien?* We round a corner, taking a sharp turn. There's light in the distance. My savior pulls us towards it, closer and closer to the laurels and lilies that light up Hell. They blossom like spring, exploding in golden sunlight as we near. Only, when we make it out of the cave, I realize it wasn't Damien who rescued me at all.

"Nadine?" In her other arm is a barely breathing Damien. His head lolls, black veins twisting around his neck and rising to his temples. He can hardly keep his eyes open. "You came back for us?"

"Of course." She pants. "Quick, move!" She pulls us back as the dragon rounds the corner and spews its flame.

If the circumstances were different, I might have considered the creature beautiful against the blackened waves—like fireworks on Lunar New Year. Only, this dancing lion is trying to *kill* us.

"Come on," Nadine says. "I know a way out."

She yanks us forward, dragging us through the water. Her nails bite into my skin as we make a sharp turn through the tangle of laurels and lilies. They twist and twine in their own unruly jungle, curling around rough coral that scrapes my arms and cheek. The cuts sting as salt water seeps into them. Blood feathers out, leaving a trace of me behind. The foliage tangles with my hair, shackling my ankles and wrists, tugging me, begging me to stay. *Don't go . . . don't leave me here alone.*

"I'm sorry," I mutter beneath my breath. "But you don't own me."

With my simple words, the spell breaks, and the laurels and lilies release their hold.

We enter the open ocean.

Damien gasps. Cool relief eases my racing heart.

Nadine pulls us back as the Kingdom of Hell explodes. It erupts like a volcano, painting the abyss with glittering tendrils as that imitation of paradise dissolves. I wait, anticipating the Devil to rise from the ashes, but the ocean is eerily still. He doesn't emerge. It's like he disappeared as soon as I denounced him. I give it another moment, wary of his reprise, but it never comes.

He's really gone.

I could almost laugh. The Devil has no power over me now. I wonder if he ever really did to begin with. Or was he just a fear, taking root and tugging? I pity him, thinking of the angel banished here alone. The same angel I considered spinning pearls and filigree for to ease his pain.

Despite overthrowing his kingdom, I don't blame myself for his undoing. His rage consumed him on his own. The Devil was wrong. He and I are not alike. He was too far drowned in his ocean to see any light, and so he took it from others. He used girls like toys and discarded us when we broke. But that's the thing. Stealing light isn't the same as creating it, and so he never truly had it. His darkness consumed him. *Blooming, blooming, blooming.* Until it went up in flame. If I don't heal now, then perhaps we would share a similar fate. But it's not too late for me yet. I don't have to burn.

"It's over," Nadine says in near disbelief. "We're free."

"Well, not just yet." I take Damien's hand, inspecting the black veins that wreathe around our skin, moving and growing like parasites.

"How do we get rid of it?" His voice rasps as he traces the vine-like texture. "It's infecting us."

"Don't worry. I have a plan."

"You do?"

I nod. "We're going to finally make our way to the stars. Right here, with the sea as our canvas."

He pulls back, releasing our hold. "I don't understand."

"Dance with me, and we'll light up the dark with stars so bright, we'll paint our own Heaven."

His eyes widen. "You're finally going to take us to the stars?"

I smile. "I am."

I pull us out from the abyss, rising closer and closer to the surface. The sirens follow as the ocean brightens from navy, into cobalt, into teal, and into aquamarine.

A pas de deux is more than just a partnered dance. Two souls. One body. Entwining together and weaving a story—evoking a sensation, a memory, a thought. I shut my eyes, remembering how Damien laid me upon the petals and joined his soul with mine. In the heat of summer, he vowed to love me, and we became a part of each other.

We separate, taking our places across the sea.

The tension pent up inside my body slips away as the darkness spills into the water. My dance was always powerful, even when I'm imperfect and fragile and completely surrendered. I know that now.

I fall into my adagio, weightless. Technique no longer matters. Instead, I'm passive to the waves, allowing the current to spin me in pirouettes. The darkness fans out, blooming like a flower.

As I lunge into an arabesque, my fingertips release a nebula. Stars explode across the darkness and create my own galaxy. I fall into a piqué manège, birthing stardust strokes. With quick bourrée steps, constellations sprout across the sea.

The water illuminates as I leap into a grand jeté, sending shooting stars as I fly. The sirens coo, and I welcome them to join me. They spin tendrils of gold into the darkness, using their fish tails like paintbrushes. As they circle me, the ragged dress I wear transforms into a glittering gown, reflecting rainbows when hit by the light. Finally, I embrace the angel I always was.

Filling the distance between me and Damien, I leap into his arms. When he catches me, his darkness feathers into the sea. We entwine, twirling in a whirlpool as the sirens hold us in a glittering lattice.

Damien caresses my body, dipping me into a fish dive. I glide my fingertips through the water, painting an opalescent sheen. The ocean comes alive with pearly radiance, reflecting under-notes of lavender and pale green. I place a palm on Damien's heart, extracting the remaining darkness slowly. His back arches, and I pluck the inky strands before chasséing forward.

He welcomes me back with open arms, catching my body as I leap into his embrace. Even without his wings, he makes me soar. We break off into an allegro, and as the ocean glows, we lose ourselves, forgetting dance steps, forgetting everything. Damien kisses me, and a Saturn ring bursts from our bodies, expanding across the ocean in a violet light. Constellations connect, and the sirens zigzag between the shapes in awe. Everything suspends in time, as if the ocean has stopped moving.

A ray of moonlight pierces the sea, so sharp it's nearly blinding. All the stars shatter at once. I yelp, squeezing Damien's hand. Stardust showers overhead. Beneath the sparkling mist, everyone transforms.

The sirens' tails turn to legs, freed from the Devil's curse. They become human again, their limbs fluttering as they rise to the surface. Damien glows while all his cuts vanish and his back is stitched together. The gold fades from his eyes, replaced by the brightest shade of emerald green. Real human eyes. For a real human boy.

"Damien!"

I lurch for him as he releases a mouthful of bubbles. He's no longer a divine being immune to nature's will. Though, through his mortal undoing, he smiles, taking my hand as we follow the trail of starlight back to the shore.

✦

Damien collapses beside me on the sand as we emerge from the sea. We rest there for a moment, our chests heaving up and down. The sirens clamor after us, goddess-birthed like Aphrodite— albeit—less graceful as they adjust to their new legs.

I grin, sitting up. "You're human again."

Nadine looks down, squealing. "Lila! You did it."

Warmth floods my cheeks, fluttering through my body. I suppose I did.

"Thank you for saving them," Damien says, moving the salt-matted hair away from my face. "Thank you for saving *me*."

He's still beautiful, still Damien. But now he's real. *Human.* My fingers trace his cheek. His skin is smooth and supple, washed clean of any scars. The ocean healed us. Our life source. It doesn't just take—it births.

"There's no returning to the stars now or being a guardian angel," I say to him. "I hate to think I robbed you of your dream."

"Lila." His hand closes around mine. "This is my dream. I can just be me now. I'm not bound to any fate. All thanks to you."

I smile, resting my head against his chest, cherishing its beating. He's alive. He's breathing and free. I wish I could savor this moment forever. Though, we can't stay here with the island in shambles. The forest, Damien's *home*, is completely burned. The trees stretch to the sky like the hands of corpses—blackened and grotesque, reaching towards the Heavens for a second chance at life.

We escaped Hell, only to find ourselves trapped in a new one.

A rising guilt crawls up my stomach. "Do you think anyone is badly hurt?"

Damien looks away, clearly not wanting to admit the truth we both know deep down. "I'm not sure," he mutters. "I guess there's only one way to find out."

"We'll start with the forest," I suggest. "That's where most of the damage took place." I can't avoid it forever. If I really want to be better than the Devil, then I need to make things right.

Before we leave, I turn to Nadine. "Are you guys going to be okay on your own?"

She nods. "We'll wait here. We need time to adjust to the land anyway. I'll take the sirens over to that cove."

I follow her pointed finger to the rocky headlands. "Okay. I promise to bring back someone special for you when I return."

There's no more time to waste. I have to make things right if it's the last thing I do.

Chapter
TWENTY-EIGHT

◆

"Lila." Damien trembles as we enter the forest's ashen remains. "There's something I need to tell you."

I stop, my fingers grazing the white-singed bark of one of the trees. Bits of it flake off as I pull my hand back. I hate the reminder of my own destruction. "What is it?"

"I didn't exactly leave my family on good terms," he confesses. "I wouldn't count on them being happy to see us."

I rub the cinders from the tree across my dress. "No kidding."

He refuses to look at me. I know going back to the commune can't be easy.

"Hey." I turn his face towards mine. "I'm here. You don't have to worry."

He smiles, close-lipped and soft. "After today, we'll never see them again."

I brush a bit of soot off his shoulder. "Are you sure that's what you want?"

He nods. "I'm sure."

"Okay. Then let's go make peace with it."

I take his hand, and we find our way back to the glade.

The forest is already haunting as it is, but what we stumble into is jarring enough to cut off my breath. Hundreds of angels kneel in silence, sitting in a circle around Mother Marguerite. Their wings are singed black, their skin dull and cut with scars. They don't glow or move or even breathe, it seems. Feathers litter the muddied glade, glinting with discarded jewels and pearls from the ball.

Mother Marguerite is laid out on her back, resting on the altar where they kept Nadine. Her chest still rises and falls in a slow, subtle rhythm, but she seems badly hurt. The right half of her face is mutilated from the fire—her eye closed shut, swollen and purple. A wave of burns travels up her arm and to her temple. White lilies and other offerings surround her—oranges, peaches, and nectarines.

A shallow gasp parts my lips. The quiet sound is enough to shift the angels' attention. Their heads snap in my direction, and I clench onto Damien's arm. His father steps forward from the crowd, narrowing his eyes in disbelief. Or, perhaps, anger.

"Damien," he bellows. "What are you doing with the Blood Moon Bride?" He glowers at me. "Leave! You are not welcome here."

Tears spring to my eyes. I hate being yelled at, even when I deserve it. My humiliation culminates, catching in my throat. Perhaps the old me would have barked back louder. I know it's what I would have done with my own father. But I'm above the pride of proving myself now. I don't need to show them I'm strong. Sometimes, it's just enough to *be*.

I sink to my knees, slowly pressing my body to the floor, honoring the angels in a bow. My lips meet the cool, wet earth. In my culture, the lower you go, the more respect you offer. This is my way of signaling I mean no harm. *I don't hate you. I forgive you. I'm sorry.*

What the angels did was wrong. There's no denying that, and I don't condone it. Though, they did what they had to do to survive. Isn't that what we all do? *Survive.* The pageant was merely a tithe to sustain life as they knew it. Seeing their home now—a crumbled, desolate wasteland—breaks my heart. All they wanted was their peace. I know what it's like to search for home. Luna Island is my home too.

"What are you doing?" Damien mutters, gesturing for me to stand.

I slowly rise, smoothing out my dress, and speak to the angels. "I know you must not be happy to see me. You're probably shocked, confused, scared—better yet, angry that I destroyed your home. But I'm not here for revenge, or to prove myself. I'm here to tell you that I understand. When you've been displaced, your whole world centers around how to preserve your comfort. It's fragile. It makes you do things you're not proud of. But you don't have to fight anymore." I take a breath, before saying, "The Devil is dead. You are free from his tithe forever."

Gasps and chatter break out across the crowd. I inch behind Damien, squeezing his arm, anticipating their reaction. A single laugh cuts the tension. It's subtle, but grows until everyone is silent except for her.

Mother Marguerite.

She slowly rises on the altar, her laughter growing as she regains consciousness.

Aurora rushes up the steps, stroking her hair. "Mother, are you alright?"

Mother Marguerite turns, smiling, and looks right at me. "You did it! We're free."

I laugh nervously. "I—I guess so." She's right. I did it. If I hadn't chosen to heal, then the cycle of abuse would have only continued with me. Now, the angels are free forever. No more tithes, no more pageants. Luna Island can finally be at peace.

"I told you this moment was coming."

I tilt my head, realizing. "You knew this was going to work out the entire time, didn't you?" That's why she was so persistent about making sure I followed through with the tithe.

She winks. "Fate is funny. Things never happen the way we expect them to."

Damien's father grimaces. "So you mean to tell me the Blood Moon Bride was never destined to be damned to Hell?"

Mother Marguerite shrugs. "We said she'd be the one to end it all, and she was. Now our family never has to serve the Devil again. Regardless of how it happened, it did. We have Lila to thank for that."

All the angels look at me, suddenly with reverence and not fear.

Aurora steps forward through the crowd. "Lila, if what Mother Marguerite says is true, then I owe you an apology. You saved our family from a curse that's followed us for centuries. How could we ever make it up to you?"

I shake my head. "You don't."

"Pardon?"

"I don't need anything from you. If you want to make it up to anyone, make it up to Damien."

His emerald eyes glimmer gold as they reflect the sun, a trace of the angel he once was peeking through. He doesn't say anything, but his smile thanks me.

"Damien," his father says, keeping his distance. His voice is cold and unwelcoming, as if it pains him to even address his own son. "We welcome you back with the highest honor. Please, tell us, how do we repay you?"

It takes Damien a while to answer, but eventually, he does. "I forgive you, Father, for the sake of peace, but I will never forget what you put me through." He looks away, his jaw clenching as he holds back what he really wants to say. Instead, he's gracious. "I won't be coming back to the commune. It's time for me to find my own path now."

His father hesitates. I almost think he's about to say something more, but he doesn't. Instead, he merely nods, accepting it.

Mother Marguerite heaves, drawing back our attention.

I rush up the steps to the altar and grab her hand. "What is it? Are you okay?"

"My time is coming. I'm afraid I'll be nothing but stardust soon."

"No, you won't." Mother Marguerite may have tried to sacrifice me, but she was only trying to protect the island. I understand that now. And if it weren't for her, I wouldn't be alive at all. She blessed me with Luna's power, and for that, I'll forever be grateful.

I take a closer look at her injuries. Burn marks trail down the side of her face and to her chest, scorching her skin with a wrinkled distortion. Her left eye is completely shut, mutilated by the fire. My magic multiplies through my body, creating a tingling, warm sensation. Damien was right—my power is connected to my feelings. My dance was only the tool I used to release them. But now, I know myself. I'm in control. It wouldn't take an entire solo variation to heal her. With careful concentration, I hover a hand over the wound, trailing the side of Mother Marguerite's face and over her heart. She arches her back with a sharp breath as I restore her life.

Coos break out amongst the angels as Mother Marguerite comes back with a glow that doubles. She rises, and a sparkling haze emanates from her body, pulsing like a wavering lilac aura. With every swift motion she makes, glitter falls from her elegant fingers. A piece of moonlight lives within her now. She smiles, doing a twirl that releases a ribbon of stardust.

"Mother Marguerite!" Aurora's voice rings out. "You're alright."

"I'm more than alright," she says. "I'm shining."

She lifts her arms into the air with a graceful motion, and the trees around the glade come back to life with lush, full leaves. A golden sheen paints each one, glinting as sunlight hits. Like a living star, Mother Marguerite lights up the dark, and the angels cheer.

"Lila," Damien's father says. "On behalf of the angels, forgive us for what we've done. How can we repay you?"

"All I ask is that you stay away from me and Damien." He owes us that much.

He nods, acknowledging my request, and with his promise, that's the last time we ever see the angels.

✦

Luna Island is worse than I imagined.

Splintered wood and broken glass litter the streets. Townsfolk huddle beneath blankets as volunteers hand out cups of soup. Boats flood in and out of the dock, taking islanders to the mainland and welcoming reinforcements.

There's one more thing left to fix before my conscience is clear.

I take a deep breath, clutching Damien's arm as we make our way towards the cottage I've grown to call home. Our roof is completely concaved, and the roses that once ornamented the windows dangle across the shutters. Laina didn't even bother to clean up the broken glass from the shattered windows. It's a mess, but in typical Laina fashion, she rocks back and forth in her bench swing, aloof and content. She's huddled beside Roisin, both of them looking off at the sea. I wonder if they're thinking about me.

I spin around, curling into Damien's chest. "I—I can't do this."

"Yes, you can," he assures me. "You just bested *the Devil*."

I swallow a breath. "This is different." This is Laina and Roisin, the two people I love more than anything. *My family*. "What if they're mad?"

"I promise you, they're not mad. They just want to know you're safe."

"Are you sure?"

"I'm positive," he says. "Go. They're waiting."

I take a moment to center myself before approaching the cottage, preserving Laina and Roisin's contentment before I shatter the scene. As I pocket the mental image, I remind myself that they love me, that I deserve them. *One breath in, one breath out.* My hands are shaking, and my knees are locked tight. *Come on, Lila, you can do this.* With a final exhale, I flex my anxious palms and make my way forward.

"Hey," I mutter. "I'm home."

At the mere sound of my voice, Laina and Roisin jump out of the bench swing, nearly tripping down the stairs as they make their way to me.

"Lila!" Roisin darts forward before Laina even makes it down the steps, wrapping me in a hug so fierce, we stumble. "Dear Luna, you're alright."

"Oh, my darling girl." Laina welcomes me into her embrace, and I indulge in her familiar lemon-and-gingerbread scent as she squeezes me tightly. "What happened to you? Last night is such a blur."

Right. The Angel Fruit. None of them know the truth about what really happened. The Starlit Ball is nothing but a fever dream now.

I place my hand on Damien's shoulder. "My friend here saved me. Laina, this is Damien."

"Oh!" Wetness kisses her eyes. "Well, Damien, I'd love to have you over sometime once this mess is resolved. Though, nothing could ever make up for saving Lila's life."

Damien shakes his head. "She's being gracious. Lila saved herself."

My brows furrow. "I'd hardly say I did it alone."

"Right." He nods. "Because you're also blessed by Luna."

Roisin tilts her head, scrunching her button nose. "A blessing? What sort?"

I look away, allowing my tumbling hair to shield my gaze. "Um, well, it's kind of a long story."

"How about you share it with us over tea?" Laina suggests.

Relief eases my racing heart at the thought. "I'd like that. But for now, I need to make things right on the island."

"Oh, honey." Laina rests a hand on my back. "Your enthusiasm is sweet, but Luna Island is going to take months to recover from this hurricane. How about we just sit back for now while things are sorted out?"

"Well, that's the thing. With my blessing from Luna, everything can return to normal immediately."

Her gaze narrows, and a wrinkle creases between her brows. "I don't understand."

I laugh, anticipating the shock. "With my dance, I can do this." I spin into a pirouette, and the broken glass on the ground restructures itself back into a window.

Roisin shrieks. "Lila!"

Laina gasps. "Did you just—"

"Yes. And I can do much more. I have a duty to the island, and I'm going to make sure the balance is restored." I look at Damien and extend my hand. "What do you say, may I have this last dance?"

He fits his palm into mine. "Always."

I smile, pulling him through the remains of Luna Island.

We break off into the streets, repairing the cobblestones with our brisk allegro. The townsfolk step aside in awe as my allongés stitch the pastel wood back into cottages and storefronts. Flowers grow from my quick bourrée steps, breathing life back into Luna Island in shades of pink and purple. Rainbows rise from the sea with my grand jeté, summoning the dolphins to leap alongside our dance. Damien catches me in his arms before lifting me into the air as I paint the sky bright blue.

We laugh as the beauty of Luna Island blooms once again, running into the forest and turning the ash into lush green trees. Color bursts in the darkness as we chassé through the angels' village and past the glade where our story first began. With my pirouettes, I add extra pink petals to the garden where Damien and I once lay.

I break into a series of chaîné turns as we make our way back down to the beach, unleashing the magic Luna bestowed upon me. The townsfolk watch in awe in the midst of the commotion, and I dust them in a veil of starlight that follows my path, healing bruises and stitching wounds until no one bleeds. They gather around me as I finish my dance, thrumming with applause and tossing the freshly spun flowers at my feet.

Roisin and Laina are the first to embrace me.

Damien plants a kiss on my forehead. "Well done, my angel."

I smirk. "Your angel?"

"Yes. My angel, my goddess, my heaven divine."

A warm flush spreads across my cheeks. I pull him in by the collar and press a kiss to his lips.

"Oh, how sweet," Roisin croons.

"We're not done just yet," I say to her. "We actually have a surprise for you."

"A surprise?"

I smile. "Come on. You don't want to miss this."

I lead us down the beach, to the cove where I left the sirens.

"Wait here," I instruct. "And close your eyes."

"Okay." She laughs nervously. "What's going on?"

"Just wait. Laina, make sure she keeps her eyes closed."

Laina giggles, turning to Roisin to ensure she cooperates. "I'm on the lookout. No peeking!"

"Fine," Roisin sighs, folding her arms.

I enter the cove and scan for Nadine. The sirens are huddled in the corner, cheering for one another as each of them takes a turn walking with their new feet.

"Hello, my sirens," I announce. "Are you ready to enter the world?"

"*Our queen, our queen!*" they chant.

I laugh. "That's not necessary. As soon as you step outside, you'll begin your new lives. You won't need a queen or a king anymore." I expect them to be excited, but none of them smile. "What's wrong?"

Nadine steps forward. "They're scared," she confesses. "We all are."

"What? Why?"

"Everything is new again. I don't—I don't even know how to *be* anymore."

"It's okay." I take her hand. "You're safe here. You're surrounded by people who love you. They'll be tender while you heal."

"How do you know?" She pulls away, turning around. "I'm so ashamed. Roisin must think I'm a fool for throwing away everything for a fate that damned me."

"Hey, remember, we're no longer blaming ourselves. Besides, Roisin has only ever wanted to find you. You can be together again."

She takes a deep breath. "Are you positive she doesn't hate me?"

"I promise, no one hates you. We love you."

She pulls me into a hug, and I let her linger for as long as she needs. "Thank you. For everything."

"No, thank *you*. You brought love back to me first. And now, it's my turn to do the same. What do you say? Are you ready?"

She nods. "Ready."

I emerge first, taking Roisin's hand, and reflect on what we vowed to do from the start—uncover the truth about what happened to Nadine, and make sure her fate doesn't happen again to someone else. Who knew I'd actually find her in the process? This is my greatest victory, above besting the Devil, above restoring life to Luna Island. I can finally bring love back to the person who taught me what it was to begin with. Nothing matters to me more than seeing Roisin happy.

I hold back a squeal, squeezing her hand one last time. "Okay. You can open your eyes now."

As Roisin's lashes flutter open, Nadine steps into the sunlight. Her bronze skin sparkles with the sun's reflection against the waves, turning her raven hair glossy as it tumbles past her waist in spiral curls. She beams a radiant smile as she approaches, just like the beauty queen she is.

Roisin hesitates, turning to me. "Lila, how did you—"

"I'll explain later." I wink. "Right now, this moment is for you." I nudge her forward, and she stumbles.

"Hey," Nadine whispers, tucking her hair behind her ear. "Remember me?"

Roisin laughs, sinking in the sand as she tries to stay composed. "How could I forget?"

"Good." Her heart-shaped lips twist into a smirk. "So then I bet you'll remember this too." Nadine runs her fingers through Roisin's rose-gold hair, before pressing a kiss to her lips.

I shriek with glee, covering my mouth.

Roisin trembles as Nadine pulls back. A bright flush blooms across her face. "I definitely still remember that too."

I smile up at Damien, content. Everything is just how it should be. "Come on. Let's give them some privacy."

"Wait—" Before Damien and I leave, Laina grabs my wrist. "I have something for you, Lila."

I tilt my head to the side. "What?"

She pulls out an envelope addressed with my name on it. "This is from your mother."

My heart nearly stops. *My mother.* "She wrote to me again?"

I glance at Damien before taking the envelope.

"Go on," he says. "Open it."

My thumb quivers, hovering over the wax seal. "I—I can't. What if she changed her mind? She could still be mad."

He shrugs. "And what if she's not? Besides, what's the worst that could happen now? You've already been damned to Hell."

I laugh, wondering if my mother ever really believed in the Blood Moon prophecy at all.

"Okay, fine," I say, ripping the seal. Only, to my surprise, the letter isn't from my mother.

It's from the Paris School of Ballet.

To Ms. Lila Rose Li,

After careful consideration of your audition tape, featuring "Aurora's Act 1 Variation," we welcome you to formally audition for the Paris School of Ballet. We were exceptionally impressed with your technique and would love for you to perform for us at the Palais Garnier this August . . .

I stop reading, nearly dropping the invitation into the sea. "Oh my god."

Damien peeks over my shoulder. "What does it say?"

"I—I got an audition for the Paris School of Ballet."

Laina squeals, jumping up and down and clapping. "Oh, Lila! How fantastic. Congratulations, honey."

I shake my head. "No. I didn't audition. I gave up on everything after I fell onstage. I never even submitted a tape."

"Well," Damien says, "it looks like someone believed in you, even when you stopped believing in yourself."

My brows furrow. "I don't understand." And then, I turn the invitation over.

Lila,
Go chase your dreams.
—Mom and Dad

Tears swell in my eyes. My parents have a habit of never saying the words *I love you.* But after seeing this invitation right here, they don't have to say it for me to know. I press the letter to my heart. *I love you too.*

Damien drapes his arm around me. "So, when do you leave for Paris?"

I brush the golden hair away from his emerald eyes. "My audition is in August. So fairly soon."

"Maybe I'll meet you in Nice. Or Monte Carlo. Or Cannes."

I laugh. "You're coming to France with me?"

He shakes his head, turning to face the horizon. "I'm going to see the world. But I'll always make the trip for a dance with you."

I lift a brow. "Will you, now?"

He puffs out his chest. "Hey, you're never going to find a better pas de deux partner than me. Besides, what we have together is magic. Literally."

I smile. "I suppose you're right, angel."

He smirks, taking me in his embrace and dipping me over the shimmering water. As the sun glimmers against the waves, we share one last kiss before the starlit sea.

Acknowledgments

✦

Writing *Dance of the Starlit Sea* began as a love letter to myself during my darkest moments, serving as a reminder that we are all deserving of love, no matter the things we've been through. I've grown up with Lila and, in writing this book, have healed traumas I've harbored for a full decade. All this would not be possible without the support of my team at Peachtree Teen, BookEnds Literary, my friends, my mentors, and my family.

To Ashley Hearn, thank you for making my wildest dreams come true. Everyone says it only takes one *yes*, and I am forever grateful for the chance you took on me. You saw potential in me and Lila from the very beginning, and you've championed me into becoming who I am today. Not only have you strengthened my craft as a writer, you've helped me come into a better, wiser, kinder, and more healed version of myself. *Dance of the Starlit*

Sea is as much yours as it is mine, and I could not imagine collaborating with anyone else on this project. Thank you for your time, dedication, and endless belief in me.

To Naomi Davis at BookEnds Literary, thank you for representing me and my work. I am infinitely grateful that you chose to stand by me throughout my career. Your constant guidance, empathy, support, and expertise is what makes this magic possible. Because of you, I have felt the utmost safety throughout my entire debut process and career thus far. Thank you for being my biggest cheerleader and always looking out for me.

To Kate Brauning, my outstanding developmental editor, thank you for your creativity, passion, and dedication. You took my story to a place I couldn't even imagine on my own and have helped me express the deepest truths within my heart. Because of you, *Dance of the Starlit Sea* is even more beautiful and impactful than I could have even dreamed of.

To Chloe Schmitz, my best friend and soul sister, who has been on this journey with me since the very beginning. Thank you for the countless writing dates, the mood board sessions, and all our brainstorming. You have seen me and Lila through every version and every draft, and your unwavering faith in me is what has kept me going strong for all these years. Thank you for being my person and always choosing to see the best in me. I love you tremendously.

To my dearest friends, who are the life source behind the themes of girlhood in this book—Alaa Al-Barkawi, Chloe Schmitz, Diana Vanessa Escobar, Francesca Flores, Heather Apgar, Imani Rae, Katharine Van Amburg, Kyla Zhao, Leanna Chan, Raquel

Boales, Saniya Sahdev, and Tiffany Lynn Thompson—you are the brightest and best part of my life. I appreciate you more than I could ever put into words, and a simple acknowledgment could never measure up to the friendship you've extended me. Thank you for reminding me what love was when I had lost it entirely. You are the beating heart of Roisin and the greatest reminder that I am unconditionally loved. They say you are the company you keep, and if that's true, then you are all the best parts of me.

To the girls who have always inspired me to stay true to my heart, embrace my passion, and achieve my dreams—Gabriella DeMartino, Heather Dempsy, Lauren Lee, and Sara Kristen Baird—thank you for helping me achieve my real-life fairy tale. Thank you, Gabi, for being the inspiration for me to write at all. Thank you, Heather, for being one of my very first readers, who read my early draft within a single sitting and made me feel confident enough to put my work out there. Thank you, Lauren, for championing this book so it can find the readers who will cherish it. Thank you, Sara, for always encouraging me to be my most authentic self and empowering me to turn to love instead of fear or doubt. I would not have the confidence to pursue my dreams without you.

To my spiritual therapists, Emily and Jessica Leung, thank you for your unwavering faith in me, unconditional support, and guidance throughout my publishing journey. The outpour of love you've extended me has kept me strong enough to continue pursuing my divine path. Thank you for healing my heart whenever it breaks, and for giving me the wings I need to fly.

To my online writing community, your support has meant the world to me, and you are the reason I first believed in myself at all. I joined Twitter during the pandemic as a way to feel less alone, and I never imagined that so many of you would follow alongside my publishing journey.

In particular, Amanda Carbonell, Bethany Lord, E. Nightingale, Elora Cook, Emma Ilene, Gillian Burrows, Gül Sinem (Rey), Hayley Dennings, Jarrard Raju, Jen Carnelian, Jenna Streety, Kaitlin Smith, Kaye Asher Edge, Leta Patton, Marleigh Green, Rachael A. Edwards, Ry Ram, Skyler Delvy, Taylor Grothe, Trinity Nguyen, and Yves Donlon—thank you for your friendship, kindness, and enthusiasm for me and my writing throughout the years.

Also, a big thank-you to the industry veterans who've extended their encouragement, support, and advice to me while debuting— Adalyn Grace, Angela Montoya, Autumn Krause, Catherine Bakewell, Lyndall Clipstone, Rachel Griffin—I appreciate you so much.

To Alaa Al-Barkawi—my angel, my sky, my stars and moon— you are the absolute light of my life. Thank you for loving me and my work in every stage. Your presence is the warmest hug, even when you're states away. Thank you for taking the time to empathize with me, learn my story, and cherish it.

To Anna Giselle de Waal, thank you for being the first person to ever read my book from start to finish, and in a single day too. Your love for this story inspired a confidence within me that sparked my career. I admire you dearly, as a friend and as a writer. You are one of my greatest inspirations and muses.

To Chantel Pereira, to this day, I still read back your comments on *Love Letters to the Sea* whenever I'm in need of a smile. Your appreciation for my story has carried me throughout my journey, and I am immensely grateful for your belief in me.

To Jamie Lilac, my heart expands with a love so vibrant when I think of how much I adore you. Thank you for having my back through every high and low—both in writing and in real life—and for always being one of the first people to celebrate my wins and successes with me. You are my angel and you lift me up.

To Katharine Van Amburg, it goes without saying, but you are the other half of my soul. Thank you for helping me and this book fly. I know what love is because of you, and I wouldn't have the ability to tell this story without your friendship. Thank you for all the aesthetic writing dates, the book immersion experiences, attending as many publishing events as you can with me, reposting anything and everything about my book, listening to my hours of crying voice notes, and holding my hand through every publishing woe—no matter how big or small. You inspire me to never give up my dreams.

To Pascale Lacelle, your critique and creativity opened my mind to the possibilities of what *Dance of the Starlit Sea* could be. I cherish your enthusiasm and encouragement for me and my writing so deeply. Thank you for your friendship and support over the years.

To Sophia DeSensi, not only are you one of my dearest friends, you are one of the most incredible critique partners I have ever had. Thank you for always gushing over my lyrical prose and celebrating my unique voice. I will always be grateful for how you've helped strengthen my weaknesses and carried me through the deepest pits of my journey. I love you dearly.

To Stella R. Marys, from the second I met you, I knew we were fated friends. No one has made me and my book feel more seen. The connection we share through our writing is so special to me. Thank you for validating my experiences, cherishing my prose, and celebrating my art.

To my BookEnds Literary fellows—Alaa Al-Barkawi, Elba Luz, Michelle Rajan, Kaitlin Smith, Ramona Pina, and our mentor, Emily Forney—thank you for growing with me in this industry. Emily, you taught me everything I know about publishing, and I am so grateful for your time, dedication, and expertise. Our fellowship is a once-in-a-lifetime opportunity that I will carry with me forever. Because of you, I found my footing, and you helped me soar. I love you infinitely.

Most importantly, to my family—Mom, Dad, and Christian. I love you with every fiber of my being, and I am who I am today because of you. Thank you for always encouraging me to pursue my passions with heart, for teaching me patience and resilience, for making me value the importance of hard work, for supporting my education, and for standing by me throughout all the highs and lows of my career. I am immensely grateful for the privileges and opportunities you've provided me to expand my craft, and for giving me the life I have today so I am able to pursue my dreams. I wouldn't be who I am without you.

About
THE AUTHOR

✦

KIANA KRYSTLE

is a proud third-generation Asian American, born and raised in California. She got her start in publishing as an editorial intern at Flux Books and Jolly Fish Press, and continued her growth as a fellow at BookEnds Literary. Through her writing, Kiana hopes to empower readers to embrace their authentic selves and seek magic in their everyday lives. When she's not writing, you can find her exploring California's coastal towns and beaches, practicing moon rituals, having tea parties, and embracing the world's whimsy. *Dance of the Starlit Sea* is her debut novel. Stay up to date with Kiana on social media at @kiana_krystle.